Also by Ellen Schwamm

ADJACENT LIVES

Ellen Schwamm

HOW
HE
SAVED
HER

Alfred A. Knopf   New York   1983

7/1983
Am. Lit.

THIS IS A BORZOI BOOK
PUBLISHED BY ALFRED A. KNOPF, INC.

Library of Congress Cataloging in Publication Data
Schwamm, Ellen. How he saved her.
I. Title.
PS3569.C564H6 1983   813'.54
82-48885
ISBN 0-394-52707-0

Manufactured in the United States of America
First Edition

HOW
HE
SAVED
HER

For Lee Schwamm and Robert Gottlieb and Harold Brodkey

HOW
HE
SAVED
HER

1

I love him in full knowledge now. I have loved him in various ways. I am convinced I loved him before we met. I am both comforted and shattered by this—and ashamed.

I had a husband and children, a mother and father, a home. I loved him more than any of them even before I knew him. Absurd. Absurd. I'm not a romantic woman. I'm worldly. I despise romance. Yet I know that if he dies I will die. I'm ashamed of this. I have not yet been able to have a single shameless moment. Determined, yes. Willful, yes. Passionate, yes. Shameless, no. Or, perhaps, yes. But hidden and walled off. Private. Very private moments. Perhaps the night I first saw him was the moment I loved him least.

Shall I tell you about love at first sight? I was blinded by shame. I didn't know it had happened. I'd been taught to place loyalty above love, which suited me because it cost more. Or so I thought then. I was a loyal wife and daughter, a loving mother. Of course, that's only part of the story. As you'll see. But remember—please—anything you may read here that seems harsh, well . . . I would take it back if I could. I wouldn't be telling any of it in the first place if they weren't still trying to discredit Lautner—I want to call him that. I can't live without Lautner—which doesn't mean I'm finished with Ned. There's a sense in which I am forever wedded to the man I left. He taught me a lot and he never stopped wanting me. I would forgive him tomorrow in spite of his hating me and outwitting me, in spite of my hating him—I would forgive my parents too—if it weren't for Lautner. As for Ned's wife—the woman I was then, that other person, that third person, she—I don't know if I can ever forgive her for what she did and the way in which she did it, but I try to love her and sometimes I succeed.

She was rich, not quite very rich, not quite happy. It was her fortieth birthday. Pauvre petite. She had lovely eyes, lovely hair. She was beautiful. She had a beautiful rich woman's face. She hadn't had a single fantasy all day. Not for any object. Not for any man. Not for a career. Not for a physical pleasure. She had no wishes except that her birthday be not unpleasant.

She was nearly ready. She was putting on a blue silk dinner suit. She was careful to dress where her husband couldn't watch her. His appetite for her was . . . well, it oppressed her. She had to struggle not to be erased by him; by his wants. His wants covered a lot of ground. He was not willing to let life be an accident. Unhappily for her, her resistance to him was what made his life interesting. She had no power over him, only the power to deny him, and that only incompletely. She sensed this, but she refused to think about it.

Somewhere, Lautner, in his advance toward her, was threading his way through crowded streets, fitfully, as if his body were being powered by a cold or failing engine. He had contrived to be carelessly dressed and there were black smudges beneath his eyes. His manner was dark and subtle but with hints of open violence in it.

Pauvre petite. Lucky woman. Nora Ingarden.

The light dimmed as though clouds had moved across the sun. Ned stood in the doorway. He shot his cuffs, then smoothed the sides of his head with the heels of both hands, a gesture reminiscent of the days when his hair had been his best feature—boyishly abundant, glossy, nearly black. He'd lost most of it by the time he was forty.

"Ready?" he asked.

"Yes," Nora said, and followed him out of the dressing room, through the sweep of bedroom, and down the stairs.

Years ago, the walls of the tiny servants' rooms on the top floor of the brownstone had been thrown down to create a unified master suite. The children's rooms and a guest room occupied the floor below. The first two floors had been partially gutted to carve out a double-storey living room whose rear wall was mostly glass and gave out onto a small, enclosed garden. The house was in the seventies off Fifth Avenue.

Valerie was waiting in the hall outside her bedroom. Valerie was nineteen, slim, long-legged, and extraordinarily beautiful—when she wasn't tormented by her erotic image. When she was, she distorted her face and slouched to conceal her breasts. "Is this dress all right, Mom?" she asked anxiously. The dress in question was a red-and-black rayon print from the 1940s with dolman sleeves, exaggerated shoulders, an asymmetrical neckline, and a drape across the opposite hip for balance.

"You look wonderful," Nora said emphatically.

Ned shifted his bulk. He was a big handsome man with large but regular features who gave the impression of a profound solidity of mind, body, and purpose. He shot his cuffs again, and fingered the button on his jacket. "If you weren't my daughter ..." he said, winking at Valerie and coughing.

Valerie's face flamed. "I'll be downstairs in a minute," she said, retreating into her bedroom and closing the door.

"Let's go, Willie," Ned ordered, throwing open the door to his son's room.

"Dad, I've asked you a hundred times to please knock before you come barging in. Is that so much to ask?"

"Sorry. Are you ready?" Ned was coughing again. The cough was persistent, unrelated to health. A raspy, dry-sounding tempest high up in his throat which maddened them all but which he couldn't control.

"Mom, is this tie okay with this shirt?"

"It's a little strong, sweetheart. The paisley would be better."

Willie tossed the offending tie onto the bed. Nora handed him the replacement.

"I'll put it on in the cab," he said, glaring at his father.

Something more binding than anger blazed in his eyes. Fascination, perhaps. Willie had an unfocused but energetic brilliance of mind that caused a noticeable crackle in the atmosphere and displeased Ned, who tried to suppress it—for Willie's own good. He was interested in Willie. Still, Nora's heart sometimes ached for her son as if he were a fatherless boy.

Valerie was waiting for them in the living room. She had changed into a pair of black trousers and an oversized white silk shirt and pulled her loose, dark curls into a pony tail. Ned appeared not to notice. Nora chose not to comment.

"All set?" Ned asked, leading the way.

Nora smiled at their reflections in the mirrored vestibule. She squeezed Valerie's hand, and gave Willie a kiss. As she picked a speck of lint from Ned's coat, her evening bag slipped from her shoulder. Ned looked down at the floor and then up at Willie. Willie stiffened. Valerie bent to retrieve the purse. The motto over the front door was incised in stone and wreathed in laurel. It read: SEMPER FIDELES.

The city flashed by. The cab driver was young and white and he drove with an easy skill that excited Nora's admiration and envy. Willie was eighteen but he hadn't learned to drive yet. They didn't own a car, driving lessons were expensive, and Ned thought him insufficiently responsible. Willie and the driver were getting on. Nora could hear them laughing through the plastic shield that separated the front seat from the rear. Willie was very outgoing.

"You take the building address, you subtract a hundred and then multiply by two, and that gives you the nearest cross street," Ned explained to Valerie.

Valerie nodded gravely. "And Park Avenue?" she asked.

Valerie was still apprehensive about getting lost. She worried about being raped.

"I don't remember," Ned said.

"The driver might know," Nora said. She was seated between her husband and her daughter. "They have that little book. . . ." The pressure of the slab of her husband's knee against hers made her uncomfortable. She pushed it away gently with her hand. He let it fall back almost immediately. She sighed.

"Here, Mom, there's plenty of room on my side," Valerie said, shrinking farther into the corner.

Nora smiled at her. Her daughter was the other half of her soul. Her son was her agent of hope. She loved her children passionately. She believed she would do anything—lie, steal, kill, or die herself—to keep them from harm. Anything less had nothing to do with love.

Ned tapped on the plastic shield. "Tell the driver to swing over to the highway," he said to Willie.

"What's wrong with Ninth Avenue?"

"Just do what I say, okay?"

"But the highway's closed below Fifty-seventh Street."

"Tell him to take Twelfth Avenue. It's the same thing."

"How can you say it's the same thing? There are traffic lights on Twelfth," Willie argued.

"It runs along the river. It goes to the same place. It's the same thing."

Willie's jaw tightened. He took a deep breath and repeated Ned's instructions to the driver. The driver made a sharp right. Nora gripped the edge of the seat for support. Ned slipped toward her, crushing her against Valerie. He took his time recovering. The two women adjusted their clothes.

Nora wasn't heavy. She didn't weigh on people. Age was beginning to blow her about like a dragonfly.

South of Canal Street the road was nearly deserted. The cab flew.

Lautner was sitting down to dinner with Mäarten Tromp.

The cab drew up to the door of one of the twin towers and came to a gentle stop. Nora saw Willie and the driver slap each other's palms. She smiled. Ned dug into his trouser pocket for money. He poked Nora with his elbow. She and Valerie got out and waited on the sidewalk.

"How come you gave him such a small tip, Dad?" she heard Willie ask.

"When you're making your own living, Willie, that's time enough to have an opinion on how much other people tip." He coughed at length.

The elevator was the size of a maid's room. It ascended rapidly and with a soft, whirring insistence. Nora's ears filled with pressure. The restaurant was on the very top floor of what had been, briefly, the world's tallest building. Nora's choice had been calculated to spare her parents the discomfort of awe and to satisfy her brother's greed without arousing his envy. The view was incomparable, the drinks generous, the food of no particular interest. New Yorkers were seldom seen on the premises at dinner hour.

The foyer was crowded with women in fur and men with suntans.

"Look around for Grandma and Grandpa," Nora told Willie.

"Are they staying the night?" he asked.

"Of course. Why?"

"I left my earphones at school." Willie was a freshman at Amherst, Valerie a sophomore. Ned had gone to Amherst.

"It's only one night, Willie."

"I don't see them anywhere, Mom," he said. He was standing on tiptoe. He wasn't as tall as he'd hoped to be. Ned was a little over six-two. The top of Willie's head was level with Ned's chin.

"Here they come now," Nora said, waving.

"I'm going up front to see about the reservation," Ned said.

"Do you think they see us?" Nora asked Willie.

"Relax, Mom. They'll find us. They're headed right this way. Besides, Grandpa's got sharp eyes."

Nora readied her face.

Her father's kiss was moist and noisy. She stepped back and smiled at him. He sent out an aura of warmth from his body to hers that was stronger than an embrace. She never looked directly at her mother. There is nothing harder than meeting the eyes of an indifferent mother, one who boasts about you to cover her want of true sympathy; a mother you're sorry for. She felt her mother's kiss feathering the air near her cheek. After embracing their grandchildren, her parents asked as one person, "Where's Ned?"

They were leashed to her but their eyes strained after Ned. They admired him even more now than they had twenty years ago, when they'd urged this marriage on her. Although Ned's proposal had come at a moment of prosperity in the family history—there was a chauffeured limousine and the worried look had left her mother's face—her father had made it plain he didn't trust his future. He wanted Nora, at least, to be safe. He thought security was happiness. Nora had admired Ned, and she'd respected him, and she'd been certain she loved him the way one was supposed to love a future husband—sanely—just as she'd been certain, absolutely certain, that marrying him would free her from ever having to do anything for money again.

On her wedding day, during the lengthy walk down the beribboned aisle to where he, Nicholas Ingarden, Jr.—Ned—waited, she thought fleetingly of running away. Her father, for whose good opinion she lived while she submitted to her mother's will—her father, as if sensing the horror building in her—her father bound her arm to his with an uncharacteristic display of physical force. With each of the steps that brought them closer to Ned, he trod heavily on the hem of her gown, forcing her into a list so pronounced that her head nearly rested on his shoulder. Only the pair of them, father and daughter, knew that if she were to straighten up, she would tear her dress open to the waist. Her love for her father was such that when he raised her veil he found only forgiveness in her eyes.

The air in the foyer was heavy with cigarette smoke. Mrs. Greene held her hand protectively over her nose.

Willie was half-leaning on Nora, his arm draped across her shoulder, in a manner that suggested affection mixed with exhibitionism, a dependence with proprietary overtones while he explained, in a penetrating voice, the physics of the sway factor in modern skyscrapers. Valerie, Nora noticed, was standing slightly apart, her mouth hanging open. Dead-eyed. Nora looked instead at the supple beauty of the line of her head and neck. In the distance, she saw Ned raise his hand. She raised her own in response and then shepherded her family past a long line of patrons to where he was waiting.

"I'm sorry, sir," the maître d' said, looking them over, "but your reservation is for eight people. I can't seat you until your party is here. If you'll be good enough to wait on line. I'll take care of you as soon as they arrive."

"You're new here, aren't you?" Ned asked.

"About a month," he said, and then, meeting Ned's eyes, "sir."

"What's your name?"

"Hugo, sir."

"Well, Hugo, is Mr. Covey around?" Covey was one of the owners.

"No, sir. Not tonight, sir."

Ned turned to Willie. "Here's a dime, Willie. Phone Jack at home. Ask him to straighten out our little problem."

"That won't be necessary, sir." The maître d' coughed. "This way, please," he said glassily.

They followed Hugo's snaking descent through the large, crowded dining room, which was laid out in shallow tiers like a clubhouse at a racetrack. Gus Greene had his hands in his pockets and was craning his neck in one direction and then another, sizing things up, his eyes as bluely alert as a baby's.

Nora, whose alertness was more delicately honed than her father's but no less insistent, saw nothing along their route to gladden her. Still, it was all right. Her first impressions were generally sober and pitiless; then, finding them unendurable, she looked away and began to embroider. The embroidery was a form of respect. She didn't think of it as lying.

Their table was on the first tier in front of the windows, a good but not quite good enough location, a bit too far off to one side to suit Ned. He coughed and looked at the ceiling and said, "This place needs a paint job."

Nora declined the chair Hugo held for her. "You come and take this, Mother. I've seen the view here so many times."

"I'm fine where I am." Mrs. Greene was standing with her back to the windows.

"Get going, Grandma," Willie said, with only half-mock sternness.

"All right, all right," she said, smiling at him coquettishly, and then she grew sad because Willie wasn't looking at her.

Ned held Valerie's chair. She gave him a quick, tense smile. Willie seated Nora, dropping a kiss on top of her coiled hair as he slid the chair under her. Ned settled in at the head of the table.

The room was walled in glass on three sides. It appeared to hang, thrillingly unconcerned, in space. Planes went by, their lights winking. A city etched in colored light fanned out at their feet. Stars were scattered like buckshot across the sky around this somehow dreary room.

"Look at that, will you," her father said. "Now that's what I call a view of Manhattan!"

"That's not Manhattan, Gus," Ned said, recrossing his extended legs. "That's Jersey City."

"Well, that's progress for you," her father said, turning

pink. "In my day, the tallest building in Jersey City was five stories high. A cousin of mine had his offices there during the Depression. He moved to the Oranges after the war."

"Ned's just teasing you, Dad. Of course that's Manhattan. You're looking toward—let's see—toward the north—Times Square and the Empire State."

Her father blushed again. He took off his glasses and cleaned them with his napkin.

"Nora, do you recommend the veal Cordon Bleu? I eat veal every chance I get," her mother said.

"Try something simpler, Mother."

"The pepper steak is good, Grandma," Valerie said.

"No, I don't think so. Steak is so boring and I don't eat pepper."

"How about roast chicken, Grandma?" Willie asked.

"No, I think I'll have the veal. How bad can it be in a place like this?"

Across the room, Nora saw her brother elbow past Hugo, leaving his wife to cope with the maître d's annoyance. Hugo shrugged. Millie smiled apologetically at him and braved her way alone. Herbert had the peach-faced look of a renaissance youth, an arrested and arresting prettiness which made him seem considerably younger than he was. And perhaps more innocent. It was hard to tell with Herbert. No one dared judge him. He had alarmingly weak nerves and that disarmingly angelic face. He dashed up to the table, already talking; he talked incessantly. It was apparent, even to strangers, that the sound of his own voice was all that stood between him and Bedlam.

"I know, I know. The baby-sitter was late, and the housekeeper didn't show up this morning, and Millie couldn't take Amanda to work so I had to drag her to the office with me, and let me tell you that was no picnic. She wiped me out. You know why she didn't have school today? You wanna know what these private schools are like? Evaluation Day. You'd think, for all the money you have to fork over, they could evaluate on their own time." He sat down next to his mother. Ned got up to seat Millie.

"Hello, everyone," Millie said, interrupting Herbert. She was a large, slow-moving, extremely pleasant-faced woman, a hard-working insurance agent; her income was three times Herbert's. Herbert had never worked for anyone but his father. Only his father was permitted to abuse him. His mother never let anyone forget that Herbert, whatever his deficiencies, had a good heart. And Nora shielded him, as far as it was possible, from her parents' ill-conceived attentions.

Herbert was still talking. "All right, all right," his father said. "You don't have to talk the hind leg off a donkey. Just say hello and wish your sister a happy birthday."

"Didn't I do that already? Jesus, I don't know where my head is today. Happy birthday, Nora. Forty, isn't it? You're getting up there. So today was the big day, huh? Today you cashed in on the big bucks!"

Millie laid a cautionary hand on Herbert's arm. "What, I'm talking too much?" He shot a look at his father. "Okay, I'll shut up, I promise." He put his fingers across his cupid's-bow lips. He had his mother's mouth and her small, delicate nose.

Nora's father said to her, "I had the lawyers send all the papers to Ned at the office. As long as Herbert brought it up. You have to give Ned power of attorney. He can't budge without it."

"Power of attorney?" She looked—and felt—very small.

"Ned said he'd handle the money for you."

"But I don't want it handled for me."

"Don't be ridiculous," her father said. "You're not a silly person."

"Why is it ridiculous? I want to spend it. I want it in a bank and I want to spend it."

"On what? What do you need that Ned won't buy you?"

Nora didn't answer. Where money was concerned—and

money, like sand, insinuated itself everywhere—well, asking Ned for money was a moral defeat. Ned was moral and without desire. She was immoral to ask. Usually, she and the children were made to feel they were asking for a piece of him, perhaps for his hands, something he couldn't do without, without being deformed. Decency required that they live simply and without money. Nora wasn't decent.

"There's no way to make money from money except by tying it up," Ned said.

Nora felt a flash of hatred. "I'm not interested in making money."

"It's not a matter of *making* money," her father broke in. His lively creased face, which generally deepened into a smile whenever he looked at her, had taken on the shady look of displeasure that was ordinarily reserved for Herbert and a slow-witted bookkeeper who'd been with him for years. "If you let a hundred thousand dollars sit in a savings account or even a mutual fund, you *lose* money."

Ah, what Ned called Opportunity Cost. As Nora understood it, or misunderstood it, this referred to the money one could have made if one hadn't bought a car or something else, and it meant that not only was nothing free but that one actually had to add this cost onto the cost of everything else, one's home, one's vacations, one's children's schooling.

"You're nuts, Nora, you know that?" Herbert said. "Don't you know how lucky you are to have Ned managing your money?"

Ned was a tax lawyer. He represented mostly foreign investors with large holdings in the United States. Ned, her father said over and over again, "is the most sophisticated man with a dollar I ever met. He's sophisticated financially. Nothing he does is simple—he's no fool. Nobody says you have to be a fool to be an honest man."

"You know Grandpa never thought you would just spend the money, Nora," her mother said.

"No, and I may not."

"Hey, why doesn't everyone lay off Mom. It's her birthday," Willie said.

Nora's money had come to her from her mother's father, a prudent Lutheran who had loved God and small children (though not Herbert): a nice sum on each of her birthdays for the thirty years their lives had overlapped, which he'd seen fit to tie up in a trust until she turned forty, an age he believed to be beyond the reach of passion. He had never liked or trusted his son-in-law, Nora's father was a Jew, after all—this was understood but not discussed. Nora was his first and favored grandchild, and the only woman in the family to have money from him in his lifetime or after. At his death, his ample estate was divided between his sons. If Nora's mother had any objections to her brothers' being enriched at her expense, she never made them known. Nor had she ever complained about Nora's receiving this money.

Mrs. Greene's eyes were sad.

"Oh, Mother, I want the money myself—oh, we'll talk about it later—money is a bore."

Herbert talked at length, and in a loud voice, about the maniac who'd laced aspirin-free capsules with cyanide, thus causing a recall of many thousands of bottles of pills and making his—Herbert's—life a misery. Mr. Greene owned a small, often-troubled chain of discount drugstores. Millie spoke warmly of her company's newly expanded health benefits, under which even Herbert's dental work was covered.

When the dinner plates had been cleared away (the veal on Mrs. Greene's plate was hardly touched), Nora took some packages from a shopping bag next to her chair. It was an eagerly awaited eccentricity of hers to give presents on her birthday.

"I never know what to buy you, Nora," her mother said, "your taste is so intelligent—you don't like pretty things. You wouldn't tell me what you wanted."

"Oh, Mother, I like this eyeglass case. I really need one. But put on the necklace."

Mrs. Greene was fingering the choker Nora had taken from her own neck a minute before and placed on the table in front of her. "But this is your favorite piece of jewelry." The necklace was made of dozens of twisted strands of tiny lapis lazuli beads and clasped by a gold hand. "Are you sure you want me to have it?" She didn't look at Nora.

"You've always loved it. Of course I want you to have it. It's my thank you to you for being such a wonderful mother," Nora said.

She saw her mother glance at Ned.

Ned said, "Nora bought it for herself, Mary—thrift-shop money—selling her old dresses."

"This isn't Gucci, is it?" Herbert, looking at the credit-card case in his hand, said. His face was girded for disappointment.

"No, but you can change it if you like. It's from a store on Madison called Bottega—"

"Oh, yeah," Herbert broke in, "when your own initials are enough, right? Thanks," he said, with genuine enthusiasm. "I can really use this." He was grinning broadly now.

"Why so extravagant this year?" her father asked, and then he said, "Never mind," and transferred his attention to Ned, who'd summoned the captain and was conferring with him behind the menu.

"I know you can't stand the heater in your car," Nora said, ducking the subject of whose money she'd thought she was spending when she'd chosen the red cashmere lap robe.

After the last of the presents had been exchanged—the children had given her *The Audubon Society Encyclopedia of North American Birds*—the cake arrived with an honor guard of waiters and busboys who ringed the table and sang "Happy Birthday." She blew out the candles with a burning face while Willie whooped, "You can do it, Momma."

"I warned Dad this was a bad idea," Valerie whispered. Valerie, who herself was acutely shy of unwanted attention, grasped Ned in a way that Nora did not. She disliked him but respected him. She respected the protection he offered.

He was like the high wall with battlements that surrounds a besieged castle behind which she had her mother's protection against him. Of course, there was a sense in which she also loved him, if not deeply then loyally.

The cake was cut and served and then the captain poured the champagne. He moved quickly around the table, but not quickly enough to foil Herbert, who stayed his wrist for a moment so he could pry back the white towel and have a look at the label. "You see this?" he said in a loud aside to his mother. "If I told you what this bottle cost, you wouldn't be able to sleep tonight."

He meant this literally. How well or badly Mrs. Greene slept was a form of currency within the family. If you loved her, you kept track.

Ned raised his glass to Nora across the table. "To a woman of valor. Her price is far above rubies." He was speaking in a sentimental voice but Nora believed he meant what he said.

In the early years of their marriage, he'd given her jewelry for her birthday. One year a crab, the next a starfish, then a pair of sea horses with ruby eyes—always small, jeweled, underwater creatures. This year he'd presented her with an electric pasta machine. Men who went on buying their wives expensive gifts, he often said, were working off their guilt about something.

Nora noticed that his eyes were moist. Dynastic sentiments were the strongest of all his feelings. His toast brought the late Nicholas Ingarden, Sr., to mind: undoubtedly it was meant to, since he was quoting the very lines that his father, a man of property, had so often invoked when speaking of women. Nicholas Ingarden had groomed Ned to marry an heiress. Ned had disappointed him. Nora had borne his rage.

"Her worth is greater than pearls." Ned got up and walked to the foot of the table and kissed Nora's waiting, upturned cheek. "Your turn, Gus," he said, when he was seated again.

"To my beautiful pussy cat," her father said. "With her

brains she should have been the boy." He kissed Nora smackingly on the cheek, close to her ear. The sound, one a shooting star might make if you were close enough to hear it—she'd thought this as a child—deafened her for an instant to the double-edged nature of his words, his sadness about Herbert and her.

"You're next, Mary," Ned said.

"Is it my turn already?" her mother asked, her prettily plump face taking on a look of mild agitation. "To my daughter, Nora, who has given me nothing but pleasure and I hope always will."

Herbert waved his glass frantically for attention like a schoolchild. Every day was the first day of school for Herbert. Valerie, who'd been designated by her father to speak next, hesitated and glanced at her mother for instruction. Nora signaled with her eyes for Valerie to wait. A private smile flickered between them.

"My turn, my turn. Pay attention, folks," Herbert said, tapping his spoon on the side of his glass, his jocularity forced and embarrassing. "To my sister," he said. "Older and richer but not necessarily prettier."

"That's enough," his father cut in, seeing that Herbert had only paused in expectation of a laugh. "Let's hear what the kids have to say for themselves."

"To my mother," Valerie murmured in her low musical voice. "And my best friend."

"What a beauty!" Nora's father said. "The women in our family have always been beauties. Not yours, Ned. Sorry, but the truth's the truth. You got good blood when you got Nora."

Her father had never stopped selling her.

Willie pushed back his chair and stood up. Nora's face came to life as she looked at him. Sometimes on the street, when she saw a young woman with small children, she quivered, remembering how happy she'd been with Willie and Val when they were small. Holding him in her arms, holding Val, the weight of their tiny bones pinning her to the earth, she hadn't felt it necessary to question anything, anything of importance.

"Mom," Willie said, gesturing first toward her and then at the landscape beyond the glass walls, "you don't know about the stars and if I say you're greater than a galaxy you won't know what I mean, so I'll say that all those lights aren't as bright as your eyes when you're not mad at me for not picking up my room." He came around the table and hugged her. His hugs were dangerous. He'd once broken a few of his great-uncle's ribs. The rest of the family applauded.

In midapplause her father turned his full attention to Ned. Fluctuations in the world economy, in the prime rate, and in new car sales were the only subjects that could hold his interest more than spasmodically. "What do you think's gonna happen in Turkey?"

"We're about to see a turnaround," Ned said. "The inflation rate's dropped—of course nobody's talking miracle yet but exports are up, and unemployment's down. I'm still cautious, but if the debt-rescheduling negotiations go okay—three-point-two billion is nothing to sniff at—and if West Germany and Japan and the IMF all come through, well, prospects there might be worth looking into. Maybe not."

"You ought to take care of that cough, Ned," Herbert said. "My sinuses give me a hell of a lot of trouble this time of the year. Steam heat does it. When it isn't my back—I haven't been able to play tennis for six months—it's the mucous membranes. And now Amanda's got nosebleeds all the time. Remember, Dad, when I was a kid, how they never let up? How many times a week you had to rush me to the hospital. . . ?"

"If everybody's ready, I'll get the check," Ned cut in.

Nora's father said, "Good idea. Grandma needs her beauty sleep."

Nora was reaching into her bag for her gloves when the captain handed her a note. She read it quickly, then looked around. Ned was skimming the check for errors.

"It's from Tromp," she told him. She'd been a patient of Tromp's years ago. She and Ned saw him occasionally at dinner parties. She was sure that Tromp was attracted to her, but his behavior had never been other than professional.

"What does he want?" Ned asked.

"To send over a bottle of champagne. He heard them singing to me."

"Ask the gentleman to join us, will you," Ned told the captain.

Tromp shook hands with Ned. He congratulated Nora. "You're looking well," he said, reaching for her hand and shaking it twice, two clean short strokes as if he were chopping wood, as if nothing like a flirtation was possible. He was a short, round-faced, restless Dutchman, entirely indifferent to his appearance but he wasn't indifferent to hers.

"I am well," Nora answered. Greeting Tromp in front of her mother, father, brother, her children, her husband, and on her birthday, her internal temperature rose several degrees. Her face grew hot and she flushed. Her voice shook as she introduced Tromp to her family. An indiscreet curiosity shone in their eyes before which she felt naked and shamed. She could feel Tromp's and Ned's sexual interest—even voracity, when she was embarrassed and quivering.

"So you're Nora's shrink," Herbert said. "That's really amazing." He stood up and went over to shake hands with Tromp, crowding in until he was unnervingly close. Tromp took a large step backward and laughingly crossed himself.

"Sit down, Herbert," Gus said, so callously that for a moment Nora was racked with feeling for her brother.

"I'll get the waiter to bring a chair, Mäarten," Ned said. He liked Tromp.

Tromp coughed. He liked Ned. He liked all rich men but Ned particularly. Ned had given him a few good investment tips, and no bad ones. "I'm afraid I've left my dinner guest alone with his brandy. I should get back," he said.

"Ask him to join us instead," Ned said grandly.

"Why not?" Tromp said. "I'll be right back."

Stay married, Tromp had advised her. Be discreet. Have an affair. He'd said, "You can't take care of yourself."

Tromp was a coarse man, inelegant, often grotesque, often unorthodox, not the sort of doctor one would expect to be fashionable but he was anyway. He had a gift for making even the dullest patients feel clever and amusing. He denied the existence of the unconscious, choosing instead to delegate the mystery of human behavior to something he called the unreflective level of consciousness. Nora was fond of this label. It suggested to her that with a little sustained reflection, one could know everything about oneself. Anyway, she'd taken his advice. She thought of herself as a happy enough woman, no unhappier than she deserved.

Tromp was crossing the room followed by another man.

Ned laid a credit card on top of the check and signaled the captain. Herbert leaned to his left, trying to get a look at the total.

Nora's father yawned out loud. Her mother took a small bottle of artificial tears from her purse and put a drop or two discreetly in the corner of each eye. She took a long sip of water. "It's smokey in here," she said to Nora.

A shadow fell across the table.

Nora looked up.

What can I say of such a moment?

The man was tall and shabbily dressed. The way in which he had no expectations touched something in Nora and made her feel less lonely. His eyes were sad. It was as if he'd seen the wrong side of every right thing. Intelligence on his face was like ice on a road—not a weapon but a dangerous footing for anyone talking to him. His features were of no inherent interest. His body moved clumsily. But then what can I say about the sensual exactness with which he moved once he caught sight of her? It is for some reason really hard for me to say that that shabby man promised a kind of truth.

She fell in love without catching his name.

The waiter brought a chair.

He sat down next to her.

She wished him gone. No, that's a lie.

She wished her family gone. Tromp, too. In Tromp's presence, and with her family watching, she felt constrained and trivial. She was crushed by the weight of her suit—it was cut in imitation of a Chinese communist worker's uniform—whose wit, in this context at least, defined her as worse than merely silly. She often judged herself to be unworthy, but she wasn't accustomed to being judged that way by others.

"So," Tromp said, drumming his fingers on the table. "What have you been up to, Nora?"

"Not much," she said. "Just trying to live in the present moment—you know, your favorite analogy—like the petals of a flower unfolding into consciousness." She smiled nervously. She wanted to assure the stranger that she was more of a person than she appeared to be. She could guess at what he saw.

Her parents looked confused and ill at ease. Herbert was staring moodily at his reflection in the window, trying out different smiles. Ned's blank eyes, the angle of his head and shoulders, the way he was scratching at the tooth edge of his gums with his fingernail made it seem as if he were planning something. Willie was grinning and cracking his knuckles, leaning forward with immense interest. Valerie, seeing Nora's face, smiled anxiously. She glanced at Tromp and then at Ned and then back at her mother, protectively now, as if Nora were in danger.

"Did you hear that, Lautner?" Tromp asked.

So that was his name. It struck Nora's ear with the force of a blow.

Tromp was tilting back in his chair and smiling with satisfaction. "The ideal analysand, wouldn't you say? Smart, practical, terre-à-terre, as Tolstoy said of women, mildly ironic, trusting. You can believe me when I tell you she wasn't really neurotic. There were some minor adjustments in attitude, that was all."

Lautner was mute, yet Nora could hear his mind swooping, and the sound it made was like a high, thin squeal in her ears.

"I don't think Lautner agrees," Tromp said, laughing. "For him, neurosis begins with duty—with one's definition of duty. Duty, you see, is never a given. One's notions about duty—to a mother or father, for example—may be totally irrational and the cause of extreme personality distortion. According to Lautner's theory, everyone is neurotic. Am I 'paraphrasing' you correctly, Lautner?"

"Close enough." Lautner's voice was indistinct, more like a mutter of stones falling than a voice.

"Wait a minute," Nora's father said to Tromp. "Let's get something straight. Are you trying to tell me that this man thinks that because my kids respect their parents that makes them crazy? Well, let me tell you something. It's the doctors that are crazy. When Herbert here was sixteen, I sent him to a psychiatrist. He was very short for his age and the school figured he needed a boost. His doctor had the nerve to ask me if I loved my children—why, he even asked me how often I slept with my wife. I punched him in the face and I took Mary home. I wouldn't let the kid go back. He grew seven inches in the next year, and he's okay."

Lautner wore a condensed look of discomfort.

Nora cringed a little. As a very young woman, she'd confronted her father's shortcomings. Her disappointment had been sharp enough nearly to extinguish her love, but the fierceness of his attachment to life and his enormous hopefulness, his capacity for a kind of joy, and her belief that he would die to protect what he loved had allied her to him— she loved him and regarded him as *wise-after-all.* Sometimes she was ashamed of him, but mostly she loved him. He was her father.

There was a long pause during which it became clear to Nora that Lautner was going to respond. He made a sort of platform out of the silence and then he mounted it. When he spoke, his voice was almost as tremolant as an organ pipe and it set up a vibration in her head that was shocking, a vibration that went on expanding and widening like the sound itself.

"For one thing, Mr. Greene," he said, "I am not a doctor. And for another, I am not a minister. I believe that any conception of the family bonds as holy laws despite the clear intention of Judaism and Christianity to make one's tie to God the only one to matter, and where the ark—the holy writ, whatever one wants to call it—is really the husband's or the father's wallet, and where any disruption of these bonds is called a sin for which one is damned is really a kind of obvious crime against the mind and the emotions." His eyes were severe and unpleasant. "Of course, I'm not forgetting that it's only these bonds that keep some of us from being outright monsters of ego. What I propose is simply that each person be encouraged to determine for him or herself"—here he paused and looked at his hands—"what validly constitutes duty—to a dishonest father, say, or to a lazy or self-loving mother, or to one's country, or to truth—and then act accordingly. And live with the outcome without complaining. I doubt you want to take this as an attack on your life, Mr. Greene. I doubt you would want to examine the subject." He smiled. "I am not a tyrant. I do not insist that anyone face anything. I wait, Mr. Greene. I wait."

The nave of Nora's reasonableness must have cracked then because without further ceremony certain walls—inhibitions?—dearly bought notions?—but not duties or actual beliefs—gave way, and it was over the din of falling stone that she heard what Lautner said, heard it quite clearly. No time elapsed between her hearing and her comprehending.

Nora's father said, "Well, you can just wait—waiting's good for eggheads." He took out his handkerchief and made ready to blow his nose. "Why are you looking at me like that?" he asked Lautner.

"Dislike," Lautner said.

Nora saw her mother stiffen as if she'd been slapped. Her brother's eyes bulged, his head shot forward. Her father looked at a point somewhere beyond the table, perhaps beyond the room.

"Do you have a family yourself?" Ned asked. His question had an angry edge as if he were being pulled in against his will. Nora thought of Ned suddenly as subject to the temptation of intelligence. He was rubbing a book of matches back and forth across the tablecloth.

"Everyone has a family but the devil, Mr. Ingarden," Lautner said.

"I want to make sure I understand," Nora said, valorously. Her pulse was beating against the hammered gold cuff on her wrist. "What is obedience to God if it isn't a model for earthly duty to one's family—the prototype of what's practiced in families, or should be—if kindness has meaning?"

"My dear interlocutor, kindness always has meaning—and while it may require interpretation, it does not lack meaning while it is waiting to be understood. Human kindness is very rare. A person can be wildly extravagant about duty on the basis that it won't be continuous—or the politics of being dutiful can lead to being the boss, to having the moral upper hand, but I doubt that this is kind. The dutiful are not automatically kind—or godly; they're often quite power-mad. I'll tell you a secret if you promise to think about it." He leaned toward her and said softly in her ear, "The person who is most power-mad, Nora, determines the level of alertness of those around him who would rather be in love."

A moment passed. He said, "I've upset you."

"Yes. But I don't think I mind." Suddenly she laughed—in an unstable way. She said, "Willie, Ned, you have to learn to be more disrespectful to me."

Val said—quickly—"You said that to me last year." She added, "But you didn't mean it, Mom."

Nora looked at Ned, at her parents. At Lautner. I think if Lautner had asked her at that moment—but he never asks for anything: he doesn't act on the basis that he is permitted love or lust—she would have followed him anywhere. But he didn't ask and she saw the folly of hoping. He was clearly of a different caste. And he thought her shabby. She ached with love and confusion, shame and dismay.

Ned was shaking his head, his jaw was pushed forward. "It's not hard to decide who's the power-mad one at this table," he said.

"Now there I'd agree with you," Lautner said.

There was a short, bleak silence. Tromp finished his champagne, thumped the heel of his hand on the table, and stood up, apologizing for having kept them. Lautner rose, smiled at Nora, and said, "I'm sorry I'm so argumentative," and they left.

"That's one arrogant son-of-a-bitch," Ned said.

Willie said, "God, Dad, did you notice that he argued from an essentially Wittgensteinian point of view? I thought he was amazing." He flexed and extended his fingers while he talked so that his knuckles cracked repeatedly.

"Stop that, Willie," Ned said. "He's some kind of fraud."

"Mom?" Willie appealed.

"He's not a fraud," Nora said.

Ned appeared not to hear her. He was concerned with a cough.

"It's late, Nora," her father said. He looked worn down and ill—hardly feisty. "Mom and I have to get an early start tomorrow."

"It was a lovely evening, Nora," her mother said. "It's a pity the veal was so tough." Had she heard anything?

Everything was changed and yet nothing was different.

She was in love but so what? She wasn't free. The moment was a coarse one to live through. There really is no limit to the ongoingness of things; to the awesome reality of a family.

She locked the front door and turned out the lights.

Ned had never actually wronged her so she wasn't free. He was upstairs, stretched out on the bed, waiting for her to thank him properly for having made her birthday so pleasant. Willie was waiting to seduce her into talking with him until he was relaxed enough to be able to fall asleep. Val was waiting to read her the concluding paragraph of her term paper on the amorality of Genet. Her parents were waiting to tell her how proud they were of her. She was waiting too—or a part of her was waiting—to see what would happen next. There was nothing else she could do, you see. She hadn't gotten to her feet in front of her family and asked Lautner to take her away with him. And she certainly wasn't going to kill herself because she had to stay. But there were conditions: there were certain thoughts she couldn't allow herself. She couldn't think about Lautner, or if she did she had to keep her thoughts about him from turning into a story.

She climbed the first flight of stairs. The walls were smudged with powdery gray-black shadows. She knocked and entered the guest room. Her parents were in separate beds, reading. She kissed her father good night and covered her mother with an extra blanket.

Her mother said, "You're so thoughtful, Nora. Daddy and I were just saying what a good wife and mother and daughter you are. How proud we are of you."

"Thank you, Mom, but if I am good it's only because I had such a good teacher."

Her mother didn't exactly smile but she let her hand stay in Nora's for a long moment.

Nora felt almost light-hearted as she walked into Valerie's room.

"I'll only keep you a minute," Val said. "What I want to read you is really short."

Nora watched the pulse beating in Valerie's throat as her voice rose and fell, one beautiful cadence after another. How much happier, how much more eager Val was when she was speaking French—how much freer.

"That's wonderful," Nora said, embracing her. "Just brilliant." But she wasn't thinking about Val's accomplishment at that moment. She was secretly shocked at having discovered, during the embrace, how narrow and fragile and vulnerable her daughter's frame was—no stronger than a bird's really.

"Bonne nuit, Maman. Dors bien," Val sang.

"Toi aussi, ma petite," Nora whispered in her ear. "Tu es super."

Willie put his head on her lap and wondered aloud about his future—whether he would live a "life of the mind" and be poor, or go out into the world and make lots of money—until the bones of her thighs went numb. She waited until he'd yawned a few times and then she moved his head onto his pillow and got up from the bed. He said, looking up at her drowsily and with a childlike smile in his eyes, "This is not a complaint, Mom, but you know the only soft spot on you is your heart."

"Thank you for saying that, darling," she said, and pressed her lips to his forehead one last time.

She climbed the second flight of stairs, her legs as heavy as stone pillars. The muffled blare of a siren filled her ears.

Hearing her enter the bedroom, Ned rolled heavily onto his side. "Happy birthday," he said softly. Insinuatingly.

There was a terrible plea for complicity in the way he drew his knees toward his chest, in the way his fingers curled toward her, toward the light, out of the crumpled blanket.

She turned off the lamp and locked the door. She slipped into bed beside him. He took her in his arms and exhaled deeply.

"I'm very lucky to have you, do you know that?" he said. "We're all very lucky to have you. The caring, the effort you make, the commitment. There's no one like you."

"Thank you," she said, hiding her face against his shoulder.

"I just wanted you to know what I was thinking."

"Yes," she said.

"We're going to have forty more wonderful years, at least. Tonight was just the first line of the first scene of the second act." He lifted her chin and kissed her on the mouth. "I love you very much," he said.

"I'm the lucky one," she said. "I married a good man."

This was her birthday gift to Ned, the important gift she'd made him for many years now. He didn't value material or physical gifts.

"We did it together, you and I," he said, adjusting her body beneath his.

She closed her eyes.

Nora was to learn that Lautner believed that what was called neurosis—or unhappiness—was often merely the reflection of evil. *Merely*—to him. That night, to Nora, the evil was in her thoughts of him. Not sexual fantasies. Those came later, in the middle of the night when she felt a terrible desire to lie on the floor and howl because he wasn't there to talk to her. The way in which he was rude—or truthful—made talking with him more interesting than anything in her life. She thought that until tonight, no man had ever told her the truth about anything. Her birthday present to herself was to stay awake until morning, thinking about him.

2

She woke very late to the sound of the telephone ringing. She was determined not to think about Lautner.

"Is that you, Nora?" Tromp asked.

"Yes," she said, instantly alert with disappointment.

"I didn't wake you, did I?"

"Oh, no."

"I'm calling to apologize for the way Lautner behaved."

"That's not necessary."

He paused. "I can't see that any of you gave him a reason to be so unpleasant."

"Have you known him long?" she asked. "Who is he? What does he do?"

"Never mind about him," Tromp said. "Tell me about you—are you well?"

"Well enough," she said after a pause.

"That sounds ominous. What are you doing with yourself these days?"

"Are you asking as a doctor or as a friend?—oh, never mind—I'm doing some charity thing. I go to long, boring meetings. I have one a little later today."

"How are things between you and Ned?"

"I haven't had another affair, if that's what you mean."

"What do you think you might like to do?"

"There isn't anything in particular. I don't seem to have a calling."

Tromp burst out laughing. "Oh, Nora. So serious. There are other things for a beautiful woman besides a calling."

"I don't think so. Not for me, I mean."

"Why don't we have lunch and talk about it? I might have some ideas."

"Lunch?" The idea of seeing him alone alarmed her.

"Yes. One day next week. Of course, we could have dinner, but I don't think you'd feel free to talk in front of Ned."

She hesitated for a moment before giving in.

"Good. I'll phone you next week, then."

"Yes. And thanks for calling. I'm relieved that you don't think we provoked him—Lautner, I mean."

Merely saying his name out loud had the effect of summoning up the longing for another sort of life, one she could barely define except that its accomplishments and its rewards would not hinge primarily on money. Or on God. The knowledge that she'd thrown away her life—and not wantonly but calculatingly—hit her now as if from behind and with a force doubled by its unexpectedness, and left her breathless. She told herself that a few people were better off because she'd existed, but in the deepest, most private sense, she knew that her life had been mostly wasted. She wanted another chance; she believed she deserved one but that didn't mean she could take it if it came.

This thought chased her from the bed. She tossed her nightgown over a chair and threw on her running clothes. She drank a cup of coffee standing up at the sink in her well-appointed kitchen. It was pointless to harp on self-hatred— self-hatred was a particularly perverse form of egotism. On the other hand, the women she knew who refused to acknowledge the ugly compromises involved in being dependent were even more odious to her. The issue was far too complex to be resolved—if she ran hard enough and far enough she got free of it. It. Self-hate and envy. She went out of her way to be nice to women who had reason to envy her her looks or her money. She avoided the company of women whom she, in turn, might envy. Boredom, self-hate—anything—was preferable to envy.

A police car was standing at the entrance to the bridle path, its engine idling and clouds of smoke billowing fatly from its tailpipe. The driver let his eyes travel slowly over her. Nora glanced at him, then away. He was burly and experienced-looking and there was resignation in his eyes tempered by the possibility of both passion and cynicism. Nora always looked at a man's eyes first, and then at his hands (she couldn't remember looking at Lautner's) and sometimes, if she was interested, at his wrists. She noticed men's groins too, imprecisely but precisely enough, and necks—she detested thick necks.

This morning, the men running toward her on the track they shared with horses and riders struck her as looking self-satisfied and prosperous, the older ones shrewd. She was uncomfortably aware of being appraised by this group. If she didn't look her best, and she didn't—her running clothes were worn and baggy, she wasn't made up, and her hair was tucked into an old ski cap of Willie's—she felt defensive and powerless. Underpriced. She didn't like being intimidated in this way but she took her running too seriously to pretty up for it, so seriously that Ned's mocking pleasantries on the subject no longer bothered her. She knew he was jealous. Running gave her possession of herself. Occasionally he boasted about her weekly mileage in public.

She was a third of the way around the track when she saw the bird-watchers. They were staring in open-mouthed astonishment at a small bird that was hopping back and forth at the edge of the bridle path. A genuine celebrity ringed by admirers. The bird seemed disinclined to fly away and yet the Swainson's warbler (she confirmed her guess in the *Times* the next day) was a known skulker, and also it was far too early in the season for it or any warbler. The whole thing was rather odd. A man standing at the fringe of the crowd caught her attention. He was peering at the bird through a pair of metal-rimmed yellow glasses of a kind invented by the French to help hunters see through underbrush, and he was listening to a Mozart opera. The music was leaking from his headphones; she heard it as she neared him. She surprised herself by stopping a few feet off and pretending an interest in the Swainson—an interest well beyond what she felt—so that she could study him. He resembled Lautner, she thought, her breath catching in her throat, but the light was so different and he was dressed so differently. Also he seemed shorter. Just imagining that he might be Lautner made her feel slightly feverish, somewhat disembodied yet acutely aware of her body, which was trembling a little. He was staring at her, she realized. His eyes through the yellow lenses were translucently green. Jadelike. The way he stared at her—she could feel his eyes drilling into her—made her feel that he knew something damaging about her of which she herself was ignorant. He looked as if he knew a lot.

She ran off to escape his eyes. He was taller than she'd thought at first sight, more or less Lautner's size, but darker and more dangerous-seeming. But then, as she passed him, he smiled at her and whatever cruelty she thought she'd seen on his face disappeared altogether. She ran the rest of the lap looking over her shoulder every now and then, thinking he might still be Lautner, hoping he might be following her. He wasn't.

After a while, with an effort of will, she was able to push him to the back of her mind. The air felt sweetly cold against her face. She looked out at the city from a snug hive of her own warmth. Whatever the cost to her nerves and her self-esteem, nowhere else in the world was she as much at home as in this Byzantium of intrigue and striving.

In a narrow strip of woods to her right, she glimpsed a pair of lovers. They were not so frivolously or so deeply in love as to interest her for long—one half-moment, a sad, envious glance. Frivolity was a trait Nora held in grand contempt, but that didn't prevent her from being fascinated by certain of its practitioners.

The woman in the trees, in the man's arms, in the dove-gray morning light, had a look on her face that suggested it didn't matter much who was kissing her. Even so, spasms of jealousy pursued Nora. To be kissed hotly on a cold gray morning . . . she shivered and upped her pace. Things were clearer to her when she ran and the clarity was a kind of freedom. Momentarily. Then it became unbearable.

At Ninety-second Street, two men in nylon running suits, one of them playing a radio, drew even with her. Their suits rustled dry-leaved as taffeta. She guessed them to be about ten years younger than she, but they were slack-bodied and gray-faced and they had dark patches on their cheeks from the exertion. She had to sprint to get away from the blare of their radio. Her senses were so honed from running that she could hear them breathing heavily over the blast of music. She knew they were trying to catch her. She willed herself to stay ahead of them. At this stage of her run she was feeling enormously strong (this happened occasionally—she was a respectable but not an impressive runner), as if she'd been granted a strength immeasurable by ordinary standards. "Fuck her," she heard one of them grunt. Keeping her pace, she turned off the bridle path and onto the Park Drive. The police car was gone. She pulled off her cap as she ran. The wind lofted two startling wings of russet-colored hair from her temples; it draped her scarf in warrior folds across her breasts. She was in a state of burning bodily immediacy, empty of thought and will, running like someone destined, her legs moving faster—say one beat faster—than she knew to be possible or sensible. No matter. It was out of her hands. If I said she was an arrow speeding toward the world's great heart and that she could almost feel its warm red pigment seeping into her pores, would that be acceptable? It was like that.

She couldn't keep it up. She stumbled or she willed herself to stumble. Simultaneously she saw she was about to collide with a large, densely muscular, foreign-looking man. She veered sharply. He grazed her shoulder. She saw the yellow glasses. His resemblance to Lautner shocked her. She addressed him questioningly. He appeared not to hear her. He disappeared around the curve. The world flattened.

In the house facing hers across the garden, someone was playing the minuet from *Don Giovanni* on a recorder. Nora pulled some clothes from her closet. Her mode of dress was that of a woman who expected to be looked at and wanted to be admired but couldn't bear to arouse the antagonism of envy or passion. She favored spareness of line, good cloth, earth colors (the paler ones) and black. If she knew the audience was a forgiving or a generous one, she would risk a measure of wit. A striped Joseph coat several sizes too large and belted like a bathrobe. She had only this limited conception of style and she was as obedient to its dictates as any master of the Japanese print.

That day she chose a checked silk shirt in tones of milky chocolate, a miniature wine-and-white pin-dot tie, a pair of pleated flannel trousers of a rich middling cocoa, and a herringbone plaid jacket in the same range of color. She dressed hurriedly, as she did everything. Excursions into the more languorous aspects of movement didn't sit well with her—things like long baths, facials, massages, manicures, especially. Bodily indulgences in general, as well as prolonged gazing into mirrors, had an effect opposite to that intended. She preferred herself on the wing, as if speed were the only beauty that had in it an antidote to vanity.

She ran a comb through her hair and then began to braid it by touch. Her hair was her glory. It was the changeable red-daubed brown of an Irish setter's coat, silky and with a tendency to fall into soft curling waves. Hair and glory, an odd but historically persistent pairing. Why, she often wondered, since hair was a dead thing? But the romance between women and their hair never stopped being interesting—and dangerous. She would cut her hair and then regret it; then let it grow again and grow to hate it—to hate the luxury, the eloquent and hampering uselessness; then cut it again and regret it. At one time, she had even dated the events in her life according to the length of her hair. Her grandfather was cooler to her when it was long. She cut it when he had his first heart attack. It was short when she married Ned. It was long for her grandfather's funeral. In college, she joked that what she hoped for in her next incarnation was to be a woman who spoke flawless French, who played the cello with enough warmth to melt the polar ice-cap, and who had hair down to her ankles.

Her hair hung to the middle of her back now, but unless it was braided or otherwise harvested and bundled—that day she favored a boyish look with her hair in one long braid—it was an embarrassment. She plucked out the gray hairs as they came in.

After a glance in the mirror to satisfy herself that the woman reflected there was not an impostor, she slung a large leather pouch across her chest and to one side like the mailmen of her childhood and left the house. On the street, traveling to her meeting, she assumed a face that she thought of as hopeful within the context of grief. She didn't care to inquire too closely into her own grief or sadness, although she was moved by the sadness of others. Her distaste for self-pity and her almost limitless admiration for hard work of any sort lent her face a seriousness largely undercut by her way of dressing. She believed herself to be a creator of style and therefore to have some limited value, but she knew she was viewed by others chiefly as a made object, perhaps even one of museum quality. Under no circumstances could she be taken for a genuinely serious person. Oh, she was immensely serious at the level of daydream—that is, in her soul. But then so are many women.

Margaret, pretty and fierce, scrupulously groomed and scrupulously clean—the way she was clean reminded Nora of a child fresh from the bath—detached herself from the throng of women around her and came toward Nora, limping slightly because of an arthritic knee. Nora straightened her back. Margaret Reed Martini Palma, depending on how much she drank—the drunker she was, the closer she ventured to the lower social classes (her dead father, a South African, was either a sergeant or a major in the British Army)—had spent years as a purveyor of art to the rich, during which she'd learned to be a lady and to be amusing. She was a careless and harsh and indirect critic of women who did not put on as good a show as she did. Margaret may have been vague and changeable about her own origins but where the lineage of her pictures and her furniture was concerned she was outspoken, accurate, even scholarly. I'm thinking of the hardly Titian nude over the yellow silk sofa in the living room (Margaret called her "the naughty Donna" and turned off the light over her when Monsignor Creedy came by to discuss the Eucharist over a glass of champagne), and the tiny Degas drawing on the foyer wall to Nora's left, badly torn but charming, and the thirteenth-century Siennese Madonna and Child in the dining room— very rare, Margaret had explained once, not because it was so beautiful but because the predella hadn't been removed and sold separately in one of those nasty eras that had a passion for small genre scenes.

Margaret, prodded by tax advantages and the high cost of insurance, had given pictures to the Metropolitan over the years as fashion had made them more valuable. This heartlessness toward the beautiful had gone to underwrite the adventures of her expensively saintly only child, her now dead son, Tony. She'd said to Nora that she missed her Tintoretto but that she could always go around the corner and have a look, although she did hate the new lighting: it was so harsh it sucked the spirit from the paint. Nora had educated herself by some weeks of looking, and then, yes, she told Margaret she agreed with her.

As for Margaret's furniture—the chaise longue, for instance, had at one time decorated one of the lesser apartments at Versailles. The other things came from the back halls and minor rooms of the Luxembourg and Schönbrunn. Authenticated pieces but quite heavily damaged so that in spite of being honorably restored (under the supervision of one or the other of Margaret's Italian husbands—art dealers who had become rich; both had been old enough to have fathered her), their full value could never be realized at a sale. In the whole apartment, only a pair of Neapolitan white bisque lamps covered with three-dimensional flowers were historically worthless. And these, Nora thought, represented Margaret's flirtatious and erotic boast.

"Hello, dear," Margaret said, taking both Nora's hands in

her own. Nora bent to kiss her: Margaret was barely five feet tall. Her white hair was neatly waved around her face, her blue eyes shone. "How marvelous you look, Nora," she said. "Like an English schoolboy. Tony once had a jacket of that material."

Tony had been dead eight years, murdered by unknown persons in Naples, two years after having married a local whore to save her from her pimp. There was a child. No one knew whether he was Tony's but Tony had claimed him. "Tony," Margaret said, dabbing at the corners of her mouth as she did when she was about to be particularly naughty, "had a tendency to rescue fortune hunters." Still, she sent the child's mother money every month. And when she died, the child would have a trust fund.

"It's your dress that's marvelous, Margaret. Almost as marvelous as the naughty Donna's skin tones," Nora said. "I know I've never seen it before. Is it new?"

The dress was pink-and-white silk, pink lilies on a white pond. A not-quite Monet.

"No, but I don't wear it except when I want to feel wicked. It was terribly expensive. It's a Chanel—but you probably know that. I had it made the spring after I gave the Metropolitan my dear, dear—dear—Duccio. One doesn't have to insure one's dresses. At least, not yet. I think it's pretty. I'm so glad you noticed."

Margaret then drew her into the front room, into the rising warmth of mingled perfumes and the murmurous hum of women's voices. "We'll be starting in a few minutes," she said, motioning Nora to an empty place on the silky couch next to Kitty Lilienthal and at a right angle to Connie Blakely, who was perched on the edge of a small bergère chatting with the woman next to her. Nora smiled in an odd way, peculiar to her enjoyment of Margaret, and sat down.

When Margaret had invited her to join the committee, she'd asked her to include one or two friends who could be useful.

"It's a dinner auction—stuff from the museum's basement. Margaret calls them demoted treasures. It's for their acquisition fund," Nora explained to Connie. Connie Blakely was the younger sister of one of Ned's childhood friends.

"I'd love to help out," Connie had said. After all, she said, her kids had practically grown up in the Museum of Natural History. Connie's husband, Bob, came from an immensely rich family, hundreds of millions probably. His father held the patents on a number of inventions that were crucial to the steel industry—"little thingies," Connie said—which the family also manufactured. The family had its own foundation. Connie was doll-sized like Margaret, blue-eyed, blonde-haired, fair-skinned, unfailingly kind and genuinely public-spirited. Her taste in clothes and furnishings tended toward clutter—ruffles and layers and puffs.

Kitty Lilienthal had refused at first but hearing Margaret's name—Kitty had a passion for the solemn, hieratic beauty of Siennese art—she relented. Kitty's childhood had been impoverished and religious. Her married life was monied and secular. Her husband, Lloyd, was in real estate. He lived on the telephone. He lived nervously but well. As for Kitty, she toiled long hours in the kitchen for secretly preferring culture to God. She pursued material simplicity as ardently as if it were a form of morality; indeed, she occasionally served all-white dinners. And her clothes were as calculatedly spare as they were expensive. The jewelry Lloyd bought her was inexplicably elaborate and possibly not at all to her taste, but she wore it loyally, as if it were. In her free time, she gave classes in the art of Japanese flower arranging. She loved her sons baroquely, though, like a woman possessed. She respected her husband. She was obedient to the religion of her fathers. She hated her widowed mother but she supported her and suffered her company. Nora loved her for her uncompromising sense of duty.

Carmela and her sister, Nunziata, who helped out when

Margaret was being ambitious, moved among the women serving coffee and small open-faced smoked-salmon sandwiches made by the latest caterer—Margaret was not handy in the kitchen. Kitty Lilienthal smiled at Nora as she settled her plate on her lap, rolling her eyes nakedly toward the fireplace, where Margaret and Anina Durant were in unlikely conference. Anina Durant (she was as luscious as a peony) was married to a wealthy Frenchman who was rumored to be an insatiable voyeur. She had a sighing manner, a vaguely Mediterranean accent, and a voice well placed for seduction; and she signaled with her eyes that she was reasonably intelligent. She'd recently had her breasts reduced and lifted. Her gynecologist, Roger Silverthorne, who was also Nora's doctor and friend, thinking to amuse Nora, had described to her how Anina had burst into his office a few weeks after her surgery to show off the results. Her breasts were stitched and seamed like baseballs and just as hard to the touch. The nipples were off center—wall-eyed—he'd said, laughing. His indiscretion and his callousness had determined Nora to change doctors, but since he was a friend and she dreaded hurting his feelings she wasn't certain she could. Today, Anina was wearing a narrowly flowing silk dress of a highly burnished satiny bronze color that shaded to a deep iridescent peacock blue around her renovated breasts, a combination of colors that was common only to the male common grackle. The resemblance didn't end there. Anina also had that overtly chilling aura of yellow-eyed shrewdness native to the bird whose colors she had pirated. Nora had been told, and she had no reason to doubt it, that the business of several governments was transacted informally in Anina's salon, where the ambience was a seductive blend of money and power and secrecy and sexual lenience. Nora never saw Anina without wondering how large a fortune was in question and what Anina had to do to keep her hands on it. Everyone agreed—Anina's husband was a snake. The really incomprehensible thing about Anina was that in spite of being associated with such a monster she seemed to enjoy her life.

"I can't think of anyone worse than that woman," Kitty said in an undertone. "Except my mother, of course."

Nora nodded with slow but impassioned agreement, the more so for having now and then been seduced by Anina's bountifulness.

Connie Blakely, who adored both her mother and her mother-in-law and didn't much care for Kitty, said, "Oh, Anina's not so bad. She and her husband are very generous. I sit on a few boards with her." She twisted her emerald ring around and around as she talked.

Kitty raised her hand to her throat and pressed it there for a moment. The large ruby on her finger glowed as if with heat. She recrossed her long, shapely legs and said, "I can't understand Margaret's asking Anina."

"Oh, Margaret can be very broad-minded, particularly in the interests of a good cause. Didn't I ever tell you that she has a half-black grandchild?"

Kitty's eyes flew open.

"And two half-Jewish ones—like me?"

Kitty's mouth relented a bit.

"And one half-Neapolitan? Her son's third wife was a prostitute."

"You can't be serious," Kitty said, pushing her slippery black hair to one side.

"I've never known anyone like Margaret—I've never known anyone so indomitable: she never complains—without being interesting: I can't imagine her being bored. She adores weak men with good minds. She's been intimate with some of the most crazed minds of her time. Men's, I mean—she adores men. Women, too—but she's easily jealous. Besides, she places a very high value on being amused. A stepdaughter in her first marriage made a lesbian pass at her—Margaret says it was a shock and it was also dull. All her male stepchildren—there were six or seven of them, and they were all older than she was—fell in love with her. I'm sure she was a terrible mother, drunk and flirtatious and domineering, but she must have been a charming wife. She had two superior husbands—well, one, anyway—and God knows how many lovers. She still has one, I think."

"At the age of eighty?" Kitty was incredulous.

"Oh, he's a lot younger than she is," Nora said, and settled back against the sofa to look around the room. To the left of the fireplace, she saw a dozen or so women who were not strangers to her but weren't exactly familiars either: women whose pictures were in the paper because they or their husbands had money and wanted to be public figures—some of them had publicity agents—and have interesting and enviable lives and who spent a lot of time plotting galas and fêtes and balls for the benefit of worthy causes: women whom Nora thought of as being more or less worthless.

After the plates had been cleared away, Margaret limped gracefully to the fireplace and clapped her hands for attention. In her delicate, slightly wavering voice—it had a sort of shimmer—she apologized for having called this meeting so hastily and without consulting anyone else as to time or place. "I can assure you, I'm not a fascist," she said. "No one has ever seen me touch a glass of beer. I'm told we've been made fashionable because someone named Happy or Muffy—some peculiarly American name or other—has endorsed us in *The New York Times* and as a result we're very much oversubscribed. Unfortunately, our underwriters have refused to increase our budget. I'm afraid we'll have to scale down the menu and the flowers if we don't want to cut into the profits. Now, I've asked Anina Durant to chair the meeting. I don't believe that anyone who weighs less than a hundred pounds should have any authority where food is concerned."

Anina rose and walked languidly to the fireplace. She called the meeting to order—throatily—and then asked for suggestions from the floor. Everyone capable of speech responded, seemingly at once, and everyone had a different opinion. Authority was claimed on the basis of an intimate knowledge of other such events. Cancer dances. Heart balls. Nora was not a veteran of the charity circuit but had come because of Avery Loudon, once her lover, now her friend— he was the honorary chairman of the event—and Margaret, because friendship had caused the two of them to say that she would be amused, and that she was needed. She sat silent while opinion slowly resolved into two opposing camps: one that appealed for chicken curry (yellow mums in straw baskets, and a California Chablis) and another that insisted on the original plan of veal tonnato (a white Bordeaux from France, and white roses in laboratory beakers) even though it would mean cutting into the profits. Good will was a form of profit, Connie Blakely argued. The tickets were expensive. "We can't afford to have anyone sitting on their hands during the auction when we want them writing those big smiling checks."

Anina Durant agreed. To find Anina on her side silenced Connie, who, though she might defend Anina against Kitty's slurs on principle—she was a good woman—had no liking for her and thought anything she said corrupt and to be opposed.

Meanwhile, Margaret and Kitty argued for the curry. With an air of martyred boredom (she wasn't enjoying herself and hadn't invited Nora for Nora's benefit, Nora saw, but out of ennui only), Margaret said that the men paid no attention to what was served at these affairs and the women paid attention only to one another's clothes. Her eyes were listless. Then she roused herself and said that Avery would see to it that "no one dare sit on his or her hands," correcting Connie's grammar.

Nora struggled to sit up straight and be attentive-looking through the long debate but inwardly she was slumped in the corner of the couch, suffering over a disbelief that any real moral rank could be earned here. On the face of it, she felt superior to Anina and all the other socially or morally ambitious women with money, yet she couldn't rid herself of the suspicion that, for all her idealism, she was of less real value than these passionate materialists who, in spite of their many poisonous defects, actually had the power to contribute something to the world's upkeep. And since she couldn't put her finger on anything that might make her any better than the women around her beyond her excessive sensitivity to human misery, a thing she acted on in her personal relations but not on any broader scale—and that she thought of as a vanity—she kept silent.

If only she could discover a real work in the world she wanted to do and could do she would certainly not be this miserable. All her life, except for the times she'd been pregnant and again during her children's infancy, she'd felt like an unemployed force, she'd been unhappy. She wasn't such a fool as to blame God or the world or her parents or men for the failure of her life to accumulate meaning. Nothing was blocking her from meaning except herself. It was some obscure resistance, a kind of dreadful inertia in herself that drew her away from meaning.

She was absorbed in her thoughts and it wasn't until Kitty Lilienthal tapped her hand that she became aware that the noisy playground of the living room had been transformed into a den of silence. She turned her head and saw the woman who had invoked it—the silence. Sylvie Rochas. The gothic effect—the haunting matter of it was from the stabbing reality of a woman's perhaps satisfactory life.

The woman's eyes were green-black and set rather shallowly above her cheekbones and at a pronouncedly horizontal angle. Her face was long and down-sloping, her nose had a dramatic jut near the bridge, her lower lip was softer and glossier than her upper. Her hair was shoulder length, very full, lightly grayed as if a glinting tissue of frost lay over it. The face it framed was moon pale. She was tall and strong-shouldered, full-breasted and oddly narrow-hipped, and dressed comfortably but compellingly in a worn leather jacket and a pair of comfortably broken-in tweed trousers. Sylvie Rochas.

Nora had met her twenty years ago at a dinner party in St. Moritz (she and Ned had been on a ski-honeymoon), a dinner where she'd been paralyzed by the meringue, silenced by the string of three-thousand-year-old jade beads (from the tomb of some pharaoh or other) that hung around the neck of her hostess.

Sylvie was French, intellectual, leftist, of course. "A young goddess," the hostess had whispered to Nora. "Courting her is now the sole project of our best men." The ones she turned down declared her a lesbian. The ones who were seen with her smiled at these reports. Sylvie's friends were silent. She was known as a creature who didn't welcome decipherment. It had been clear even then that there were certain compromises Sylvie would never make. She would never stay very long in one place. No one would ever own her. She'd had that terrible rawness of will that demands submission; and something in her eyes suggested punishment if she didn't get it. That something was still in place. Sadistic women have a lot to teach the rest of us. Nora had never stopped suffering the effects of her brief exposure. Sylvie's success was her punishment.

Margaret hurried past her to welcome Sylvie. Anina Durant followed. Nora saw a man shake Margaret's hand and bow to Anina. She was as if ignited by his presence: the slum of her feelings caught fire. Someone spoke a few words to him and he burst out laughing. He was still laughing when he bent to kiss Sylvie's cheek, and then he was out the door, gone, leaving Nora to the holocaust in her.

Anina Durant announced Sylvie Rochas to the gathering, citing her achievements, her books, her current project—a lecture tour of American colleges and universities—as if Sylvie Rochas were the featured speaker at this forum and something of a personal trophy as well. "Sylvie's staying with me," Anina said. "I've managed to persuade her to lend her eminence to our little affair." She put her arm around Sylvie's shoulder.

"Get me a cup of coffee, will you, cherie," Sylvie said.

Anina dropped her arm. Margaret signaled one of the maids.

"A touch of cream, please," Sylvie said, extending her cup to Anina. Anina took the creamer from the tray at Sylvie's elbow and poured.

For a while, Sylvie stood at the center of a cluster of bright-haired women like the dark and throbbing heart of a sunflower, sipping her coffee with a crooked half-smile on her lips. Then she began to move around the room, offering her free hand to one woman after another, greeting them in French-accented Oxonian English that greatly enhanced her already vast style. Her speech was musically inflected, Mozartian. Her brief arias floated on currents of air across the room—"Thank you so much. I'm so very pleased. Mais, bien sûr! I know them very well. Be sure to give them my regards."

Nora noticed that she constantly urged her lower lip forward between phrases. When Sylvie reached her, Nora extended her hand, but she couldn't speak and she only glanced at the dark eyes that looked appraisingly into hers and then when she did smile—clearly in a way that said she knew she wasn't someone a woman of distinction would choose for a friend, she was insignificant, harem-bound— Sylvie with a cool, slighting, sudden blindness moved on. Nora tried to imagine Sylvie as depressed, as having smiled in an ill-judged way, as having in her an oven of sighing female secrets, and she failed. She began to shake inwardly— this had to do with Lautner. It had been possible for her to know that Sylvie existed and still carry on with her own meager life, but not now.

Oh, God, competing with her for Lautner, even if only in her imagination—no, it was impossible to live. Nora was about to faint. Sylvie was so huge in the perspective of the room, so much larger, in a sense, than the furniture—than Margaret—than Lautner—than anyone but the devil—that it felt to Nora as if she'd used up all the available air and Nora went dark.

But she remained upright. She came to, knowing just how mediocre she was.

Have you ever wished, not for the death of another woman—that wasn't possible for Nora—but that the woman, the idea, the lived life had never occurred—been born or made actual in any degree? What else could Nora wish for? She couldn't submit to Sylvie's will—kneeling to Sylvie was out of the question: Sylvie had no authority for Nora—yet she had too much honor to tear down what was so clearly superior. Nora again began to tremble inwardly. The thing cut so deep today. She looked searchingly, despairingly at Kitty, and then across to Connie as if to reassure herself that the struggle they had undertaken so many years before in the service of an inherited vision—the struggle to remain selfless and yet not to wither—that this struggle was a valid one. She was confirmed only in her doubts. Her friends' eyes, as they regarded Sylvie, were coldly self-defensive, the way her own were, no doubt.

She didn't want to think of Claire, Claire, with the bland brown eyes of a calf, the large, bare forehead that gave her a defiant, mannish look, and the waist that could be encompassed by a pair of male hands. One autumn morning ten years back, after sending her children off to school with a kiss and giving her husband his second cup of coffee, she locked the bedroom door, weighted herself down with all her jewels, a rich woman's version of Virginia Woolf's stones—Claire had been too literate for the life she was attempting—opened the window, and leaped out.

Or that other woman whom she'd known only slightly, the mother of a shy little friend of Val's—the name slipped her mind—a wild, lithe, and beautiful woman, a siren who was married to a frog-faced brute with the body of a lizard. What was her name? Never mind. The day before her thirty-seventh birthday in the midst of scandal about her promiscuity she hanged herself from the topmost rung of the banister of the staircase in their country house in Vermont. She'd had to pull her legs up so her feet wouldn't touch the floor. Gloria. That was it. Gloria.

Nora felt herself beginning to dissolve with a dubious finality. This time she made no move to control what was happening to her. She had no wish to save herself. To preserve an insight of any honesty is, in one sense, to lose everything else. She summoned to mind her children, her parents, Ned, even the poor beautiful creature who was so inessentially her brother. They had the brazen immobility of stick figures. They were supposed to represent the human meaning of her life. This really frightened her. She excused herself and went to the powder room. A circle of tinted bulbs threw a rosy light, a warm and fortifying pale gold tinged with red that plunged Nora into a state of illuminated emptiness. She put on some lipstick and checked her eye liner for smudges. She penciled her sparse eyebrows. She recognized the woman in the mirror briefly. She was someone crucial to her. It was as if a familiar word was repeated over and over until the word, from being merely doubtful, moves to a point where it loses all meaning and at the same time remains hideously familiar, as if it had meaning.

She thought: Something apocalyptic is happening to me. She told herself: No, it isn't; I can manage this.

Sylvie was gone and the voting was under way when she returned. Things were moving at an amazing speed. Chicken curry, yellow mums, California Chablis, maids fetching coats, the elevator summoned, the women crowding on, Margaret smiling as the doors closed, a flurry or two of mutual congratulation, several hasty offers to drop anyone anywhere, many, many air-blown kisses, and bang—they were all on the street.

"I'll be late for my ladies," Kitty said, waving. "I'll talk to you tomorrow."

"I've got to run too," Connie said, kissing Nora goodbye, boredly: Nora wasn't Sylvie. "The Duchess is going to buy me a set of Sèvres fruit plates in New Jersey." The Duchess was what she called her immensely rich mother-in-law, affectionately. The Duchess of Omnium.

Look how Sylvie had terrorized them all merely by refusing to be inferior. Oh, how boring their lives must seem to Sylvie—to Lautner—like children's games, lives that had no cutting edge, lives in which, on the contrary, the whole point of existence was to blunt the edge of anguish, to lie about accomplishment. Still, she couldn't help loving them any more than she could help loving her own children, or her mother, another child. It was with an almost maternal sense of dread that Nora saw them go. As if off to school. They were as fragile as her own children, weren't they? Wasn't she? As needful of adult protection? As frightened? If you'll grant love-mixed-with-contempt the status of love, then she loved them.

If not . . . well—she hated them—fondly.

She hadn't the strength to maintain her own sophistication.

Nora, you see, found herself in an awkward position. Her loyalties were all toward women, but the body of her respect, along with everything she knew, the corpus of her knowledge, and everything she was, her bodily and moral self, were—indeed, had always been—in the service of men—even though, at bottom, she believed men were rarely good to women. She'd been tyrannized, so to speak, by centuries of male genius. She loved the male mind. She loved male courage. She loved the male body.

I doubt she can change this. Her God is male.

3

She stood alone and uncertainly on the street. She considered returning to Margaret's but rejected the idea after a moment's reflection. She had once spoken a few words of complaint to Margaret about her life. Behind the lawn handkerchief that was part of her arsenal of good manners, Margaret had permitted herself a very discreet yawn, more a shifting of facial muscles than a yawn, but not so discreet that Nora failed to see it. Nora, thus patronized and humiliated, had blushed and quickly changed the subject.

There was no place Nora cared to go; there was no refuge. She began walking aimlessly down Fifth Avenue. Lautner's shadow darkened her thoughts; Sylvie's face bloomed on every façade. Perhaps, she thought, she could console herself by shopping. Shopping, for Nora, was a bit like a holiday, a brief, sunny holiday, a somehow illicit step outside ordinary life. Sometimes shopping made her so happy that she felt guilty afterwards, as if she'd spent the time with a lover. There was something of the bandit in Nora when she went shopping; she became ruthlessly focused. Shopping was not a game, partly because she had to defend her purchases to Ned, but mostly because she'd chosen to let her clothes express the sort of woman she was.

She walked around the corner to Madison Avenue and went into a store she liked.

"How nice to see you, Mrs. Ingarden," the proprietress said. "Some wonderful sweaters arrived just this morning. Perhaps you would care to see them?"

"I'm looking for an evening dress, Madame. Something simple in a solid color. Perhaps silk or matte jersey. I need it for next week. There won't be time for any major alterations."

Madame Hupert led her to the appropriate rack and left her. She kept track of who liked close attention and who did not. Nora rifled quickly through the size sixes. There was one magnificent dress: greige, matte jersey, Athenian-looking. Although it cost twice what she'd ever spent for a dress, she was ready to buy it. She could wear it to the dinner auction and to the surprise birthday party Kitty was giving Lloyd next month at the Harmonie Club. Let Ned howl, she thought, surprised at the depth of her callousness. He benefited materially from her beauty and her style even if he wouldn't acknowledge it.

"Ah, yes," Madame Hupert said, pushing aside the curtain and entering the fitting room. "I thought as much. Shall I call Louise?"

"Please," Nora said.

"What height heel will Madame Ingarden be wearing?" the fitter mumbled, her mouth filled with pins.

"An inch and a half," Madame Hupert answered, smiling at Nora. She was vain about her memory for details. "And, Louise, a touch less fullness in the skirt. We won't take more than a quarter of an inch," she said to Nora. "Louise will see to it."

Nora stood as still as a statue while Louise ran a row of pins down both sides of the skirt and then marked the hem, turning up the front for her approval.

"The length is fine," Nora said. "Thank you."

She remained immobile while Louise slid the dress down her torso to her ankles; then she stepped out of it as gingerly as if a prick from one of the fine steel pins might change her destiny. She was too old to sacrifice another lifetime waiting. Louise gathered up the dress and left. Nora slipped rapidly into her shirt. She was just fastening her trousers when suddenly Madame Hupert's voice rose with a shrill urgency over the fitting-room partition.

"Come out quickly, Mrs. Ingarden."

Nora drew back the curtain. A man stood in the narrow passageway. He was pointing a small black gun at her.

She regarded him with a calm smile. The encounter with Sylvie had brought her nearer a feeling of death than this gun which had no more power to affect her imagination than a toy.

"Out," he said, waving the gun. "I don't want any trouble. I don't want to hurt anyone."

Nora studied him serenely without moving. He was quite tall. As tall as Lautner. His face was covered with a stocking—disfigured—almost as if his features had melted. He was dressed all in black. He wore gloves.

"I said out. Move. Follow the old bitch. Raise your hands in the air."

Nora passed in front of him. She felt the muzzle of the gun in the small of her back. Madame Hupert led the way to the stockroom. Louise was there, eating her lunch. The fork fell from her fingers and she began to scream. The man in black put one gloved hand over her mouth. He pointed the gun at Nora's head. "Take off your ring and your watch and give them to me," he said.

She slipped off her wedding band and put it in his outstretched hand, alongside the gun. She gave him the watch.

Then he said, "Up against the wall, the three of you. Don't move until you hear me leave. I don't want to hurt anyone. Give me five minutes before you call the police. If you don't, I'll come back and kill you."

They heard the ring of the cash register opening. They heard the jingle of the door closing. Louise collapsed in a chair, sobbing. Nora poured a glass of Apollinaris water that Madame Hupert kept for the clients and gave it to the fitter. She patted her hand. Madame rushed to the telephone. "The second time in two weeks," Nora heard her scream. "The same man."

The police arrived a few minutes later.

"Was he black or white?" one of them asked Nora.

"I don't know. He was wearing a dark stocking over his face."

"What about his hands?"

"He was wearing black gloves."

"His neck?"

"The stocking was tucked into a black sweater. He was wearing a black rain slicker. He was thin. Maybe a hundred and forty-five pounds. And tall. A little over six feet, I think. He was wearing running shoes."

"That's quite an eye, lady."

"I work at it. I always hoped Starsky and Hutch would find me useful."

Both cops laughed. "How much did he get?" one of them asked Madame.

"Several thousand dollars," she said. The taller cop whistled.

"Many of my customers prefer to pay in cash," Madame said.

The cops nodded, knowingly.

"He took my wedding ring and wristwatch," Nora said.

"You'll have to come down to the station to report that," the shorter one said.

"Maybe later," Nora said.

"We'll send the dress when it's ready, Mrs. Ingarden," Madame said. Her voice cracked like a choirboy's. "We won't charge for the alteration this time, hein?" She shrugged her shoulders and threw up her hands. Her face was crumpled, papery.

"That's very sweet of you, Madame Hupert, but let's just leave it as if nothing had happened. Perhaps they'll catch him. Who knows?"

"I wouldn't count on it. These guys vanish into thin air," one of the cops said. The other shook his head in agreement.

"The second time in two weeks," Madame Hupert was repeating hysterically as Nora left. "The same man."

Nora stepped off the sidewalk; her hand shot out; a taxi squealed to a stop at her feet. She climbed in and gave the driver her address, but when he pulled up in front of her house, she found she couldn't go in. "Please hold your flag," she said. "I'd like to go on to Broadway."

He dropped her at a store that was famous for its hectic atmosphere and for the variety and quality of its foodstuffs, and for its low prices. She moved mechanically through the crowded aisles, filling a wire basket with Javanese coffee beans, French goat cheese, Greek olives, Italian pasta, Portuguese anchovies. When her basket was full, she joined a long cashier's line near the exit doors. A large heater mounted on the ceiling over her head whirred and clacked. The coils glowed, red as coals. She unbuttoned her coat and took off her scarf. She shifted her weight impatiently and stared empty-eyed at the hat of the man in front of her; it was loden-green velour, narrow-brimmed, and dotted all over with tiny enamel ski pins; it reminded her of wildflower season in the Alps. The heat was fierce; ovenlike. The line was restlessly in motion but not advancing any. She sighed. A gap opened. The man in the green hat made no move to close it. She edged as near to him as she dared, her version of a confrontation, and then, as if sensing her disapproval, he turned around.

Seeing him, she shuddered. His physical presence had the alarming insubstantiality of extreme old age. At the same time, his nearness to death made him seem terribly young, the doomed youngest child of an inbred mountain family, a case of acute feeble-mindedness, or perhaps it was only that his clothes were so big they looked as if they'd been handed down from a much older brother. Nora couldn't say who he was but she knew she knew him—or that she'd known him once. She gagged on her certainty.

He stepped out of the line and with a sort of ghostly gallantry gestured to her to take his place. Oh, he was a big-headed, nearly fetal thing, heartbreaking and disgusting all at once, and as terrifying as a murderer in the blatancy of his association with death.

She knew who he was before his wife spoke her name.

"Nora?"

"Hello, Marjorie. God, it's been a long time, hasn't it?"

Marjorie ignored her remark. There was no malice in it, just common sense mixed with the exhaustion that comes of being the victim of other people's clumsiness. "Matthew had brain surgery a couple of weeks ago. He's doing really well, aren't you, Matthew?"

Matthew removed his hat and inclined a shaved and partially bandaged head toward Nora as if presenting his identity papers. He tapped the right side of his skull and smiled with a nearly unbearable sweetness.

"The change in him is a shock, I know," Marjorie said in a low voice as they embraced. "Just try to be natural." Marjorie was tall and large-boned and her directness and honesty were as impressive as she herself had become with the years.

Nora nodded. Her legs were trembling and her mouth was sharply dry. She was mute with the horror of deep feeling. She tried to make her eyes speak instead but she couldn't tell whether or not she succeeded: deception was an aspect of Marjorie's extreme graciousness.

"You remember Nora, don't you, sweetheart?" Matthew looked blank. "From the old days, darling. You went to high school together."

"Sure, sure," Matthew said, and his eyes took on the light of recognition. He seemed not to be looking at her so much as at something in his mind. "Nora, Norrie Greene. Hey, how about that?" he said triumphantly. "The boys against the girls, right? The softball game of the century. The Aces against the Rockettes." He looked at Marjorie excitedly. He was squinting with the effort of memory. "Sure, I remember. Norrie played . . . second base. Right?"

Nora nodded. He half-saluted her.

"Hello, kiddo. How're you doing? How's the arm holding up?"

"I always wanted to play shortstop," Nora said. "I wanted to be Pee Wee Reese. But Dolarita Barriscale had the arm."

"Me too. Me too. Pee Wee Reese is the one. Oh, hey, Pee Wee Reese. Small and speedy like us, huh, kiddo? A speed demon but with an arm. Dolarita Barriscale? Wait a minute—don't tell me—a blonde with a helluvan arm. Big shoulders, no tits, taller than me, right?"

"Right," Nora said.

"Hey, kiddo, remember Dougie Moriarty—the tall, skinny kid with an Adam's apple the size of a fist—his father was a cop? What d'ya suppose happened to him? I dream about him sometimes."

"He lives in New Mexico. I think he teaches at a university. He's a poet. Remember? He was at the reunion a few years ago. We all sat at the same table, Dougie and the four of us and Danny Wald and his third wife."

Matthew was supposed to have been the poet. He'd gone into advertising instead. Marjorie had trained as a flutist. She'd become a mother. Nora had dreamed of a moral life. I'm not ready to draw any conclusions yet. I'll venture this, though: fewer people than you think really want their dreams to come true.

Matthew didn't answer. He put his hat back on. Nora could see him feeling with his eyes for a grip on the face of the recent past. It was too sheer. He slipped; his empty hands agitated the air around his chest. He bounced from sentence to sentence. "No, I don't remember—I don't remember that at all—maybe it'll come back to me later—sometimes that happens. . . ." He looked wildly about him as he spoke. Marjorie took his hand and smiled reassuringly at him. He shook his head. His eyes filled with tears at his failure to comprehend his life.

"He's not in any physical pain," Marjorie said, "but we'd better go. This is the first time I've taken him out of the house. Put this somewhere for me, will you?" she asked, handing Nora her basket.

The line hadn't grown any shorter. An elderly cronelike lady with the habit of war starkly imposed on her face was demanding her money back on a loaf of bread that had gone stale overnight.

"Why don't I take care of it? I'm on line anyway. I'll drop the bags off at your apartment in a few minutes," Nora said. "I can leave them with the doorman."

"That's sweet of you, Nora, but there's no need. The shopping was just an excuse to get Matthew interested in something. Thanks anyway. I'm glad we ran into each other."

"Are you in the phone book?" Nora asked.

Marjorie nodded.

"I'll phone you soon—is next week all right?" Nora asked, but Marjorie didn't answer. Perhaps she hadn't heard. She was elbowing her way toward the exit in pursuit of Matthew, before whom the crowd had parted, almost melted, as if he were a pope or a leper or a blind man. Nora put both baskets of food on an empty counter and followed her out. She carried Matthew's face, his bandaged child's head, with her.

Beneath the traffic light, a sign flashed red. Nora froze. Eventually, it flashed green. She stepped off the sidewalk. She had the strong habit of obedience. She thought of Jenny, who didn't. There are things for which there is no consolation; still, she had the urge to try. She telephoned Jenny from the street and was grateful to find her at home.

Jenny lived in the west forties, a few blocks from the Hudson, next door to a welfare hotel. To Nora's great relief, the fallen-as-if-in-battle bodies of the neighborhood addicts that usually blocked the entrance to the building—one had to climb over them to get to the door, an exercise that put Nora into a sweating state of fear mixed with disgust and then self-reproach—were absent. The day had turned bitterly cold. Jenny buzzed her in and she climbed the dimly lit, rubbishy flight of stairs. The air she sipped was sour; the halls doubled as a urinal. Jenny lived alone in a tiny apartment—"too cranky to inflict herself on anyone on a daily basis," she said. Morally self-exacting is how Nora thought of her.

As she approached the landing, she heard the bolt being slid back, she saw the door scrape open, and then Jenny was embracing her in the hallway. "Come on in," she said. "I'll make us a pot of coffee and we can put our feet up and relax."

"You have no idea how glad I am to see you," Nora told her. She had known Jenny only a year. Avery had introduced them. Jenny was a fund raiser for a private famine-relief agency—Avery was on the board. Jenny had just returned from a field trip to Somalia, where—as she'd put it, a kind of dull wonder in her voice—"millions of people are living under tarps and plastic sheets stretched across branches. When the sandstorms come, well, forget it. There aren't any blankets, there's no wood for fires—everything's been used up. If you think of the moon jammed with make-shift tents—that's what it's like. And it's all women and children. It's a land of women and children—nearly three-quarters of a million of them, and they're all sick, all starving slowly. It's the worst refugee problem in the world and no one even knows about it."

Nora begged Ned for a thousand dollars to buy a solar-powered well pump for one of the camps, but when he turned her down, she sold the pair of sea horses without telling him. She was haunted by the image of an endless line of barefoot, starving women covered in ghostly dust, carrying sick and dying babies down a road that was no more than a track, toward refugee camps that were already massed with other dying women and their children, and by what Jenny had said to her: "I don't understand how people can know about such horrors and not do anything."

"You have to forget," she answered. "If you open yourself to pity to that extent, you risk going crazy."

"So what?" Jenny said, and her eyes were as hard as agates.

A week later she sent Jenny a money order for twelve hundred dollars.

Shortly after that, Avery, knowing what it must have cost Nora to raise that much money, had said in a brotherly sort of way, "Don't go overboard, Nora. As far as I can tell, Jenny likes you, but she's been describing you around town as a nice, bright, good-looking woman—'you know the type, somebody's pet.' " The phrase "somebody's pet" had the effect on Nora's body of a stampede. Every cell of feeling trampled. She put Jenny out of her mind. Months went by. Then one day Jenny called and asked her to dinner. Nora accepted without hesitation. She was still searching for a better way to live and although she was too proud to take instruction, she wasn't above stealing what she could. In return, she was eager to offer Jenny Ned's protection—access to good doctors, financial advice, things like that. Possibly she exaggerated the purity of Jenny's relation to life, but she couldn't help worshiping her as a romantic figure, a woman unaided by men or children or money, making her own way, trying to be useful and self-sufficient in a world that was mostly thin-crusted and criminal, a stubborn, melancholic waif—no one was ever as sad as Jenny—moving alone among the rich and intellectual and near-famous in the poor-girl clothes she affected—which were somehow startlingly chic—and appearing to see through the phoniness and pettiness around her with her long, narrow eyes, eyes that were the color of almond skins. Nora admired Jenny and told her so often. She hungered for Jenny's good opinion. Jenny hardly ever praised anyone.

"What's new?" Jenny asked, taking Nora's coat and tossing it over a chair.

"I don't know where to begin," Nora said.

"Start at the good part," she ordered, and picking up a

battered enamel coffeepot she moved toward the kitchen, actually more an improvisation at one end of the tiny living room than a kitchen, but then the whole place was improvised and deliberately makeshift. Everything was old and indecipherably worn, and nothing matched, no two patterns or colors or styles. Acquisition was clearly not the object.

Nora followed her and sat down on a bar stool pulled up to the island of low, rickety cabinets that divided the kitchen from the living room. "What if there is no good part?" Nora asked.

"Then start at the end."

"Which end? Death? Robbery? Jealousy?"

"Stop the questions. Start with death. Get it over with."

"That's easier said than done," Nora said, smiling for the first time.

"Credat Judaeus," Jenny said.

"That's not fair. You know I never studied Latin. You're worse than Sylvie Rochas for making someone feel inferior."

"Sylvie Rochas? I didn't know you knew her." Jenny's voice was strained.

"I don't really. I met her once twenty years ago, and I just saw her again at Margaret's."

"Consider yourself a lucky woman then. She's a horror," Jenny said. "I hate her."

"She doesn't look like a horror. She looks infinitely superior—which I suppose comes to the same thing."

"Oh, you—you never hate anyone. Well, I hate her. But, then, I'm not a nice woman."

Nora couldn't help smiling at this unlooked-for comfort. Some of the bandaged tightness in her chest eased. "What makes you hate her?" she asked.

Jenny tossed her head. She had straight, baby-fine hair that swung limply about her face. Physically, there was something altogether childlike about Jenny. Her coloring was monochromatic to an extent one hardly ever saw except in small, bronzed children at the beach, her eyes and skin and hair being confined to a narrowish range of topaz which made her wonderfully arresting to look at. Her forehead was a trifle too high to be considered benign, but the parched lips she worried between her teeth when she was upset, and the small, rather pointy chin, and the stubby child's hands which, in the grip of an emotional moment, she would clasp together and hold to her chest in a bouquet of concern— these things softened the effect of the forehead and gave her a friendly look. "La Grande Rochas?" she asked. "I hate her because she peddles revolution while she lives like a queen. Someone told me she bought Pompadour's childhood house in Paris and that she holds court there on Bauhaus furniture for all her leftist friends." There was nothing Jenny despised more than the tricking out of radical ideologies in fashionable decor.

"I don't know anything about her except what I've read in the paper," Nora said, meaning to be conciliatory and truthful both. "I don't know how she does it, but she's glamorous without compromising her seriousness. I didn't think that was possible."

"Maybe she's not serious. We're old enough to know that people are rarely what they seem to be."

"That's true—but if you give up hoping, there's no reason to get up in the morning."

"A lot of good hoping does." Jenny pressed the empty coffeepot to her lips and sighed. "Look at me. Suffering humanity on the one hand, and then all these bleats in the dark that don't turn into love on the other. I'm getting too old. . . . " She put the coffee grinds directly into the pot of water and then added some cracked eggshell. Nora was reminded of the movie cowboys of her childhood, fixing their own grub in the absence of skilled female hands. She felt a surge of love for Jenny. And pity.

"Maybe you should think about getting married," she said, only half-joking.

"Don't be silly. Who would marry me? I'd make a terrible

wife. I've made a terrible wife. And I'm not significantly better as a significant other. You know what a brat I am to Laurence."

Jenny had been married once—briefly, as a girl—to someone named D'Amato (she used his name), and seriously in love on another occasion, as a woman. The man who was to have been her second husband had drowned in front of her eyes three summers before on the eastern end of Long Island.

"How is Laurence?" Nora asked. Her elbow was propped comfortably on the counter and her chin was cupped in her hand.

Jenny sighed again, a sideways skid down an octave of melancholy. Her eyes were lowered and her lashes rested on her broad cheekbones. She struck a match and lit one of the burners, then bent to adjust the flame.

Laurence was an Anglo-Indian and a visiting professor of economics at Columbia. He was a few years younger than Jenny, an amusing talker, and desperately good-looking in a self-consciously overripe mode: thick, dark hair, a sallow complexion, angular features, clandestine black eyes. It had been Jenny's intention to save Laurence. Salvation was an exotic notion for him, as it turned out. When he was two, his Church of England mother abandoned him to his Indian Hindu father for a career as a cellist.

"I'm through with him—for all but practical purposes, anyway. You know—what you were saying earlier—something to get up for in the morning. I have to tell him as soon as I can find the courage." Jenny put two age-cracked mugs on the counter and then straightened up and squared her shoulders, gestures of self-rebuke meant to strengthen her resolve, but, as they both knew, stoicism, no matter how devoutly practiced, was no solution to melancholy.

There was this thing, this immense grief about being a woman—not unmixed with the often electrifying joy of being one—that they had in common and that was at the root of their friendship and which they joked about but never discussed seriously. I don't mean to suggest that Nora claimed special status for women's grief. Men, Nora believed, had their own versions of grief and women nursed them because they perceived this. It often seemed to her that the women she knew spent most of their lives trying to dissipate the grief of one man or another, of one child or another—along with their own. A man Nora loved and respected once told her that on the whole he thought men's lives were harder but women's were more painful. Nora found in this an odd kind of comfort.

"Milk?" Jenny asked. Nora nodded.

Jenny poured the coffee and then they took their mugs into the living room. Her ostrich-trimmed peach satin high-wedged slippers, brothel footwear and really odd for her, Nora thought in passing, slapped as rhythmically as castanets against the flat of her heels as she walked. The sound reminded Nora, unaccountably, of Lautner. She drank her coffee quickly and then leaned her head against the padded and stabilized porch swing that Jenny had turned into a couch. She sighed. She felt suddenly and giddily depleted. She was an island of silence around which everything seemed to be in noisy motion. The steady rumble of the passing trucks had set the windows vibrating in their frames, and she could feel the oscillations of a moving subway train through the soles of her shoes even though the tracks were a few blocks to the east. She had moved so far from ordinary sense, and so swiftly, that it didn't strike her as a joke to claim that she could actually feel the lurch as the earth shifted on its plates.

But Jenny threw back her head and laughed. "Didn't the coffee help?"

"Some. It must be exhaustion. I didn't sleep well last night. And I've had a slight headache all day."

"How was Margaret's—apart from Sylvie?"

"Margaret was amazing, as usual. The rest was a waste of

time." Nora closed her eyes. She wasn't going to think about Lautner anymore.

"Ah, yes. The endless territorial battles of the rich and bored," Jenny said, refilling their mugs.

"What happened after I left Margaret's wasn't boring. I don't know what to call it—unreal, I guess, or maybe surreal," Nora said, reaching forward for her coffee.

"I'm waiting," Jenny said. "You're not going to make me beg, are you?"

Nora took a sip. "I was held up at gunpoint."

Jenny laughed. "Seriously? Where?"

"I was in a store on Madison trying to recover from the effects of you-know-who—when a man came in to rob the place. He was all in black. He looked like a cat burglar, or like someone in the movies playing a cat burglar—really glamorous—well, that's not quite accurate: he had a stocking over his face. The cops think he's a junkie. If he is, he's a middle-class one. He didn't ask for my pocketbook. He took my wedding ring and my wristwatch, so, metaphorically anyway, I'm unattached and immortal. He said he didn't want to hurt us and I believed him. I wasn't frightened at all."

"Only you could believe the best about a mugger," Jenny said, shaking her head.

"Oh, come on."

"All right—but you know you always excuse the worst. Certainly with your friends."

Nora didn't excuse the worst, not really. She simply filed it away for future reference. If her list of grievances grew to be insupportable—that is, if she thought she was being overly ill-used (she counted a certain amount of ill-use as part of friendship)—she cut herself off from the friend completely and irrevocably and without warning, in the style of Louis XV. What choice did she have? She couldn't fight. She couldn't even protest.

"They didn't catch him, I suppose?"

"No. He disappeared into thin air, to quote one of the cops."

"They should transport some of those creeps to Somalia. It's worse than any prison."

"You want to hear the rest?" Nora asked.

"There's more?"

"Unfortunately, yes. I ran into someone I went to high school with. He's dying."

"Cancer, I suppose," Jenny said, pressing her coffee mug to her chest as if it were a lead shield.

"A tumor, anyway."

"Where?"

"The brain."

"Oh, my God," she said, shuddering.

"It's terrible. His memory's been affected. He had no idea who I was until his wife reminded him we went to school together, and then he remembered all about that but nothing later."

"How did we get onto this subject?" Jenny asked.

"He has a wonderful wife. I'd like to do something for her but ... well, we were never friends, and jumping in at this late date seems sort of cheap. . . ."

"I have to change the subject," Jenny broke in. "I can't think about cancer. I won't sleep tonight. How's Ned?"

Jenny didn't have much to say to Ned, but she thought that for a rich man he was amiable enough. At least he didn't try to make every pretty woman he met.

"I'm thinking of leaving him," Nora said.

"Are you serious?" Jenny didn't sound surprised, but Nora was stunned by the words that had come, unbidden, from her own mouth.

"Oh, I don't know. I don't know why I said that. I feel weird. I'd better go home. My headache is much worse than I thought." The roar of the traffic from the street had risen in pitch and volume, upped by the insistent blare of an ambulance siren to the point where her eardrums felt as if they were vibrating at an inhuman speed, literally rattling the bones in her face and bringing her—or something very fragile in her—close to shattering. The pain in her head sharpened as she spoke. It was as if a shaft, a spear, or a sword of light—the hardened light of her own escaping truth?—were burying itself in the loam behind her eyes. She stood up shakily. She was sweating and swollen about the face. Her tongue felt wooly in her mouth.

"Are you sure you're well enough to leave? Why don't you stay here? You aren't in the way."

"I have to go," Nora said. She felt skinned; her flesh was too raw to bear the touch of eyes, even those as kind as Jenny's.

"I'd better go with you and help you get a cab. I don't like the way you look."

"Yes, I think so," Nora said. She was like someone drunk or dreaming, lost to conscious life. She was aware of herself standing in front of a dingy street vendor's supply store— she could smell the hot dogs and sauerkraut—aware of Jenny, her hand raised and wagging as she stepped off the curb into the sludgy flow of rush-hour traffic toward the dismantled West Side Highway, but her awareness was of a very low order. She wanted urgently to be in her own bed. Time, however, was passing as slowly as if she were a child waiting for the grownups to tire of this party or that dinner and take her home. Eventually Jenny arrived, inside a taxi.

"Call me when you get home so I can stop worrying," she said as they changed places.

The cab ride was slow and uneventful until, at a red light a block from home, as she was burrowing deep in the confusion of her leather pouch, looking for her wallet, the door of the cab was jerked open from the street side and a man jumped in and pinioned her in one swift motion, a motion swifter than memory or recognition. She was flung halfway across the seat by the force of his entrance, her scream was stifled against his broad chest, her arms bent like twigs in his grasp.

"Surprise," Ned yelled. And then: "Hey, why such a terrified face? Don't I even get a kiss for trying to make you laugh?"

It was one of the worst moments of her life.

4

Nora undertook the evening's obligation as little refreshed as if she, not the short man holding her arm, had been the one to fly across a continent. Ned's client, Bernardo Maldonado—he'd asked her to call him Nardo—was irritatingly energetic. He gripped her arm with the wiry strength of an antic monkey, tugging her here and there as it suited him, his rhythms so completely out of phase with Ned's plodding ones—Ned had hold of her on the other side—that she was jerked and bounced, now on her feet, now off them, with the stagy, exaggerated movements of a marionette.

They were walking down Eighth Avenue with their heads bent low against the freezing rain. A hooker whose baby fat was corseted inside a pair of skin-tight designer jeans emerged from a doorway and walked alongside them for a few feet. Nardo patted her bottom and sent her away. A couple of pushers were braving the rain to hawk loose joints and nickel bags, chanting their prices with the unintelligible speed of tobacco auctioneers. Nardo yelled some words in Spanish and they backed off. He was a small man with worldly, sinister eyes. His family dealt in metals. He'd come from Venezuela to attend an International Maritime Conference on the ownership rights to sea-bottom metals like the manganese nodule. He also headed a group of Venezuelan investors who wanted to increase and diversify their holdings in the United States.

A bare step from Gold's Gym (boxing, Nardo had told her, was his enduring enthusiasm), in front of a topless bar, a stranger staggered up to them, one of his hands clutched to his heart, the other raised as if to stop the traffic of their objections. "Can you help me?" he asked. "Please help me. I don't feel well."

He was neatly though shabbily dressed, gaunt as a drunk, clean-shaven, a marginal man, not clearly one thing or another. Rain pelted his face, one side of which was badly scarred, his right eye pulled into a vulture slit. His cheek and ear had a look of the arrested volatility of melted wax. He reminded Nora of the man-in-black. And of the man-in-yellow-glasses. And of Lautner.

Nardo, accustomed to beggars and unburdened by doubt, turned his back quite easily. One can be so quickly pulled from one's nest, comprende?

Ned understood perfectly.

Nora temporized and then allowed herself to be led away. Her face and neck were burning with shame. She felt small-hearted, morally stunted.

Stenciled in gold on the battered door that Nardo held open for them were the words GO D'S GYM. The "L" was completely worn away or had been erased by one of the local wits. The gym was crowded with men, rank with male smells. Cigars and sweat. Nora could tell at a glance that she was the only woman present—and she was not just any woman, but a lady-in-black-silk. She felt menaced even though no one had yet noticed her. What had possessed her to wear her hair loose?

She prepared to enter the room by arming herself with a prim smile and aloof eyes. This rarely worked as a strategy, but she had no other. She tried to bind her breasts, mentally, to her ribby skeleton. She tried not to focus on what was be-

tween her legs, as if it were still hairless and therefore without significance, as if her future, the one to be lived with a
man, had not yet presented itself to her as a serious notion, as
if she were still a tomboy. Matthew's friend.

Nardo was talking to someone at the door. She used this
delay to look around. The gym was L-shaped, about the size
of two tennis courts. There were men everywhere, banging
away at the speed bags and the heavy bags, dancing on
sneakered feet in the foot of the "L," where a ring was
set up, a jittery sort of dancing, left and right, forward and
back, throwing silent, taped fists at shadows, standing
around in front of the mirrors, turbaned and robed and
watchful.

Nardo had loosened his tie and stowed his hands deep in
his trouser pockets and he was stooping a little. Nora liked
him better in this context. It was clear from his smile, locker-
room conspiratorial, bonded, that he felt entirely at home.
Nora wondered what there was to smile about. She saw
nothing but the unhappiness and the violence of emptiness
on every face. Her shyness and her fear made her humorlessly self-defensive. She had a prim abhorrence of all contact sports.

Nardo plunged into the crowd, using his elbows, hips,
even fists to make his way, leaving them to follow as best
they could. Every few seconds someone waved at him or
reached out to shake his hand or grab him around the shoulders and pound his back. "Hombre! Qué tal? Cómo estás?"
When he reached the ring, he poked his upper body through
the ropes and slapped one of the two young contenders, the
one wearing red shoelaces, slapped him familiarly as one
would slap a horse, on the nearest flank. He was about ten
yards ahead of them. Nora was clinging to Ned's arm in a
way that seemed to displease him. He moved off a bit, held
himself physically apart from her as if any show of concern
would compromise his standing in this all-male atmosphere.
He had never done anything like this before, but then he was

nearly as out of place here as she was. She tried to smile or at least to look cheerful as she trailed after him.

A bell rang. There was a sudden surge of bodies into the space around her; a wave of sweaty, almost sexual turbulence broke over her head, struck her from behind, a curling wave of excited greed, in the midst of which she felt a hand grab her thigh. A tentacle. She sobered up instantly. The sleeve she tugged at should have been Ned's but it wasn't. She couldn't see him anywhere. The hand moved caressingly to her buttocks. She shuddered and plunged ahead into the press of bodies, the jungle of bodies, hoping to catch up to him. She was accompanied in her flight by the sound of a long-drawn-out kiss. It was taken up and passed along, sustained by one pair of lips after another, a sort of purgatorial basso continuo. She stared straight ahead, not daring to meet the eyes that were stripping her naked as she went. The hand was in her hair now, fondling her hair. Perhaps it wasn't the same hand, she didn't know. Lizards of disgust crawled across her scalp. Sweat beaded her forehead and ran down her cheeks.

A large black punching bag dangled from the ceiling in the corner a few yards away. The anatomical details of the head and torso of a man were diagrammed on it in white. It was armless and legless, a sandbag man, a man nevertheless. She fixed her eyes on him like a dancer spotting turns, a trick to keep herself from succumbing to the vertigo of shame and rage, to keep herself from screaming out loud, and she didn't let go of her concentration until she reached him, until she was hidden safely behind him.

It took her a while to stop shaking. She dried her face with a handkerchief. She straightened her skirt, which had twisted nearly halfway around her waist. She tucked in her blouse. She shook her hair as if to free it from the memory of having been violated. And then she stepped out and looked around. Her boldness shocked her. Novelty was not her customary medium, particularly novelty experienced as fear.

She'd been schooled from birth not to see things that should not be seen. And yet she looked.

There was a slight thinning of the air along the half-mooned arc of her thoughts, so to speak, nothing more, as his absence modulated by slow degrees into presence. Or perhaps it was simply that she hadn't noticed him until that moment. He was unmistakably *who he was,* and at the same time not at all what she would have conjured had she done the conjuring, for he was less rampant and more ambiguous than her imagination required. That is, at first sight he made a lot more sense than, say, a pyramid.

I'm talking about the devil.

Nora had the oddest feeling she'd seen him before. Her first impression was of a tall, strongly made, iron-gray man whose physical presence had the highly specialized eroticism of heavy machinery. Something in him called to mind the cool, dense smoothness of steel and the oiled decisiveness of a complexity of intricately moving parts the purpose of which is to produce something. But while his body had this quality of utmost decisiveness, his face—or so it struck her at the time—was daringly inconclusive, somewhat the way the face of a boy emerging from adolescence is, a face whose features and expressions are still only aspects of a phenomenon. I suppose that is as accurate or inaccurate a description as any to follow, since, as she would learn, his face and body and temperament were so mobile that he never gave the same impression twice.

"Do you know who I am?" he asked.

There was nothing natural in the manner in which he asked this question. He seemed to be all startling agreeableness while harboring feelings of unsympathetic, even contemptuous reservation, and however deep and sonorous and welcoming his voice was, there was something blatant and metallic in it as well which suggested that, in the end, like church bells, its unrestrained tolling might give more pain than pleasure.

Nevertheless, she answered him.

"No, I don't think so. Should I know you?"

"What if I told you I was the devil?"

"Fine," she said. A giddy smile threatened the corners of her mouth.

"You'd accept that?"

"Why not? For a woman it's as believable as war."

He threw back his head and laughed, the skittery, up-spiraling laugh of an overtired child, a laugh that contained the threat-seeds of tantrum.

"Seriously, I think I've seen you somewhere before."

He looked directly into her eyes and smiled. His smile was like the gift of a caption on a rare species of tree. It made him slightly more comprehensible. It was enough.

"Lautner?" she asked, with some excitement. The same man but with every difference.

"If that name suits you, certainly."

"You're not Lautner?"

"Do you find my presence disturbing?"

"Are you Lautner or not?"

He put his hand across his own mouth and looked at her over it and waited until she grew polite.

"Please—tell me—are you Lautner?"

Nothing.

"In what way are you Lautner?" she tried.

Nothing.

"Are you interested in me?"

Nothing.

She said, "You're so real. . . ."

"Am I? Americans are so reluctant to acknowledge that I am that I often wonder. They seem to see me only in blacks—and mass murderers. I wonder why the existence of evil is so embarrassing except to liars. Have you noticed that bullies hate tenderness—and forbid it? Are you as willful as you seem?"

His smile was cordial but the words fell from his lips a

shade more slowly than was necessary for clarity or even for emphasis. Nora felt a kind of jolt of impatience in her chest. Her right eye began to twitch. Presuming an intimacy somewhere between that of lover and physician, an intimacy it didn't occur to her to forbid, he pressed his left index finger firmly against her lid, and immediately the tidal pull of muscle on skin ceased.

He said, "I suppose originally it was a matter of hope—and of real estate. You sold land by its godliness: you ought to see the old advertisements—this blessèd land. Its blessèd affluence. But the movies are helping me, and so are some left-wingers: I hope you've noticed—haunted suburbs, haunted backwoods, pollution. I've always had support in Hollywood. I wish I liked Hollywood. I wish I liked my own humor. But I don't like anything which is easily and slickly available—like the devil's humor. Just how frightened are you?"

She had never been so nervous or so interested in her future.

She proceeded as though this were a flirtation. She couldn't conceive it to be anything else. "I'm sure I should be frightened but I'm not. Believing in your existence doesn't exactly make you real."

"I see your point," he said. "You're more honest now that we've chattered a bit. But you are aware that some people have found me quite painfully real? Of course, 'real' is such an ambiguous word. Now, supposing I were 'real,' as you put it—in what way would I interest you?"

His power interested her. She liked it for its guardedness, and its formality, and its latent, teasing enmity. It was natural to him, to the extent that speech is natural to us—that is, inherent but needing to be learned—but with this qualification: whatever language he spoke, and over the course of time she would hear him speak several, none, not one, appeared to be native to him and perhaps his power was as foreign to him as it would be to a woman.

There were traces of bitterness in his pronunciation, a gritty, clinging sediment of many accents, just as there was a suggestion of syntax forced, trimmed with topiary diligence into ornamental, unnatural shapes. She could have told him what she thought, or she could have said that everything about him interested her. She didn't. Instead she fired off a fusillade of short, provocative sentences, a kind of verbal raid that was meant to leave him dazed by her charm and adroitness. She liked to flirt. She wasn't bad at it.

"Of course, if you are who you say you are, I don't think you'd interest me on any grounds," she said. "You're outside my sphere of appreciation."

"Ah, Nora, sooner or later I interest everyone, even if only by the light of self-love—and name-calling—and perhaps the spirit in the beloved—as you know."

"Well, yes," she conceded in a drawling voice. "Certainly, you're fascinating as a dramatic conceit. I didn't know that was what you meant. For one thing, without you there wouldn't be any wit." Her eyes were brilliant with gaiety, almost feverish.

"That's it, then? A dramatic conceit?"

"Well, I'm half-Jewish. I know the Jews more or less invented you, but they've never taken you all that seriously."

A smile, this one as emphatically brief and panoramically illuminating as a flash of lightning across a black sky, streaked across his face and blooded it. A transfusion of light. Nora caught sight of someone, someone who was not at all one-of-us and yet was irrevocably wedded to us. She saw the partial humanness of his condition and she was both moved and stung.

What does one do with such a glimpse?

Here. He had a singular forehead, high rather than broad, very high and etched with deep horizontal grooves and giving off onto a cliff of a nose. Eyes the color of rain. Ears small and close to the head. A mouth eroded to the point of abuse.

Lips hard as rind. A long, thrusting jaw, slightly underslung. All ranged in a narrow passage of a face. An isthmus. Hair cropped close at the base of the neck but curried to fall in long, thinning strands across the crown. Ashy newborn blond mingled with a sheenless silver. He was tall but not immensely so. The feeling of height was augmented, perhaps, by a broad-shouldered if otherwise Anglicized slenderness. His clothes weren't terribly interesting in themselves—trousers of cavalry twill, a gray turtleneck sweater, a shabby corduroy jacket the color of hay—but he wore them with an indifference massive enough to be indistinguishable from true style. Or maybe that is what true style consists of.

For the duration of his smile, he stooped deferentially toward her, holding himself profoundly still as if to encourage her scrutiny. His manner was as unself-conscious as that of a young child being adored. She tried to take him in. Time passed, and yet the longer she looked the more there was to see. She couldn't begin to fathom the depths of his purposes. How could she? He atomized before her eyes even as her mind tried to make him cohere. She found the concentration exhausting. When she was able to tear her eyes from his, it seemed to her the parting was of tape from skin. But if relief was what she sought, she failed to find it. There is no relief from the extraordinary.

"I don't know you well enough yet to read your mood with any accuracy, but if you'll permit me, I'll tell you what I see—what I see—" His eyes moved as he repeated the phrase.

"Why not?" she said, trembling slightly—but only slightly. She stood as still as someone of her physical temperament could. She lent herself—in imitation of him, perhaps, but with intense self-consciousness—to study. His eyes seemed actually to touch her. She waited in a steadily growing state of unease while he lit a cigarette and twirled it thoughtfully, assessingly, between his thumb and forefinger just inches from his lips. I wonder now whether in those days she ever loved him more than she feared him. Yes. But I suspect she loved him for his severity—his contempt and his perversity. I may as well say this now: his interest in her, from the start, was flatteringly beyond her grip. It was somewhat as if she'd become a superstar overnight, that is, hideously vulnerable to compliments and insults unmitigated by perspective or truth; but, being a sophisticated citizen of her time, she tried to keep up an appearance of normalcy. She tried to pass herself off as someone-who-knew-better. She knew nothing.

He said, "You're in no mood to consult your pride."

She experienced a mild loss of equilibrium: she placed her palm against the wall for support. She wasn't exactly ill but she wasn't well either.

Real desire is the only temptation; the rest is sham.

"You're willing that you be permitted to be helpless for a few hours only—then you want your will and your life back—nothing having been lost. Well, am I close?" he asked.

"Say something," he said after a moment.

"Who are you?" she asked. This was possibly the first serious moment of her life.

"What I can give you," he said, and paused, "is the gift of being open about what you will. And what you are."

"Who are you?" she repeated. "What is your name?"

"Trust your intuition," he said.

She was silent.

"Well, who am I, Nora?"

The anthracite of resistance, a lump of mute coal, was in her throat. The pause between question and answer expanded; so did her unease. His manner of looking at her was so unnerving in its expectancy that she found herself longing for something, anything, even a drastic illness, to come crashing in and free her from the double peril of being prodigal with his time while strangely aching for the power to slight him. Who was he? Did she believe in devils? Was he truly the devil? What did she know of the truth? Perhaps only that nothing less was required of her here. She laughed with pleasure at her insight and immediately, under the ice of panic, she could feel the warmth of thought beginning to move and then, in a moment she would never forget for its voluptuous clarity, she glimpsed the idea that truth might be a problem of details of address between herself and a man as well as of a matter of substance and that was reason enough for her to remain mute. She shook her head.

"I said earlier that I could give you the gift of *openness* of will—you could talk now if you believed I was honestly real. Well, are you interested?"

His offer, this time, had a lazy rhythm, a slow-running tempo, like a river. She should have kept silent and fallen to her knees. But she came from the merchant class. She bargained. "A gift like yours?" she asked. She meant the gift of resonance which came from his being an almost ultimate power, after all—not a woman.

"I have no particular gift," he said. He drew deeply on his cigarette and sent a lasso of smoke at her head. She stepped to one side and its noose passed harmlessly by her neck. They exchanged smiles.

"If you are who you claim to be, then coyness doesn't become you. Everyone knows you have gifts, many of them—" Then: "I've heard you quoted all my life."

"Reading *The Life of Johnson,* one makes the acquaintance of Boswell's gift as a note-taker."

She laughed. She wanted to say that, given the identity he hinted at, his gift was that he existed with such resonance— he was strongly endowed with the power of creating a belief. Simply that he existed was a guarantee that within one meaning he could forge a multiplicity of other meanings. Was this the gift he was offering her? She couldn't ask; she was afraid of appearing ridiculous in his eyes. What if her way of being smart was simply a roundabout and pretentious way of being stupid? Like the student Willie had jokingly mentioned to her, the one who'd invoked Wittgenstein on language in philosophy class to explain why he couldn't write his paper on Wittgenstein. Judged harshly enough, all human minds were flimsy. The devil was hardly a lenient judge and Lautner seemed bent on judging her. But what if his way of looking at things, the unknown standard by which he was judging her, was the gift he was really offering?

"Well, is it yes or no?"

"No," she said, with an air of regret ennobled by principle, as if he'd offered her an expensive piece of jewelry. She wanted it understood by this act that she was a free agent. Free to continue to doubt.

"Fine," he said. He was still smiling when he said: "I'll say this once and only once, Nora. Poses bore me and I don't choose to be bored. Furthermore, I am not enchanted by modesty, and still less by fake vulnerability. Such traits may constitute a politically valid expression of personality for a woman, but they are to the mind what blasphemy is to a pope. Do you understand what I'm saying?"

"I don't know." On the surface, of course, his language was decorous, but then, as she would discover, slowly and with some pain, he often used language to conceal vile thoughts, as he often gave her ideas to prevent her thinking.

"If you want me, Nora, you have to interest me."

"You're not here on my say-so. Whoever you are. I didn't ask you to come," she said. But gently.

"Didn't you?"

"Certainly not." Her view at the time was that, far from being invited, he'd crashed her life as casually as if it had been a party. She accused him of this.

"You're a liar," he said, in a mild voice. His eyebrows, however, had assumed a furious divinity.

"I don't lie," she said. Earnestly. Gently. Her voice was staunch, but she couldn't control her chin, which was trembling over the justice of his accusation.

"Everybody lies," he said, even more mildly than before. "I am not A Liar."

"Ah. Well, let me put it this way. Would you by any chance agree that you're often careless with truth?"

"I would not." Of course she was, and, knowing it, she blushed.

"You must be quite an extraordinary woman." He stubbed out his cigarette against the wall, where the imprint of her damp palm still lingered.

She didn't rage or protest. Or even sulk. She languished. The blossom of her eagerness closed under the violent downpour of the sarcasm, of his sudden look of extreme boredom. "Perhaps I am extraordinary," she then said, not believing it. "Perhaps that's why you're here."

He'd said he didn't value modesty but she couldn't support her boast and she could tell by his face that he knew it. She had no notion of what she was worth in the world and she fought having such a notion. As it was, the degree of her self-esteem was largely dependent on her mood. She was in one moment an undiscovered beauty or genius, in the next an imbecile or crone. How could it be otherwise? Her standards were as hidden, as volatile and unilaterally arrived at as Lautner's.

"Perhaps you are. Perhaps you are extraordinary at that," he said.

She could tell this was not a true concession or even the appearance of one, there was something so polite in his tone.

Then he sighed as if from exhaustion, and his sigh carried him inward out of her reach to a place rich in remoteness and focus, a singularly male geography of mind which she envied men above all else. Even the most distracted among them seemed to have this gift. He had lowered his head—or it had fallen forward of its own accord—so that she couldn't see his face. His was not an uncommonly large head, yet at that moment it gave the impression of being a killing burden, as if the weight of such an immense consciousness could no longer be supported by the mere stalk of a neck or by one soul alone. She sensed, or he lured her on to sense, a near-fatal depletion of the marrow of life in him. It might have been an elaborately adroit pretense, she didn't know, but it had the feel of simplicity.

She was not a woman much given to prophecy. Nevertheless, she said to herself: Usually things come to nothing. I am a liar and a fool but I interest him. This will end in something.

He raised his head. The eyes she looked into were no longer his. She didn't know whose they were; they were just eyes. Thus did the cleaver of his loneliness pass through her bone and bite into her heart.

She became sensible of her surroundings a little at a time. A pair of brown legs, a pair of white. The dull thud of leather hitting flesh. Gobs of spittle strung like webs between a pair of peanut-yellow gloves. Knightly headgear bobbing. Her own body damp with sensation. Jostling. Jeering. Shouts of encouragement. The ice-pick stabs of Nardo's voice? Ned's laugh? The noise was vast.

"Ready?" Ned asked her.

He patted her shoulder.

"Ready?" he asked again.

She nodded and took his arm. The light, falling from the high ceiling, cast odd blue shadows. True shadows. It hollowed out Ned's face, scooping flesh from under his eyes and cheekbones, turning him into a demonic stranger, and in the strange light, in the drenching silver-blue light, Nora seemed to see a woman standing beside him lost in thought. She was thin, almost transparent, the other woman, the sort of woman who'd always been thin and who had a dreamer's thin-boned sense of hazard. Her silhouette was lissome with bones angled like spears, spears sheathed in silk. A "V" of skin, too taut and not creamy enough to satisfy a connoisseur, was visible from the hollow at the base of her throat to the bony hollow between her breasts. Small breasts. Tense shoulders. Boyish hips. Long legs. A flourish of wild rusty hair massed from a narrow skull. And bones again. In the corded neck, in the face. Oh, admirable bones. Blue eyes muddied with green, madonnaesque; the sadness possibly calculated as part of the beauty, possibly not. Heavy-laden eyelids. Sparse eyebrows. A straight nose. A soft mouth. All in excellent order—except, Nora thought, staring, recognizing herself at last, except that everything can still happen to this woman. She is one of those women who have been waiting all their lives for something to happen.

"So what do you think of my muchacho, Nora?" Nardo asked, coming up to her and slipping his arm through hers. The woman vanished. Nora was mute.

"He's going to be somebody," Ned said, hurrying to answer for her. "You can see it."

"He's somebody already," Nardo said, over his shoulder. He was clearing a path to the door. "I own him."

The restaurant was moon-colored, commercially chaste; the mirrored walls dripped rivulets of light. A dust of cumin was in her nose; she breathed in, inhaled the dust, the dust of waking dreams.

Perrier for the ladies, tequila for the gentlemen and, of course, the state of the world. Babies for the ladies.

"Seven," Nardo's wife was saying. "Five hombres. Two girls." Graciella's very plumply blessed by God and Nardo.

"Two. One mujer. One boy." Nora's also blessed, if bonily.

Isn't this a banquet for the mind?

"The President of Venezuela?" Graciella's cousin-by-marriage is brother-in-law to the wife of the President of Venezuela. Of course he's dead, muerto, the cousin is, but still, they can vouch for their President. Ned can vouch for his.

One of the breads was smooth and flat as a skimming

stone, the other puffed like Victorian sleeves. Orange chicken and green dahl and a necklace of lime wedges around a bowl of white basmati rice. Sounds of chewing. Nardo's limpet eyes on Graciella's (Chella's) mouth. Her fork, her head, hanging in obedient shame. Napoleon-Nardo raised his arm. A sari billowed at his wife's milky elbow. A brown hand cleared away her half-filled plate. Ah, Graciella, you have our sympathy and our contempt.

"The diet works by hypnosis?" Ned asked.

"Sí," Nardo answered. "I'll show you. Come, Nora, look into my eyes. It's easy."

His eyes were as narrow as Ned's. Everything in his face was narrow: eyes, lips, nose, chin. He was a small, shrewd, narrow man with a sabered will.

She shook her head.

"Sweetheart, just look into his eyes. What can happen?"

"Sí. What can happen? Listen to your husband, Nora."

"No." Nunca jamás. En la vida.

"Just for fun—no?—we will make a small demonstration. Chella!"

Nardo snapped his fingers twice. Chella's head jerked to attention. His fingers again, pinky and pointer, a pair of horns. He, Taurus, lowered them, charged twice in quick succession at Chella's eyes. Chella's head lolled, a moment only, then dropped to one side, a heavy-lidded flower on a broken stem.

"Bueno." Nardo smiled at her like a bad priest. There was a fine veining of blue on Chella's alabaster lids for which one could love her. He had boned the rest.

Nora glanced at Nardo, then away, quickly. His eyes had been waiting for hers. They were as deep as the ancient cenotes. One could wait a lifetime and not hear a stone hit bottom.

Nardo threw back his head and laughed at her. Ned picked his teeth and smiled.

"You see how simple, Nora?"

"Please wake Chella up."

"Seguramente." Two snaps. Chella opened her eyes, lifted her head, unfurled a thornless, wide-eyed rose face to her particular sun. Not God's work, not any of it.

"Your turn, Norrie." She was addressed by her husband. He was leaning far back in his chair. Tantalizingly far. He was trespassing on her childhood name.

"I said no."

"Entonces, a bit later, no?" Nardo crossed his arms and smiled at Ned. A rank complicity.

"No. Not later."

There was the yogurt, cool in her throat, and there was the feel of cucumber between her teeth like the bones of small birds breaking, and there were her eyes sentenced to the jail of her plate. And there were her thoughts, running free.

Are you listening, you? YOU OUT THERE. YOU KNOW WHO YOU ARE.

With thee conversing I forget all time.

AM I KNOWN TO YOU, LIAR?

Everybody lies.

"Broiled bananas for the señora, fried milk balls for the gentlemen, ice cream for me, and my wife will have ...?"

"Kheer, please."

"An excellent choice, madam. A sweet fit to pleasure the palates of kings and brides."

Pleasure forgets itself. She raised her careless, pleasured head and it was done. Nardo's eyes affixed to hers as if with tape. A crack. The leak was warm and slow and blue.

A ripe smile split her husband's melon face. Chella clapped her pink and spoiled hands. Once. She giggled. Three oh-so-tiny rushes of girlish breath.

Nardo snapped his shrewd and foolish fingers twice. His horns in place, he charged her eyes.

A hand flicked out and addered his, midair. The hand was hers. She bit down hard. The cucumber bones were crisp between her teeth.

He gasped and tried to pull his fingers free. She bit down harder still.

"Cōn," he shrieked. Cunt.

Chella's eyes were strained to bursting disbelief. She sucked her own plump fingers in dismay.

Ned hissed: "Let go, damnit. Are you out of your mind?"

She opened her mouth. She parted her fingers.

A bowl of fragrant raisin-studded rice was set between her elbows. Across it lay an unbroken tissue of the thinnest silver, a sheet of foil moonlight.

A dish of broiled bananas appeared beneath the señora's stricken eyes. Nardo checked his fingers. No blood. Syruped, reddish-brown jamuns, fried balls of dried milk, awaited his plucking.

"Say something, for godsakes. Apologize." Ned's breath was hot. The cardamon-scented kulfi, the ice cream, melted. His eyes were on his plate. All eyes were on all plates save hers.

"Apologize. Now."

She looked at her husband. His shoulders were as stiff as a hanger on which hung her grandfather's voice, her father's shadow.

Rising, she said, "Excuse me." A hand held her chair.

The ladies' room was dominated by a glassed painting. Rajasthan, c. 1800, a vision of the universal form in all its manifestations. The universal form. Boundless Krishna: manifold arms (14) and stomachs (3) and mouths (14) and tusks and eyes (kohl-rimmed, 28) shining in many colors. Not a he or a she but a thee. A tree.

A shelf of black marble held tissue and powder, hairpins and cologne. A small white ashtray was filled with coins. A maid waited attendance. Two black Barcelona chairs faced each other like a bored married couple. The toilets were hidden.

Nora smiled at the elderly maid as if her smile could help confer the wealth of visibility. There was sympathy in her eyes. Twenty years ago, she saw a short film in which the hand-held camera followed a men's room attendant, a worn-down, silent, expressionless old Polish woman, as closely as a detective. At first, the scale of the woman's life seemed pitiful; her life would have fit under the heel of a boot; but gradually the detective work uncovered an infinity of possibility, and by the film's end the woman had become a Joan of Arc of possibility, and as such she could no longer be overlooked by anyone, anyone of merit, that is. Anyone with a soul. Nora had never forgotten this film.

She closed her eyes and pressed her fingers to her temples. Her face was pale and drawn. Something foreign was prowling within her, slippery as mercury. It moved from temple to throat. She fingered the hollow at the base of her neck, then pressed her palm flat against her breastbone as if to trap it. It eluded her. She dug for it with her thumbs, uselessly. She sighed, stood up, dropped a silent bill in the white dish, smiled again, and said good night.

The Maldonados' empty chairs rebuked her for her fall from taste. A sermon shaped Ned's back. His fingers drummed the table in an irregular, staccato rumination with distinctly moral overtones. She braced herself.

"I'm at a complete loss," he said, hoarsely. His voice descended a ladder of short coughs. He stared at the tablecloth. "I didn't know what to say to the Maldonados."

He was enraged but he was frightened of her too, she saw. He'd never been frightened before. She could hardly stand the responsibility. "He was badgering me," she said. "He wasn't going to stop with you encouraging him. I didn't know I was going to bite him. I don't know what came over me."

It was true. She didn't know. Just thinking of it again, though, caused a rocket of elation to explode in her chest. Little insects of exhilaration crawled across her body. How could she make this stranger understand that she was trembling with the necessity of ACTION? Kirillov bit Pyotr Stepanovitch's finger for scorching his face with a candle. For invading the privacy of his SOUL. She said this to her husband. One look at his face told her the analogy was self-serving and beside the point. The standard here was not ethics or chivalry or literature. But she went on anyway. She told her husband that reading a novel was as much of an experience as making money. That was a mistake. Ned never read. He disapproved of the self-conscious, psychological men and women in fiction, fools looking for meaning, for completion. He threw up his hands, a clannish gesture meaning WHAT CAN YOU DO WITH A WOMAN LIKE THIS?

"All you had to do was tell him to stop."

"I did, if you recall. Several times."

"You could have made it clear you meant it."

"I tried."

"Really clear."

She wondered whether she was as incomprehensible to Ned as he was to her.

"Nora!"

"Yes," she said.

"Nardo is one of my most important clients." He was speaking a little more slowly and a trifle louder than necessary, as if she were a foreigner or a child to whom he was giving directions. "I have to give him a plausible explanation and I can't do that until you've given me one."

For some reason, after twenty years of pathological politeness, she was not able to take this quite serious incident seriously.

"Tell him I'm epileptic and that was the start of a seizure."

He leaned toward her, his nostrils flared ever so slightly. Hair up on a cat's back; ears back on a dog's head. She knew what was coming next. The system was worked out eons ago. She bared her neck.

"Oh, God, can't you tell him the truth?" she cried out, in despair.

"And what is that?"

"That he's a creep."

"The truth? What does the truth have to do with this? Who cares about the truth?"

"I do," she said.

"Just how badly do you want to hurt me?" he asked.

"I want to love you," she said.

5

In the dream, she carried the woman like a papoose; or the woman's body was joined to her back like wings. The woman was not her own mother but the Mother. Nora knew her by her density. It was forbidden to look at the Mother's face. Sometimes the Mother spoke to her from her position on Nora's back, sometimes, without taking her body from Nora's, she spoke to her face to face. The face Nora saw through her closed eyes was indistinct, blurred by a veil of command, and yet of a magnificent sweetness that was in itself an immense power. The Mother's weight bent Nora to the ground as if she were a sapling. At the same time, the fact of the Mother's being there endowed Nora with a more than humanly explicable strength.

Bits of dream narrative were still clinging to her when she woke, but language slowly sapped the oracular power in the

pictures that were the lifeblood of the dream, and by the
time she was fully conscious, what had been revealed to her
was mostly gone.

She glanced over at Ned. His eyelids were twitching; there
was a dreamy half-smile on his lips as if sleep were a nightly
vacation, and the bed a wide veranda on which he took his
ease. She was as tired with alertness as if she'd passed the
night in a sentry box. She tiptoed to the window.

Outside, the sky was being sheared: starry bits of fleece
descended everywhere. She pushed open the window and
took a deep breath. A flurry of snow blew off the sill into
her face. The freshness made her think of Lautner. The haul-
age was only mental but no less tiring for that. Trying to
move the idea of him, of Lautner, from the shelter of her
consciousness into the world on the rig of language, she
made a darkish leap into discovery. Since there was no way
to present him in speech, no way that would not simultaneously raise and decide the issue of her sanity, she was
forced to conclude that he was simply not a linguistic possibility. And if this were true, then who knew what else of
grave, even singular, importance existed that could not be
made visible in Euclidean space or calibrated in diachronic
time because of the impoverishment of language which
when you needed it most turned out to be only another
metaphor.

She held her head in her hands.

Too many root ends multiplying too fast can crack a clay
pot. Virginia Woolf's definition of a crackpot.

She closed the window and stood there a moment, her
arms crossed below her breasts as if she were waiting for
something. The world outside went on gleaming, trafficking
in purity. Her heart began an odd sort of parade. There was
a sudden, prodigious, sweeping movement across the plain of
her chest. She had never felt anything like it before. She
pressed her forehead to the pane. She closed her eyes. Ned's
voice from the bed, insisting on a world of sensible pur-

suits—his coffee, his newspaper, his life—roared in her ears like a rising wind. The dust blew, and the mysterious beauty, the barbarian regiments of her love, a woman's love, were obscured for the moment, although a more sentient observer than Ned might have caught the gleam of ardor in her eyes, the quick flash of desire in the turning of her head. She went on with the familiar motions of morning but Lautner was never out of her thoughts for a moment.

She and Ned took breakfast together as usual. There was no residue of bitterness in their behavior toward each other. You ask how this can be? Well, a memory for grievances is deeply uncivilizing; therefore, they conspired at forgetfulness. To appear content, after all, was the highest compliment they could pay to society and to themselves. I am not being ironic. No one says these things, and yet any number of us are forced by circumstances and upbringing to live out our lives this way.

"You want to sign these for me wherever you see an 'X.' " Ned pushed some papers across the kitchen table.

The sounds of breakfast were in her ears—the click of Ned's cup fitting to its saucer, the envelope of buttered toast disappearing crisply into the slot between the mitred bones of his jaw, and then earlier sounds: her mother's furtive sparrow-pecking at their leftovers, and a lament that could only be her brother's. Herbert was six, he was raising his arms over his exquisite head, his shirttail lifted out of the waistband of his corduroy trousers, he lowered his head and screamed, he stamped his feet. Her mother rounded him, rounded the Maypole stick of his body, his small, fragile body, tucking and weaving. He raised his arms again, the shirttail lifted, the process repeated itself. She would be late for school again, the object of a thousand sniggering glances. She was the firstborn. Someone had appointed her her brother's keeper, her poor, weak, terror-stricken, angel-faced brother. It would never be otherwise.

The phone rang.

The caller spoke her name. She couldn't speak his.

Ned raised eyebrows of inquiry. She said, "Excuse me," and covered the receiver. "It's Tromp," she said.

"What about the papers?" he asked, looking at his watch impatiently.

"They can wait until tonight, can't they? I want to look them over anyway."

"You mean you want to read them?"

"Yes." She never read what she signed—to do so would be a sign of distrust.

He frowned. "Every day we lose costs money."

"I'll take care of it tonight."

"All right. I'll talk to you later." He called her once or twice a day whether or not he had anything on his mind.

The front door slammed. She put her feet up on his vacated chair.

"I'm sorry," she said.

"You sound terribly young on the telephone. . . . Why is that?" Lautner asked.

She said, "It's something I've learned.

He said, "It makes people more polite?"

"I don't know—I haven't thought about it."

"So young," he said.

"My perceptions or my voice?" she asked, taking care to flute each word: she wasn't comfortable but when he laughed, she blossomed with confidence.

"Your voice," he said.

"I'm a hopeful person," she said without hesitating. "I suppose it shows in my voice."

"Can you tell me how you manage to associate the telephone with hope? It seems so American of you."

"I don't know. Maybe it's in my father—my father's a hopeful man. I'm very close to him. I don't think it's cultural. I've written my life off any number of times but here I am, still hopeful."

She realized after a moment that Lautner was bored.

He said, "Your dark thoughts are a species of hope?"

"That depends on what you mean by my dark thoughts."

"Suicide, say."

"God, no. What a legacy for my children. Anyway, before I get around to contemplating suicide, I have to think about cancer, which comes and gets you. My relatives die of cancer. I think about that right before I fall asleep."

She was growing tired. She hurried to reverse the verdict. "Well, I suppose it's crossed my mind," she conceded. The memory of Sylvie surprised her, slipping like a knife from her own hand, cutting into the soft flesh of her mind. "A part of me has always been able to keep a certain distance from suffering," she said.

"And if one day you can't?"

"Why are we talking about suicide?"

"And then?"

"My pride is sufficient to prevent it. . . . I have a lot of pride. It's gotten me through—I trust it."

"Two thousand years of Christianity calls pride a sin."

"That's fine—for men. A woman needs it to survive."

His laughter was a reprieve. She confused it with approval. She leaned back in her chair and took a sip of cold coffee, and felt willfully happy.

"Survival is not my joy, Nora," he said.

"What?" A note of panic entered her voice. She'd lost the thread.

"It's not terribly complicated, Nora. Let's say I have a crisis—I may not want to keep a certain distance, to use your words. I may prefer an intimacy with my condition to survival. My hopefulness goes. I wake up each morning in a state of despair—but I still have my pride. What then? What does my pride rest on—on your hopefulness? On that of people like you?"

"Well," she said, feeling her way to the end of the sentence like someone looking for the door in a dark and unfamiliar room, "I suppose if I fell below a level of autonomy in the way you're describing, I'd have no choice but to contemplate suicide. I can't see myself leaning on anyone—on anyone's folly, if I thought it was folly."

"Your family?"

"Oh, they're perfect, in their way—yes, really: I'm not joking—they are very perfect."

"How imbecile you are."

"What do you mean?" She'd been feeling pleased with herself for having confirmed, without actually lying, his apparent preference that life not always be worth the trouble and for putting her family beyond his judgment.

"Your refusal to be interesting to me is laudatory."

"Don't tease me—why are you teasing me?"

"I'm not teasing you. I'm bullying you, don't you feel bullied?"

"I don't know what I feel." She was feeling the beginnings of confusion and fear.

"What do you want out of this conversation, Nora?"

"I don't know that I want anything." She wanted to impress him. And she couldn't.

"What do you want out of life, at this moment?"

Men and their questions. Still, she didn't question his right to ask. If he'd been a woman, she would have been deeply offended. "I want to be useful," she said. "That's all a person can ask, really."

"Do you mind not being essential?"

Suddenly she said, "I've been essential. Compared with Mothering, Art is clutter."

"Do you know how confused you are? And occasionally brilliant? And how little you trust your children?"

She didn't answer. She said, "Flattery comes from the devil."

He said, "I never said that. I said someone, a woman like you with *perfect* children, distorts and hates their reality."

She felt sick and angry. Emotion robbed her of her voice.

On what basis could she argue with him? He had an infant's immunity to self-doubt. He was certainty itself, a Stalin of certainty.

"Let's hope you don't destroy my hopefulness," she said, warningly, as lightly as she could. Her coquetry was systemic, like her need for security, not a scarf of skin that could be sloughed off at will. She didn't quite realize she was threatening suicide.

"Do you know how complicated what you've just said is?"

"Is it?" She did and she didn't.

"You're a very complex woman. You're a cold bitch by nature, you know."

She waited in cheerless silence, not knowing whether to admit she was or not, whether to admit she felt complimented by his observation.

"Don't sulk," he said. "All athletes are cold. All mothers are bitches."

"How did you know I was an athlete?"

He didn't answer.

"You're not a comfort, you know."

"Is comfort what you ever ask of a man, Nora?"

In a very childlike voice, after a pause, she said, "Are you angry with me?"

"I don't think so but I'm never sure about these things until later."

She cradled the receiver to her neck. Her relief was such that she might have stopped trembling except for the chagrin, the chagrin of being powerless, the sort of feeling one has in the presence of a great celebrity—like the devil.

"I'll speak to you tomorrow," he said.

Tomorrow. She replaced the receiver and stood up and then was forced to sit down.

By early evening, the city was engulfed in a near-delirium of white silence. A brief country winter before the rotting of the snow. So much of what was familiar—markers, curbs, islands, crosswalks, signs—had been obliterated or had its proportions altered by the heavy snowfall that the streets had a quality of being unmapped, possibly unmappable. Nora couldn't stop the tape in her head; she couldn't permit herself to understand it—her sense of isolation as she made her way to the theater, partly on foot, partly by subway, was tumultuous. She was, as she'd never before been, at one with the weather.

Ned arrived as the houselights were dimming. He inched his way toward her across the row of knees. "What's first?" he asked.

She shook her head and put a warning finger to her mouth. A wasted, reed-thin young man was standing on the stage, a clarinet in place between his lips. A throng of young dancers joined him. They hurled themselves into the first sequence. Seeing this, Ned sighed. His expectations, though low, weren't low enough. There followed an interval of poorly tutored confusion during which he coughed incessantly. Nora wanted to shake him.

When the company's founder and principal choreographer, its star, padded in on his old-dog's feet, things quieted down, onstage and off. He made his way slowly through the corps to the center of the stage. The clarinet stopped; expectation throbbed in its place. The corps melted away, leaving him alone onstage, encircled in a moon of white light whose rim he chose to explore. When he had traversed the circumference, he stopped and cocked his massive, shaggy head. His large, sorrowful eyes lifted and his face assumed the fixed look of a great Dane hearing astral sounds. The audience strained with him. After a moment, he shook himself free and his pelt, which age was loosening from the bone, rippled. He entered another universe of stillness, one in which only movement as condensed and allusive as haiku was permitted. The clarinet partnered him. An indissoluble union. A revelation.

Ned yawned. When an occasion required something of him that he didn't have, or when a situation wouldn't yield to the imposition of his will, he simply withdrew.

The old man padded off. The corps resumed its chaotic investigation of space as if nothing had happened. But it had. Something quite astonishing had happened. After the drenching economy, the gorgeous discipline of the founder, his essentiality, a word that came to Nora with the force of a blow, this display of youthful flailing vigor represented a serious breach of taste. A litter of puppies let loose in a drawing room. The audience broke away willfully, detoured into private conversations, into uncontrolled, almost sullen fits of coughing. The clarinet badgered them for their attention but the disapproval was too strong.

At intermission, Ned stood up and stretched. "Let's go," he said. "This is a bore and I've had a long day."

"You go," she said. "I want to see the rest."

His lips puckered with suppressed rage. Usually Nora confined herself to the timetable of his wishes; this was one of the forms her fidelity took.

"Don't be difficult. It's not worth seeing."

"I don't share your opinion."

"I'm not asking you to share my opinion. I'm asking you to leave."

"Why don't you stay? You might get to like it."

"I've told you. I'm dead tired."

"I really want to stay, sweetheart."

"Suit yourself," he said, grimly. "I'll see you at home."

She took up a position against one of the spindly columns and looked around. The crowd was mostly in its twenties and thirties. A number of men were dressed for hiking, an expression of sanity given the weather. A few, however, were studies in retrospective elegance. One young man was wearing an ancient tuxedo and patent-leather pumps; another, celluloid cuffs and a green eyeshade. His shirt had a detachable collar.

The women nearest Nora—there were about a dozen, forming a loosely knit group—their faces and bodies, the various ways they displaced the air around them, everything about them in fact, converged in a display of earnestness toward culture which she found both repellent and touching and which marked them as fairly recent arrivals in the city. She supposed they'd come to the city for the same reason she had when she was their age—because objects worthy of such earnestness could be found only here.

To judge by the way they were dressed—peasant skirts, shapeless sweaters, clumsy boots—it seemed a good bet that they worshiped hand labor, seeing in it the egalitarianism of Christ-in-the-common-clay. Why not? She still felt that way from time to time and she was old enough to know better. Still, it angered her to look at them. Natural gifts aside, what was one to do with a woman who lacked the wit or the considerateness to make herself attractive? With an entire group? She felt saddened by the waste. The faces of these young women weren't shining with the wit of selflessness; they didn't have the nun's ruthlessness or the saint's. They were pasty with low self-esteem and, at the same time, reddened with the effort of pulling down what was above them while eagerly straining toward it. And yet they thought of themselves as "nice" women. Well, perhaps they were. Perhaps she was. But of what value was niceness?

A bell chimed. She took her seat. The lights dimmed. The curtain rose on the clarinetist and a pair of winged men. Father and son. The playbill said that the program for the second half would be announced. It wasn't. She recognized the founder beneath his feathered mask. She wondered who was dancing Icarus.

Their wings were made of feathers and linen fastenings and wax. Spread, they might have spanned the stage.

How can I say what it was like? It's history now. I'll try to be brief.

At the start, there was the son, touching his father's wings with wonder—then his own with a kind of mad joy; and there was the father's caution, a sense of the project as ill-fated because presumptuous; and there was the engineer's caution—will it work?—and this was amplified by degrees to include the father's love for his only son and his great pride in the brilliance, the daring of his own invention. Then came the beginning of the journey: the exhilaration of escaping earth, the great weightless leaps, one after another, which somehow linked up to become a form of flight—one believed them actually flying, the son behind the father—and one cheered. Oh, we all cheered: it was a glorious moment. Something had been accomplished, truly accomplished, there was no question.

The pair flew on, though one hardly knew how—the dance seemed beyond human strength—over a stage that had become a sea. They had left Samos and Delos and Naxos behind them; they were just passing Paros. In another moment the son would have begun his fated climb toward the sun, when the father, the founder, suddenly plucked crazily at his breast. He looked down at the stage from the height of his great pain—there was terror in his eyes—then he plummeted. His scream was cut short as his face hit the boards. The thud was terrible. The great wings rose and settled. They covered the fallen body like a shroud.

Icarus removed his mask.

She knew who he was.

She fled the chaos of the theater, the screams, the falling curtain, the rush of living bodies toward the stage.

Do you know the story of the maiden who was so fleet she could outrun the swiftest men? It's an ancient tale and well known. The one who was finally defeated, detouring for love? A poor thing who didn't know the detour for what it was. The ending? Oh, she kept her life, but she lost herself, exactly as the oracle had forewarned.

Stories are wonderful things.

It was a vile night, the wind driving the snow before it

with steel-threaded whips, the snow prying into secret places, but Nora was not alive to the cold. She was running hard to make the bus. The back of her neck was sleetily wet and there was a narrow cuff of frost around her wrists. Her face was a fire that warmed her, her face was burning. Her mind was burning too, with the idea of him, an undoomed Icarus, with the idea of that unfathomable originality embodied in a living man, her face was burning just to think of the elegance of mind, the beauty of face, the caprice of spirit, to think of the journey of love enlarged to the point of death. She should have been worried. She should have been in mourning for herself, but no, she felt joyful and safe. She was protected, you see, by the immensity of her desire for him. She had nothing to lose. Everything but the desire was lost already.

In this mood, she began to plot: how she would kidnap him, break into his very soul, and seize him by force, if necessary.

The woman pounding on the door of the bus to be let in was so indelicately changed by love, so mentally shattered, that even I would have had difficulty recognizing her.

6

I hesitate to speak of this—who speaks willingly of the darker things that belong to love?—but she felt a sort of madness growing on her.

When she asked him over the phone—"Will I see you today?"—and he ignored her question, she wanted to chain him to a wall. Time was flowing as it did in dreams: from the peak of one event to another, the valleys of connections seemingly buried: weeks, even months, omitted and then a minute split into seconds, each the length of an anxious lifetime.

She repeated the question in a different voice. "Will I see you today?"

"Probably," he said.

After a long pause, she asked, "When?"

"Now," he said.

Arriving: the door opened from the inside as she was fumbling with the room key. They faced each other without speaking: an intense, trembling woman with worried eyes, a passionate woman, barely aware of her surroundings—one of those anonymous residential hotel rooms on the Upper East Side—dressed in hiking boots and heavy clothes; a haggard, gray-faced, slightly stooped, ceremoniously disheveled man still in evening dress, vibrating with fatigue or nerves, who nevertheless, just as he was, commanded the woman's fiercest hopes.

In the stifled light of the foyer, his eye sockets appeared nearly hollow, making him look as if he'd lost the will to live. So much the better. She would supply the will. Her dream had always been to attach herself to a man of immense gifts and incorruptibility and power (they would be attached to each other with her as his indispensable tenant), to find a tortured genius, someone exhausted by inner greatness, and rescue him, elevate him, crown him. Her fantasies, such as they were, were never set in rooms. They were set in empty space. They had nothing to do with what happened in one minute and then in the next. They were edited by the mind and will of a willful, spoiled woman and they consisted mostly of embraces, as in reunions, after prolonged and involuntary separations. Great stabs of feeling like lightning truths in a great man's arms. If she tried to move beyond this, her imagination bogged down in the mud of the real.

The imperfection. The confusion, the anger, the error, the hurt. In the paucity of what actually would happen as compared to her hopes.

He smiled and took her face between his hands and held it for a moment. Then he kissed her on the mouth. His lips were warm. He drew her into his arms. She leaned her head against his chest. How long was she in his arms? Long enough to change her life.

He brought her to the bedroom without a word. Not even her name. He walked over to the bed and took off his clothes. She was apprehensive about the silence but happy too in her awe, a child watching a magician. His unclothed body seemed enormous, like an extent of meadow, and like a meadow he was covered with a golden furze across which there played a kind of ambulating shadow, and each hollow and crevice the shadow fell upon darkened still further while all the rest blazed gold as if in full sunlight. Who could have imagined a body like his? A mind?

He drew her toward him with his eyes.

She moved like a woman sleepwalking in snow, a blind woman zigzagging toward him across a great white field of snow. He was buried under centuries of snow but she was obsessive and eager and ruthless. The next shovelful was sure to be the crucial one, the one to uncover his ancient Trojan splendor, her ancestry, her discovery—his true self.

Pulling off her sweater, she shrank with discomfort. Ah, what she wanted at this moment was a means of treating her body without irony and with the degree of care appropriate to it as one of the instruments of her destiny—as she imagined dancers did. She felt him judging her. She glanced up at his face. It was stitched together with silken threads of weariness, an embroidery so impersonal it was hard to pity him. He opened his mouth to speak but he was incapable. His face jerked, his eyes bulged horribly. The seizure—if that's what it was—lasted a moment then passed away.

"Are you all right?" she asked urgently.

He didn't answer.

He closed his eyes. His face took on the immobility of Asian statuary. She trembled, waiting for the great eye to open. The awning lifted, she was exposed to the elements. The eye was wintry. There was no pity, no mystery to be seen in it, only a kind of eloquent, crackling scorn that said that everything she was was in the way of everything she ought to be.

He left the room without a word.

Despair loomed up before her, an actual granitic mountain, cutting off her view of everything. It was so hideously large, so solidly exhausting to contemplate that she couldn't even attach a word to it. God help her, she didn't see how she was to live with it there, pressed against her eyes.

It was a vengefully true moment from which she emerged naked, scattered, sightless, inwardly running through the apartment searching for him, sobbing his name, a creation of the wild Brontëan moors. She couldn't disavow him. She couldn't even hate him for having the power to humble her.

She found him in the living room, stretched out on the couch. In the dim light, the room was all mellow blues and dull, syrupy reds. His body rippled with long, silvery muscle shadow. He lifted his head with unexpected suddenness and caught her looking at him.

"How curious are you?" he asked, not unkindly.

His first words.

She'd been in quiet anguish over his silence. She was used to confusing silence with disapproval; that was one of the forms her paranoia took.

"You're very beautiful," she said, blushing.

He lifted his penis by the crown from its cushioned place on his thigh. It was pale mauve, long, the right length for its thickness, and straight. She blinked. Her curiosity was making her miserably shy.

"There are networks of hollow vessels under the skin that

fill with blood," he told her. "That's why it is so much darker when it's erect."

She nodded, instructed.

"This part," he said, indicating the rim around the base of the head and the long seamlike vein running from it to the root on the side facing away from his torso when the thing was erect, "this part is especially sensitive."

She ran a finger along the route he indicated. The thing lifted its head, briefly.

He put his penis to one side, took up the scrotum, the pouch of skin. "This holds the testicles. Feel. There are two of them. They're ellipsoids."

She had them in the cup of her hand. She thought of the soft spot on the skull of a newborn. He pulled up on the skin. "When men get older, the scrotum loosens some."

There was a great deal more. He told her the rest. Of course, she knew all of it—she wasn't a novice in that sense—but having him explain it so unself-consciously made all the difference. This was the friendliest a man had ever been to her. What must it be like, she wondered, to have such a highly visible addendum, a thing that was at once a toy and a friend, a playmate with the power to amuse and betray you both. One would have to stay on excellent terms with such a companion. But how? Men's humiliations, she thought, had to go far deeper than a woman could ever know.

She knelt between his legs. She made one long cylinder of her mouth and throat. She guessed at a rhythm, not knowing what would please him. After a time, he moved his hand to the back of her head, he took hold of a hank of her hair, and by pulling on it he instructed her in the tempo he preferred. She began to see. She was crouched between his legs like Cinderella in her ashes. He was all the finery she would ever need. There was no one in this life she envied now. Behind the pleated fan of her womanhood, she was smiling. She had the power of the future in her, and I say that power in whosever hands—or mouth—is rarely innocent. If I say she—

Nora—wanted the power to do good, I mean she wanted to be the one to define what constituted goodness. And, then, she wanted him to love her for her goodness.

For all the encouragements and ministrations of her mouth and lips and tongue, he was not fully erect. The lining of her mouth was abraded, there was a ridge of raw, upended flesh in the space between her lips and nose, and all the while his hand was lifting and falling to a cadence that did not allow her to breathe in synchrony with her needs. She couldn't shut her mind to the notion that this had become some sort of test of nerve and skill. Her jaw ached, her throat was in spasm. She continued to worship anyway, in her clumsy way—she wanted so to give him pleasure—but the foreboding that her enterprise might not be blessed with startling success had become a certainty and, to be truthful, she was a bit desperate.

He sat up and motioned her to lie back. When his tongue touched her, she jerked like a hooked fish. She was unnerved by excitement, both shut up in herself and scrupulously alert, like a woman fearing for her chastity. The muscles of her buttocks were as tightly clenched as fists. She yielded to his attentions very slowly, and the yielding surprised her by turning very slowly into pleasure.

"Tell me something," he said, as she was recovering from the experience—they were sitting side by side on the couch, companionably, she thought—"now that you've discovered that pleasure has a validity of its own, how are you going to live any other way?"

The question nearly stopped her heart. She didn't want to live any other way and he knew it. He knew she had to be with him. He knew she was obsessed with him and that she wasn't ashamed of it. Insights that are profound enough often take the form of obsession. The question really was, would he have her or not? Was he telling her he wouldn't?

"I don't know," she said weakly, feeling the strength ebb

from her body at the thought of life without him, "but if I have to I'll manage somehow."

"You're lying," he said, pushing her face away with a disgust that was slashing. "Can't you ever tell the truth?"

The cheek of her fear opened. She recanted. "Yes, I'm lying." Her readiness to confess, to acquiesce, frightened her. It wasn't a lie—it wasn't rhetorical. But it didn't seem to satisfy him. She didn't see any end for herself but death. Was it her death he was after? Did he hate her that much? No, she couldn't believe that. She didn't believe in hate. Where she lived, as far as her poor power extended, *there was no hate.*

He was studying her. The moment, she felt, was crucial. She tried to convey to him without words that what he called her lying was that but it was something else as well. An aspect of her wholeheartedness, maybe, and of her desire not to hurt anyone, particularly him. She couldn't tell if she succeeded or not.

A strand of silky hair fell forward across his eyes like a sudden shaft of light. He reached up and brushed it away. The gesture had a sacerdotal resonance: clearly he had the power to brush away all barriers, even her lies, even her fright. His eyes glowed, reflective as mirrors. They seemed to swim in a film of liquefied crystal. The lids were only partially retracted, as if the porcelain behind them might crack with full exposure to the light, to any sort of light. He could see through her and apparently he didn't like what he was seeing at that moment. There was a cruel curve to his faintly pouting lips. The smile that flowered on them might be worse than a sneer. Or maybe not. He put on his clothes purposefully as if to say she was not his final destination.

Leaving: the sharp chill of the outdoors reached her as he opened the door to the corridor. It penetrated to her bones like the chill of an unpleasant truth. Had she given him any pleasure at all?

Now that she was leaving she was desperate to know. She

loitered in the doorway for a while with the eyes of a beggar. He offered nothing. Finally, she said, "If you tell me how you want me to behave, I'll try to change. . . ."

He didn't answer and his smile as he said goodbye was as forced, as verging on the hysterical, as impersonally and tauntingly suspicious as it had been when first they'd met.

On the walk home, she took a vow: if she couldn't make him happy as she was, she would invent a woman who could. Short of success, life wasn't worth the trouble.

While she was in transit back to the ordinary, the snow turned to rain. The sky was cat-gray and plump; its belly sagged with the weight of sudden heat. All around her she could hear the suck and pull of moisture as the top layers of snow, pelted by rain, began to melt and run off. Within minutes her clothes were soaked through. She appeared not to notice.

There's an architecture of weather in this city, a second city almost: narrow, intensely vertical cylinders of rain wedged between buildings, the visual echoism of rain on lights, the way they fattened with blur like a bird's rained-on feathers in plump concealment of the frail, lurking skeleton. Magnification to conceal. A second city, slick with danger.

The slim book in Nora's hand was by a contemporary German and boasted of a single life of incomparable mental athleticism, in which climate paradox grew like a weed and dead flowers and freedom were made to seem conciliatory. The fat book at her elbow, within the fan of lamplight, was by a dead Japanese. The climax of ten thousand years of empire was a woman's fleeting smile.

Rain slashed the window.

Her husband's head and shoulders as he leaned urgingly over her took on the hateful, autocratic density of Late Roman portrait busts of senators and the like. Had it always been this way?

"Sign here and here and here," he said, flipping the long white pages and coughing in elaborate sequences.

"Let me ask you something first," she said, the pen he'd handed her poised in the air.

"What?" He turned his eyes from the document to her, suspiciously.

"I'd like you to put the house in both our names."

"That's not possible."

"Every married woman I know has joint ownership and a joint bank account."

"Our situation isn't like anyone else's. My financial affairs are extremely complicated, and there is no way I'm going to complicate them further. It's out of the question for you to write checks on my account."

"I haven't asked for a joint checking account."

"You have no idea what the tax implications of joint ownership are for someone in my bracket." He walked around and around the table like a sheepdog patrolling the perimeter of its holdings.

"Please explain them. I'm interested. I'd like to understand." She put down her book.

"Why all of a sudden now? You've never given a damn about my affairs before." He wouldn't meet her eyes. He shot his cuffs, he thrust his jaw forward, he pulled his shoulders back, he coughed.

"I was wrong. I regret it."

"Well, you can just put it out of your mind. I'm not turning over half the house to you."

"Don't dismiss it out of hand like that, Ned. Please."

"Don't sign. It's all the same to me."

"Am I being so unreasonable?" she asked, her will collapsing. "We've been married nearly a lifetime."

"Don't you trust me, Nora?"

"Of course I do. But when you went away last month, I had to ask my father for five hundred dollars so that I could run the house until you came back. You're always late with the children's money."

"You think I like doing that? You think I do that on pur-pose? You know how short of cash I am, but it doesn't stop you, does it? My worries don't interest you."

"You're never so short of cash you can't cash a check. I didn't start this. All I want is to keep my own money and spend it as I see fit. I don't care if it isn't productive."

"Half this house is worth at least ten times your inheri-tance."

"Just what am I worth to you, Ned?"

"That's a stupid question." He shrugged dismissively.

"Please give it some thought anyway," she said.

I still ask myself: Why did it have to be that way for them—that needless proliferation of misery?

7

She ran at dawn. The wind was so cold it burned her eyes. Her throat stung. Quills of ice pierced the skin on her face. She returned home an hour later and waited out the morn-ing for a call that never came.

And then it was time to dress for lunch. She scanned the contents of her closet and concluded that she had nothing to wear. Everything she owned defined her as someone she no longer wanted to be: a woman who couldn't kill her enjoy-ment of clothes, a woman who *knew how to dress*—a shallow woman. Nora dreaded being thought shallow or vain, unap-proachable or aggressive. Hoping to escape classification, she subscribed to Montesquieu's advice: she did her best to fol-low fashion from afar. Not too far, for even that was a state-ment. What was not? And strong statements were barriers.

Nora hated barriers. Clothes were a barrier. Money was a barrier. Any sort of privilege was, really. Intelligence, in a twist of logic she couldn't quite defend, was the only defensible barrier. Nora was a mind snob of the worst sort: one whose own mind was not as well developed as her snobbery. Still, she was eager to rise above all social distinctions and to recognize greatness of soul as the only legitimate basis for a hierarchy. At the same time, she would never be seen wearing cheap shoes. A woman whose husband paid a little too much attention to Nora said to her once, only half in jest, "It's hard to think of you having a mind, Nora, the way you look."

I don't mean to exaggerate her beauty. It was never the kind to disrupt the natural order of things. Rather, it was the sort that had to be discovered, and when it was, what claimed the eye was the subtlety of her bone structure. Some people found her face a bit too cool, and it was true that she'd been turned down by more than one caricaturist on the grounds that her face didn't offer any opportunity for exaggeration. I can see the argument, but for the most part I think those men lacked talent or—equally constraining, given their profession—malice. Anyway, Nora was inclined to slant her face rather cold-bloodedly toward the ideal. That way she didn't have to take full responsibility for her looks.

She decided to risk Valerie's red-and-black print. She swept her hair into the pompadour that the dress demanded. A sort of fictitious beauty attached itself to the person she saw in the mirror. Some people call this glamour.

The phone rang after she'd locked the front door. She was so clumsy-nerved she could hardly reinsert the key in the lock. She dropped her gloves rushing through the house; bending to retrieve them, she stepped on the edge of her scarf. It tore at the skin of her neck. The phone toppled to the floor under her assault.

"Nora? I'm glad I caught you in," her father said. "What's

this Ned's been telling me about you wanting him to put the house in your name?"

"Only half," she said. Her disappointment was physically painful. Her heart hadn't slowed yet. "Can we talk later, Dad? I'm going to be late for lunch."

"This'll only take a minute. Norrie, Ned bailed me out of a very tight spot a while ago. He put up a chunk of money in return for a part-interest in the business. Sign the power of attorney, pussy cat. You know he'll always take care of you. He's a good man. What does it mean, half a house? The man carries a fortune's worth of life insurance. He fixed your teeth. That's the kind of proof that counts."

"Is the house in Mother's name or yours?"

"What does that have to do with anything?"

"Dad, I'll call you later. I don't have time now."

"What do you mean, time? Just sign the papers."

"I'll call you tonight, okay?"

"Don't call me. Just sign. Don't make problems for me, Nora."

"Why is my not signing a problem for you?"

"Sweetheart, just do what I'm asking, okay?"

"I'd better call you tonight."

The restaurant had a buttery warmth. It was a narrow room lined with U-shaped banquettes, perhaps twelve in all and all occupied. The tables were covered with white homespun cloths, and a bud vase holding a single white narcissus was centered on each one. The walls were the color of Devonshire cream, the wood floors were bare and dark. The austerity was of a humane, encouraging sort. The owner was quite amiable. Avery had chosen well.

She had no difficulty recognizing Kasim. He bore an anguished resemblance to his photographs. The face locked up on his book jackets was no less a prisoner for breathing. His eyes carried out what seemed a self-imposed sentence, being dark and calm and cold, used to looking inward. He had a long, sharp nose, the nostrils disproportionately large, dark wiry hair, graying sideburns, a sluggish complexion, and emphatically molded lips. He was Lebanese, half-Christian, half-Moslem. He'd been schooled in London. He wrote in English.

Nora had presumed a large man and, seated, he met her expectations. His shoulders were that broad, his torso that long, but when he rose to introduce himself she saw that he was considerably shy of even medium height. He was dressed with obvious care in a fawn-colored shirt, a red wool tie, oatmeal twill trousers, and a brown-and-green tweed hunting jacket.

When Nora considered the padded assertiveness of her own dress, her cheeks reddened, her composure faded. "I hope this place will do," she babbled. "It's only just opened but I've heard it's quite good."

"There's no doubt in my mind," Kasim said, smiling.

The captain pulled out the table and she slipped in beside Kasim.

"Shall we have a drink to ease this nasty business of getting acquainted, or shall we wait for the others?" he asked.

"Oh, a drink now," Nora said. She rarely drank during the day.

Mahmoud Kasim was the author of a number of novels set in the Middle East and two books exploring the Palestinian question. And now he'd written a play. Jenny had met him recently at a conference. She had been half in love with him since reading his first book, and had hopes of persuading Avery Loudon to back his play. Avery was a full-time philanthropist, and Nora, she knew, had considerable influence with him.

While she and Kasim waited for the others, they discovered they had in common a tendency to headaches, the habit of punctuality, a deep interest in the Japanese print, and the "mongrel-thing," as Kasim put it, of being half this and half that.

"I was at that Sotheby auction a few months ago. The Met was selling some of its prints. I bought a Hokkei. Do you know him?"

"He was a pupil of Hokusai, wasn't he?" she asked.

He was. His Hokkei was very elaborately executed, even by surinomo standards, he said. It showed Kintaro with a knife, riding a giant carp. "I paid more than I wanted to, but it's a good impression. There's some slight wormage in one of the corners or it would have been out of my reach."

Years ago, Avery had given her a print by Eishi showing a courtesan seated in front of a mirror painting her own portrait, which lay on the floor at her feet. The odd thing about it, and what Nora loved, was that the reflection in the mirror was of the back of the courtesan's head, but the woman herself, at the moment she was captured by the artist, was looking at the viewer more or less full face. And the completed portrait at her feet was just as the viewer saw her. But upside down and miniaturized.

By the time Kasim opened his shopping bag and brought out two new shirts for her approval, they were old friends. The shirts were quite handsome. Nora made excuses for Valerie's dress. He understood perfectly, he said. Innovation was the mark of an artist; one must expect failure in the transitional periods. He confided to her that he felt unappreciated as an artist.

"You're a hero to my family," she said.

"I'm quite bitter, actually," he said, looking into her eyes, smiling thinly. "I've no money to speak of. My audience is recalcitrantly small. And next year I face the unspeakable prospect of teaching . . . unless . . . "

He had hopes for his play, he said. It would help him spread his wings a little, assuming good reviews and a bit of luck. Nora had read the play. She saw no possibility of a commercial success. As for a succès d'estime, she couldn't say; the characters seemed wooden to her. But she didn't venture an opinion, she liked him too much. She liked his viyella shirts and his mind and his caustic lack of modesty and his inverted pride and even his ungratefulness. She liked that he was the sort of person who stressed what he had in common with you. Others might dislike these things. It was a fact that in some circles Kasim was held to be an insufferable prig whose fictional characters had no fictional blood but were simply icons for his ideas. She also knew that Kasim's work aroused little serious antagonism among the critics because although it was good, it wasn't good enough to constitute a threat to any established body of ideas in either literature or politics.

Jenny turned up with a smile and a damning word about the weather. She sat down on the banquette at a right angle to Kasim. Under her long lashes, her eyes were glowing softly. "I like what you've done with your hair," she said to Nora. "And the dress is wonderful."

She gave her hand to Kasim. He raised it to his lips and looked at her significantly. Avery arrived minutes later. Nora was continually astonished by how tall he was. Jenny introduced the two men and they shook hands. Avery sat down next to Nora and leaned over to kiss her. Even seated, he was apologetically tall. His bald head gleamed pinkly. His blue eyes conveyed a finely detailed warmth.

Nora had met him years ago at one of Margaret's dinner parties and she'd placed him, in her mind, at the head of an easy dynasty of stables and children. The facts were otherwise. His wife was a formidable eccentric who lived in seclusion in Fiesole and permitted Avery to visit her only at Christmas. His son preferred the South Pole to Beekman Place. His daughter was a Christian Science healer in East Texas. The family interests were mining and lumber, the fortune demonstrably vast and diversified, the lineage impervious to assault. He kept a house in London and an apartment at one of the more fashionable hotels in New York.

"You've changed your style," he said to Nora. His tone was mildly charged with disapproval. He could never disapprove of her entirely—or so she thought then.

Nora shrugged. "I was in an odd mood."

"Well, I like the way you look," Jenny said, firmly.

A crease of annoyance appeared on Avery's smooth, shining forehead. For the first time, his overt cleanliness struck Nora as a form of repentence not unlike Margaret's.

"By the way," Avery said, "I took the liberty of asking someone to join us. He'll be along when he can. There's no need to wait lunch. His name is Lautner. You'll find him interesting, I think. You particularly, Jenny."

The others went on talking. Nora heard everything but understood nothing. Her emotions were succeeding on each other so quickly that she couldn't put a name to them. A kind of internal chaos prevailed—a thudding, irregular heartbeat and a noisy buzz in her ears as of insects in summer, thwarting for a time her best attempts at self-control.

When she was able to attend to the conversation again, Avery was saying, "I'm a great admirer of your writing, Mr. Kasim, but to be perfectly honest, I couldn't disagree more with your politics."

It cost Nora something to keep her eyes, which kept drifting to the door, on the two men. Her nerves were so raw with anticipation that Avery's mild voice grated like sandpaper. Even so, she didn't give much weight to what he was saying. His directness was of a soft, drawling kind that could easily be mistaken for honesty, especially when paired with the look of candor in his blue eyes, but those who knew him well seldom took his remarks seriously because of his tone, which was that of good-natured raillery—his way of flirting or staying amused. "Baiting" is too harsh a word.

Kasim said, "Thank you," and then, audibly biting off the ends of his words, and with his fingers bridling the stem of his wineglass, he added, "But I'm curious to know how you manage to admire my writing when my morality, or what you choose to call my 'politics,' is inseparable from my work."

"Why, Mr. Kasim," Avery said, affecting a mild astonishment, "everyone says you're a superb stylist." He made this remark in the weight of voice one used when praising the decor to one's hostess over drinks.

Kasim's head reared as if a whip had been cracked silently across his neck. He squared his shoulders and put down his glass. His fingers smoothed the length of his crimson tie. And then, with an attempt at ideological laissez-faire that curdled in the heat of his temper, he said, "Chaps of your sort usually deplore my views."

"And what is a chap of my sort?" Avery asked, holding his head far back, a look of deep amusement in his eyes.

"Much as you won't like hearing the truth, the fact is that you Americans have become a nation of very ordinary men. You've no special destiny. You're not uncorrupted survivors from before the Fall. Your greed is out of control. You haven't the moral authority to tell anyone what to do anymore."

"Yes, we know your opinion. We've read your books."

"It's not just my opinion," Kasim said, pausing to sip his wine. His plump sausage fingers were trembling. "It's the world's as well."

"Come now, what makes you think you speak for the world?" Avery asked. "You're only one—and not even the most famous—of any number of stateless intellectual terrorists who let others pay in blood for your beliefs. Nobody in power pays the slightest attention to you." Avery twirled his wineglass. "And you call Americans naive. . . . "

"The rich are always naive," Kasim said. "Money is insulation. The richer you are, the more protection you buy yourself—property, servants, art—the less you're able to feel anything." His voice had a practiced burrlike insistence and his words were calculated to rub rawly in the sorest places.

"Oh, nonsense," Avery said. "It's a cheap shot to pose as poor if you have the sphere of influence you claim. You're as insulated in fame as I am in money, if we use your argument. You can't have it both ways, you know. And besides, even if you were poor, and clearly you're not, to judge by your clothes, your sort of self-righteous poverty is more reprehensible in the sight of God than what you call the naiveté of the rich." Avery's voice was as mild as ever, but his eyes were shining with unfamiliar fervor. Nora saw that this was an entirely serious moment for him. Jenny had flinched at his words and then looked at Nora, the cords in her swiveling neck as taut as the strings of a loom, her face more catlike than ever.

"In the sight of God? What sort of God would condone things as they are?" Kasim said. "I have no time for an indifferent God." His anger was edged with a fierce contempt. Jenny flashed Nora a worried look.

The smoothness of Avery's accent, the mild look in his blue eyes, the affable smile that never left his face, even the genial angle at which he inclined his head, a head so well shaped that the lack of hair was merely one more advantage, the tapered, immensely strong hands—oh, the sheer size of the man: he was six feet five inches tall—all this, coupled with the deep natural propriety of his self-assurance, created an impression of unassailability that went well beyond Avery himself to suggest a long-enthroned structure of legitimacy, the closest thing we have to divine right.

By contrast, Kasim seemed the most vulnerable of men, dangling sourly, humorlessly over a chasm, secured only by the frayed rope of his own words. He was in a light, oily sweat and his chest was barreled with tension. His fingers searched the tight knot of his tie and then withdrew without easing it. Nora saw the choked face of a very ambitious man who was being forced by conscience or pride to undergo a kind of death for the sake of his ideas. She felt sorry for him and angry with Avery. The inequality between them was chasmally fierce as only social inequality can be. Lineage is not rectifiable even when mitigated by intelligence and taste, and it was precisely Avery's pedigree, generations in the making, that was hardest on Kasim. Avery was too self-possessed to have to humiliate anyone. He hadn't deigned to pull intellectual rank, though he could—his intelligence was certifiably extraordinary—which meant things could still be resolved if he wanted them to be. Nora urged this course on him with her eyes. He nodded discreetly.

Kasim, trembling and flushed, tried to stand up, but being so closely confined to the inner side of the table, he was caught in an unfortunate sort of crouching bow, a geishalike posture from which he begged to be excused, pleading jet lag and the beginning, the aura, of a migraine which could not be ignored. The captain appeared to pull out the table but Avery waved him away.

"Why such a fuss over our differences?" he said. "Sit down and let's talk, shall we? That's the reason we're all here." His smile spread patriarchally, like the arms of a green bay tree.

Julien Sorel and Kitty's Levin were at war for Kasim's immortal soul, or so Nora read the moment. Kasim was deeply interested in securing immortality, which these days required a certain amount of publicity. His contradictory needs made him veer like a drunken driver from one side of his personality to the other. He sat down. The ax was laid unto the root of the tree.

Avery was drumming his fingers on the table—idly, he would have them believe, but Nora saw that he was deeply aggrieved. Kasim had insulted his virtue. Kasim, who had been thoroughly outmaneuvered, humiliated by greed and ambition into staying, was mute with self-loathing and rage against Avery. Jenny had leashed her immediate destiny to Kasim's. Her face made plain that he was one of her heroes. She could scarcely muzzle her ill-will toward Avery, yet she tried for Kasim's sake. For the sake of his play. She looked questioningly at Nora.

Ah, but Nora's eyes were elsewhere—following the progress of a tall man wearing a shabby black suit, a man whose eyes burned through her like live coals, a man whose face was fraught with the potential for the ultimate.

She gave him the smile meant for Jenny, a lunatic smile. "Lautner!" Avery said warmly, getting to his feet. "Come, let me introduce you to everyone."

Lautner? Why call him Lautner? He wasn't Lautner. He wasn't anyone but himself. It was pointless to chain him to a single identity.

Lautner shook Jenny's hand and smiled at Nora. "Mrs. Ingarden and I met the other night. Tromp introduced us too. She has a very impressive family—as families go." No one could doubt his sincerity, not even Nora.

"I'm glad to see you again," Nora said.

"I don't think you know Mahmoud Kasim," Avery said.

"Well, in a manner of speaking, I do," Lautner said, grasping Kasim's hand.

Kasim took this as a compliment and smiled politely.

The waiter brought a chair and Lautner sat down. The expression on his face was sweet-natured and slightly foolish. His manner suggested the near-heretical simplicity of Saint Francis among the birds, a posture that would surely bring him to harm anywhere outside the gates of his pretty garden. His performance, if it was a performance, was of such sincerity and oddity that it was almost dreamlike. Was it possible that she was dreaming it? That at any instant she chose she could leave the stage and be free of him? That the harshness, the terror, the caprice were inside her? Were her doing? Hers alone? She jerked herself back from the edge of that possibility with the violent inner shudder of a dreamer rescuing herself from the plunging free fall of sleep.

"I'm afraid I interrupted something," Lautner said, and whereas Nora remembered his voice as having been a sort of glacial rumbling, now it had a gentle artlessness that left her doubting her memory. She simply couldn't grasp him in his proliferations. How could she? She was a woman who believed that the aphorism was the most exquisite flower of human thought, and she wanted all language and probably all meaning to rush toward compression, as if compression and meaning were indissolubly linked, as if a thing once true was true forever, as in the words of the Austrian general Conrad von Hötzendorf, whom Avery was fond of quoting: "Everything that is not as simple as a slap is no good for war."

"You interrupted Avery in the act of provoking Mahmoud," Jenny said. She delivered this slight with a gracious smile to Avery.

Kasim was silent. Nora was silent. Avery smiled wearily and patted Nora's hand. Jenny's sincerity tired him. Still, he was fair-minded enough to respect her for her decency.

Lautner saw everything. Nora wanted to lay her head on his breast and weep. I am the woman you see. This is my life. This man was my lover. This woman is my friend. Help me. She hardly understood the sudden darkness of her mood.

"I know your work," Lautner said, turning his attention to Kasim. "And, of course, knowing Avery's position, I'm aware that it's fatuous of me to try to reconcile your two points of view. But, assuming for a moment that material appearance can sometimes express the profound truth of things, let's say that if truth has the shape of a giant carp— you know, the ones in Japanese prints—then perhaps it can be said that each of us gets a brief hold on the tail before the thing wriggles away."

Was his simplicity a tactic? A form of irony? A species of contempt?

"Yes, well, I'm afraid my assumptions don't go in the direction of parable," Kasim said, somewhat condescendingly. "Unless the carp can be eaten, I'm not inclined to consider it."

"Kasim isn't critical enough of how the carp gets on the table," Avery said. "That's the bone I have to pick with him—if you'll excuse the pun."

Nora couldn't help smiling. Jenny clenched her jaw. Lautner's benign expression was unaltered. "For all his theoretical eagerness to take sides," he continued, as if there had been no quibbling, "I'm sure Kasim would agree that no highly regimented society—on the right or the left—has a place for the artist except as propagandist or apologist."

Kasim would, of course, agree.

Avery finished his beef and put his fork down with a thoughtful look. Kasim wiped his mouth of the traces of bouillabaisse, almost daintily, it seemed to Nora. Jenny, looking from one to the other, relaxed her shoulders. She smiled gratefully at Lautner.

Money was never mentioned. When Jenny and Kasim got up to leave—together—Avery suggested that Kasim drop by his offices at the foundation sometime later in the week.

"That man is too easily humiliated to be anyone's friend for long," Avery said to Nora when Kasim and Jenny were gone. "I hope Jenny knows what she's doing."

"I have to be going too," Lautner said. He reached across the table to shake Avery's hand. Nora, seeing his wrist catch the rim of his coffee cup, lunged for the cup but she wasn't quick enough. The cup tipped over and, in falling, it toppled first his own untouched wineglass, then the salt shaker and pepper mill, then Avery's water goblet, then Avery's cup of espresso. The contents of everything between them, liquid and solid, Avery's own half-finished plate of zabaglione and strawberries—everything—ended up beached on Avery's gray pinstriped suit.

For such a dinosaur of a man, Avery had amazingly swift reflexes. He leaped to his feet, but then, surprisingly, this proved to be the extent of his adaptiveness. He stood help-lessly erect with his nostrils pinched and his arms held away from his sides in a sort of convulsion of fastidiousness and mortification, as if his body had suddenly acquired the stink of centuries of sewers.

The owner approached at a run. He dabbed at the Easter Island–sized monolith with a napkin, and when this proved inadequate he signaled for reinforcements. Two busboys rushed to assist him. Amid a vast confusion of hygiene and blame, Lautner rose to tender his apologies. His clumsiness, he announced in a voice made even sweeter by embarrassment, was unforgivable. It would be best if he went back to his hotel and tried to get hold of his nerves. New York was sometimes a bit too much for him. He was really only a country boy. He turned to Nora and asked if he could see her to a taxi.

Something black and gold gushed in her chest. "Yes, thank you," she said. She made no attempt to take her eyes from him.

Avery looked from her to Lautner and back, his face registering polite surprise, then suspicion, and then, seeing that Nora's eyes were still in thrall to Lautner's, angry comprehension. In that brief interval, Nora saw that she had earned his hatred, probably forever.

He said goodbye to her, clamping his lips around the words and uttering them over his shoulder as if a frontal attack was more humane than she deserved. And then the owner and a small battalion of waiters escorted him, shocked and spattered, from the front.

It was barely two-thirty, but the sky was an indeterminate gray, a color that neither proved nor disproved her watch, a gray as remote from reality as the gray in photographs. The wind was on the increase. It was snowing again, the snow falling in dismal slanting lines, each flake as heavy as if weighted with ash.

They walked a block. Lautner held her arm. She was as saturated with pleasure as if they were strolling on a faraway beach under an idyllic sun, one that warmed without burning. There were no taxis, no buses in sight.

"Are you feeling any better?" Nora asked shyly. His face was very pale.

He shook his head. "I do find the world a vile place," he said. "It's not a trick. Hell may be ugly but it's just."

"I love you so much," she said. "Does that help at all?"

"Not yet," he said.

"I know I'm awfully small but you could lean on me a little—and I can arrange for a car if you'd like."

There was a slight increase of pressure on her arm.

"My hotel is on the next block," he said. "But thank you."

She left him at the entrance and forced herself to continue walking. Seeing the carriage lights of a small bookstore aureoled in mist, she thought numbly that she might go in and browse, but the hand she placed on the doorknob refused to turn it. She walked on. Solitude, it seemed, was the only fit condition for someone in her shoes.

She returned home to find her parents' suitcases in the foyer. She was not in a mood to receive anyone, least of all her mother and father, from whom she tried to conceal all emotions but those that attached themselves to filial love.

She went upstairs to her bedroom and lay down, but she was unable to rest. She picked up a book, but within a few pages she understood that there was nothing to be learned from its author. She was in the kitchen preparing dinner when she heard a key in the lock. She recognized her mother's quiet tread. A hanger rattled in the front-hall closet and was quickly silenced.

"Mom?"

"I'll be back down in a minute."

She dashed into the hall in time to take the suitcases from her mother's hands. "Ned will take them up when he comes home. They're too heavy for you."

"That's silly. Let me have them."

"Where's Dad?"

"He'll be along later with Ned. They were finishing up some business. I went shopping." She picked up one of the suitcases.

"Please, put that down, Mom."

"I thought I'd change clothes. The stores were overheated. . . ."

"Then let me take it up for you."

"Why? You're not any stronger than I am."

"I don't want you to hurt your neck again."

"Careful of the wall on your right side, Nora. My bag leaves black marks on everything."

"Why didn't you let me know you were coming?"

"Ned knew."

"Is something wrong?"

"Not really. Daddy wanted to talk to you."

Her mother took a shabby nightgown out of her suitcase and slipped it under the pillow. "I'll just go in the bathroom and put on the robe you gave me for my birthday. I save it for traveling; it's too elegant to wear at home."

"What does Dad want to talk to me about?" Nora asked through the closed door.

"Nora, I know Ned's not the easiest man in the world about money. I have some savings I want to give you after you sign the power of attorney. There's one thing, though. Daddy doesn't know anything about my little bank account and I don't want him to." The door opened and her mother came out of the bathroom tying the belt of a sky-blue-and-peach silk robe. "Nora, if you knew how much I love this robe."

"About the money, Mom. It's wonderful of you to offer and I appreciate it, but why can't Dad know?"

"The money gives me a little security. It's only ten thousand dollars, but you know Daddy. One day there's a chauffeur and a limousine and the next he's mortgaged the house to raise some money."

"Then how can I possibly take it from you? I should be giving you what Grandpa gave me."

There was an odd-feeling pause and then her mother said firmly and without looking at her, "I just wanted you to know that the money is yours for as long as you need it."

"Mom, I'm not going to sign my money over to Ned. I just can't."

"That's a big mistake, Nora. You're his wife."

Nora jumped up and dashed from the room.

"Nora, where are you running to?"

"I forgot to lower the flame under the rice. It's probably boiling over."

"This is some mess," her father said, surveying the damage in the living room. Two weeks earlier, a pipe high up in the wall between the master bedroom and bath had sprung a leak that had gone unnoticed for a few days. "This is gonna cost a fortune to fix up. The wall has to be scraped and canvased. The ceiling too."

"It's even worse upstairs," Nora said.

"I picked out some swatches for you today, Nora," her mother said, putting down her Bloody Mary and reaching for a large manila envelope on the table beside her. "I thought as long as you have to paint you might want to re-cover the built-ins. How long has it been? They're awfully shabby for such a beautiful place."

"Oh, eighteen years, I guess. As long as we've been here," Nora said.

"I still remember when *Better Homes and Gardens* did that piece on the house. I was so proud. I still have the issue."

"It was the magazine section of the *Times*, Mom."

"Well, you know my memory."

"As soon as the walls are dry, you can get someone in here to do the job," her father said, testing for dampness with his palm.

"It's going to take time to settle this, Gus," Ned said. He put his feet up on the coffee table and crossed his ankles. "The insurance won't cover the costs. I've decided to sue the plumbing contractor."

"Has an adjuster been here yet?" her father asked.

"The other day. For hours," Nora said.

"Well, then, you can get started—" her mother said.

"We aren't going to do anything, Mary, until this thing is settled," Ned said. His cough gathered slowly, deep in his chest, building in volume and speed until it crested and broke over their heads. He put down his drink and gave himself up to the paroxysm.

Her parents were staring at him as if hypnotized.

"I'm sorry, Ned. I hope you don't think I meant to interfere," her mother said. She was blushing.

"You mean we're going to go on living like this for as long as it takes to settle with the plumber?" Nora asked. "A court case?" She burst out laughing.

"We aren't going to do anything for the moment." Ned was stony-voiced. Clearly, he expected an argument.

Nora refused the challenge. The house, which as recently as a few days ago had thrilled her with its comforts and proportions, tonight struck her as being unloved, uncared for, pretentiously grand, unworthy of serious attention. "I have a few things to do in the kitchen," she said, rising abruptly.

Her mother jumped up.

"Stay here, Mom, and keep the men company."

"You're sure?"

"I'm sure."

The table took up most of the dining room. It was kidney-shaped, awesome and silly both, a whale with legs. Nailed along the length of its apron were a dozen highly polished brass tags. Like markers at Arlington, they were engraved with the names and dates of the deceased—in this case, the twelve original members of the board of directors of Nicholas Ingarden's chemical manufacturing company, for whose meetings this table had been created. A dozen high-backed chairs, stiff and demanding as thrones, were drawn up around it. Four places had been set at the widest end.

Nora was serving dinner from a tableside cart when, without any warning, her mother lowered her head to her crossed arms and began to sob brokenly.

Nora put down the artichoke and looked at her father. Her eyes were wide with alarm. He whispered to her across the table as if across a deathbed, "It's better not to pay any attention. That way she won't be so embarrassed later." He glanced at Ned. Ned's narrow blue eyes were riveted to the opposite wall.

After a while, Mrs. Greene raised her head. She wiped her eyes and blew her nose and smiled bravely without looking up. Nora put an artichoke in front of her with trembling hands. Her mother tore off a leaf, dipped it in the drawn butter, and brought it carefully to her mouth, hiccuping a few times as she swallowed the last of her tears.

"What do you suppose got into your mother, crying like that?" Ned asked as he closed the bedroom door. "It was really awful."

"I don't know. The second drink, I guess. She hardly ever drinks."

Ned sat down heavily and took off his shoes. He yawned. He seemed to grow, to accumulate bulk, before her eyes. She felt herself sickening with dread. "I just can't give you power of attorney," she said abruptly. "I'm sorry."

He pulled off his socks and dropped them on the floor. "It's immaterial to me," he said, examining his toenails. "You and your father can handle the transfer between you. I was just doing him another favor."

"What transfer?"

"That note of his that Lloyd is holding—it's due next week."

"I don't know what you're talking about."

"That's because you never listen. You're not interested in how money's made—only in how it's spent." He began to unbutton his shirt.

"Please explain what you're talking about," she said.

"Why don't you ask your father?" He heaved himself out of the chair, took off his shirt, and dropped it on the floor next to his socks and walked into the bathroom. She couldn't take her eyes off his body.

"I'd rather hear it from you," she said.

He returned from the bathroom with a nail clipper and resumed his place. The chair's swiveling pedestal was broken, and the seat wobbled unsteadily on its base.

"Please, Ned." She wondered how deeply her father was indebted to her husband.

He bent over his feet and began to clip his toenails. "All right," he conceded. "I'll make it as simple as I can. About a year ago, your father came to me for help. He was very tight for cash and he couldn't get a loan through regular channels. I agreed to lend him some money—unsecured, of course. Unfortunately, I couldn't lay my hands on that much cash," here he paused a moment to cough, "so I went to Lloyd Lilienthal and asked him to put up a hundred thousand for me for a year. You understand that without the money your father would have lost everything. Lloyd was very reluctant but in the end he did it for me."

Nora found she had to sit down.

"Are you still with me?"

She nodded. She tried to feel gratitude toward Ned. She succeeded only in hating her father. She remembered what Lautner had said to her father the night of her birthday. "I am not a tyrant. I do not insist that anyone face anything. I wait, Mr. Greene. I wait."

"Lloyd said he didn't like the idea of holding a friend's note—it invites trouble. We structured it so he would lend the money directly to your father. In that case, of course, the loan had to be secured. You guaranteed the note. Do you remember now?"

"Vaguely. But I don't remember signing anything."

"You signed. I explained it to you at the time."

"Yes, but didn't you tell me that it was a technicality—that my father was good for it and that anyway Lloyd would always extend the loan if it turned out that my father couldn't raise the money when the year was up?" She spoke slowly, trying to trap the shadowy, fleeting memory.

"What are you trying to say, Nora? That you wouldn't have guaranteed the note for your father if you'd known it would turn out this way?"

So she was to be penniless after all. "No, of course not."

"Then what are you saying?"

"I guess I'm asking why you didn't borrow the money from a bank and then lend it to him yourself."

He laughed incredulously, as if to say how much beside the point, how childish her question was. "Why should I jeopardize my credit position? He's not my father. If you're looking for someone to blame, start with him. He got you into this, not me. I put myself out to help him when no one else would go near him."

His words stung. "I'm sorry," she said.

"You should be." He took off his trousers and tossed them over the back of the armchair. They slipped to the floor. "Why don't you get dressed for bed?" he asked from the bathroom doorway.

Penniless. She went over and picked up his discarded socks and crumpled shirt. She put them in the hamper. She hung up his tie and trousers. She opened her lingerie drawer and took out the black lace brassiere that was cut out around the nipples and the matching G-string that had a pink satin tongue appliquéd on it. His gifts to her. She began undressing slowly. "Have I signed anything else I've forgotten about?" she asked, sighing as she took off her shoes.

"We can talk about it tomorrow," he said thickly, hurrying past her to the bed, where he quickly pulled the sheet up over himself.

The first few times he'd undressed in front of her, he'd turned out all the lights. Twenty years later, he was still uncomfortable with his clothes off. She wasn't sure why. Maybe he believed that nakedness lessened his authority.

"I'll be out in a minute," she said, retreating to the bathroom.

She brushed her teeth and washed her face; she ran a soapy washcloth between her legs; she slipped into the G-string and brassiere; she took her hair down and pulled it forward to cover her nipples. She clenched her hands, digging her nails into her palms to distract her from the long, silent scream of pressure in her head. As she was struggling to open the bathroom door—it had swollen badly as a result of the leak—she heard a sharp crack that reverberated uncannily. She looked up at the ceiling. She had the impression that the light fixture was closer to her head. She looked again and saw that the ceiling was actually sagging in the middle. She tugged open the door and poked her head into the bedroom.

"You'd better come in here and take a look at the ceiling," she called to Ned. "I think it may be dangerous."

"There's nothing we can do about it at this time of night," he said. And then, in a thicker voice, glimpsing the triangle of black lace, the wriggling pink tongue, "Come to bed."

She heard another crack, more splintery-sounding than the first, more like thunder. Unearthly. She left the bathroom, closing the door firmly behind her. Her mind felt preternaturally clear. "How many of your loans have I countersigned?" she asked Ned. "How much am I in debt for?"

His mouth tightened. "The banks require the wife to be a guarantor as a matter of form."

"Am I on the children's college loans too?"

"They're no different from any other loans."

"If you should die," she went on, amazed as much at her mental grip as at her temerity, "what would I be left with after all the debts were paid?"

"I carry plenty of life insurance."

"But if I'm a guarantor they can take the insurance money, can't they?"

"You can relax," he said. "You'll be well taken care of." She heard a low rumble on the other side of the closed door. It emboldened her. "With what? Do you have assets I don't know about? A numbered Swiss bank account, maybe?"

"Don't be ridiculous." He began to cough.

"Where's the money going to come from?" she persisted. "What about the children?" The rumble was louder now.

"What's that?" Ned asked, sitting up.

"Nothing," she said. "You can't do anything about it at this hour anyway. Remember?"

He jumped out of bed and raced across the floor. She blocked the door to the bathroom. "Get out of the way, Nora," he said. "Something's going on in there."

"Please answer my question," she said. "Where's the money going to come from?"

"Nora, I have to see what's happening in there. It may be dangerous. This discussion will keep."

The noise was ominous. Still, she stood her ground. He shoved her impatiently to one side and flung open the door. Nora, peering over his shoulder, took in her breath. It drew down an avalanche. Great chunks of soggy gray matter broke loose and dropped as if off a cliff, smashing to pieces on the tile floor. The light fixture trembled on its wire a moment, then plummeted like a felled white bird. A cloud of choking dust rose from the rubble. Ned began to cough.

Observing herself and her husband from some dispassionate corner of her mind, seeing herself tricked out like the centerfold of a girlie magazine, seeing Ned meatily naked, she felt the stirrings of an ugly knowledge. Her saliva tasted of bile. Her eyes burned as much from shame as from the dust. She waited for the dust to settle as if for a revelation.

In the absence of a ceiling, the grid of structural steel that supported the roof of the house was laid bare to the eye. It was tawny with rust, a crumbling fur or fungus of rust.

"Jee-zus," Ned breathed. "Jee-zus Christ," he said, shaking his head.

Nora looked up and grinned. Her little ripple of a smile acceded rapidly to the rough surf of hysterical laughter. She began to cackle, her stomach convulsing.

"Stop that," Ned said, but she was beyond his reach, drowning in laughter.

An hour passed before order was restored. Ned summoned her father for an opinion. Her mother, wakened from a deep sleep by the avalanche of plaster, doubted she would be able to close her eyes again. Nora got hold of herself and went downstairs to find a book for her mother to read and to fix her a cup of honey and warm milk. She returned to the bedroom to find her father prodding the exposed steelwork with the iron head of a sixteenth-century lance that Ned had inherited from his father, one of three such weapons that hung on the walls of their bedroom. He declared the steel sound, the roof secure.

What does it matter, really, Nora said to herself when at last she was able to turn out her bedside light. Money wasn't real to her anyway. At least not the way it was to her father or to Ned or even to Kitty, for all her religious observances. Last summer the two couples had been lazing around the Lilienthals' swimming pool, the men talking idly of the financial ruin of a mutual acquaintance, when Kitty, with startling vehemence said, "I can't imagine how they'll go on. Life without money is so dreary."

Maybe for someone like you, Nora wanted to say, shocked, truly shocked, but surely not for everyone. Difficult, yes. Uncomfortable, yes. Painful and harsh and terrifying, but not necessarily dreary. Of course, she'd said nothing. For one thing, she felt implicated by having money; she was Kitty's accomplice, wasn't she? And then too, her manners prevented what her temper urged. Outwardly nothing had changed between the two women. Except that, in the deepest sense, Nora was through with Kitty. But if Kitty's motives couldn't stand scrutiny, then neither could her own. And if she couldn't respect Kitty, then how could she respect herself? Who did respect her? she wondered. Ned? Hardly. Her parents? Her children? Of course they *loved* her, but so what? Everyone knows that love without respect is only charity.

8

Although it was the dead of winter, the world was melting around them. The briny smell of the ocean, borne to the plaza of Lincoln Center on the back of a herd of slow-moving clouds, suggested the approach of summer. Drops of water beaded the strands of their hair like ticks on dune grass. The snowstorm, in its southerly migration, had netted new fish. Ned was among those beached in Baltimore, and so Nora informed their guests as they crossed the plaza and made their way toward the opera house.

Three sullen camels, their saddlebags festooned with bells and stuffed with pledges, were stabled in slush under the arcade of Philharmonic Hall. Nora's companions paused and pointed and laughed. The camels, Nora explained, were a fund-raising attraction for the Central Park Zoo. "Ah, you Americans," one of her guests said. "So inventive about your charities."

The sound of the bells followed them a short distance before being absorbed into the toplike hum of people engaged in the genial motions of enjoyment. When filled with a crowd as it was now, shortly before curtain time, the plaza had a sprawling, almost pastoral feel, as if it were a mock-village green, but the anomaly of a large open space surrounded by low buildings in the midst of such general Alpine verticality testified less to a longing for the warm glow of a more intimate past than to the city fathers' faith in the economic generating power of the arts.

The man with the fleshy, humorless face and the leaden physique was Herr Hermann Nernst, a Swiss publisher. The tall blonde striding jerkily by his side was his wife. She was twenty years his junior and she danced, she said, when she wasn't entertaining moody writers for Nernst. Her eyes were sexually enraged.

On Nora's left, as they climbed the broad red-carpeted staircase to their box, was the communist mayor of a middle-sized Italian city. He was a mild-faced, courteous man with a felicitous accent which was shown to its best advantage as he explained to Nora the ways in which he encouraged Mahler—the music, that is—to exploit his emotions. The mayor's wife, who spoke no English, turned her head and smiled and smiled.

Then there was Eva. She was fifty, an Austrian intellectual, the widow of an Italian industrialist who had been a Catholic and a communist with supposedly strong connections to the Mafia. The husband had been dead five years. Shot once in the head—the official story was suicide. Eva was a round-faced woman with a frothy hairdo and pastel eyelids. She was wearing a pale yellow chiffon dress of great delicacy and expense. The skirt was cut so that it furled like the petals of a tea rose. Eva, Ned said, was his shrewdest client.

Nora shepherded her group past the ticket taker to the corridor outside their box, where she left them briefly to find an usher to unlock the door.

She installed the three women at the front of the box and placed herself between the two men in the row behind. As the motor-driven chandeliers of crystal and ormolu ascended toward the ceiling, she sighed happily at the prospect of an evening filled with the solacing brilliance of Mozart. She glanced at the box next door and noted with some surprise that it was still empty. It belonged to the general manager of the opera house.

Frau Nernst and Eva were apparently too compatible for silence. The curtain of words they so mercilessly drew around themselves rustled as maddeningly as static. Periods of silence alternated in a snorer's rhythm with bouts of whispering and weakly suppressed laughter. Elvira's threatening lament—*"Ah, chi mi dice mai quel barbaro dov'è* . . . Oh! Who will ever tell me where that monster is who stole my heart away?"—moved Eva and Frau Nernst to the excess of adding gesture to sound. They waved their arms about for the next few minutes. Nora fumed but did nothing.

At the first intermission, they were shown to the table generally reserved for Ned, and there they raised their glasses to their absent host. Eva adored Mozart, particularly *Don Giovanni*. She said so very vigorously, adjusting her chiffon petals around her as she spoke.

Frau Nernst hated modern music. The structure of her outer ear was not adapted to assimilate such sounds of discord and violence.

"Except for my wife, we in Europe have learned to live with discord and violence. We have our ideologies, you know." Nernst addressed himself to Nora.

"For this very reason, my dear Lotte," Eva said to Frau Nernst, "I force myself to endure it." Modern music.

"Modern music is your form of penance then, Eva, Liebchen?" Nernst's voice was flirtatiously naughty. "All of Europe knows how bad you are!" The dome of his belly shook with self-approving laughter.

"One doesn't do penance for certain kinds of violence, caro," Eva said in a tone of tranquil gossip. "Without violence there is no earthly salvation."

"For a woman wearing such a superb chiffon, to sanctify violence—I find this terribly amusing, Liebchen. No?"

"Pay no attention to Nernst," Frau Nernst said, tossing her helmet of cold blond hair, her face as impassive as a warrior's as she hurled her javelin of heavily accented words. "He has become a hun-derd percent American. Nothing is serious but the money. We are every day on the verge of divorce because of his *cynicisme.*"

This intimate piece of news was translated by the mayor, sotto voce, for his smiling wife, whose smile faded, whose nostrils widened, then pinched, as if something having a very bad smell had passed beneath them. The mayor's look was one of rehearsed attentiveness. Years of political training.

Herr Nernst took no wound at all, protected as he was by the shield of his skin, its dark, hairy hardness.

"Reasoning thus, my dear Nernst," Eva said, and here she lowered her pale apricot eyelids a trifle, took a compact from her purse, and opened it, "men with big bellies who give outcries to the public on the subject of world famine are rather more ridiculous than a poor woman to whom no one listens anyway." She closed her compact. It latched with the clicking finality of a door.

The chimes sounded. The party rose. Nernst bowed to Eva. They exchanged the easy flirtatious smiles of good competitors who, if they are not honorable adversaries, are certainly ex-lovers.

The house lights dimmed. The mayor leaned toward Nora and whispered, "We in Europe have had also to learn to live with failure and contradiction, Signora Ingarden. It takes much time and a sense of history—but you Americans, you are so impatient!" Nora nodded. She glanced idly past him at the next box.

Lautner sat there, smiling at her.

The conductor raised his baton.

The music shot through her head like stars, a great crashing waterfall of stars, and it was as if through a curtain of mist that she looked into his eyes. He submitted to being adored. It was she who had to turn away.

He was seated in the second row, between two women. Margaret was on his right. She touched his hand and he bent his head to receive her whispered words. A tall, long-boned woman in her fifties with a narrow face and coarse dark hair was on his left. She was swathed in an immense paisley shawl, like an Indian woman in a blanket. Behind them were two men, both standing, one blond, young, handsome, smooth-faced; the other, his lover possibly, a few inches taller, thirty years older at least, wild white hair, startled blue eyes. There were two women and a small, frail-looking man in the front row. Sylvie was one of the women.

A low upholstered wall was all that separated the two boxes, and yet Nora felt as completely sealed off as if she were in a tomb. She was not above remaining where she was, even now, if only she could find some honor there. A round of whispering sprayed her box like machine-gun fire. Lautner's eyes registered something graver than annoyance. Margaret looked over. She saw Nora and shook her head disapprovingly. The whispering continued. Nora passed from one grade of anger to another until she was physically hot with rage. Her armpits were wet, the sides of her nose slippery; reason was skidding across her palms. She reached forward and tapped Eva on her bare, coquettish shoulder. Eva looked up expectantly, a pleasant smile on her face. Nora put her finger to her lips, the snake in her mouth coiled a silent PLEASE. Eva smiled and nodded her head. The pounding in Nora's head slowed by degrees; by degrees the music entered.

The next battery aroused Lautner to a pitch of temper that cauterized his face. Nora read a searing indictment of her life in his eyes. Frau Nernst was shaking with audible laughter at something Eva had said. A snarling hellcat sprang to life inside Nora. It broke loose and rampaged through her parlor of manners and song. It gripped Frau Nernst by the shoulder and shook her. It hissed, "That's enough—both of you—get out—right now. Out."

The two women drew in, first their breaths, then their skirts, as if Nora's words might spatter them with filth. Even Nernst came alive, licking his thick lips. The mayor's wife made herself extremely small; she was hardly visible above the railing of the box. The mayor was preparing a conciliatory speech. Why bother? It was known he was too moderate for the left and too radical for the right. So what if his city was the only one in the country still functioning. It was too late for reason, far too late.

The two women stood up as one. Their faces were cold with rage. The mayor's wife glanced uncertainly at her husband and, seeing him already on his feet, she hastened to hers. A red-faced, sputtering Herr Nernst brought up the rear. Nora stayed behind long enough to glance at Lautner. What she saw in his eyes gave her reason to hope.

Once she was outside, her rage died as suddenly as it had flared. She sat down at the edge of the fountain in the center of the plaza and waited for Lautner, although it seemed unlikely he would join her. A short distance off, a Puerto Rican cyclist was making ever tighter circles on the rear wheel of his bicycle, the front end erected like the head and shoulders of a prancing Lippizaner. He held the handlebars as if they were reins, loosely but with great authority. His tee-shirt said: STATEHOOD SUCKS. FREEDOM SINGS. Yes, of course. But did he know how much the world hated a free man and his privileges? As for a free woman, something worse than hatred was reserved for her. Ridicule. Still, Nora would have done significantly better, as things turned out, to have observed that history treats the free and the imprisoned, the oppressors and their victims, with an equality of contempt.

Never mind. I say "never mind" because she hadn't yet lost the final flash of her beauty, and with the fountain playing prettily behind her and the glow of borrowed light illu-

minating her great sad eyes, I can tell you she made a
charming picture, charming enough to stir more than a few
passing hearts. Her beauty was always her ace in the hole,
the point at which serious contemplation stopped. Besides,
in truth, nothing of what had just transpired, for all its rag-
ing drama and all her trembling emotion, was of any real
consequence to her. She was quite indifferent to the world in
the absence of Lautner. Her old life was dead. The quivers
were all reflexive, and shortly even they would be stilled.

She walked home alone. Time was as much an element to
get through as the weather.

She adjusted the shower head in Valerie's bathroom so that
it shed its needles of water directly onto her uplifted face.
She was a pale and skinny squint-eyed girl again, one who
had no husband. She didn't hear the bathroom door open
and close, admitting the man she would later marry and her
family would argue was all the husband she deserved. She
had been admitted to the parlor of memory. Her twenty-
year-old boyfriend was there with her. "A rose," he said, and
his hand curved more closely around her waist. "Have the
guy put it on your . . ." Her ass. He couldn't say the word.
No. Too visible. What would her mother say? Or the doctor
with his antibiotics? "What about the inside of my thigh?"
Thinking furrowed the unbroken ridge of his black eyebrows. The heart-encircled mother on his biceps rippled. She
knew about the destroyer on his chest, the naked girl on his
ass; her own hands had cupped the blonde beauty, and when
he clenched and unclenched his glutei maximi, medii, and
minimi, the girl wriggled like an adorable fish.

Where to put the tattoo was less important than what to
have engraved on her skin. And what if the tattooist
wouldn't do a girl, a sixteen-year-old girl? He would though.

"A rose," the boyfriend urged. "On your . . ." He pointed
to her breasts. They both blushed.

"No," she said. "I'll have whatever I choose—here." She pulled down her jeans, exposing a sharp hip bone. "Under here and as low to the groin as you can get."

"What'll ya have, miss?"

"I'll have—Sa'ad al'Din Saood."

"Come again?"

Shahrazad's villain, drop-leaped from a tree. A big, slobbering blackamoor with rolling eyes that showed the whites and who futtered the Queen on command whilst the King was away pleasuring himself at the royal hunt.

No image can survive the transfer to flesh without becoming a lurid version of itself. But what if the trashiness was what interested her?

"Maybe this isn't such a good idea," the boyfriend said. On second thought, he wouldn't have a girl whose skin had been violated.

That was all right with Nora. She wasn't playful by nature. Even her flirtations were highly sober affairs from which she could be easily dissuaded by the threat of abandonment.

Was it the streaming water awakening her skin to the memory of being young again that made her husband's large apartment suddenly feel too small to contain her? Where to go was not the question—she saw herself, a skirted Odysseus, tied to the mast of a loom—the wandering was implicit. But the means by which to leave troubled her. The winding staircase she'd climbed to reach her watery retreat was barred at one end by two smiling warriors sprung from acres of baby teeth and guarded at the other by the Gorgon's head of guilt. To escape, she'd have to raise an army. Or be one. She thought about what she'd be leaving behind: friends and language and belongings and the security of dying where she'd been born and knowing where she'd be buried and among whom.

The heavy downpour of water and possibility was too much for the old drain. She was ankle deep in tub water when her feet, grown strangely light, began on their own to do a steamy, shuffling little water-kicking dance, and she found herself going round and round under the glow of the moon-shaped ceiling light to the reedy music of her own voice while her breasts and back streamed with water like those of a fountained nymph, and this went on and on until her nails and bones had softened to paste and her legs and feet had nearly dissolved, until what ran through her veins was no longer blood but water, until finally there was nothing left of her for anyone to hold. And then someone pulled back the shower curtain, one of those mercifully quick, but hideous pulls as if it were a bandage, and, stepping over the tall tub sill, tried to take her in his arms.

She screamed and she clawed but she had no lips and her nails were as soft and translucently papery as the skin of an onion.

What did it matter who he was? Whether her husband or a naked stranger? Whether a bull or an eagle, a swan or a satyr, a flame, a shepherd, a mottled snake, a ram? Why not a rearing stallion? Or a dolphin, a hawk, or even a lion? He was someone returned unexpectedly to find her chastely alone and irresistible in her innocence. And so, shortly, another piece of deceitful business would be practiced on yet another mortal girl.

"Let's dance," he said, and he pressed his naked body to hers and closed his eyes while the water beat and stung her about the face. She tried to surge beyond him in her mind, to pretend for the moment that he didn't exist, but he blocked her or she was contained by her pity, which was like a sandbagged wall against which she foamed and along which she was diverted, dripping, down the corridor and up the stairs, to her marriage bed.

What happened there's a matter of interpretation. A ravishment, if I'm true to rage in her heart. As his fingers approached, she thrust the body of her deepest knowledge, the soul of her truest passion, beneath the bed, and she did it in terror and in haste, as another woman in another century might have stuffed her lover into a wardrobe at the approach of her husband.

He positioned her mean remains beneath him and mounted her. The surface of her skin was as cold as marble. She was a statue of herself. He came on entry. Far off, between the stone pillars of her thighs, she felt the seeping proof of his claim.

"Are you awake, Nora?"

"Yes."

"I love you."

"I know you have a need to show you love me, Ned, but it doesn't come across as love."

"I don't know what you're talking about." He coughed a little.

"If you love me, if you love the children, then behave so we can respect you. Stop the evasions and the double-talk and the tics. And stop coughing, for godsakes. You only cough when you're not being honest."

"On what grounds do you think you're justified in attacking me? I'm not the one who's making trouble. You've been crazy ever since your birthday."

"Oh, Ned," she sighed. "Please—just stop it. What good is love if it harms people?"

"No—you stop it—you listen to me, Nora." More coughing. "You don't know what you're saying."

But she did. And he knew it.

9

Once upon a time, in a great city, there lived a beautiful lady who was unhappily married and expected to remain so and who, although she had been around long enough to be convinced that nothing more of importance could happen to her than her death, was nevertheless dumbly and persistently hopeful.

I say "a great city" as another would say "a great beauty," one whose face and form seize your breath in your throat. To be sure, there are flaws, but in such cases they merely add that element of soul which breaks true hearts and without which beauty is meaningless. A great city, then, with hardly enough air to go around and what little there is carrying the reek of other mouths. A great city, the heart of the modern world, unsafe and corrupt but splendid, too. A great city, one that belongs to those who pursue their dreams, not to those who rehearse them.

Now it came to pass that on a certain day in the twenty-first year of her sojourn in this city, even as the beautiful lady was congratulating herself on how well she had weathered the comforts and consequences of a privileged life, the devil suddenly appeared to tempt her.

Why her?

Why not her?

When she saw him, her wits were waylaid and her senses stormed, but not so thoroughly that with the little that was left her she couldn't still scheme, and she said to herself: This is my chance and I'm going to take it.

It was no surprise, waking to the idea of him. This morning he was wearing white flannel trousers and a cocky smile.

He had one foot on the dashboard of a roadster convertible and his arm around a pretty woman with bobbed hair who had just consigned her future to his care. This morning she was nineteen, the age her father was in the photograph beside her pillow, and she was driving north along a dark country road, about to ram her mother's car into an old jalopy that was pulling out of a dirt driveway in front of her, turning south with its headlights off. She was driving slowly but even so she didn't see the thing until she hit it—broadside. Her car folded up around her, the steering wheel broke off, her ribs cracked like nutshells. She couldn't get the door open. She rolled down her window and crawled out into the night. She was in pain. It was very dark, not even the sliver of a moon.

The driver of the other car was sprawled on his back in the middle of the road. She thought, Oh, God, I've killed him. She knelt by his hard-faced body, afraid to touch him. He was her age; he stank of cheap whiskey. She knew he was poor, she knew he was dead, but, God, how she hated him for lying there, for being drunk, for being poor, for being dead, for being her responsibility. She wanted to scream at him to get up. What right did he have in his wanton, drunken poverty to ruin her life?

Lights went on, doors opened, other cars appeared in this wilderness of country dark. There was the sudden babble of voices, then "tsk"s of disappointment, grunts of disgust. HE ISN'T DEAD. HE ISN'T EVEN HURT. DEAD DRUNK IS ALL.

Someone took her to a house and put a phone in her hand. She heard her father's voice. The police arrived. There were questions. She answered them. She was extraordinarily calm. She was terribly nervous, perhaps even in mild shock, but mostly she was embarrassed—no, mortified—to have caused such a fuss, to have been so clumsy.

There was a ring of strangers around the passed-out boy's body, another around her. Their faces were fizzy with excitement. A man patted her shoulder, a woman took her into her arms. She didn't know how to protect herself from this party atmosphere. Then her father pulled up in his limousine. He was driving it himself, a thing he rarely did—he was poor once; he was convinced he'd be poor again—but this was an emergency. He was wearing his vicuña coat and it had the smell of money. Who could doubt his rights to her? He broke into the circle. The woman stepped back, the man withdrew his hand. Her father took her into his arms. So badly did she want to be true to herself that she stiffened with resistance. She tried to interlace her pride in the cords of her spine. But her father, in love's name, was forcing her face to his chest, cradling the back of her neck as tenderly as if she were newborn, saying: "It's all right, it's all right. Daddy's here. Daddy's here." She felt the sureness of his coat against her cheek, the strong fingers urging her to surrender, and, oh, God, how she hated herself for crying, more than she hated that stupid, drunken boy for lying there in his obscene poverty, more than she hated her rich father for rescuing her. She was sobbing with love for him and hate for herself. She'd wanted to do this on her own. She'd almost done it.

Ned was asleep when she left the house. Her run went so badly that she shortened it by two miles, cutting across the baseball diamond from the South Drive to the North at a slow trot. She was feeling dull and heavy, even bleak, exhausted by the opulence of her emotions of the night before. A small bird with the black bib and bill and white cheeks of a house sparrow was hopping around in the snow, pecking at the scattered crumbs alongside her path. Nora noticed the bird but there wasn't time enough between her noticing and her bearing down for the bird to fly off—or for her to retract her leg. Her foot hit the ground, carrying the dead weight of the log of her leg. The bird's streaked and feathered back broke like a twig.

She screamed then. She choked on her horror as if the bird

itself were stuck, flapping, in the cage of her throat. She shuddered away from the knowledge of what she had done, undoing her own balance and toppling into the snow beside the body of her twitching and convulsively chirping victim. Its mate, the female, was hopping wildly about, a frantic back-and-forth sort of movement, a short distance away, heedless of its own safety. Nora scrambled to her feet, fighting the impulse to run. She stood over the thrashing, dying bird for a long moment. Then, gritting her teeth, she raised her foot and stomped.

One thing that can be said for hatred: it was nearly always honest. Nora couldn't bear too much honesty. Still, she knew now that she hated her husband. It was an old and settled anger. She hated him partly as one hated one's victim, as she'd once hated that drunken lout for playing dead on a country road. She hated him for being someone she couldn't love. And, oh, God, she despised herself for being his lout, for playing dead beneath him all those years on all those dark roads of their marriage.

Ned called to her from the dining room. "Sweetheart, when you send my gray suit out to be pressed, remind them to sew up the change pocket, will you? They forgot the last time."

She could see him from where she stood. He was looking at the paper over the tops of his half-glasses, hitching his shoulders forward and coughing.

"I'll pin a note to the pocket," she said, wheeling in his breakfast.

He touched his neck gingerly as he raised his glass of juice. "I nicked myself," he said.

A tiny bloodstained shred of tissue hung from his Adam's apple. It waved like a little white flag of surrender when he spoke or swallowed. He would never surrender.

"I stepped on a bird by accident during my run," she said,

shuddering at the telling. "The thing was dying. I had to kill it. It was horrible."

"Really? That's too bad," he said, without looking up from the paper.

She poured his coffee and handed the mug to him. "Last night at the opera was something of a disaster."

He raised his eyes then. They grew more serious and more disbelieving as the details became known to him. "You threw them out for talking during the performance? What in God's name are you doing?" He slammed the table with such force that his coffee sloshed over the rim of the mug.

What am I doing? It's this, my dear husband, just this: Eva is a horror, or almost one. And the men are fools. And, dearest husband, heart of my heart, I say that talking during Mozart is a kind of end-of-the-world, and no, I will not apologize and if you dare to do so on my behalf I will call them up and retract every word. I will make a scene bigger than any you can imagine with your tiny mind.

"Answer me," he said.

She shook her head.

"Shaking your head is not an answer."

But why should she defend herself?

He sighed sharply like a cold wind. "I want it stopped! Do you understand? I want whatever is going on here stopped!"

She nodded.

But she was incompletely mastered and he knew it.

Her parents had spent the night at Herbert's; they prided themselves on being fair. Their notion of fair-mindedness (which Nora endorsed) meant that they constantly busied themselves with Herbert. He was a late bloomer—her father's phrase—and he required the sort of care one gave a sickly child. For the same reason, they occasionally put up with his attempts to give them pleasure. The pleasure thing never turned out very well. Herbert became overexcited, pushy, silly. The more he performed, the more irritating he became. He didn't want to have to amuse anyone. He just wanted to stand there and be applauded. These little forays into Herbert's territory ended with her father shouting at Herbert that he was an imbecile, that if he didn't grow up soon and begin to act like a man he would kill them both, while her mother stood silently in the background, casting the enormous winged shadow of her pain over the battlefield. She didn't attempt to protect Herbert from his father, though. Not once. What did that make her? What does that make most of us? But if you protect your son, you castrate your husband. Or so they—men—say.

Her parents had just returned from Herbert's and now they were waiting downstairs to be fed—Ned's pets but her responsibility—but Ned, coming in from the office with a grim look on his face, had summoned her to the bedroom and with no more than a grunted hello had started up the stairs.

As she followed after him she tried to think what was the worst she could say of her husband. That he was a liar? Everyone lied. Even Lautner said so. That he was a dull companion? Most of the people she knew were dull. They used money and position to create excitement, and they managed to create some—Ned too. It was the absence of all passion she couldn't forgive him. What had he done, what had been done to him—what awful things—to make him so calculating, so without spontaneity? But how terrible was that? How else could he have survived a childhood spent entirely in boarding schools and summer camps, except by closing down? Then why did she shudder whenever he came near her? And why was it that the further removed she was from him sexually—as when she thought of him as a blood relative, or the father of her children, or when he traveled—the more she felt she loved him? Perhaps what she loved was the idea of a good man. Granted, he was obsessed with her, but did he love her? How could he love anyone? He was really only concerned with imposing his will, without effort, on those around him. He was lazy in that way but as stubborn as a bulldog. His will might falter in the world but at home it was absolute. How far would he go to ensure that his will triumphed? She could barely ask these questions of herself. Answers were beyond her. She could summon a crazed amount of courage if she had to, but she wasn't an honest woman. Her notion of loyalty wouldn't permit her to be.

Ned's bearing as he climbed the stairs was rigid around the shoulders; he held his head disturbingly erect. The second flight was much narrower and more winding than the first. His body took up the full width. He was like a wall. The wall wasn't visible to the naked eye. Society saw him as an agreeable man. But, visible or not, the wall existed, even as the sound barrier existed. She couldn't go through it. She didn't have enough speed or force or honesty or will of her own—whatever. And she couldn't explore ways of going around it; that would mean leaving her children unprotected. It was stay or go.

"Sit down," he said, motioning her to the broken chair. It rocked drunkenly on its pedestal in spite of the cautious way she eased herself into it.

"Where were you the day before yesterday?"

"Why do you want to know?"

"Just answer me, Nora."

"The day before yesterday? Let's see. I went running in the morning. Or did I? No, I don't think I did. Wasn't it raining? Well, anyway, I had lunch with Avery and Jenny and Kasim at that new place I told you about, off Madison. My parents were here for dinner. And then the ceiling fell in."

"Someone saw you on the street with a man. You were behaving in a way that attracted attention."

"I walked a few blocks with Kasim. We were arguing about his play."

"I don't believe you."

"No? Why don't you call Kasim? He's at the Westbury. I'll look up the number for you." Beneath his silence she could feel the whiplash of his jealousy and vindictiveness, but she doubted that he would press the point further. The indignity to himself of having to ask for anything was worse than not knowing the truth.

"Is that all?" she asked. Her head was pounding. She wanted to fly at him with her fists.

He didn't answer. He looked at her with narrow eyes and without a change of expression.

"I have to get dinner," she said. And left the room.

She couldn't sensibly blame him for keeping her prisoner, could she? Any more than a convict could blame his guard? She heard his heavy-heeled tread on the stairs behind her. She moved more quickly, at the same time rubbing her hand along the wooden banister that ran the length of the second-floor landing, onto which the children's bedrooms and the guest room opened, to remove a trace of dust the cleaning woman had overlooked. At the head of the flight of stairs leading to the living room, where her parents waited, she stooped to pick a thread off the carpet. As she was straightening up something slammed into her from behind with terrific force. The impact sent her plunging, nose-diving through the narrow, sharp-edged sky of the stairwell. She grabbed wildly, unthinkingly at the wall and knocked one of the many steel-framed family photographs off its hook and brought it sharply down on her head. There was a huge, muffled explosion inside her skull as if she'd thrown herself on top of the live grenade of whatever was happening. And still she fell, spinning crazily out of control, the ground seeming to climb to meet her, bursting into flames at the shoulder, the hip, the ankle on contact.

A century passed, during which she raised her right hand and pressed it to the seam that had opened in her skull. A millennium trickled away—a drop at a time, like the blood between her fingers—while she looked first at Ned, who was as if icebound on the stairs and *smiling,* and then at her parents, who, like children playing statues and having been commanded to freeze, were waiting in arrested postures of concern.

And then Ned yelled her name and the film started up again. They were moving toward her now, at least their voices were getting closer; nevertheless, she continued to see them as they had been, saw them on the screen of her closed eyelids. The frame was still frozen on her retina. Ned smiling. Her parents hostage to his wishes. She felt Ned lift her hand away from her head and spread the sides of the gash. She felt the blood running down her face. She opened her eyes. She saw her mother wobbling grayly. She saw her father put his arm around her mother's shoulder. Ned said something to her—she had no idea what—and then disappeared. He came back with a plastic bag filled with ice cubes. He pressed it to her head. A continent away, her ankle swelled with unnatural lightness and heat. It seemed to be floating above her leg like a tethered balloon.

"Can you sit up?" Ned asked.

She attempted to oblige. A tomahawk of pain slashed through her shoulder. In her weirdness she imagined a wing being torn off a bird. Was she bleeding on the rug? she asked Ned when she could speak. Please, put something under her head. It would be a pity to spoil the prayer rug. Blood doesn't wash out.

"If she's worried about the rug, she's okay," Ned said to her father. His face loomed over hers like a giant sunflower.

"I need help," she said. "Get someone to help. It's my shoulder."

Luckily Roger was home. He lived down the block. He would be right over, Ned said. Would he tell everyone that Ned, seeing her crumpled at the bottom of the stairs, had smiled? He'd told about Anina's seamed breasts, her relocated nipples.

The shoulder was an agony; she stifled the screams that

cut like razors in her throat. And then Roger's big, shaggy head was beneath her chin. When she did scream, her hot breath ruffled the longish hairs at the back of his neck. He lifted her up and sat her in a chair that her father brought from the kitchen. She could hardly see her father. He was obliterated by her tears. She was weeping helplessly with pain. Roger said, "Hang on, Nora. This will only take a minute but it's going to hurt." He jerked her shoulder between his hands with a twisting violence that was like another explosion of the grenade and that should have torn her shoulder off, but in fact returned it to a state of painless function. "Thank you," she wept, seizing his hand and kissing it. "Oh, God, thank you."

"The head wound is superficial," he said. "The scalp is very veinous. It bleeds a lot. Is anything else bothering you?"

She pointed to her ankle. He bent and examined it. He ordered her to stand up, put weight on it. Ned helped her to her feet. He put his arm around her waist to steady her.

"Just a mild sprain, but it means a couple of days of not running," he said, shaking his head sympathetically. Roger was a runner. He put a piece of tape over the cut on her scalp and ordered her to bed. "Call me tomorrow if you develop a headache or feel dizzy or nauseated, and we'll take an X-ray. There's always the possibility of a concussion."

"How did it happen? Did you trip?" her father asked while Ned was seeing Roger to the door.

"I don't know," she said. "How's Mom?"

"She's okay. She's in the kitchen. You know she can't stand the sight of blood."

She limped up the stairs, followed by Ned. The bedroom was vast, level, treeless. The air was chillingly cold. She crawled under the covers and closed her eyes. She saw Ned smiling, her parents cowed. She opened her eyes.

Ned said, "For godsakes, Nora, why did you stop short like that at the top of the stairs? You knew I was right behind you."

"You smiled," she said, dully.

"What?"

"You were *smiling*. I looked up and saw you."

"You're crazy. You're imagining things. If you saw me smiling it was nerves."

"Then you admit you smiled?"

"Don't be ridiculous. All I said was that what you took for a smile was obviously nerves. You frightened me," he accused.

"I assume what happened was an accident, but I'll never forget that you smiled." The room was colder than ever. She began to shake beneath the blankets. She'd forgotten that the heat was voluntary on his part, as was the food, and the medical care. She needed the comforter, but she was helpless to get it for herself and she shrank from appealing to him. He stood by the side of the bed, looking down at her. She gazed up at him. The silence between them was more ominous than the noise of war. "You smiled," she repeated and then turned on her side away from him.

"You can think whatever you like," he said. "I certainly did not."

10

My subject is hunger—empty spaces, the kind that clutch at you as you pass by; dying cities, the eyes of the very old, the eyes of unhappy women, a child's fingers. The longing to be full is everywhere, and everywhere it urges one to pity. But if the hunger's too shrill, one's pity curdles, turns to hate. How else can one live without renouncing the world?

The wife of an Indian client of Ned's was driving Nora through an ancient part of Calcutta some years ago when the car's air conditioning suddenly failed. Within seconds the heat became unendurable. Nora rolled down her window just as the car stopped at a traffic light.

"Nora, quickly—close up your window!"

Nora wasn't quick enough.

Two small children, girls of perhaps eight years, appearing from out of that vast nowhere to which the mobs of the poor are consigned, had jumped from the street onto Nora's side of the car and, clamping their dirty hands over the half-lowered window, were now demanding money in high-pitched birdlike voices: a sort of squabble of sound.

"Go away," the driver told them in Hindi.

But they hung on. She gunned the motor, ran the light, sped up, trying her best to shake them loose.

"Roll your window up all the way, Nora," she ordered. She was nearly hysterical.

Nora obeyed, thinking the girls would let go when they saw her intention, but no, they continued to cling to the window; they continued to demand what they would have. Nora couldn't go through with it, obviously. She let go of the handle and reached for her purse. The other woman leaned over, enraged. She slapped Nora's wallet from her hands and then, still speeding, steering one-handedly, crazily, taking them from one side of the road to the other, she began rolling up the window in Nora's stead.

The two little girls were shrieking with pain as the window closed on their fingers, but still they hung on. The driver cranked the handle as far as it would go, her face reddening with the heat in the car and the physical and emotional exertion of inflicting such pain, and on children. The girls' expressions were terrible to see, the eyes fixed and coldly brilliant as the eyes of birds, the lips drawn back in a howl, exposing rows of small, rotted brown teeth. Nora shrank back from the shrimp-curled fingers that clawed at the air near her head inside the stifling car, fingers that had turned the same liverish blue as the drawn lips.

By then the children wanted to let go but the pressure of the glass against their fingers made it impossible. She put her hand over the other woman's and forced the window open a scant inch. The two small girls dropped from the car as if they had been shot by a sniper—they rolled like bundles of laundry into the gutter.

Nora was too stunned for speech.

"I make no excuses. You either live your life or you don't," the other woman said, in a coldly superior but still hysteria-ridden voice.

Nora, wearing an intricately cut black coat, a witty piece of needlework, emerged from a taxi and looked around. A fleet of garbage trucks was huddled under the rusting canopy of the abandoned West Side Highway like a herd of behemoths waiting their turn to feed at the river's edge. The air was warm and fast-moving; brushing Nora's cheek, it had the feel of feathers. Rain clouds barreled across the sky. The mist that hung in the air was as fine as a scrim.

She crossed Twelfth Avenue, limping very slightly. ("Like you," she'd joked with Margaret on the telephone. They had, of course, discussed the opera. Margaret thought she'd done the right thing; Margaret hardly knew Lautner but she found him "irreplaceably charming"—her words. Essential to her, Nora knew she meant.) The slush was nearly ankle deep and it had been plowed into furrows by the tires of passing cars. She traversed the full length of the pier but no one was about. A vacant and paint-flaked cruise ship was secured at two points to the dock by yards of stoutly braided cable the color of wheat which was as beautiful in its function as the fat plaits of a schoolgirl.

The river on which the ship floated was strangely luster-less. While she waited, she let her gaze wander to the other shore, where smokestacks and factories and cement plants sat low and squat in the water.

The indifference of men and women to the natural world was hateful and the color of ash.

Soon she heard footsteps at her back and the world was suddenly dyed with color, Venetian color, and dowered with possibility. She whirled around, an involuntary twirl, her arms lifting from her sides with joy, everything else forgotten for the moment. He emerged slowly from the shroud of the past, a small figure, gray as the sky, a splash of brightness the color of buttercups wrapping his neck, growing larger with every approaching step until, standing in front of her, he blotted out the rest of the world.

She searched his deeply socketed gray eyes for a sign of inhumanity, but without success. She searched behind the façade of the jutting nose and the long, narrow jaw, back of the hollow of his cheeks and across the steeply rising forehead, for a hint of the monster he claimed to be, but she found only a man of vast intelligence and changeable temperament.

He embraced her without a word. She didn't dare lean against him this time. She exerted just enough pressure in the opposite direction to keep a straw of air between her cheek and his chest. His surface was as rough as raked earth, no, as crushed stone, which sucked up light and gave back shadow, bits and chips of shadow, and in the glade of shadow within his arms she sensed the extremity of his separateness, the incalculability of his value. He was a creature utterly unlike any other, one who'd never had a childhood, who would never know age or failing powers, for whom there were no seasons, not even in the mind, only the climate of self and the direness of falling—each instant was a falling— and the isolation of falling, which he wore as proudly as if it were a crown. It was a crown of sorts. To reconcile this man with the other, that frail, exhausted, more-mortal-than-mortal being who looked out of this one's eyes whenever he chose, was beyond her powers, and yet she saw clearly that neither side of him could be maintained in the absence of its opposite.

He said, "Beautiful, isn't it?"

In his presence it wasn't difficult to be persuaded of the beauty of the sullen buildings and the stinking river. She merely had to squint for it to be as he claimed, and so she nodded and said, Yes. He bent and kissed her wounded head. It was sweet, no mother's kiss was ever sweeter. The thick syrup of love was in her veins, warming her. The perfume of a shocking sincerity was in the air. With each breath she took she received something from him and with each one she expelled she tried to give something back, opening herself to him from head to toe, opening herself toward him from her spine, as a book opens, as a butterfly spreads its wings and reveals its hidden columnar self.

He breathed her name. A million powdery, sun-warmed microspores of life settled on her. His lacquer-yellow scarf was like a small ridge of sunshine on that gray day, and the world around him seemed to come alive with the odors and buzzes of creatural things bursting with an urgent hunger from their shells and cases and pods into a world of inquiry and imperfection.

"Come," he said, taking her by the hand, and it seemed to her, swaddled as she was in his warmth, and with her hand safe in his, that they moved as magically from that place to the next as thoughts through a restless mind.

Was he real to her at all?

Was he as real, say, as a fireman come to pull her from the flames?

He was more real than that. He was as real as the absence of heat when one was cold or the want of food when one was starving. Her connection to him was as real as pain is real.

The slit between the buildings was barred by an iron gate. He took a key from his coat pocket and unlocked it. The cobblestoned alley down which she followed him would not have accommodated the width of an open umbrella: they might have been in Venice.

The place he brought her to suited the enterprise of love, she thought. It was as different in tone from the city on the other side of the narrow gate as childhood is from what comes after. Several beautiful, large-spirited red brick federal houses were nested together in a fan-shaped opening at the end of the courtyard. Potted evergreens were posted every few yards like sentries.

They drank strong tea from white ironstone cups in a celadon green parlor, sitting side by side on a rose-colored, watered silk sofa.

Lautner was looking at her, his mouth and eyes smiling. His attention put flesh on old bones. Nora, unaccustomed to the padding of pleasure, was moving and thinking more slowly than usual. The cords in her neck were slack as if her moorings had loosened.

"I'm curious about something, Nora," he said, leaning forward to put his cup and saucer on the tea table. "I'm curious to know how you would define evil."

"As an absence of good," she said promptly. And then, after a pause, "The way blindness is the absence of sight."

"That's too abstract for me—I'm not sure I know what you mean. Is your husband evil, for instance?"

"Evil? Ned? I don't see how," she said, laughing. "He's insensitive and stubborn and, by your standards, he's a liar but he's not evil. He's hardly a Hitler."

"Am I evil?"

"You? I don't know."

"Are women evil? Children?"

She was silent a minute. "I don't think they have the force," she said, finally.

"Of what possible use is your definition?" His face darkened a little.

She didn't answer.

"Do your thoughts and your life have any connection, Nora—any connection at all?"

"Yes," she said, beginning to tremble. "It's Ned's that don't."

"Then you've lived too long with him. You're infected."

Something in her chest plummeted. It might have been something that had outlived its usefulness, but at the moment it was happening, it was as if her life was over.

"I'm waiting for you to say something."

She swallowed the stone in her throat. "According to the definition I gave you, my husband is evil—so either I'm lying about him or I'm lying about what I think evil is."

"Well, which is it?"

"I don't know." She remembered Ned's smile as she lay at the foot of the stairs.

"If you use Hitler as your standard, it's the same as saying that evil doesn't exist anywhere else. On what level do you want to live your life, Nora? On what level do you want your children to live theirs?"

"On your level," she wanted to say—but how could she or her children live on his level? Faced with him, with a culture whose systems of reckoning and measuring were too advanced for a mind like hers bred to rigid tribal notions of conduct, to duty and family and God, what sort of answer could she make? She might as well have been facing Ahasuerus and all the intricacies of etiquette of the Persian court. But she wasn't Esther. She had only herself to defend and it was too presumptuous and so arbitrary, being embattled on one's own behalf. By now she doubted she was worth defending. But he was waiting for an answer.

"I want to live on a level where I don't have to hurt anyone," she said, finally. "I guess I want the same thing for my children."

"Then you're not worth my time," he said. "You want to be innocent, do you? You want to be above reproach?" He threw back his head. She waited for the characteristic jerk at the end of the arc, for the spill of lemon-white hair, for the gonging laugh. "Oh, no, my dear sweet spoiled little pet—it's too late for that. You're too self-righteous and too ambitious, both. And you get your own way too often. Any concession that involves mere prestige is one you're willing to make, even eager—that's your version of democracy, I suppose—but there isn't much else you'll yield. You do have an appetite for submission, but that isn't the same as a longing. I'm afraid you're not a saint, Nora. You're too smart for that."

She didn't protest. She felt penitent in the face of the truth. She wanted to atone for being unwilling to distinguish between lies and truth. She made no attempt to escape from his steady gaze, dull gray as pewter.

"You know," he said, "sometimes I think that your obstinacy in clinging to this notion of girlish innocence is less an act of insistence on what you know to be true than it is an effort of your mind in the direction of faith."

Was this meant to excuse her? What was going on here?

"Sometimes you're really a very stupid woman."

The room was filled with the long shadows of afternoon. In the absence of confidence, she contracted to a hard pebble of hurt, one so small it could slip between the dark lips of adjoining rocks and never be seen again: slip, not metaphorically, but in such a material way that one of her hands was actually slipping from the arm of the sofa, the other was falling from its nest in her lap, and her head was dropping slowly toward her knees. The crevasse she'd entered was squeezingly narrow, as suffocatingly narrow as the way she lived, and there seemed to be no bottom. This experience of falling—she wasn't fainting—and of being horribly and perhaps mortally bruised as she hurtled from one jagged surface to another of the upended black volcanic slabs that confined her, was not a mental game, not a trick of consciousness. She was as much there in her person as she had been on the stairs the other day. How could she sustain the direness of another fall? Perhaps she wouldn't have to. Lautner was reaching across the deathful distance that separated them with a look of penetrating concern on his face. His fingers were at the base of her neck and he began a deft, rhythmic kneading. The knot of terror in her mind, intricate enough to have been tied by a king, loosened.

"I'm going to play a record for you before we leave," he said. He rose and crossed the room to a cherrywood cabinet on Queen Anne legs.

Schubert. The Piano Trio in E-flat Major. The piece of music that had had the greatest claim on her imagination when she was a girl and which hadn't lost any of its power to burden her with ecstasy. She never listened to it by choice. She settled a bit deeper into the silk cushions and closed her eyes, playacting a bit at first—a woman sensitive to music is an attractive companion and she was eager to change his opinion of her. He had to see how genuinely sensitive she was, how feelingly decent. Her eyes brimmed. From time to time, a few comforting tears spilled. And then, just when she'd given up expecting transport because of his closeness— he'd taken her hand in his—she was sucked under by a wave of music. Overmastered. Helpless. She couldn't get her footing in that ocean of sound. She was whirled head over heels; she came up choking and gasping for air while the music rushed on, overflowed the sea wall of her mind, and was lost—sucked up by the waiting desert of everything-that-wasn't-music, and was lost to her forever.

It took her a few minutes to get hold of herself. The music had long since stopped and for a while the only sound in the room was the one the needle made grazing the surface of the record. She didn't hear him cross the room to attend to it. She heard the silence once he had. And she felt his eyes on her. She raised hers expectantly.

His face was startlingly beautiful, long and thin and full of pain, and his gray eyes were radiant. "It's time we were going," he said gently.

"Oh, not yet," she begged, or bullied. "Please, can't we stay a little longer?"

He shrank back from her voice as if it had touched him

physically; he shuddered as if it were some crawling thing. He shuddered away from her as she did from her husband. "What is it you want, Nora?"

"Just to talk."

"Talk? You haven't offered me a single intelligent sentence; all you've done is feel sorry for yourself. What you're asking is more time to sit at my feet. Well, let me warn you, I have all the disciples I want. The act of learning is too ruthlessly self-centered to be of much interest to anyone but the student. Also, you might keep in mind, being the sort of woman you are, being as jealous and possessive as you are, that to be a disciple is to be someone on whom polygamy is practiced."

His remoteness of mood was an almost unbearable infidelity, and she couldn't find the words to bring him closer. The density of what had to be mastered each time they met—no more or less than a foreign tongue—made her feel like a perpetual beginner in the language of her life.

"Let me love you," she said, finally, but so softly that it was almost a whisper. "Let me take care of you."

"You don't know the first thing about love," he said.

"Then teach me," she begged. "Please. I want to learn."

"Do you? All right—start by telling me a story."

"A story?" Her mind shut down, snapped closed like a trap, trapping nothing.

"I'm waiting," he said.

"Once upon a time . . . " But she couldn't invent a story that wouldn't bore or enrage him. She knew only one kind of story: her own. Women in kitchens and nurseries, behind cash registers and typewriters, and in the beds of men not their husbands, women married to dead men, indebted and full of grief. A colorless heroism. What if she were to call them goddesses? No, she couldn't do that. Men, invoking goddesses, might choose to forget that goddesses were capable of doing evil (this was what separated them from other women), but she couldn't forget it. Evil, she told herself, willing herself to believe it, was not merely an abstraction. It had physical dimensions, physical force. It wasn't the absence of anything—it had the horribly real, even glittering presence of gold, and it couldn't be transmuted into a more banal metal no matter how many brilliant minds tried a reverse alchemy. But then why did every dawn bring an unstained world to her eyes? Why did she refuse to live with what she knew?

Lautner stood up.

At the thought of being parted from him, great chunks of her pride began to loosen. She opened her mouth to beg but something prevented her. She could bear the humiliation of begging but she didn't want to disgust him. It was one of those moments, for a certain kind of woman, when if she couldn't pick up a gun and kill her tormentor, she had to faint. It took all her strength to remain upright, there was such a desire in her to give way.

"When will I see you again?" she allowed herself to ask. Unwisely.

"When I know, you'll know," he said, and his condescension was manifested in the clearest articulation of syllables she had yet heard from him.

Her face darkened; rage reddened her skin but she forced it toward hurt instead, toward the grayness of hurt.

"If you could see the self-righteousness in your face," he said, smiling unaccountably. And then, conversationally, as in "how are you," he asked, "How angry are you?"

"I'm not angry at all," she said. "I'm hurt."

"Yours is not the face of a woman who's hurt. Yours is the really tiresome face of a woman who's thinking how much finer and stronger and more worthwhile her love is than the sort her lover is offering in return. It's best you don't mistake me, Nora—I am not one of your lovers. Don't blackmail me," he said, stabbing the air near her face with his finger. "You won't like what happens."

His anger, a sudden wind blowing up again, scattered her

thoughts like dry leaves. Anything he did, everything he was, scattered her thoughts. She ventured, ill-advisedly, to tell him this.

"I know that in certain circles incoherence is thought to be the highest compliment the infatuated can pay to the beloved. I don't travel in those circles."

"I'm sorry I upset you so often. It's not my conscious intention to make you angry."

"What do I care about conscious intentions? My conscious intention is to leave you. I'm still here, however."

She was too bewildered to answer.

"And one more thing," he said. "Don't you ever say you're sorry again unless you know what it is you're sorry for—and you're prepared never to do it again."

If that's how it is, she thought, then revolution is the only authentic apology.

The sound of the bolt shooting the lock told her he was gone. She stretched out on the couch and lay there for a time. Eventually, she raised her head; she measured the room with half-closed eyes. It fit around her like a coffin. The curtains behind the couch were imprinted with dusky cabbage roses. She stared at them until they became animate, until they danced for her like fat snowflakes and she was caught in a storm of swirling rose-colored snow or star-tossed icicles of confetti. She closed her eyes and waited for the storm to subside. When she opened them again, she was dragged along a dizzying network of paths between the sentry rows of coarse, gargantuan-lipped cabbage roses, in a joke garden, a childhood garden. Her teeth were on edge. She was very small. The mildewed roses had bitter, enormous hearts. Adult hearts.

Do you think of yourself as having had a happy childhood, Nora? Was that Lautner's voice?

Tracing the outline of the space enclosed by the particular

quartet of roses nearest her with her eyes and one outstretched finger, she accidentally reinvented the Chinese
vase. She discovered the peculiar integrity of that which
waits to be discovered. The vase was gray-white and it had a
crackle glaze of alarming delicacy, alarming because it suggested to her all over again the ease with which beauty could
seep through the world's frail shell or the egg-walls of the
mind and be lost. She sat up. She sat on the edge of the rose-
colored sofa; she trembled on the edge of the perception that
the insanity of extreme individuation, as when one was
in the throes of creating or responding to a work of art, to a
masterpiece, to her Chinese vase, to her falling lover, this
kind of insanity was a response to the insanity inherent in
the work, to its originality. She struggled not to lose the moment. She held the image of the vase in her hands. It was
cool to the touch. When she placed it next to all the other
images of vases and bowls and cups and pots stored in the
cupboards of her memory, she was suffused with a feeling of
high purposefulness, a feeling of nearly boundless hope.
That's the point of art, isn't it? she argued. Art is the soul's
bridge, isn't it? she said to Lautner, addressing him as if he
had materialized there. It permits one to cross safely over
that great, gaping uncertainty to "everything we know to be
the case"—so Wittgenstein characterized the world—and to
stand augmented in the presence of what is good, what is
beautiful—call it deity, deity in any one of its manifestations. Art is a form of prayer, she insisted. So is love. All language tends toward prayer; Lautner had told her that. All
utterance is aimed at power. That too. If this is true, then
can it also be true that her silence means she has relin-
quished her power in his favor? If he were here, she would
ask him. She would dare.

In the next instant she was thinking, almost idly, and with
closed eyes, that it was time to get up and go home. Or, if not
home, then somewhere away from here. Not heaven or hell
but wherever Lautner was waiting—in his world of trans-

sense. She opened her eyes. The Chinese vase was gone. In its place she saw a large, bruise-colored fist, the fact of a cabbage rose smugly clenching and unclenching its petals.

She stood up too quickly and suffered a moment of extreme giddiness. She sat down again and dug her nails into her palms, and, with her head hanging between her legs, she forced herself to take a few deep breaths. The equilibrium she recovered was insufficient for her purposes.

Let's say that story ended and that someone else, a city woman living for a time in a country cottage, a woman who was watching a flock of disorderly and fiercely honking geese pass overhead, began another. She too had only one story. She told of a woman like herself, filled with rage against herself for being the sort of woman who couldn't live without a man, a woman left to her own devices in a strange house, and ready to ransack it, and the universe if necessary, for clues as to the true nature of the stranger she had taken for her lover. But, finding the house to be protected against her violation by its very emptiness—a really sinister emptiness, one that spied on her with the obscene eyes of a voyeur—she drew a shade down over her intention and left in great haste, passing through courtyard and alley and gate as if in a dream, turning south, away from home, and then, after a time, east, aimlessly following the modest curve of the street past tenements and small townhouses, a blur of darkish reds and browns, until she reached the gash of an avenue, where a river of purposeful traffic dragged her, along with other small bits of life, from the narrow side street into its agitated center, even farther off course.

This woman wandered up one block and down another, her mind enveloped in a growing mental dusk, following the dim shape of an idea, while just inches away, in the world, street lights came on and the sidewalk filled up with homegoers and seekers of pleasure.

Turning, she saw her reflection in a shop window. She was doubly dead now, conveniently dressed in black and spattered with the wet ash of city snow. She entered the shop because the tiny red Vermont farmhouse and its barns, nestled among snowy hills in the store window, sang of a good life encompassed, and made her achingly homesick for something she'd never had.

"I have a dollhouse," she said to the salesman. "Rather, my daughter has. Of course, she's grown and gone but still—it's a Newport mansion with a stucco exterior. It's enormous—too large for a dollhouse, really—and it's only partially furnished. My daughter never liked it. It's terribly pretentious. But, seeing the things in your window, I thought it might be fun for us to fix it up after all these years. . . . "

Oh, yes, do let's air it—do let's open the doors and windows to the sun, and paint, and paper. Let's restore it to its original purpose—do let's show how far one can push extravagance—and *cynicisme.*

"What scale, Madam?" The salesman's scalp showed a well-bred pink through his thinning hair. His head was shaped like Ned's. His voice was dryly condescending like Lautner's. His eyes strayed toward the ceiling.

"The scale? Oh, dear—I don't remember, but why don't you show me some things in a range of scales and I'm sure I'll be able to tell you."

The woman in the story wasn't able to decide on scale. The mound of tiny objects, chairs and tables, brass candlesticks, chandeliers, mirrors and clocks, service for twelve in Coalport china, a silver tea service, a set of hand-blown Venetian stem glasses, grew until the salesman's disdain was as visible as his scalp, until the other customers' impatience had turned to resentment and her own scant interest in the project had faltered completely. And still the heap increased. A cache fit to accompany the kings of Egypt to the distant, but nevertheless domestic, world of death.

"I'll leave Madam to decide."

Decide? The woman had decided ages ago. She wanted nothing. The shop was overheated and overcrowded and she was in a sweat of obligation. Oh, take something, anything. Here, this is a pretty thing, isn't it? This rosewood grandfather clock with its brass fittings and leaded-glass door and tiny swinging pendulum. The woman's grandfather stopped the pendulum whenever the family visited him because the woman's mother couldn't sleep for the noise time made, passing. Yes, it was pretty, so pretty the woman found she really wanted it. She needed it. She'd lost her means of telling time—or it had been taken from her. The clock fit effortlessly into the niche of her palm, into the niche of her memories, as well.

She signaled the salesman again and again. It was clear from his cold and studiously averted eye that he was a practiced tyrant of scorn and condescension. Well, she—this woman, dreaming of devils—refused to be kept waiting any longer. Fifteen minutes was grace enough. She'd have her clock, one way or another. She looked straight ahead. The furnace of her heart was cold. All her body heat was in her face. She slipped a sly thief's hand into her pocket and she walked, soundlessly as an Indian, out of the store.

Some kind of reason came over her once she was on the street. She thought of rushing back to the store with a rich woman's plea of forgetfulness, but she didn't take a step.

Can it be? Is my heroine to be a woman of temperament? Is she to be a variable, an unaccountable, a law-breaking female? It seems she is. It seems she is going to be a black-robed, black-hearted, stocking-faced crook.

She stood her ground for some time at the edge of the curb, allowing wave after wave of the slush churned up by passing cars to break across her coat, her legs. She was as clearly a woman in need as one who'd fallen onto the subway tracks, and yet there was something in her eyes, something pleading and at the same time willful, that alienated sympathy and made passers-by look the other way.

She walked to the middle of the sidewalk and stood there, needing to be jostled. But no one touched her. Was she invisible? Had she too disappeared into thin air? And then someone she might have known an hour before, a young mother of obvious means, a shopping bag filled with toys over her arm, walked by. The woman in black stretched out her hand. She had no wish to detain the young mother, or to know her, only to feel the warmth of a familiar life on her skin. She let her fingers trail lightly across the fur of the woman's coat as she passed. It was enough.

11

Despite the chilling rain, Jenny was waiting for her on the street in front of her building. Her eyes were red, her mouth was swollen, and she was shivering. They embraced.

Nora followed her across the small, grim lobby and up the stairs. There was a dull thud somewhere over their heads.

"It's only my neighbor's husband. The welfare checks came this morning. He's usually drunk by evening."

Jenny pointed to her door. It was bent out of shape. It hung open on one hinge. Nora took a deep breath and followed her into the apartment. At first sight, everything in the small room appeared to have been broken or slashed or, failing that, sprayed with red paint.

"Savages," Nora yelled, the madness of rage sweeping over her, but even as she spit the word out, the thought of scrubbing and straightening restored her to a sanity of purposefulness.

Jenny hadn't moved from the doorway. She was withered

and at the same time upright, like a stalk of dry, unharvested corn.

"Have you called the police yet?" Nora asked.

"There's no point. I'm not insured. They never catch these guys. They don't even try."

Nora walked around the apartment, shaking her head in disbelief. "I'll get started in the bedroom," she said.

Jenny nodded and leaned against a wall.

What Nora found in the bedroom sent her unsteadily back to Jenny. "I need a pail and some newspaper, and if you have a pair of rubber gloves . . . "

"What for? What's in there?" Jenny asked, suddenly alert.

"The same mess that's in here," Nora answered.

"What is it?"

"It's better if you don't know."

"What are you talking about?" Jenny yelled. "This is my HOME!"

A sacred eggshell, home.

"Don't go in there yet, Jenny."

But she was already at the door. "People are filth," she said, arriving. Her fists were clenched. "People are monsters."

Nora pushed past her into the tiny room that held only a mattress and a low bedside table. She scraped the piles of human feces into a pail with a wad of newspaper. She held her breath.

Jenny threw herself onto the bed and stared at the ceiling. Bits of stuffing poked through the slashed mattress. Her eyes were dry and dead.

Nora brought the pail to the street. She returned to find Jenny fixing tea, moving around the kitchen picking things up with the exaggeratedly slow movements of an invalid.

"I want to kill someone," she said in a toneless voice, as she filled the mugs.

Nora blew the steam from her cup and said nothing. What could she say? She lived in a fortress; what could she say that wasn't a boast?

"Senseless," Jenny muttered. "So senseless." As if reason were the issue. "There's nothing here but junk—the whole place is nothing but junk—and they knew it—they didn't take anything."

"I suppose they were angry because there was nothing," Nora said.

"I have to figure out some way to live with this." Jenny put her mug on the counter and pressed her fingers to her temples.

"You will," Nora hurried to assure her.

Jenny shrugged her shoulders.

"I know you'll manage."

"Oh, God, Nora—if you knew how tired I am of just managing."

Of course. Who wants merely to manage? One wants to be touched with perfection. One wants to be blameless and successful and well loved. One wants to shine. Oh, one wants and wants and wants.

"Being a woman is shit," Jenny said, sweeping her tawny hair off her face into a knot that added years to her age. When she was unhappy, her broad cat's face with its narrow chin went worrisomely pale. Her gold-tinged eyes turned a jaundiced yellow.

"You mean being alive is shit," Nora argued.

"Oh, that too. But in the end, there's no compensation for being a woman—at least a woman without a child. I can't speak for mothers."

"What's the compensation for being a man?" Nora asked.

"Psychologically? Not being a woman, I suppose, although God knows I never wanted to be a man." She undid her barrette and her hair fell around her face. She sat on the edge of the battered, paint-splashed stool, cupping her head between her hands. "Just look at this place," she said, the tears streaming freely at last. "What am I going to do?"

"We'll clean up and then you'll get a painter to come in," Nora said.

Jenny shook her head. "You have no idea how exhausting

it is to live alone, Nora. To have to hire a painter is more than I can think about. And, besides, I don't have the money."

That was the nearest Jenny had ever come to reproaching her to her face. Nora knew that by Jenny's standards she was spoiled and overprotected, but to discover that she was tactless as well, so wanting in delicacy as to suggest that money could right everything—that was bitter knowledge, and she wondered how often in the past she'd offended Jenny in this way. One of the hardest things for the rich to conceive is the extent to which a lack of money affects every aspect of daily life.

"God, it's cold in here," Jenny said, standing up. She lit the oven and all four burners. Then she began to sift through the wreckage of the room with a melancholy determination. "If I ask you a question, will you promise to tell me the truth?" she asked, as she piled some papers on the coffee table.

"Of course," Nora said, doubting that she could do otherwise: she approved of Jenny so entirely that she couldn't imagine a question whose answer would not be welcome.

"Do you think I've aged noticeably in the last year?"

"Why?" Nora asked.

"Oh, just a feeling I have when I'm with men that I have less to negotiate with. But you haven't answered me. Or is your question a tactful way of saying yes?"

"We've all aged," Nora said.

"Thank you. It's a relief, knowing. Sometimes I think I've made a terrible mistake, choosing to live the way I have."

"Well," Nora said, risking a smile, "you can always marry a rich man."

"I just might—assuming I knew one who was free."

"It's not hard. I know dozens."

"What would a rich man want with me? I'm bad-tempered and self-centered and I hate to wait on anyone and I have rotten depressions that last for weeks."

"None of that's a problem," Nora said. "It's your honesty that would cause trouble."

Jenny sighed and squared her shoulders. Her physical concreteness, the slope of her long back as it dipped to meet her buttocks, the power in her thighs, and her stride, almost flamencan in its assertion of heel, had never seemed greater.

"Are you in love with Kasim?" Nora asked as they tilted the porch swing onto its frame.

"If you mean, do I have a future with him, the answer is no. He has a dependent wife. He can't afford a divorce. I am sleeping with him, yes, and yes, probably I'm in love with him. I always love the ones where there's no future, haven't you noticed?"

"I'm going to leave Ned."

Jenny barely paused. "I'm shocked but I'm hardly surprised," she said. "Is there someone else?"

"I should have left him a long time ago. I should never have married him in the first place."

Jenny bent to hold the dustpan. Nora swept great chunks of broken crockery into it.

"It isn't Avery, is it?"

"Oh, God, no. I don't think Avery will ever talk to me again. It's nothing that can work out."

They both sighed and positioned the rug crookedly and sighed again. In some ways, the room looked worse when finally, a few hours later, they finished. The drama of the assault was gone and what was left had the sadness of something that had once been marked for slaughter.

Nothing Nora could say would induce Jenny to come home with her. She left her lying on the bed, waiting for the locksmith, listening to the rain on the windows. Perhaps it's enough for me to say that what has not happened to her will never happen now. It's enough to break the heart. But so what? as Jenny would say. Hearts break every day.

. . .

She'd always known that one day she would take this road. It had only been a matter of time, of course, but as late as this morning she hadn't known it would be tonight.

I can still see her serving dinner, a meal like any other. I can see Ned rubbing his hands together and smiling, his eyes absorbed with solitary pleasure. Meals added a certain kind of satisfaction that was missing from the rest of his life. Nora couldn't take her eyes from him. She shuddered. He ate.

She cleared the dishes, moving mechanically back and forth from the dining room to the kitchen. Wisps of the past, drifting foglike across her line of intention, obscured her purpose. When she was finished cleaning up, she took an icy bottle of vodka from the freezer and walked toward the kitchen table, where a crystal shot glass waited, throwing prisms of light onto the wall. The bottle seemed to repulse her touch. She bent her knees and dropped close to the floor to shorten the distance the bottle would have to fall, hoping to save it. It bounced harmlessly, then spun for a time on its side. She watched but she made no move to retrieve it. At length, she blinked. A shutter snapped, trapping memory, and she asked her husband to join her upstairs when he was finished with his paper. No rush, she assured him, just something she had to say to him.

Observe her, poised at the bottom of the narrow, twisting flight of stairs. Her eyes were shining. The stairs were quite steep and absurdly beautiful to her. She took them slowly, bloodying every step with her need, with the breaking of her faith, determined, nevertheless, to be pilgrimlike in her disregard of pain.

When she reached the top she was breathless and at the outermost edge of intelligibility. Her throat had become a reed set in vibration by a column of anxious tropical air. A jungle of words was on her tongue, and the yellow eyes of the past, gleaming and dangerous, were everywhere.

She entered their bedroom and closed the door behind

her. She sat on the bed, hands joined and resting in her lap, as coldly chaste as if she'd taken final vows.

Eventually, she heard his tread on the stairs. Each thud of his heel was a cleat digging into the flesh of the past. The door opened; he walked in and flung himself onto the bed beside her, innocent of the future she was about to bequeath him. He was stretched out full length on his back with a pillow folded under his head.

She pivoted on her knees to face him and, looking directly into his eyes, she said, "I've made up my mind to leave you. I can't stay married to you any longer." She hadn't taken a deep enough breath to see her to the end, and the last few words expired in her throat. Still, he'd heard enough.

He stared at her without sight. His chin began to quiver; the flesh of his neck trembled.

"No," he said, as if she'd merely asked his permission.

"Yes."

"I don't believe you."

"It's true. You can believe me."

"Why? Is there someone else?"

"It's me," she said.

"But you hate selfishness and irresponsibility."

"I know that."

"Then why?"

"I don't love you."

"My God, that's just a word. You're a loving person. I feel loved. Everyone who knows you feels loved."

"That's not true. How long has it been since I've made you feel physically loved?"

"I can live with that. I know you have problems."

Let that pass. She would protect him to that extent.

"But I don't want to live this way anymore. I'm bored and unhappy."

"Bored?" The word crumbled in his throat. He cleared away the particles with a scream. "Bored?"

She nodded.

"Bored? That's enough of a reason to break up a marriage? To throw away a lifetime?"

"I suppose there are kinder ways to express it. But boredom is serious. It makes everything trivial."

"Why should you be bored? You have children, interesting friends, and your books. You always say a person lives in their imagination."

"Yes—but the imagination has to take an attitude toward life, and if one's life—"

"I don't know what you're talking about," he broke in. "You're not making any sense."

"Well, I can try to explain it to you."

"Forget it," he said, closing his eyes and squeezing the bridge of his nose as if two fingers could block the meaning of what she'd told him from penetrating.

They were both quiet for a while. There was the sound of the steam sizzling in the radiator.

"So," he announced, averting his head and gazing at the window, "it was all for nothing."

"What was?"

"All these years—they might as well never have happened. You know what you're doing, don't you?" he said, turning toward her. "You're robbing me of my life."

"No," she said. "I don't believe that. It's not true."

"Oh, yes it is. Because what was it all for if not the future? I lived a certain kind of life because I believed . . . oh, what's the use—" He broke off and shook his head.

"So did I," she said. "But marriage isn't a pension plan."

"Goddamnit," he wept, "it's supposed to be."

He slumped against her. She put her arms around him and stroked his head. "Stay," he said.

"I can't. I need to be on my own."

"That's just a lot of romantic crap."

"Possibly. Maybe that's what's wrong with me."

"What is?"

"My romantic sensibility—my refusal to see the wrong

side of anything—it distorts everything. It makes me self-righteous. It makes me a liar and a fool."

"That's not true. It didn't distort the children. They have real depth because of you."

She was silent. She couldn't accuse him of the crime of defending her.

"Well, what about them?" he asked. "Don't you care about them either?"

"Of course I care. But they're grown, they're nearly adults, they'll be all right—it's not as if I'm deserting them. I haven't died. I'll still be here."

"And me? What about me?"

"You won't admit it, but you don't like me very much. You haven't for a long time, if you ever did. I know you're vaguely proud of me and you like what I stand for—you like the idea of me—when it doesn't interfere with what you want, but that's not the same thing as love. We have no passion for each other—we never had any—and we're not friends. Friends talk to each other. It's funny, but the only thing we have in common is the need to be blameless."

"You can't speak for me," he said.

"You're right. I'm sorry. I know I do that all the time." She disengaged his arms and got up.

"Where are you going?" he asked, with real alarm in his voice.

"To get my nightgown and a book. I'm going to sleep downstairs tonight."

"No," he said, and grabbed her wrist. "You'll sleep here."

"Is it that important to you?" she asked, twisting her arm free.

"What do you want me to do—beg?"

"No, I'll stay."

She undressed where he couldn't see her. The Victorian nightshirt, slipping past her shoulders in a voluminous and nunlike fall of heavy white linen, scoured her soiled imagination, making her feel as if she'd cleared herself of a crime.

When she stepped out of the dressing room, Ned was stretched out on the bed. Seeing her, he cleared his throat.

"I don't know what to do," he said, and turned his palms up like a child.

Instantly, absolution fled. She felt dirty and inferior in the presence of his grief, which, being strong enough to rob him of his pride and his authority, gave him a certain nobility in her eyes, a nobility that had been missing until now. She could almost not remember why it was necessary that she leave. Her decision might have been made by an unfeeling outsider who had no knowledge of her character or her desires. She sat down mutely beside him.

"Tell me what to do," he pleaded now, in a new shrill voice. He raised and lowered his head rapidly, little bird-jerks, and his eyes darted away to the corners of the room and back.

She was silent.

"Goddamnit, I said tell me what to do. You're always giving advice to everyone else."

"What can I say?"

"Oh, God," he sobbed, and knocked the back of his head against the carved headboard, softly at first and then harder and harder. "Oh, God. Oh, God."

"Let me help you," she said, and reached for his head to cushion it.

"YOU?" he screamed, pulling away. "You? Ha!"

"Yes, me. There's no one else."

"That's right. There isn't anyone else, there never has been. Not for me. But that's not true for you, is it? IS IT? WHO IS HE?"

"Not now, Ned. Please."

"Yes—now."

"I won't do this. Not now."

"Then help me," he begged.

"How can I?"

"Love me," he whispered.

"But I can't. Not the way you want."

"It doesn't have to be the way I want."

"That's not true," she said. But what did the truth matter in the presence of so much pain? His suffering seemed more acute than any she'd ever felt, and it was enough to humble her. He took her in his arms. He pressed his mouth to her ear. His tears stung her cheeks. The air around their heads was hot with his breath. She kissed him as she would have kissed a child, but he mistook her meaning and, raising her nightgown, he fell onto her.

"Oh, no," she breathed, and stiffened, but the ether of his misery anesthetized her will and left her limp with obedience.

She was so dry he couldn't enter. He licked his fingers and wet her but it didn't help. He made small, yelping noises and rubbed frantically against her thigh like a dog against a table leg. She endured it from the great distance guilt puts between people, sick for both of them. He came at once, spraying her stomach and her legs and her breasts. When he finished, he heaved himself off her and spit.

"I hate you," he said.

She lowered her nightgown and looked at him. His eyes were narrow and nakedly mean. "I've known that for a long time," she said, and wiped his spit from her cheek.

"Go ahead. Sleep downstairs. I can't stand the sight of you."

A hollow-eyed likeness of the man she'd married, a man who, without particular joy or ambition, had exhausted himself in the execution of his duties, this man was seated at the kitchen table the next morning.

It can be said, honestly, that the two who were about to meet as if for the first time—the first meeting in the cycle of ending—had, in their long years together, given each other some pleasure and much pain. They had been the unloving witnesses to each other's shortcomings. Appreciation had been left to others.

The sun would shine only briefly that day.

Ned's face was swollen as if with reabsorbed tears; it had softened without losing its toughness like a sponge.

Standing in the doorway, Nora felt as if she were laden with dust. She had the disused air of a thing that has been covered in sheets: summer furniture. The cold stove, her husband's folded hands marked the place where their story came to its close.

Seeing her, Ned sighed, the sigh of a sleeper. Sleepers had no past, he had no past, the past was all deception to him now; and the present was a heaving groan, and he'd lost track of how to calculate the future. He was thinking he would like to sing a funeral song for his life, he would like to get to his feet and sway from side to side and wail some ancient words for the comfort of his soul, but where was a man to get the strength? The words? He was thinking that perhaps she could have given them to him.

He cleared his throat. Even so, when he spoke his voice cracked and the crack widened until at times his words all but disappeared into it. "Look," he began, "you haven't been yourself since your birthday. Obviously this has been on your mind. What I'm saying is, why don't we take a little vacation—go off somewhere warm for a couple of days—and see if we can't work things out. I'll find the money, somehow."

She denied him with difficulty. The desire to love abides.

"Please," he said, looking at his folded hands. "Please."

She shook her head again. Now she was one of those who tore living branches from the trees, who pulled down the houses of the landed, one of the monsters, a marauder, someone who'd chosen herself over civilization. A cunt.

This was not the ending her husband had been led to expect by the mother of his children, and he was terribly bitter. He had a right to his bitterness, I suppose. But he had no outlet for it—for the bitterness—only a tone of voice that he loaded with all the blows and slashes he couldn't inflict on his wife bodily.

"Do you have a lawyer yet?"

She shook her head.

"Don't waste the money. You're not going to get anything out of me. You can take your clothes and some of the kitchen stuff and any wedding presents from your side of the family. Make a list of what you think is yours and give it to me. I'll let you know. The jewelry's out. I bought it for you. I'll give you a food allowance for a couple of years—until your father returns your money." Here he sneered. "How soon can you be out of the house?"

"Me?"

"Yes, you. You want out, you get out."

"But what about the children?"

"They stay with me."

"Isn't this something we ought to discuss?"

"There's nothing to discuss."

"It's not as simple as that. Nothing is."

"Don't lecture me. It's simple enough, as you've made clear. You've told me you're leaving and it's not open to discussion. I'm telling you I'm staying. I see no reason for further discussion either."

"But the children are involved. You can't just decree what you want. You're not the judge."

"Sue me."

"Please—why can't we talk?"

"I have nothing more to say to you, Nora. This is all your doing. You know I love you. If you fight me, I'll cut the children off without a penny."

The belt of his robe had come undone. He made a great show of overlapping the edges, of retying the belt; he gave the job the deliberate attention he gave all matters requiring resolution. He began by reducing the matter to its units, to its atoms, so to speak, and then he broke those units down further until the thing or the problem was disassembled and lay in pieces in the mind like a jigsaw puzzle. He believed everything was susceptible to being reduced in this way; reassembly was mistaken for discovery. Discoveries weren't made in little gray units, Nora wanted to lecture him, but in leaps that were white with the heat of intuition and illumination. The world didn't move toward meaning, toward God or whatever, in neat little units. It progressed from illumination to illumination as one leaped from rock to slippery rock across an icy stream. This man would never make a discovery in his life. To hell with his money. Of what consequence was it to her now? Lautner was all that mattered.

He turned at the door and addressed her coldly. "I don't want this made public until you actually leave. I'll see you at the Duttons' tonight. I want you out of here in two weeks. If you can't find a place that quickly, I suggest you move in with your parents. Oh, and if I were you, Nora, I'd start looking for a job right away." His bearing as he crossed the threshold was sodden but military in its conformation. He didn't look back.

She heard him sobbing on the stairs.

12

A great change had come over Nora while the rosewood grandfather clock she carried around with her like an amulet ticked away sixteen bare, unfurnished hours, a stark infinity that marked the absence of any word from Lautner, whose name, like a mantra, had not for one instant been out of her thoughts. On the contrary, his name had become an instrument of thought, and with it she was dissecting, as if for purpose of an autopsy, the corpse of her husband, a man whose emotions had died but whose appetite for money had survived and who took his authority from the ownership of money rather than from the practice of virtue.

As for Lautner's authority, however punishing it was to her sense of her own worth, she was convinced it was the expression of something valid. She perceived, however dimly, however presumptuously, that the pain she was suffering at his hands was the pain of resurrecting sense, which she experienced as an in-bursting of light, a light that was hot enough, white enough, to kill her—certifiably, not rhetorically; coffin, graveyard, mourners, all of it—or to reimbue her with life, but not, she hoped, the kind of life that was meanly bounded by incomprehension of her past. Nevertheless, this was what she feared; it seemed so likely. She was far enough advanced in her thinking to see that not-to-comprehend her past would be to achieve only a partial resurrection—to be returned to life, but so horribly maimed that she would be unable to die by her own hand if she couldn't endure the pain.

The volcanic nature of such thoughts as these had altered the landscape of her mind almost beyond recognition. She took as proof of the extent of the change Ned's growing revulsion toward her as toward someone from whose mind he was in danger. But although it was true that the further she removed herself from him the more clearly she could see him, and although she knew that the quality of her future depended on her seeing him honestly, still, with half her mind, the half that remembered the defectiveness of her devotion to him, the half that gave him every benefit of every doubt, she clung to the belief that, at bottom, he was, if not a good man, at least not a bad one. The other half was playing detective, collecting evidence, building a case.

This was Nora's state of mind when, promptly at eight

that evening, she rang the doorbell of the Duttons' Beekman Place apartment.

"Welcome," Maudie said, opening the door. Maudie always began with "Welcome"—it was her trademark. She liked trademarks, and her throaty voice made a kind of burrow of the space she occupied. Maudie was small and very pettable, if one was willing to risk being bitten, and very alluring in a World War II pin-up-girl way. She had plump, old-fashioned breasts, and a soft round face that had begun its sag toward the monstrous but was still quite pretty. She pirouetted slowly at one end of the immense foyer, showing off her dress.

"It's meant to be a relief map of the Grand Canyon," she explained. As she whirled, layers of black and ocher chiffon upended and fell; red rockslides and boiling black lava and a teal-blue ribbon, the Colorado River, cutting a gorge from Lees Ferry on her left shoulder to Lake Mead, a turquoise puddle at the edge of her right ankle. "Don't you just love it?" she asked.

Maudie was an heiress. The family fortune had been made, originally, in umbrellas or zippers and shrewdly enough invested to afford Maudie the many indulgences of which her life consisted, among them the maintenance of an art gallery bearing her name, and the indescribable exultation to her material nature of commissioning all her important clothes from the most celebrated artists of the day, male artists. It was her long-standing habit to sleep with her "men," as she called her artists, claiming that the intimacy was beneficial to their art and her business. She forgave them when they left her bed as long as they didn't leave the gallery. Not many did—Maudie made reputations and money. She was willfully open about her love of intrigue. She was intelligent and often amusing and sometimes vindictively honest. It was pointless to feel sorry for her, Nora told herself, but she did anyway: Maudie was, after all, as unhappy as a sane woman with too much money could be.

Nora kissed the soft cheek Maudie offered and then gave her coat to Maudie's housekeeper, Ida, a silent, devoted, almost ghostly presence who'd been with Maudie since childhood and still forced her to attend Sunday mass. Or, so Maudie said.

In contrast to Maudie, Nora was wearing a slender, unornamented column of fluted black silk, a specimen of Jeffersonian simplicity. There was approval in Maudie's scrutinizing glance, but she didn't comment; her generosity didn't extend quite that far, or perhaps the doorbell, ringing just then, distracted her. She was easily distracted.

"Well, look who's here! What do you think of my dress, Ned?" she asked, laughing. She had a wonderful fizzy sort of laugh. "Do you recognize the terrain?" Ned had taken Willie rafting down the Colorado some years before.

"Terrific," he said.

Nora turned and saw him slipping bulkily out of his coat. She looked at him uncertainly. He walked over and kissed her forehead with a shallow readiness to cover his true feelings that caused contempt to brim like tears in her eyes. Then he turned to Maudie, whose lips were waiting for him. Maudie liked to be kissed on the mouth. Tonight, for the first time, Ned obliged her. She raised her eyebrows. He blushed. She withdrew from his embrace, more than a trifle stunned, to greet Jenny and Kasim. Jenny was lank-haired and carelessly made up, her cheeks and mouth swollen as if she'd been crying steadily since the night before. Her chin trembled when she tried to smile.

Maudie hugged her warmly. "I heard all about it from Nora," she said, of the break-in. "It's just terrible. Still, I'm glad you could come." And in the same breath, "So this is Mahmoud! I can't tell you how I've longed to meet you."

Kasim smiled curtly and drew back a half-step. His sallow face wasn't easily read. There was no hint at all of an opinion in his cold, dark eyes, but Nora saw that they were registering everything; each blink was like the click of a camera.

The pictures, she thought as she shook hands with him, would not be flattering.

"Well, well, well. So we're all here!" Chester said, in his clipped manner, and waved to them from the front porch of the small and architecturally undistinguished house in which he'd grown up, a copy to scale of the façade—the structure filled one end of the huge foyer—which Maudie had commissioned for his fortieth birthday a few years ago. He was standing behind a terrifyingly lifelike wax replica of himself, a pleasantly dandified man in a dark suit and narrow tie seated comfortably in an arrow-back rocking chair. One of his hands rested on the dummy's shoulders. Behind the owlish metal-framed glasses, the real Chester's blue eyes were brightly vacant like his twin's; his mustache was less smartly trimmed, the bulb end of his nose a trifle more swollen, probably from his most recent bout of drinking.

When you think about it, I suppose, an individual life doesn't make much sense. Overhearing others talk about your own life, for instance, is a terrible shock: fascinating and horrifying all at once, like the replica of Chester. You want to keep interrupting with phrases like "Hey, that's not right" or "You're leaving out all the things that make it make sense." But if you put in too much, it makes even less sense.

Take Chester. He'd been born and raised in rural Vermont—or was it New Hampshire?—where, to hear him tell it, what most distinguished him from his schoolmates was not his mastery of Greek or Latin, but his subscription to *The New Yorker*. He'd married Maudie shortly after arriving in the city. Marriage had given him the leisure to find himself, and, failing that, to go on searching indefinitely. Maudie's trust fund easily covered the dizzying expenses of their kind of idleness.

The first thing he did, with Maudie's backing, was to write and produce an evening of three one-act plays. He'd put his whole soul into them, he said. The characters drank a great deal of champagne while delivering endless perorations in the style of P. G. Wodehouse. The playwright and the leading lady—Maudie had dreamed of being an actress—were denounced as horse thieves, the evening as a vanity production. It may have been Chester's talent for the third-rate or for theft—he lusted after the wit of a Mencken or a Woollcott, but although he was cranky and even dark on occasion, he wasn't smart enough or callous enough to achieve it— that prompted his agent, many years and many failures later, to suggest he try television. Whatever the reason, he conceived, wrote, directed, and produced, with some critical success, two hour-long specials on the subject of trivia.

Chester was a passionately sociable man, but his experience, his comprehension of human life had remained as shallow as a boy's. Still, his vanity and silliness, when applied to the art of conversation, sometimes resulted in a lively and amusing style, rather like that of a eunuch or a geisha in its freedom from certain unpleasing aspects of reality. He could talk anecdotally about food and obscure moments in history, moments so obscure that they were all but forgotten, so that he had no obligation to be scrupulous in the retelling.

On the darker side—that is, when he was unable to believe in himself as anything but a schoolteacher's son—he drank heavily and monologized tiresomely, a provincial Hamlet, bored with everything and spoiled and unlovingly passive. It was then he fell in love with purposive young women, or so Maudie said, as he'd once fallen in love with Maudie, women whose main assertions were in the direction of marriage. Maudie got rid of them for him.

Talking of him to Nora, Maudie often wept.

"I can't imagine what's kept them together all these years," Jenny wondered aloud after meeting them a few months ago. And then, ascribing some tinge of her own temperament to Maudie, she went on to offer as an answer the Duttons' eighteen-year-old daughter, who'd been institutionalized since birth, and who lacked even the animal capacity for recognition.

"Well, they certainly aren't happy," Nora said. In her opinion, the Duttons trifled too rigorously in sensation—their May games were fatal to happiness. "But they do protect each other in some way."

Nora went up the steps onto the porch and said hello to Chester. He put his arms around her, out of nerves, she supposed, since ordinarily he avoided touching. He gave Ned, who both bored and intimidated him, a jittery half-salute, but Ned seized his hand and shook it forcefully and then introduced him to Kasim. Chester grasped Kasim's hand eagerly; he'd been waiting for Kasim, was Nora's guess, and his eyes moistened a little in the presence of world-class fame. To be fair, Chester did value a fine mind. He compounded his embarrassment by kissing Jenny expansively. His face was bright red.

Nora saw Kasim take a wary look at his surroundings. Perhaps Jenny had told him the story of the oaf who mistook the hickory construction by the fireplace for a woodpile and tried to separate the parts for burning, or the one about the barbarian who wiped her lipstick on a paper napkin signed by Oldenburg and then crumpled it—imagine! crumpled it—and threw it back onto the tray of soft-sculptured partially consumed hamburger and fries that, in those years, had occupied the place of honor on the steel-and-glass coffee table.

"Well, well, well," Chester repeated, rubbing his hands together. He had the owlish, awkward look of a studious Boy Scout who, though pledged to obey the rules of conduct, was not at home in the woods and never would be. He led them through the screen door at the back of the porch and into the living room of the apartment, which was furnished principally with a trio of oversized chocolate-brown suede couches and a pair of grand pianos and a rotating collection of art.

"All right," Maudie said, "all of you stand in front of the fireplace facing us and close your eyes tight."

The Duttons were known for plotting surprises. She and Chester sat down on one of the couches. A large painting draped in white hung on the wall behind her head. She reached up and grasped a corner of the cloth in her small, fat paw. "All right, you can open now."

"My God," Jenny breathed, "look at that!"

The Duttons' living room, their furnishings, their artwork, their objects, the Duttons themselves seated just as they were at this moment on their couch, had been re-created in paint with a shattering fidelity. Under the microscope of the artist's talent, or malice, or both—or perhaps this was simply where accuracy of reproduction led—the Duttons had become indistinguishable from their possessions, as mired in the dreamless sleep of objects—Nora thought, borrowing the words of Ponge—as the objects themselves.

Nora and Jenny glanced at each other. "Wonderful," Nora mumbled. Jenny lowered her eyes and murmured something inaudible. "Terrific," Ned said, with a broad, unappraising smile. The trace of amusement mixed with contempt in Kasim's dark eyes was unmistakable. Maudie and Chester took his silence for awe.

When Chester went to get the drinks, Ned smiled initiatingly at Kasim, and the two men withdrew to one side of the fireplace and remained there, talking animatedly. Nora could hear Ned outlining his thoughts on the economic rehabilitation of Lebanon. He was faintly pink with the exertion of courting Kasim. What was he up to? Nora wondered. Eventually, his cough, rustling steadily in the thicket of her conjectures, warned her that the trap being set was not for Kasim but for herself.

In the dining room, Maudie, knowing how public displays of sexuality embarrassed Ned, and being devoted to mischief-making, seated him, as usual, facing the wall-sized group portrait of herself and Chester and an artist friend, picnicking nude in Central Park. Her breasts, Chester's organ were served up with more self-conscious elaboration than the talent of the artist, even for parody, could accommodate—although the platters of Chester's food, and the artful way they were arranged on the Venetian lace cloth, through which blades of green grass poked in a crazed erotic striptease, nearly redeemed the picture from emptiness. More than once during dinner, Nora saw Ned's eyes stray to the canvas and linger there almost studiously. From time to time he shook his head as if to dislodge something bothersome that was rattling inside. She thought it likely that he was trying to calculate who knew what about their situation—how far she'd betrayed him. When he finished eating, he looked down at his plate, at the hollow, whitish bones that lay there, and then up at the picture once more. His jaw tightened decisively. He thrust his head forward out of the casing of his shirt collar and caught Kasim's eye and smiled. Kasim smiled back. The conversation throughout dinner had been desultory, Chester's eyes chaperoning each morsel of food from their plates to their lips and obligating them to the narrowest conventions of flattery.

"What's in this dish, Chester?" Ned asked. "It's wonderful."

"You can't get an ordinary meal in this house," Nora said.

"Don't ask Chester about the food, Ned," Maudie broke in. "You don't want to know how much time it took him, the guilt will ruin your appetite."

"Oh, guilt's all right—it's sort of self-congratulatory, don't you think?" Jenny asked.

"It's remorse that's the bitch," Nora said.

"Well, I don't know about that, but this is Nora's recipe for osso buco. I added a few anchovies, is all. What do you think, Nora?"

"It's delicious, Chester. Much better than Nora's. Really delicious," Ned said before she could answer.

Chester turned red with pleasure at the compliment.

"Mahmoud," Maudie said, licking her fingers greedily, "now that the food's out of the way, tell what your play is about. We're dying to know. Jenny said Avery was interested. Of course, Jenny must have told you—we're interested too."

"Yes—well it's *about* terrorism." Kasim put his knife and fork across his plate and leaned back in his chair.

"That can't be all you're going to say," Maudie wailed, pulling a few strands of hair free of the pompadour, a sign of the tempest that would follow: sleeves pushed above the elbow, dress front unbuttoned to reveal a deep, moist gorge.

Kasim smiled and patted at the corners of his mouth with his napkin. "It's difficult to talk *about* one's work at the dinner table," he said, cuttingly, but then he softened his expression and said in a somewhat more conciliatory tone, "It's about a political kidnapping."

"You know, a think tank in California just finished a study that supposedly proves that one of the main side effects of centralization is terrorism," Chester said, leaning forward earnestly.

Kasim put on a look of weary disbelief. "One thing about American intellectuals, they never let reality interfere with their thinking. I was actually booed off the stage at an American university a few years ago for saying that people had more freedom in the United States than in the Soviet Union."

"I couldn't agree with you more," Ned said, shooting his cuffs and pulling back his shoulders. "I know first-hand how these studies are done. You can prove anything you want with numbers; I've done it myself. If I wanted to, I could prove to the satisfaction of everyone at this table that all evil results from buildings that are more than one story high."

"Speaking of centralization," Chester said—he hated being cast as an adversary to a great man—"someone told me that there's this primitive tribe someplace in Africa that has no power centers at all—positively none—no hierarchy of any kind."

"That'll be the day," Ned said, smiling conspiratorially at Kasim.

"No, seriously, I mean it," Chester said. "The guy's doing a book on the place."

"You mean a place where no one is more beautiful than anyone else, no one is richer, and no one is smarter—or taller?" Kasim asked.

"Where did you say this place was, Chester?" Jenny teased.

"Queens," Nora said, quickly.

When the laughter died down and Jenny explained the joke to Kasim, insofar as it was explicable, Maudie asked Kasim to "tell what you really think of Avery, his politics being so different and all."

"I don't go in much for gossip," Kasim said.

"But gossip's such fun," Maudie cried.

Her lighthearted challenge was met by a weighty sigh from Kasim. As a sentinel of culture, he refused to filthy up his mind with "he said"s and "she said"s—I'm quoting Jenny now, from a later time when she also told me, and rather bitterly, that Kasim's taste for the universal as opposed to the human connection didn't prevent him from being as petty in his dealings as any Italian duke in the Stendhal repertoire. He'd never in his life, he boasted to her, overlooked a slight—even an imagined one (Jenny's addition).

Maudie wasn't accustomed to being thwarted. She looked at Ned, hoping for an ally, but he made it clear by shaking his head that he was incorruptible. Seated as she was between two paragons, Maudie rebuttoned her dress and, with a sigh matching Kasim's in its humorlessness, struggled to resign herself to something she dreaded more than insomnia—an emotionally economical evening. She appealed to Chester with her eyes. Surely Chester, her beloved Chester, smoothing his mustache with several short downward strokes of his index finger and thumb, would rescue them from this monotony of seriousness.

Chester rubbed his hands together, but this time over the tinder of his imagination. "I have a proposal to make, friends," he said, winking at Maudie. "Let's improvise a little radio show." Something in his voice caught, and enthusiasm spread as quickly as a brushfire.

Maudie's face inflated with pleasure. "Chester has been doing research for a documentary on the old radio soap operas," she said.

"There are so few ways to amuse oneself that aren't culpable," Chester said, appealing to Kasim, who, surprised to find his own view so succinctly put to him by a frivolous stranger, inclined his head and smiled freely for the first time. Observing this, Maudie clapped her plump hands together. Liveliness squirted from between her fingers. Promise had returned to the evening.

Ned's eyebrows were raised in wings of pleasure. He excelled at games—charades and the like. Jenny appeared not to have heard. Tonight no one was her equal in despair, and in this blackness of mood she was slow to recognize the merit of amusement. "I don't know if I'm up to it. What do we have to do?" she asked.

"We invent the story as we go," Chester answered. "Come on, it'll cheer you up. I'll start and we'll move clockwise around the table. Speed is the important thing."

"Wait a minute," Ned broke in. "You haven't told us any of the rules."

"Just keep the story going," Chester said. "You have to pick up where the person before you leaves off, and you have to make sense—more or less."

"You mean you can stop in the middle of a sentence?" Nora asked. The idea that closure wasn't mandatory gave her the feeling of being disadvantaged and at loose ends, law-abiding in a lawless society.

"You can stop in the middle of a word if you want to," Chester said, making the prospect even worse for her. "Oh, and one more thing—if it's okay with everyone, I'll do the sound effects."

"But this isn't fair to Mahmoud," Jenny said. "He won't have any idea what we're talking about."

"Oh, don't worry about me," Kasim said. "In one respect, anyway, I have the advantage over all of you. You see, there are only two basic plots in all storytelling and I'm privy to both of them."

"Please—tell what they are," Maudie urged.

This time Kasim answered without resistance. "Either a stranger comes to town or someone we know goes to a strange town."

Jenny smiled. Nora saw the light flicker in and out of her tiger eyes and the grieving primness of her lips soften in something like forgetfulness.

"Bravo," Maudie said.

Kasim was smiling broadly now, in an undefended way, as if there were no tariff on frivolity. As for Nora, she thought, although she didn't dare instruct Kasim in her views, that he hadn't pushed his idea far enough. There was only one plot: expulsion and return.

There was a general holding of breath in the face of the possibilities before them—a sort of hush before creation—and then Chester raised his hand as if it were a curtain and the folly commenced.

CHESTER (*Speaking with a mock-British accent*) Inspector, I found this body blocking the doorway this morning when . . .

NORA . . . this morning when I left the bedroom to . . .

NED . . . to collect the newspaper from the front door.

MAUDIE (*Using a deep voice, introducing the inspector*) Did you recognize the deceased, sir?

KASIM (*Smiling gravely*) Yes, Inspector. I'm very much afraid it was my wife. Allow me to introduce myself. My name is Felix Downunder.

JENNY (*Attempting the deep voice used by* MAUDIE) You're very calm about it, my good man. Tell me, when was it you last saw your wife alive?

CHESTER (*Looking thoughtful*) I don't know that I can answer that question. You see, we'd been estranged for some weeks and . . .

NORA . . . and she wasn't at all herself when she left.

NED She was completely out of control, irrational to the point of making up things that weren't true.

MAUDIE Can you give us an example of what you mean, Downunder?

KASIM Yes, of course. Her voice had altered, for one thing. Changed registers completely. I hardly knew what to make of it. My first thought was . . .

JENNY . . . that she'd taken a lover, but . . .

CHESTER . . . but it hardly seemed likely that anyone would have wanted her in her condition. You see, she was . . .

NORA . . . she was . . . well . . . going through something tremendous. One night when she was undressing, I was stunned to see a strange bird tattooed on the inside of her thigh. There were other things . . .

NED . . . such as her suspecting everyone around her of stealing from her.

MAUDIE When I questioned her about the bird, she denied that there was such a thing on her body even though I could see it—it was a sump-tu-ous red-and-green parrot with a brilliant yellow bill.

KASIM (*Leaning forward, toughening his voice, looking at* JENNY) But isn't it possible, Downunder—odd name, Downunder—that, in fact, this parrot was a figment of your imagination? That quite possibly the strain of your work produced this particular—hallucination? You know, of course, that in Marxist terminology, a parrot . . .

JENNY (*With energy*) . . . a parrot is not merely a feathered example of some genus or other with zygodactyl feet—no, in the Marxist lexicon . . .

CHESTER (*His face bristling with pleasure, looking at* KASIM) . . . in the Marxist lexicon, parrot spelled backward is torrap—pronounced toe-wrap, a wrapping for one's toes—specifically a wrap for the toes of those who throughout history have been unable to afford shoes. Ergo, a code word meaning a member of the masses, one of the exploited of the world, a slave, if you will. (*He takes a bow before continuing.*) However, the third and final meaning is the most interesting, because . . .

NORA (*Groaning*) . . . because . . . because . . . it's vaguely theological, older than the Egyptian Book of the Dead and more esoteric than *Finnegans Wake*. It doesn't make sense to ordinary people—one would have to be an initiate to . . .

NED (*Shooting his cuffs, coughing*) Never mind—we're getting away from the point, which is the dead body that Downunder here reported to us at the Yard. Let's have a look at it, Downunder.

MAUDIE (*Clicking her nails on the table to simulate footsteps, but stopped by* CHESTER*'s glare.* CHESTER *stomps his feet.* MAUDIE *retracts her nails. She laughs, a low bubbly laugh, and then she speaks.*) By Jove, that's the damnedest thing, Inspector. The body seems to have disappeared.

KASIM Incriminating evidence, Downunder, can always be made to disappear if there's enough money.

JENNY Inspector, are you suggesting that I had anything to do with the murder of my wife?

CHESTER (*Loosening his tie*) Voltaire said if he had not been a writer he would have been a murderer. Just what is your profession, Downunder?

NORA (*With an intensely concentrated expression on her face*) My profession? You mean what do I do for a living? I'm an . . . I'm an archeologist, sir.

NED (*Looking hard at* NORA) That's no proof of innocence, Downunder.

MAUDIE I'm innocent until proven guilty, Inspector. I know my rights.

KASIM Yes, but do you also know your responsibilities, Downunder?

JENNY The evidence will show that I do, Inspector.

CHESTER   What evidence, Downunder?

NORA   (*With a vehemence not entirely justified by the situation*) It doesn't matter how cleverly you interrogate me, Inspector. You'll never get the real truth. The selection of evidence is always arbitrary. It's in the nature of things. In the end, all evidence is inadequate and suspect.

NED   You can't double-talk your way out of this, Downunder. We have laws in this country.

MAUDIE   Exactly what am I accused of, Inspector?

KASIM   Of reporting a crime.

JENNY   And that's a crime, Inspector?

CHESTER   Yes, unless you can produce the evidence—in this case, the alleged victim. You're an archeologist, Downunder. Can't you dig up the body?

NORA   (*Amid the groans of laughter*) I know. This is a job for Mr. Keene, Tracer of Lost Persons. (*There is a burst of nostalgic laughter.* KASIM *has an outsider's determinedly cheerful but blank look.* JENNY *whispers something in his ear. He nods.* CHESTER *imitates a phone ringing.*)

NED   Keene speaking. Yes, of course. I'll be right over. (CHESTER *simulates footsteps, doorbells, etc.*)

MAUDIE   The dead body of my wife has disappeared. Unless I can produce it, I'm bound to hang. Can you help me, Mr. Keene?

KASIM   A most unusual case. My staff and I will get right on it. We should have some news for you very soon. First, however, I'll need your wife's name and last known place of residence.

CHESTER   (*Overeager and speaking out of turn but waved on by* JENNY) Her name was Mirabelle, Mr. Keene. I have no idea where she lived after she left me—but . . .

NORA   . . . but I do know she had a friend named . . . Persephone. Also, there may have been a lover but I don't know his name.

NED   (*Tightening his jaw, looking away from* NORA) We'll get right on it for you, Downunder. I'll phone this Persephone myself. (CHESTER *makes dialing sounds in his throat. They are so good that everyone laughs.*)

MAUDIE   Yes, Mr. Keene, I was Mirabelle's best friend and I'll tell you everything I know even if it . . .

KASIM   (*Whispering*) . . . even if it destroys my career. I'll begin with the parrot.

JENNY   The last time I saw Mirabelle was a few weeks ago. I drove her to a broken-down house in Hoboken. She asked me to wait in the car, which I agreed to do, but I was hurt. We didn't have any secrets from each other. I waited hours. When she came out she was very pale and shaky. I asked her if it was very bad. She said yes, more painful than she'd expected. Then she pulled up her skirt and showed me the tattoo. I was too shocked to question her, but later that night I decided to . . .

CHESTER   . . . I decided to pursue the matter. I admit I was suspicious, Mr. Keene. I called the Tattoo Club of New Jersey, hoping to find out the name of the tattooist, but the office was closed. A taped message said Mr. Webb was out, but to please leave a name and Spider would be in touch. (*Laughing protests as the name Spider Webb becomes clear.*)

NORA   I sat by the phone for hours. I had a feeling my life and Mirabelle's depended on making contact with Spider. Finally he called me and we agreed to meet the next day, but when . . .

NED   . . . when he failed to show up, I drove to the Tattoo Club. The door was unlocked. Spider was lying on the floor at the bottom of the stairs, in a pool of blood. (NORA *looks hard at* NED. *He blushes and looks at* MAUDIE.)

MAUDIE   He was naked to the . . . my God, what's that? (*The crash is loud enough to startle them all.* MAUDIE *runs off to the kitchen to investigate.*)

KASIM   (*Picking up as if nothing had happened*) He was naked to the waist, Mr. Keene, and there was an immense but quite lifelike spider tattooed on his chest, which, by the way, was freshly shaved. I noticed that the spider itself was located on a thread over his heart and that the bullet that killed him had passed directly through the body of the spider. (KASIM *makes no effort to conceal his pleasure. Success becomes him. He has the sort of look on his face that small children get when they perfect the art of pumping and realize they can power a swing themselves.* NED *whistles appreciatively.* CHESTER *makes a victory sign. The women applaud.*)

JENNY I'm afraid that's all I can tell you, Mr. Keene, except that there was a scrap of paper next to the body with a phone number on it. I memorized the number and destroyed the paper. 864-6346. (*There is a round of applause for* JENNY's *advancement of the plot. By now they are bursting with mutual approval and there seems to be something at stake in bringing the game off.*)

CHESTER Thank you, my dear Persephone. You've been most helpful, and at great personal risk. My client won't forget your generosity. (CHESTER *makes sounds of hanging up the telephone and dialing another number.*) 864-6346? Good. This is Mr. Keene, Tracer of Lost Persons. To whom am I speaking, please?

NORA You are speaking with Mirabelle.

NED How can I be sure you are who you say you are? We have a report here of your death.

MAUDIE (*Just returning to her seat, and using a Mae West voice*) Why not come up and see for yourself, big boy? (*Then whispering to* CHESTER *who is looking questioningly at her*) Four of the wineglasses and two dinner plates.

KASIM (*Obviously having no idea who Mae West is*) I'll be there directly, Miss Mirabelle. (CHESTER *knocks on the dining-room table.*)

JENNY Mr. Keene, is that you? Thank God you're here.

CHESTER (*Looking at* JENNY *in astonishment*) It can't be! I must be mistaken! (*And then, aside*) I'll have to ask her some questions to which only she would have the answers. By God, if she's who I think she is, then my life's work will not have been in vain. (*Turning to* NORA) Tell me, Mirabelle, is that your real name?

NORA   Of course it's my real name. Why should I lie to you, Mr. Keene?

NED   Obviously—to cover your other lies.

MAUDIE   My mother taught me not to lie. Lying is vulgar, she said. Always tell the truth even if it's unnecessary. And especially if you don't know what's going on.

KASIM   (*Looking significantly at* CHESTER *as if they were bridge partners*) Your mother, Mirabelle, did she have any distinguishing marks?

JENNY   I seem to recall something odd . . . wait . . . yes, of course. I was only six when my family abandoned me, but, yes, my mother had two different-color eyes. One was blue, the other brown. Yes, I'm certain of it.

CHESTER   (*Smiling at* KASIM, *then addressing* NORA) Shall we sit down, child? I have something of the greatest importance to tell you. I was not always as you see me now, a Tracer of Lost Persons. No, I was once an ordinary man going about his business in an ordinary way, a simple Peer of the Realm with a wife and two children and a house in Bourbon-on-Water. All that was changed forever the day my daughter disappeared. She was only six at the time. (*Smiling at* JENNY *for her contribution*) Her mother, my wife, died of a broken heart. Her brother, my son, ran away to Australia and changed his name. (*Smiling at* KASIM) Though all my attempts to find my children ended in failure, I never ceased to believe that they were alive and that I would one day find them. Behind every case I took lay the desperate hope that the lost person would be one of my own dear children. That day has finally come. You, Mirabelle, are the daughter taken from me so long ago. Your mother's eyes. Indisputable proof!

NORA   Father! Mademoiselle said you'd all gone to America to live, that you never wanted to see me again. She took me to France with her.

NED   Can you explain why you pretended to be dead? And what about the parrot your husband spoke of?

MAUDIE   Don't call that man my husband, Father. Fond as

I am of him, our marriage was never consummated. He was more like a brother to me. . . . Oh, Father, do you think it's possible?

KASIM   In this life, Mirabelle, many things are impossible, yet they happen. So said Saint-Simon. But let's get back to your supposed death and the parrot.

JENNY   (*Smiling*) Well, I thought that if my husband believed that I was dead I could start a new life. As for the parrot, well . . . actually, it wasn't a parrot at all. (*Throws up her hands.*)

CHESTER   What was it, then, my dear? (*Turns to* NORA *with a wicked smile.*)

NORA   If you promise not to laugh, Father, I'll tell you. It was a . . . phoenix.

NED   (*Laughing, throwing up his hands*) That's my Mirabelle. She hasn't changed a bit since she was six. The only thing she liked more than reading books was spending my money. (*Uneasy looks around the table.* CHESTER *knocks on the table.*)

MAUDIE   (*Using her own voice, uncertain of who she is expected to be*) Yes. Who's there?

KASIM   Open up, Mirabelle, I know you're in there. I'm still your husband and I demand an explanation.

JENNY   I think perhaps Mr. Keene should explain.

CHESTER   Downunder, I'll get right to the point. This has gone on long enough. Mirabelle—rather, Mary Belle—is not your wife, she's your sister. And I am not just some cheap detective you hired. I'm your father. The governess did it! (*Laughter and applause.*)

NORA   Father! Brother! How I look forward to spending the rest of my life caring for you both in our little house in Bourbon-on-Water. (*More laughter, more applause.*)

Nora shocked everyone by bursting into tears. Everyone was terribly solicitous and knowingly circumspect. But Nora couldn't stop. She was thinking of Jenny's sanctuary, violated, of Maudie's imbecile daughter, of Chester's feebleness, of Kasim with only his wits to live on, of Ned's coldness, of her own corruption. She saw each forehead as if marked for death. She saw no reprieves. She stood up and said good night. Ned took her home.

Lately, I've wondered why suffering inspires such respect. I suppose because we've been taught to regard suffering as a sort of tonic for deepening the soul. Joy is equally effective, but this is a very recent discovery. It's awfully easy to invoke suffering. Just having some Jewish blood is enough. Or being a child of the Atomic Age. Never mind one's privileges—a Trotskyist with a country house still suffers. Joy, on the other hand, is harder to achieve and, like embarrassment, is nearly impossible to fake. And its depths are difficult to plumb. I like that about joy.

13

Nora, looking out her bedroom window, and seeing the last rays of the sun rouge the sky, was as solitary as a woman in a poem. Poised as she was on one leg in a pool of watery shadow, she might have been part bird, part woman, a creature of legend. She felt like one—a sharp-eyed, long-necked feeder on darting minnows of insight and despair. She was pulling on her hose, actually. And contemplating her husband with the intensity of a woman at her prayers, as if the only way to purify herself was to comprehend him and make sense of twenty years. She wanted to comprehend and yet not to blame.

She pictured him standing in front of an open refrigerator with his arm hooked over the top of the door, as he undoubtedly was, shifting his bulk from one foot to the other, popping cracked green olives, a few at a time, into his mouth as he contemplated what to eat next. She imagined him penned up in a mental corridor by the fact of her decampment. Attempting to escape, he tore open the flesh between the ribs of his thoughts. A sob gathered in his chest around the wound, like blood. He selected a small wheel of goat cheese from the shelf and peeled back the briny green leaves, exposing a creamy white interior. He took a few rapid bites and replaced the leavings. A moment later, he seized the disjointed leg of chicken and brought it to his mouth. His appetite wasn't obedient to the reins of reason; he was bucked and thrown by it again and again. She minded his gluttony only mildly; it was his lying about it that enraged her. The way he was shrewd and unconceding in his denial so that his conduct never looked ugly to himself.

He didn't want to know the truth about himself; that much was clear. The world was filled with things he didn't want to know about, she decided as she began making up her face, and a lot of what he did, she saw suddenly and clearly, was done to stave off knowing. And when she faulted him for having no personal reference or connection to anyone around him, he curled into a spiny, armor-plated ball; he could be an armadillo of contemptuous certainty, and it wasn't a metamorphosis that horrified or shamed him—he was shameless in that way. He simply waited until the threat had passed. Hunkering down, he called it.

What did she want of him? was the question in his eyes as he searched the well-stocked shelves of the fridge. He wasn't emotionally ambitious, but then when did he ever claim to be? The bottom line—his phrase—was this: he came home every night, he paid the bills, what he did he did for the family. When did he contract for more than that? He believed life was a problem capable of solution. But unfortunately for

her and for Valerie and for Willie, his Aristotelian disposi-
tion of parts hadn't led to wisdom but only to a deathful obduracy, to stasis. He called this consistency a virtue. And
didn't he always defer to her in matters of the heart? Ah, but
there was a catch here, she saw as she rouged her cheeks.
Matters of the heart were, in his view, diversionary. And by
ascribing an enormous tonnage of sensibility to her—as opposed to an equal weight of intelligence—he set up an equa-
tion in which he could be honestly proud of her and not have
to take into account her mind. He conceived of sensitivity as
a kind of playpen of the heart around which she was welcome to toddle. She was not welcome, however, to wander
into the great world where things are not just thought of but
actually transpire. Of course—Ned still speaking—he knew
that in her terms he was the illiterate, but then he didn't live
on her terms or in her world. In fact, hers could hardly be
called a world, or if it was, then it was a world he built for
her. What sort of life could she have without him? She and
her friends, mostly women but some men, lived at that essentially frivolous level where the strength of one's feelings
on any subject overrode the soundness of one's argument. If
Ned thought in such terms, he could accuse her and her
friends of being Emersonians; that at least would be amusing. But the worst part of prolonged contact with him, she
decided now, was that he laid claim to virtue while actively
taking advantage of innocence wherever he found it.

Why has she devoted twenty years and all her charm and
wiles to legitimizing a pretender to virtue? she asked herself.
Her heart was pounding. She wanted to stop a minute to answer this question, but her mind leaped ahead as if it had
been let off a leash. She reddened her trembling mouth,
trembling with awful knowledge. If a man grinds you down
into accepting less than fair value, and still requires that you
be grateful, isn't he worse than a common thief who breaks
in and steals what you have? More cowardly? Why hasn't
she wanted to know any of this before? Because a wife who

questions isn't loyal. But he loves her, he really loves her. So what? Who cares? What is his love worth? Love means you give permission to the loved one to live. Otherwise, what's the point?

She asked these questions of the woman in the mirror as she fastened the tiny hooks on the bodice of her splendid, one-shouldered, draped jersey evening dress; of the woman who, for two decades, had willingly aided and abetted Nicholas Ingarden in the systematic and fraudulent appropriation of what innocence could not defend. She was corrupt too, she told herself, but surely her corruption wasn't equal to his: he was still unrepentant, while she was remorseful nearly to the point of death.

The click-clack of her high heels on the polished wood floor of the foyer would alert him, she knew. She was right. She heard the refrigerator door slam; she pictured him wiping the back of his hand across his mouth to remove any lingering crumbs. That he was standing innocently at the sink when she entered the kitchen, holding a glass of water to his lips, didn't fool her. "Ready?" she asked.

"Not quite," he said, taking a long, slow sip of water.

"I'll get my coat," she said, and left the room. She pressed her throbbing forehead to the mirrored wall of the vestibule and waited.

He took his own good time.

The museum, a spired, half-inspired Romanesque revival, imitation castle-on-the-Rhine, pink granite, four square blocks roofed in red tile, covered what, in the 1870s, had been a muddy campground for squatters and goats. A hundred and some years later, dozens of taxis and limousines were jockeying for position in front of the Beaux-Arts entrance to the site, while an equally combative crowd of expensively rigged-up ticket-holders was maneuvering for precedence on the sidewalks and steps.

Inside, the crowd, enlivened by expectant female faces and the sweep of long dresses against the solid ground of black dinner suits, flowed slowly but good-naturedly—like a placid river—toward the Hall of the Northwest Coast Indians. Ned stepped out of the current onto the bank to take a look at one of the posted floor plans. That Nora could easily direct him was of no consequence; he wouldn't move until he'd gotten the lay of the land himself. What a presumption, to think you could know where you were at any given moment. Nevertheless, when he stopped, she stopped, and when he advanced, weaving skillfully around and between the richly dressed processionists, she followed after, squawlike. A few seconds later she heard Maudie's voice soar over the general buzz of conversation. "She is sweet, I agree with you. What I'm saying is, I don't like sweet women. You can't trust them for shit. They'd rather be sweet than honest."

Ned shook his head. "Oh, Christ," he muttered, rolling his eyes at Nora, a forgetful relapse into their married idiom. She was expressionless and silent. The bridge of language leading back to their old communality was too seductive. She allowed herself to be carried toward Maudie's voice by the current of bodies.

Seeing them, Maudie squealed and waved. The lines of welcome in her face deepened, pouches of warmth opened under her eyes, tiny cracks appeared around her lips, and Nora was gathered into Maudie's round arms, soft as chamois and twitchy with excitement. She could never tell whether Maudie was genuinely glad to see her or just acting out her notions of those gestures to be included in a dimensional life—as she put it (her therapist was a Rankian).

Maudie handed her off to Jenny, who smiled wanly. Jenny did look a little better. Her skin had resumed its natural color—that of ripe wheat—but her eyes, set widely apart under her low amber brows, had violet smudges under them. Worrisome. Ned dispatched air-kissed greetings to the two women; his embrace, Nora decided, was more a shrugging off of contact than a seeking of it. She noticed that he didn't attempt to meet their eyes. He shook hands with Chester, met his eye boldly, and smiled with the professional familiarity of a politician. He made no such effort with Laurence, Jenny's rejected lover. (Kasim was out of town.) Apart from being useless to him, Laurence had eyes whose pleading and succulent feminine quality plunged Ned into adolescent awkwardness. Not that Laurence wasn't a little difficult for everyone. Jenny said he was self-involved to an exaggerated degree; everything between them was geared to his moods, his fears, his work, "Oh, you know, he's like a difficult child—but wonderful in small doses." If he was a child, he was an appealing one, a cherub with a dark side, a child whore of Egypt. His eyes were an odd purplish brown like the shiny skin of an eggplant, ovular, and as heavy with imagined juice as the bacchanalian grapes of a Caravaggio, and his gaze had tendrils.

"Nice to see you again," Ned said, not looking above Laurence's jaw and extending his hand cautiously.

"Hello, Ned. How's everything?" Laurence said. His touch was as tenacious as Ned's was transient.

Ned coughed and cleared his throat and said, "Fine, fine," and then he turned hastily and in some confusion and took Maudie's arm. For the occasion—and Maudie had a rousing sense of occasion—she was gorgeously panoplied, truly deserving of praise, but Ned seemed not to notice.

"It's a Chilkat dance shirt," Maudie announced as they walked. "I borrowed it from a friend who was a friend of Max Ernst and started collecting these things when Ernst did, way before they were fashionable. He bought the stuff for next to nothing. Can you tell that the design on the front is meant to be a beaver?"

The others laughed. Nora watched a vacant smile appear on Ned's face. Maudie's conversation had never been more than a series of unconnected soft and giddy ploppings of sound to him, and never more so than tonight.

"Well," Maudie said in a loud, goading voice as they neared the Hall of the Northwest Coast Indians, where tables had been set up under the totems, her eyes glinting with mischief—it amused her to punish inattention—"if beaver doesn't interest you . . . "

Ned was still smiling, the stiffish smile with which one greets the not-heard-or-grasped, sunk as he was in the layers of his own bereavement.

"Obviously I should have worn the headdress that goes with this," Maudie said, disregarding Ned as hopeless and addressing Nora, who was on Laurence's arm. "The full regalia's every bit as powerful as Wolsey's red and gold. Except here, of course, the power's all in the design. Even on the hanger, the damn thing's alive."

The crowd, which had been flowing along at a leisurely but regular pace, suddenly and for no apparent reason formed a massive clot, and they were hemmed into physical intimacy with strangers. Ned's eyes met Nora's. Abruptly, his mouth crumpled. He turned his head away, pinching his lower lip between his thumb and forefinger, to keep it from trembling, she supposed. His eyes watered. Then he got hold of himself and the face he'd aired for that instant was shut away again. The logjam broke; he walked off stiffly with Maudie.

Nora shriveled inside her chic, colorless dress. To be an instrument of oppression was hateful. For herself, she preferred the status of victim. She acknowledged the truth of this while she adjusted the pins in her hair, one long tendril having escaped at the nape of her neck, and then she paid Laurence a very delicate compliment about his looks. He smiled with pleasure at her remark.

"Do you know," he said—he often began with this inquiry; it was his notion of friendliness, perhaps—"do you know, I was appallingly fat as a child." His voice was low and confiding.

"Impossible," Nora said, flatly. Underneath his loosely

cut clothes, an Indian silk pajama, he appeared to be quite rangy.

"Actually, I was fat until I was seventeen. I still have no musculature at all. I look dreadful in a bathing suit. I'm pear-shaped."

"What happened when you were seventeen?"

"I had my first lover. He starved me. Well, actually, that's too severe—we did fasts together. He was both physically and spiritually fastidious."

Nora burst out laughing.

"Why is that funny?"

"Weren't you making a pun?"

He looked puzzled.

"Fast and fastidious?"

"It wasn't intentional, but it will be in the future."

"Do you still fast?"

"In my Indian periods, yes."

"And in your other ones?"

He laughed. "In my Anglo ones, you mean? I lust."

They were passing the prow of a canoe carved from the trunk of an enormous tree and paddled by American Indian slaves in the Seventy-seventh Street lobby—the others were a few feet ahead—when Nora felt a sudden and startling increase of pressure inside her skull, something like the buildup of aerodynamic drag that occurs when the speed of an aircraft approaches the speed of sound. When the two speeds were synchronous, she heard the boom of her name. She whirled around. Who wouldn't have, being summoned in that extraordinary manner? Ned turned as well.

Her knees hardly served to hold her up. She pressed her hand to her heart, and the dome of her milky-blue sapphire, catching the light, cast a star on the ceiling over Lautner's head. She smiled at the joking appropriateness of the image, although her emotion was such that she was close to tears. She and Ned saw him at the same moment. Ned turned away. He was not a man to have his feelings mauled by a sight.

Whether or not Lautner was truly beautiful, his appearance caused a certain devastation. His face was extremely powerful in spite of nothing in it working properly: the nose was hardly Roman, the eyes were vastly intelligent but not well formed. He was tall—not rearingly, like the man accompanying him, yet he outshone this man in boldness and size. He glittered from within with something like high purpose. He was possibly ridiculously serious in this setting but he had an air of independence and self-companionship that silenced ridicule.

"Nora," he said, extending his hand. "I'd like you to meet a friend."

"Orlando Blok," his companion said, making a slight bow. He was very tall, and thin as a saint. He had a showy mane of white hair and a deeply lined face, long and narrow like a stallion's, startled blue eyes, and remarkably muscular hands. He had been in Lautner's box at the opera.

"Nora Ingarden," she said, careful not to look at Lautner.

"Orlando Blok the composer?" Laurence asked, tightening his hold on Nora's arm as if he were a tenor reaching for a high note.

"Yes," Blok said, blushing furiously, and with a daunting shyness.

"Laurence Ghose. It's an honor to meet you, sir," he said, extending his hand. He was flushed with hectic gaiety and so blatantly affected in his manner, so far off key, that Nora shuddered for him. "I grew up on your music. My mother's a cellist. I believe you know each other."

Blok smiled but said nothing. Laurence was struggling to interpret Blok's silence, plucking at the edge of his white silk tunic.

"Aren't you going to introduce me to your friend, Nora?" Lautner asked.

"I would but I only know your pseudonym," she answered, playfully.

"Are you a writer?" Laurence asked.

"Well, that's quite an oversight," Lautner said, ignoring Laurence, taking a deep breath and exhaling noisily. "Why not amuse us by guessing my real name, Nora?"

"Beelzebub?" she asked, recklessly. "Mephisto?" She cocked her head. "How about Old Nick?"

Laurence was enchanted by this Rumpelstiltskin game. He looked with his dark changeling's eyes from one to the other of these two mysterious strangers, and then at Nora with new respect.

"Come, let's walk," Blok said to him. "You haven't told me your mother's name yet." His accent was unplaceable by region; entirely American, though. They did as Blok commanded, Laurence having surrendered all rights but those of a retainer; they stepped into the mainstream and were carried off.

"Well, Nora, here I am as you wished," Lautner said as he led her through a narrow opening in the press of scented bodies, close by the display cases. "You want me to be undeniable, don't you? Or am I now simply a figment of the collective imagination rather than of just yours alone—no more susceptible to proof in the world than virtue or beauty or God?"

Was she being teased? His tone was scolding, but it seemed more affectionate than usual.

"Blok's extraordinary, isn't he? Everyone you know seems to be extraordinary. Sylvie—those other people at the opera . . . " It occurred to her then that she had it backward, that in fact it was one's contact with Lautner that brought the extraordinary within one's sight if not one's reach. So that was his gift—what he'd meant by the gift of language—a grammar that radically enlarged the realm of the possible by insisting on honesty—not honesty as a simple-minded principle, out of reach and static, but as a very complex project in which the whole point was to make increasingly finer distinctions and then live as if the distinctions really mattered.

"How would you define 'extraordinary'?" he asked.

"Well . . . original," she said lamely. It was more a question than an answer.

"Possibly what you take for originality is merely a different set of clichés from the ones you're used to."

"I don't think so," she said, with a sigh. But then how would she know? She knew nothing anymore. Everything was in fragments, really—her thoughts, her life—and she had nothing to put in its place, nothing to offer him, not youth or wisdom, only a fading beauty—and love. She was frightened and exhausted.

"How jealous are you?"

Did he read minds? Often. And faces. And situations.

"I'm jealous of everything you do, everyone you know—every minute." There was a heady freedom in admitting this. "You see, you're making an honest woman of me," she said, only half-joking.

He was silent.

"Well, it's happening, isn't it?"

"Is it?" he asked, and his beauty grew frighteningly precise.

"I was honest with Ned. I've told him I'm leaving. All those episodes I thought added up to a life are over. Finished."

"Oh, Nora, you're hopelessly literary."

She'd heard that before, from Old Nick himself, whose head she saw a short distance away, bobbing up above the others like a cork. He was sneaking furtive glances at her over the shoulder of his dinner jacket like a third-rate detective who'd somehow gotten ahead of the person he was tailing.

"Nothing is ever finished for the living. Even the fact of death isn't final. There's always memory. There are no endings except in books."

"I don't know. You've overwhelmed me before but that's not the same thing as convincing me."

The crowd had thickened again, making headway difficult. He circled her upper arm with his fingers, and he steered her with his hand, which was like a rudder of bone, not only steered but pushed her, keeping her an arhythmic half-pace to his right and forward of him so that she constantly had to renegotiate her balance. She didn't question his intent. She assumed he had his reasons for strong-arming her, just as she had hers for allowing it; she took it—the rough handling—as a sign of interest. They walked. She was on the verge of falling with every step: she maintained her balance by an effort of will, much as when she went running. Eventually, something in his stride—it was long-legged, and his ankles were as loosely sprung as a skier's—transmitted itself to her, vibrating into her legs and up her spine to her neck, steadying and strengthening her so that balance was no more an effort than breathing.

They reached the Hall of the Northwest Coast Indians sooner than she wished. The vaulted ceiling rose an emperor's distance over the inlaid tile floor and was supported at regular intervals by a dozen monumental totems carved from the trunks of virgin trees that once guarded Indian villages from harm. The room was as shadowy as a sacred grove; a haunted music filtered through the leafy-feeling air. Beneath the watery babble of voices and the rustle of silken dresses and the scraping of chairs as the guests took their seats, she could hear the recorded tranced voice of an Indian singer offering his monodic a capella song—the cry of the raven, the call of the killer whale, the wolf—the narrative beat as relentless as a pulse.

Laurence and Blok were waiting for them just inside the room. Laurence's eyes were fixed on Blok with a puglike devotion, as if in the iconography of Blok's face he'd finally found his purpose and the world's fused. Blok's narrow horse-face was as tightly woven in its mesh of wrinkles as one of the nearby Tlingit baskets, finely enough wrought to hold water. No spillage, no clues as to what he thought of Laurence.

"May I call you tomorrow?" Laurence asked. His fascination made him incautious.

"I won't be in town tomorrow, I'm afraid." Blok looked around the hall with a certain weariness.

"May I call you when you come back?"

"I don't know when I'll be back." Blok tossed his head. His white hair settled wavily, like seaweed.

"That must be hard on your friends."

"They're accustomed to my ways."

"I could learn," Laurence ventured.

"Perhaps another time," Blok said. He was not unkind, merely indifferent.

The muscles in Laurence's face tightened; he bit the inside of his cheeks like an adolescent boy being snubbed. Lautner nodded at her and then withdrew his arm, moving from her side to Blok's. A key slipped into a lock and turned had no less an air of finality than the manner in which he engaged Blok. He was a man of few gestures, each one seemingly conclusive—this in spite of his conviction that nothing was ever finished.

Nora hurried Laurence off toward the bright signal flag of Maudie's arm, which waved them home as if from space travel to the comfortable desolation of the everyday. Ned and Kitty and Connie were already installed in their chairs. They sat listening to Chester with lifted chins and lowered eyes and their brows contracted somewhat closer together than usual, following his gesticulations—the short swipes of his bent arm, the hand that moved from his heart out toward them and back again. There was a short burst of laughter when he finished his anecdote with the words "because the King of Prussia said so." He laughed with them, little clipped ho-ho-hos.

"Have you seen Anina?" Kitty Lilienthal asked.

"Not yet," Nora said.

"She's with a very handsome, very young man who keeps whispering in her ear."

"Maybe he's her son," Connie said—wistfully, Nora thought. Connie had four sons, who shared their father's slight regard and enormous need for women.

"Oh, of course," Maudie said, nodding. "And that gorgeous feathered creature at the table next to hers is Rima the bird girl, and the distinguished-looking man with her, the one with the soulful eyes, is her father."

Nora turned her head sharply. At the sight of Sylvie and Lautner and Blok—and Margaret as well—at the same table, something in her chest was thrown down and a flood of jealousy and appetite and rage and despair rushed through her—even to her limbs. Margaret fluttered her fingers. Nora waved back.

"Who's the man with Margaret?" Ned asked.

"Never mind the man," Maudie said. "Who's that woman in the feathers? She's epic-looking, isn't she? I'll bet she doesn't have a single kind bone in her body."

At that moment, Sylvie raised her eyes and caught Nora's ransacking her. She might have been a wrestler for the holds she used—she pinned Nora at once. Sylvie, it seemed, was able to subdue everything, even the least promising object, to her style; a kettle, a chair, someone else's life—anything unsubdued or not worth subduing didn't exist for her. I say she's an artist, the sort of artist who breaks with tradition so as not to risk being an imitator. Heroic? Not to everyone, maybe. But to Nora, surely. One thing is certain, though. Wherever such an individual asserts his or her rights, there the supremacy of the family is ended. Don't ask what takes its place. It's not an accident that a woman without a kind bone in her body is regarded as a traitor to all her sex.

"You must have heard of her," Nora said. "Her name is Sylvie Rochas."

"A leftist with a town house," Jenny said.

"Oh, yes," Maudie said, thoughtfully.

"Who's the man next to Margaret?" Ned repeated.

"Orlando Blok the composer," Nora said.

"The man on her left," Ned persisted. "The one you were talking with."

"That's Lautner."

"The man we met with Tromp on your birthday? I would never have recognized him. I don't remember him looking like that."

"Would you like me to reintroduce you?" she asked, almost hoping he would accept the challenge.

"Hardly," he said.

Nora looked into the empty eye slits of a rope-haired Tsimshiam starvation mask whose beaky nose and full lips thrust as sharply out of its sunken face as the prow of an ice cutter, as pointedly as if its reason for existing was the head-on breaking of physical barriers to the other world.

"Are you okay?" Maudie asked her.

"I'm a little tense."

When she'd told Maudie she was leaving Ned, Maudie had said, "Well, it's about time. I don't know how you stood it. A man who doesn't ever get drunk or make a scene or make a fool of himself is hopeless."

"Lloyd's looking for a parking space," Kitty Lilienthal said. "The parking lot was full. We wouldn't have brought the car, but we're going to the country after we leave here." The Lilienthals owned a weekend house in a compound upstate. They alone of the original settlers had survived. Divorce, not Indians or plague, had decimated the utopia of dogs and children. The easy communality of swimming and skiing and blueberry picking was gone. Strangers moved in and out. Their house was up for sale.

The news that Nora was leaving Ned had brought out the worst in Kitty, who had no loyalty to life outside the limits of family. Kitty's maid had been at the sink peeling back the thin green spines of a hundred snow peas. Kitty hadn't dismissed her; she hadn't suggested that they move to another room. Nora had been forced to speak very softly. She'd broken down a few times. The phone rang twice while she was there. Kitty had answered it herself; she'd spoken at length both times. In the middle of the second call, as she was detailing her technique for reviving tulips, Nora had gotten abruptly to her feet and said she was leaving. Kitty had flushed but hadn't hung up. With her hand over the receiver, she'd explained to Nora that the call was urgent. Lloyd's sister's centerpiece had fallen and her company would be there any minute.

Lloyd Lilienthal, the man approaching the table, the man who, yesterday, had come into possession of Nora's inheritance, was small and barrel-chested. He strutted like a bantam rooster. He had an oversized head, thinning reddish hair, short legs, and a coarse-featured face. Connie Blakely's husband, who was a few yards behind, overtook Lloyd and they arrived at the table together. Bob Blakely was tall and muscular and smugly big-shouldered. He ran the family business, he played racketball competitively, and he spent his spare time with women. He was a man of few and grudging words; when he spoke it was usually to give orders. But he liked to laugh. Laughter broke through his narrow lips like water through a cracked dam.

They talked about the woes of mass transit for a while; one of Lloyd's friends was the present chairman of the city's Transit Authority. The waiters exchanged clean plates for dirty ones. The guests ate their curried chicken and drank their California Chablis and talked about crime. "The average drug-free criminal commits two-point-three crimes a year," Lloyd said, with his mouth full of food. "The addict criminal, one hundred and sixty-seven." Ned opened his mouth to respond and fell into a violent fit of coughing. His grief, or self-pity, or malice—perhaps all three—scraped rawly against the walls of his chest. He waved off Nora's attempt to help him. He gave himself up to one paroxysm after another. The rasp of his cough combined with the grainy sound of the tribal music formed a kind of sand that worked between the fibers of her nerves and grated there. She gritted her teeth and narrowed her eyes and wished the evening were over.

Ned turned aside, took a handkerchief from his pocket, and buried his face in it. His coughing broke down gradually and deceptively into sobs. When Maudie realized what was happening, she leaned her tousled head toward him and laid a soft white hand on his heaving shoulders. Jenny half-rose from her chair in sympathy and glanced at Nora. Chester raised his eyes to the ceiling and muttered, "Oh, dear, oh, dear." Lloyd and Bob, for all their outward dissimilarities, looked at their respective wives with the raised brows and horrified eyes of a pair of twins. The wives shook their heads warningly. Nora was silenced by the outcry of contradictory feelings within her.

"Is there anything I can do for you?" Maudie asked, moving her chair closer to his.

He shook his head, coughed one final time, and blew his nose. Seeing Maudie's warm and slightly bulging eyes on him, he gave her a damp smile of gratitude. Jenny resumed her chair. The waiters poured coffee. Chester swiveled away from the table and tilted his head to one side to catch an announcement being made by Anina Durant, resplendent in a ruffled and brilliantly patterned dress of watered silk that had huge bouffant sleeves and a skirt so vast that an army of the blessed could be accommodated beneath it. This, Maudie whispered, at an age when she really ought to be cultivating simplicity.

"Anina says we're to finish our coffee and then follow the crowd to wherever it is they're holding the auction," Chester said, smoothing his mustache.

Ned pushed back his chair and got to his feet. He took Maudie's arm, using her sympathy as if it were a cane he could both lean on and brandish at Nora, and he walked off with her. Nora hardly noticed. In the throng of compliance with Anina's command, she lost sight of Lautner and his party; they disappeared into the belly of the crowd. She sent her friends on ahead on the pretext that she had to give Margaret a message and she continued searching, but without success.

By the time she took her place between Ned and Jenny in the center of the third row of chairs, the first few items were being carried down one of the side aisles toward the stage, where Avery, the honorary chairman of the evening, waited to open the auction. The loonskin ring that hung around his neck, the bear dancer's grisly claws that fell aslant his scrubbed pink head might have prompted laughter worn by anyone else, but Avery wore this shamanistic regalia with the same easy distinction as he wore his name and his dinner jacket. His eyes were dancing as he raised the leg bone of a small bird to his lips and blew it a few times. The tiny, piercing sound carried all the pathos of an infant's cry, and the audience of parents and grandparents responded to it as if to a beloved child, exhibiting something like a fawning rush to attention.

"I want to welcome everyone to the world of the Northwest Coast Indians. I would like to urge all of us to regard the occasion not as bargain hunters might, but, rather, as members of the community whose space we have usurped for our festivities—that is, to conceive of the proceedings in the spirit of a great potlatch. To do so means to compete with one another, not to get the most for our money, but to see who can give the most. Remember, we shall be enriching not just ourselves but future generations of our own tribe. This museum is a unique resource. We must preserve it by enabling it to grow. In other words, lunatic bidding is in order!"

Avery's remarks were greeted by good-natured applause. A few "bravo"'s were lofted into the air and picked up and passed along in a kind of contagion of good will. Avery was beaming, his large, firm cheeks red with pride, as he turned the microphone over to the investment banker who would act as the first of several auctioneers.

"What a farce," Jenny said, under her breath. She sat on her hands—her version of an obscene gesture.

Nora attempted to applaud along with the rest, but her hands faltered. Not so long ago the man on the stage had been her friend, but she had authorized a certain clock to tick and now he refused her phone calls, he ignored her letters. And in that same not-so-long-ago, the man seated next to her had been her protector. The hands of the clock had jumped the bridge of minutes and now he was her adversary. And as she waited in this newly time-ridden world, waited for the bidding to start, she could feel great drafts of their ill-wishing blow across her skin. It penetrated the folds of her flimsy dress as cold penetrates, sharply and to the bone. She shivered, understanding the extent to which she'd been shielded from the world's malice, from the experience of terror, therefore from life itself, by Ned's money and his obduracy. Seeing this, she laughed, a bitter inward laugh, for it was only now, having forfeited the protection of men, that she saw how hopelessly needful she was of it. There was no rest—no safety—for her anywhere but in the eider of a man's arms.

Someone tapped her shoulder just then and she jumped as if burned. Marjorie was seated behind her, with Matthew half-propped at her side. He was mostly bone now, and his head seemed larger than ever. Nora smiled sadly at him and squeezed Marjorie's hand. Marjorie gestured to the stage. Nora saw two volunteers in tuxedos, stockbrokers whom she knew slightly, hoisting a five-foot-square plank onto the viewing box. The plaster casts of a dozen uncommon, very protuberant animal snouts were mounted on it. Anteaters and the like. The item was greeted by whistles of approval, a smattering of applause, and a few catcalls. Nora turned around again and said hello to Matthew. At the sound of his name, he looked up eagerly, with his head cocked and his

neck wagging. His eyes were blank. Loyalty to the girl she
had been was there, though, only awaiting recognition.

"He still likes to be out in public. It keeps his spirits up,"
Marjorie said, softly.

"I've been meaning to call."

"His sense of things is very primitive now," Marjorie continued, as if Nora hadn't spoken.

"I wish there were something I could say besides I'm
sorry."

"Consider it said."

"You're a very generous woman, Marjorie."

"No, not really. The circumstances are extraordinary, is
all."

"I wish there were something I could do."

"No, everything's been done that can be done. It just
wasn't enough." She looked at Matthew and then she
crossed her sturdy legs.

"No, I mean for you."

"Well, I have a couple of kids who aren't in very good
shape, and there's not much in the way of life insurance, and
I have no job prospects. Of course, Matthew's parents have
some money, but they've never accepted me—they still
haven't forgiven Matthew for letting me raise the kids as
Quakers. Are you still interested?" She ran her fingers
through the fine frizz of her hair, changing nothing.

"Why don't you call me when you're ready to look for a
job? I know a lot of people. Maybe I can help you find something."

"Thanks, I might. And forgive me if I sounded mean.
Sometimes I get fed up with . . . oh, you know, the . . . "

"Anyone would."

Nora turned back to the proceedings in time to see Chester's hand fly up. Maudie was squirming in her seat with excitement.

"I have three hundred and fifty dollars from the gentleman in the third-row center with the mustache and the

glasses. Do I hear four hundred?" The investment banker's voice was strident with nerves.

Chester was so carried away that he topped his own bid.

"I have four hundred dollars from the same gentleman for this priceless collection of snouts," the auctioneer said, smiling at Chester. "Perfect as a Christmas gift for your favorite plastic surgeon. Do I hear five hundred?"

Five hundred dollars from the rear.

Eight hundred dollars from Chester.

Jenny shook her head, implying she would spend Chester's money quite differently. Maudie giggled and pulled a few dark strands from her upswept hair as she calculated the impact on their guests of a wall of white plaster snouts. Ned was plucking impassively at the skin of his neck. His eyes and mouth were at cross-purposes: the eyes ready to wound, the mouth soft, begging.

"Nine hundred dollars? Do I have nine hundred?"

One thousand from Chester.

One thousand it was.

There was a solid, prolonged burst of applause. The Duttons rose and took a bow. A spotter, wearing a red carnation, reached across the row to hand Chester a ticket for his thousand-dollar snouts.

It took three interminable hours for the lot to be nearly dispersed—a small-town-parade–like flow of rolltop desks interspersed with flocks of stuffed songbirds, followed by several fourth-rate animal bronzes, a crate of mismatched dinosaur bones—the plaster casts—useless as the odd sock, a number of fine duck decoys from the thirties, a Plains Indian ball-headed war club, which, to Nora's astonishment, Ned bid on and bought, yards and yards of windowed mahogany bookcases, a fossilized Ice Age leaf, sacks of arrowheads, bits of comets, and, finally, toward the very end, a mate to the Duttons' snouts—a frieze of rumps and tails. Maudie stilled Chester's arm, rescuing him as she always did—often tactless but a rescue nevertheless—from the folly of creating a a world in the image of his self-indulgence, and saving him from the ridicule of friends. She bore that burden, the susceptibility to ridicule, for him.

At this point, the lawyer who'd been doing his stint at the microphone yielded the stage to Avery.

"Thank you, Richard. You've been splendid," Avery said, and then he addressed himself to the audience. "I know how restless-making these affairs tend to be. In our battle against the clock, I'm reminded of what the French wag Fontenelle once said in a drawing room—I hate war because it spoils conversation." When the laughter died down, he went on. "Now, here we have a true conversation piece"—the play on words went unattended—"and I hope you'll all speak out. The museum is very interested in what you have to say. The monster you see being wheeled in is called an orrery, so named for Charles Boyle, Earl of Orrery, for whom the first one—not this one, however—was made. An orrery is a mechanism devised to represent the motion of the planets about the sun by means of clockwork. This very rare and valuable object—the only others I've ever seen in this country are a pair in the dining room of the Vanderbilt Mansion in Hyde Park—was given to us by someone who wishes to remain anonymous. I'm going to open the bidding at ten thousand dollars and request that we jump by increments of five hundred. Here it is," he said, running his hand over one of the solid brass orbits, "a trifle out of date and, to be honest, not in working order, but no less valuable for that—the heavenly universe as men hazarded it in the late eighteenth century!"

"We've done our share," Ned said. "Three hours is long enough."

"Do I hear ten thousand dollars? Yes? From the gentleman in the right rear."

"I'm not ready yet," Nora said, raising her hand and keeping her eyes fixed on Avery. Her impulse to bid shocked her.

"Thank you, Nora," Avery said, showing as little surprise

as if she'd raised her hand to pass him a teacup. "I have ten thousand five hundred from the lady in gray in the third row."

Behind Nora's head other voices, other hands rose and fell.

"I have eleven—do I hear eleven five?"

Nora raised her hand.

"Put your hand down," Ned said.

A squadron of spotters took up their positions.

"I have twelve thousand from the same gentleman in the right rear. Do I have twelve five?"

"I don't know what sort of game you're playing, but I'm warning you—you'd better stop."

"You can always sell at a profit," Nora said, raising her hand again. Twelve five.

Ned left his seat. He went straight to the spotter at the foot of the stage, a tanned and fit-looking woman, a golfer, perhaps, wearing a red carnation and a chiffon dress the color of a sickle pear. He whispered something to her. The woman dashed up the aisle. Nora continued bidding. It was going very quickly now. Maudie said there were dealers in the crowd.

"I have twenty-five," Avery said, pointing to someone across the aisle. "Do I have twenty-six?"

Nora nodded.

"Yes, I have twenty-six. Do I have twenty-six five? Is the gentleman in the right rear making a bid?"

Nora turned around to see her competition. The two men standing in the extreme right rear of the long, narrow room, raising their heads and gesturing with their chins, were known to her. One was Blok, the other Lautner. The crowd had begun to murmur. Nora saw Anina rush down the aisle as rapidly as her dress would allow. Her face was blooming with important news. The spotter trailed behind her. Anina crossed the stage and whispered at some length in Avery's ear. Avery nodded and exhaled sharply into the microphone. The sound he produced was the sort a whipsaw makes, many times amplified. "I'm terribly sorry," he said to the squinting audience, but no one heard his apology, since he'd belatedly covered the head of the microphone with his large, well-tended hand. "I'm terribly sorry," he said again, this time audibly, "but it's been brought to my attention that one of the bidders for the item now on the block is not bidding in good faith." Here he took a moment to wipe his forehead with a handkerchief. "If it's agreeable to everyone, I propose to assume the responsibility for her last bid, so that we can continue as if nothing had happened."

Nora slipped quietly from her seat and left. She was gone before the audience, caught up in the thrilling buzz of conjecture and debate, had a chance to gather its collective wits, to realize that she had been the only woman—the "her" Avery had mentioned—bidding.

"I won't forget what you did tonight, what you made me do," Ned said to her half an hour later. She was waiting for him in the living room.

Nora, who had always known she was helpless in his hands but until a short while ago had shrunk from proving it by any sort of confrontation, said, quietly, "I won't forget either."

"Why? Why did you do it? You couldn't have wanted that piece of trash."

"Tell me you love me, Ned. Tell me how much."

"What does that have to do with what we're talking about?"

"You win. I'll sign whatever agreement you draw up. I understand now how badly you need your money."

"Nora . . ."

"Get away from me, Ned. Get away. And don't ever come near me again, not ever, not as long as you live. You're a horror. You make my skin crawl. CRAWL."

"My God, Nora, how can you say things like that? Why

can't you understand how I feel? I have feelings too. You respect everyone's feelings but mine."

"Get up! FOR GODSAKES GET UP! I won't be a party to this. I am not a sadist. Ned, don't do this. I mean it. If you love me, get up. GET UP!"

"Stay with me, Nora."

"Oh, God, I don't believe this. Just think of the deal you're getting! You've negotiated me down to nothing. Everything's yours. The children, the house, the money, our friends. That should make you very happy, it's the deal of a lifetime, it's worthy of you. I'm not costing you a penny. NOT ONE RED CENT!"

"Nora, I said please."

"GET UP. Oh, God, WHY WON'T YOU LISTEN TO ME? I SAID I WON'T FIGHT. YOU WIN. I forfeit everything. The children, the dishes, the silver, the pictures, the money—HARD CASH—my share of your life—for not having loved you enough to have made a decent man out of you. But then you can't grovel at my feet like this. You can't starve me and cheat me and then ask for my sympathy too. It's disgusting, it's morally disgusting."

"Listen, you—you whore . . . it's you who's disgusting. You're the disgusting one. I wish I'd never met you."

Someone, a small figure in stained white, slipped between the sheets of a cold bed in a dark room, an ancient, crumbling nursery. Music silted the cracks in its wall, the thin reedy sound of a song from the twenties. "After You've Gone and Left Me Cryin'." She lay motionless, not wanting to break the balloon of feeling inside the music, or inside herself. She listened very closely to one song after another. For all their sophistication and wit, the lyrics were so painfully naive; they were filled with hope on such a grand scale, hope against all the odds, hope against sanity. She smiled a little. And then, without warning, a very young Fred Astaire began to sing "Night and Day." Oh, God, how the song hurt; his voice hurt her, and the hurt ballooned inside her until she was stretched to breaking. Tears ran down her face. It was funny—they were both so worldly, she and Fred Astaire, they knew everything worth knowing. How could it be that their dreams had been so innocent?

14

The carelessly dressed woman who was slumped in an armchair in Tromp's office early the next morning was not quite credible as the birthday girl of a few weeks ago. Her face was lined with something deeper than exhaustion, unless one speaks of an exhaustion of all purpose. Under the influence of the memory of the years she'd spent in this office, she felt herself falling backward in time, into lies, into childish dependency. She straightened her back and resisted the urge to lower her eyes.

Tromp was leaning forward on his elbows and looking at her with concern.

"I'm leaving Ned."

"Have you told him yet?" Tromp's vitality was of a jerky, startling nature, expressing itself in a somewhat hysterical restlessness rather than the glow of good health. Nora found herself wishing he would sit still.

"Yes, a few days ago."

"And?"

"He threatened to cut me off without a cent. As if I were one of the children." She laughed.

"Can he do that—legally?"

"I'm not going to fight him."

"He'll lose the children, you know."

"No, I don't think so. He'll tell them I don't want anything from him, that I have a hundred thousand of my own that I can always get back from my father. He knows I won't expose him. He's made it quite clear that if I try to take the children away, he'll cut them off without a cent. He can do that legally—they're over eighteen. He may be bluffing, but I can't take the chance. I want them to have the money— and a father."

"Why not let them choose?" Tromp asked.

"No. I want them protected." She sighed, and a hollow laugh broke from her lips. "Some people would say I don't trust them."

"And you accept all this with a laugh? Ah, Nora—you're in an even worse position to leave him now than you were ten years ago. You still don't know how to fight: speaking your mind to someone isn't fighting, fighting is winning, changing things in your own interest. You haven't any stake in the world. You told me on the phone that you'll never see the money you lent your father. And you're ten years older. You'll have a life of sitting at home by the telephone waiting for the world to remember you, you can't imagine how you'll suffer. But perhaps I'm wrong." He put down the pencil with which he'd been scribbling and looked at her. "Perhaps you are in a better position," he said, excited as a hound, with his body in motion behind this trace of suspicion— head, shoulders, chest, hands.

"That's not the issue. I can't live this way anymore. I'm too old. It's too filthy."

"Infidelity is not, a priori, filthy, Nora."

"I'm talking about my marriage," Nora said, sighing heavily. "Ned doesn't know what honor is. Whatever he says is so, is. No outside standards are ever brought to bear. It's like a Gulag. He tricked me out of my own money in the guise of helping my father and then he took the credit for it. I'm convinced he did it because he couldn't stand me having the autonomy."

"Is there someone else?" Tromp was looking at her intently, his pencil poised above the blotter.

"There's Lautner," she said. The relief of finally saying his name—invoking him—brought tears to her eyes.

"My God, Nora," Tromp said, banging his fist on the desk top, "you can't leave your husband for someone after—what is it?—two weeks! You're not a girl anymore. You think your children need money and protection, well, what about you? You of all people can't live without money—or a man who comes home to you at night."

Someone like Ned, he meant. Once, years ago, she'd told Tromp that she felt like a boarder in Ned's house. "What makes you think it's any different for me?" he asked.

"May I ask you a personal question?" she asked now.

"Of course."

"I know you don't love your wife. Why have you stayed married all these years?"

"My work is my life. The rest is programmatic. You'll learn the hard way, Nora. The fact is, nobody loves anybody enough. In time, everybody loves somebody else."

Yes, she knew that, he'd told her often enough; she'd quoted him for years. "You may be right, but this is something I have to do. If I suffer, I suffer."

"Why not wait a little longer? See where the thing leads. Give yourself a chance. Lautner could be gone tomorrow."

"It doesn't matter if he stays or goes. Just knowing he exists makes my present life impossible."

On her very first visit to his office, he had told her there were three things to be had out of marriage for a woman: money, children, and love. Any two out of the three made for a reasonable marriage. She had endeavored to prove him right. Now she wondered whether Tromp knew anything about the needs of women. How could he know? He was "only a man"—and the sort of man who believed that biology had a hand in shaping destiny. But if this were true, and she was more than ever convinced it was, then how, being a man, could he presume to guide her destiny without at least acknowledging that his authority in these matters was limited by gender? They weren't enemies, were they? In the end, all discussion between the sexes came to the same thing: men laid down the law and women were evasive.

"Some risks are idiotic, Nora. You'll ruin yourself. You're not strong enough to live with the consequences."

"Perhaps not, Mäarten," she said, using his given name for the first time since she'd known him, not even thinking about it, "but since I met Lautner, I haven't been lonely."

"Lonely! What makes you think Lautner will stay with you? You're very pretty and you're very smart—possibly too smart to be Ned's wife—but you're not young anymore and you have children to cope with and no money."

"Are you saying it's too late for me?"

"In this particular situation, yes."

"You know I respect you, Mäarten, but I can't accept your advice. It's wrong for me."

"Nora, this courage of yours, it won't last a minute past Lautner's leaving you."

"So what?"

"So what! Do you know what that means?"

"But I don't have the choice anymore. I'm dead either way. Maybe you can understand it better if I tell you that when I get into bed with Ned my skin crawls. Literally crawls. There's a reason for that. It's not my imagination."

He shook his head sadly. "What are your plans for the immediate future?" He leaned back in his chair and swiveled from side to side.

"I have to tell the children, and then my parents. And I have to be out of the apartment in two weeks."

"Those are not plans, Nora. Those are the demands of the situation." He shook his head again. "It would have been better if we'd done this over lunch. The patient-doctor relationship is clearly over." He drummed his fingers on the desk. An odd smile hovered around his mouth and made it quite ugly. He looked at her pointedly. "Why don't we have lunch in a day or so and continue this discussion?"

"I don't think so, Mäarten," she said, rising. "I don't think you understand the nature of my attachment to Lautner."

"Isn't it possible that you're the one who's mistaking the nature of the attachment?"

"I'm not aware that I've claimed to know what Lautner feels for me. Not a whole lot, at least not yet, I would guess. He's interested though. But I do know what I feel for him, and that's all I'm talking about." She bent to retrieve her coat from the chair.

"You're making a big mistake, Nora." He emerged from behind his massive desk and saw her to the door.

They said goodbye coldly and without looking at each other.

The next morning was particularly bleak. Nora, boarding the bus for Amherst—she was too distraught to drive—knew now that there was something as strong as mother love: the drag of desire; the self one was meant to be. If there was anything colder or more barren than the certain knowledge that mothers too could be terrorists, it was actually being one of the parties to the plot. There was the "I want—but" of the mother. Then there was the "I want" of the terrorist. Jenny once said that you didn't become an adult until you'd wittingly caused pain for someone you loved and both of you had lived with the consequences.

Valerie's smoky coloring and narrow Byzantine face were unattributable to either side of the family. She was a very private, possibly cold young woman who loved her mother passionately, far more than she loved her father. She was, therefore, deeply in his debt; Nora knew this much.

"What you want to tell me, is it about you and Dad?" Valerie asked. They were sitting in her room, in her dormitory.

Nora nodded. Her scalp tightened.

"I guess it's serious. I guess you're splitting up."

"Yes," Nora said. Her right eyelid began to twitch.

"Does Dad know you're telling us today?"

"Yes."

"Then I guess I should call him. Is he in very bad shape?"

"Yes. I'm the one who wants to leave."

"Is there someone else?"

"Not exactly. I mean, yes . . . sort of. But I'm not leaving for him."

"I thought there might be. You look so . . . I don't know—wonderful and terrible both. Is he your first lover? Do I know him?"

"No. There was someone else when I was much younger."

"Did I know him?"

"No. Look, Valerie, this is something I should have done a long time ago. Dad and I aren't suited. I waited this long because . . . well, for a lot of reasons."

"Then I'm glad for you, Mom. I really am."

Valerie's willed, emotionless sanity frightened Nora.

"Are we staying in the house or what?"

"You and Willie and Dad, yes."

"Dad?"

"He wants the house."

"But what are you going to do? Are you going to move in with this guy?"

"It's nothing like that, Val. Dad's very short of money. I'm going to look for a studio."

"Why doesn't Dad live in the studio?"

Nora shrugged.

Valerie's eyes went deader and deader as she made the connections.

"You'll be ready for a place of your own soon anyway, sweetheart."

"Don't worry about it, Mom. I'm hardly ever home these days."

Willie was slipping a record out of its jacket. His room was a lively mess. His roommate had discreetly disappeared.

"I came up to tell you that Dad and I are separating, Willie."

"You're kidding me!" He spun around, holding the record carefully, spanning it with his thumb and forefinger as if it were a basketball or an octave on the piano.

"No, darling. It's true."

He was racked with sudden laughter. He had to put the record down. "I'm sorry, Mom. I don't know why I'm laughing. I know it's not funny."

"It's all right, darling," she said, her own mouth slipping toward the shapelessness of hysteria. "It's understandable. It's just nerves." She was laughing with him now.

"Hey, promise not to tell Dad, will you?" he spat out between laughs. "He'd never understand."

"I promise."

She wiped the tears from his face. Her own grief, being older, was viscid, not soluble. They embraced. They discussed living arrangements. Through it all, Willie wore the frozen, uncomprehending look of a man struck by lightning.

Do they understand it yet, the laughing young man and his grave sister?

The next morning the sky was a brittle crystalline blue. Empty of life. The highway was glazed with ice across which a slow-moving caravan of cars skidded in a kind of balletic improvisation of no mean beauty. Nora, on her way to her parents' house in New Jersey, felt like a carsick child on a compulsory Sunday drive. The interior of the bus was chafingly hot; the heat blasted from a source directly under her. The driver was smoking a cheap cigar. Her stomach rebelled.

"Can you open the window for me, please?" she asked the man in the aisle seat after struggling with it desperately. "I need some air."

"They're sealed," he said.

"I think I'm going to be sick," she warned him, leaning abruptly over her lap.

He leaped to his feet but wasn't quick enough. Large chowderlike splotches appeared on his glistening black shoes, and the legs of his dark trousers were spotted with bits and pieces of stuff dredged up from the bottom of her stomach. She raised her head and saw him standing, shudderingly, in the aisle. His face was twisted with revulsion. He was at some physical limit himself, ready to throw up at the slightest intensification of the reality of the moment—another whiff of the thickly shifting oatmealy pond at their feet would do it. He rubbed at his trousers with a monogrammed handkerchief. J.G.

"I'm so sorry," Nora said. "I don't know what to say." She made an effort to clean up the mess with some tissues from her bag. She sprayed the floor with breath freshener. She gave J.G. a packaged moist towel. "I'm sorry there aren't any vacant seats," she said.

J.G. nodded curtly. His fastidiousness forbade their becoming acquainted. She studied him from her corner. He had narrow, deeply set, dead brown eyes, a sharp nose underlined by a pencil-thin and melodramatically sinister black mustache, and tight lips. The true shape of his mouth was hidden by disgust. His sideburns were very long and thin and meticulously barbered, descending from his hat brim almost like strings. Gaucho stuff. He kept his hat on even though it prevented him from leaning his head against the seat. His eyes reminded her of Ned's.

How can she leave her children behind?

Dear God, how can she take them? They're no more fit for the world—for Lautner—than she is.

The driver braked suddenly and the bus skidded sharply to the right. From his curled-up position in the far corner of his seat, J.G. bounced against Nora like a hard-hit ball. He recovered with an effort, cursing under his breath. Nora saw that a look of malice had replaced the horror on his face.

She leaned her head against the window and closed her eyes, passing the next hour in a daze of motion-induced misery, tangled as if in strands of sound—many different shades of gray yarn. There was the high-speed whine of the tires, the hum of the engine, the rushing water sound of air pressure as it built up outside the window and dissipated and built up again, sounds that were indiscrete and uninterrupted, deadeningly regular, seemingly without beginning or end. A universe of sound. She felt heavy-lidded and slack-jawed. Her head was in a slow, druggy whirl. She surrendered herself to a state that was not quite willed forgetfulness, not quite boredom, or sleep, or motion-sickness, but which had strong elements of each. Still, the dose wasn't heavy enough to eclipse the painful awareness that she was about to shackle her parents with an irreversible grief.

The arrival of the bus changed everything, imposing a velocity and a strictness, a sort of military discipline, on what had been loose and flabby and haphazard. Outside the bus window, she could see her mother waving eagerly. She felt as if a pair of hands cuffed her neck. She realized she had never before approached her mother except subserviently. Her head began to pound with a fierce, surflike monotony. Her lungs ripened with the pressure of discovery; she thought they might burst the skin of her chest. She clawed at the garrotting panic as if it were an actual assailant.

She wiped her mouth and buttoned her coat. J.G. fled. She waited until the bus was empty. When she stood up, she felt slippery and dizzy, mildly astonished by her body's treasonous behavior. Even with her mother's concerned kiss burning on her cheek, she had difficulty believing in the approaching moment, the moment-of-harm, even while the thick-fingered bandit in her was slipping on his dreadful gloves.

"Before I forget, Nora," her mother said as she pulled into the driveway of a gloomy, Tudor-style house, breaking the silence in the car, "I found some more swatches for you. A new fabric place opened in that shopping center outside town where Dad has a store. These are lighter than the other ones. I thought with the children away at college you might risk something pale."

"That's very sweet of you, Mom. Thanks."

"I wish you'd given me a little more notice," she said to Nora some time later. Nora had taken a shower and washed her hair. She felt better but she had no appetite. "These are just some leftovers from a dinner party I had last week. I took everything out of the freezer right after you called." The table was covered with platters of food.

"It looks delicious."

"Well, it was better last week, but with so little notice ... "

Nora was too preoccupied to carry her protest any further.

"You're very thin," her mother said. "And you have circles under your eyes." Her mother grew thin in front of Nora's eyes. "Haven't you been sleeping well, Nora?"

A broad band of cold brilliant sunlight entered glitteringly through the mullioned bay window as her mother spoke. It lit up the painting behind Nora's head, her father's favorite object—a maiden in a diaphanous robe sitting in a ruined, desolate garden, sadly plucking the strings of a harp. Nora's mother sat off to one side, robed in shadow like an inquisitor.

"I have some things on my mind, Mom."

"Well ... here are the swatches I told you about." She arranged them, off-white to beige, like a hand of winning cards, face up on the dining-room table. "You can look at them while I bring in the coffee."

"What do you think of this one?" she asked when she was seated again. "It has the barest touch of khaki. I think it's my favorite."

Nora took a deep breath. "I won't be needing any fabrics, Mom. I'm leaving Ned, and he's going to keep the house. The children are going to live with him."

"That's impossible. Don't say that, Nora! Not you and Ned! You're different." She swayed a little as if she might faint. She returned the serving spoon to the platter of rolled and stuffed chicken breasts. Then she sagged back in her sky-blue velvet chair.

"It's true, Mother. I'm sorry."

She stared at Nora in disbelief. "I knew you were unhappy, Nora, but that was so many years ago." She shuffled the swatches without looking at them. "Do you remember, you brought the children to stay with us for a few weeks? Daddy and I talked it over, but we were sure you could work it out, and obviously you did. You never looked unhappy after that. I'm sure you can work it out this time. Nothing's perfect. And think of the unhappiness you'll be causing everyone. And what for? What's it all for? Whatever it is, it can't be worth it."

Nora was silent.

"What's going to happen to you, Nora? You're only a woman and you're not a young woman either. Who'll marry you now?" Her mother paused, a vicious-feeling pause, and then, with a look of horror not unlike J.G.'s, she said, "Don't tell me there's another man!"

"It doesn't matter if there's another man or not, Mother. It's not even a matter of happiness. There's a more decent way to live, that's all. That's the issue."

"Decent? Your life is more than decent. What you're doing *now* is what's indecent. It's pure selfishness. Not live with your own children? You'd hurt so many people for your own pleasure?" She stood up and walked around the table to where Nora was sitting. She stood over her, shaking with emotion.

"I can't do it anymore, Mother."

"Do what? Live a decent life? What's wrong with your life? You have everything a woman could ask for—a lot more than I ever got. You wouldn't do this if you loved me." She began to cry and then, astonishingly, to pummel Nora's head with tiny, ladylike fists, a rain of small, bitter blows.

"Mother, please!" Nora cried out, covering her head with

her arms, but her mother was past hearing, in some realm of private indulgence, in an ecstasy of self-expression. "You wouldn't do this to me if you loved me," she said with a scream, drumming at the bowed head under her hands.

Nora couldn't move. She couldn't breathe for a minute. Something huge was happening to her, happening right on top of her, so that she couldn't describe it or even take it in. But she could embrace it, and she did. She stood up suddenly. "You wouldn't do this to me if you loved *me!*" she said, seizing her mother's wrists and immobilizing them.

"I'm asking you as a mother not to do this," her mother sobbed.

"And I'm asking you as a daughter—let me have my life." She was sobbing now too.

"I deserve some respect. I'm your mother."

"Don't I deserve any? I'm your daughter."

"What are you doing?" her mother screamed.

"I'm doing what you're doing—bullying you with my pain."

"No, no, you're not. I would never hurt you like this. I never hurt my mother. Never."

"Then why are you hurting me, Mother? Why aren't you helping me? Why are you doing this? Do you hate me that much?"

"I only want you to be happy."

"You're lying. You can't stand the thought of my being happy. You want me to stay with that dead man. You don't care what it costs—that's your idea of virtue. You're just like him. Oh, God, you're just like Ned." She flung her mother's wrists away from her as if they had suddenly become snakes. She sank down in her chair.

"I don't know what you're talking about, Nora. You're too smart for me. You were always too smart. You have your father's mind and you twist everything. EVERYTHING!"

The front door slammed, silencing them both.

"I'm home," her father called out.

Nora wiped her eyes with a napkin.

A moment later her father walked into the dining room, alternately smiling and blowing on his hands. His blue eyes were tear-glistened with cold, his cheeks appled like a child's. He gave Nora a smacking, star-ridden kiss. And, then, straightening up, he glanced at "his picture," the one behind her head; he'd "discovered" the maiden in a junk shop shortly after Nora's marriage to Ned. "How come the visit?" he asked. And then, seeing his wife's face: "What's the matter, Mary?"

"She's leaving Ned. She came to tell us she's leaving her husband and her children," her mother said, and walked out of the room.

Her father sat down heavily, like an old man. His color faded. "It's true?" he asked.

"Yes."

"You're sure you know what you're doing?"

"I'm sure."

"I suppose Ned will do right by you financially, but if you or the kids ever need anything, you know I'm here. I'll take care of you just like I always have."

"Thank you, Dad." Her voice cracked, and she turned her face away to hide the tears. "I know how much I'm upsetting you. I'm really sorry." She was a lesser Isaac risen from the altar without God's permission. But isn't it her duty to live? She doesn't believe in a God of torment. A God of vengeance and of justice, yes, and a God who confronts you with injustice as a test of humanity, but not a God who hates women and children. Not a barbarian.

"We'll have to straighten out the business of the hundred thousand. I don't know when that will be, but as soon as I can free up some cash I'll see you get it back." Her father's sigh fell on her like a sack of wet ash.

"There's no rush, Dad. I know you're very tight for money just now. I can manage."

"What's Ned giving you?"

"I don't know for sure. The lawyers will work something out."

"Nora, he's a very hard negotiator, a tough man with a dollar, a real nickel-and-dimer."

"Yes, I know."

"There's no chance this is just temporary?"

"No. I won't go back under any circumstances."

"Is there someone else? Is someone else going to take care of you?"

"No. No one else is going to take care of me. There may or may not be someone, but it's not on that basis."

Her father's concern for her showed in his face, but she could feel his disapproval growing. "Who's the guy? What does he do?"

"It's nothing definite. I'd rather not discuss it."

"Why? Is he married?"

"It's nothing like that."

"There's no sense kidding you, Nora. You're gonna have to be patient. You know, Ned owns a big piece of me."

"I didn't know. Does that mean part of my money is going to pay him off—and not just Lloyd?"

"I can't cut him out of my life just because he's not my son-in-law anymore. I need him. You know how delicate Herbert is."

"I see." What she saw made her sick.

"As long as you understand how things are. And if worst comes to worst, you know you always have a home with Mom and me."

A stooped, gray-haired man buzzed her into the vault. She signed his book. He compared her signature with the one on Ned's card and then smiled cordially, granting her a momentary citizenship in his little principality of wealth and secret documents. She followed him down a narrow aisle. He used her key and one of his own to unlock the door to Ned's box, and then, after sliding it from its enclosure, inch by scant inch, he carried it, with achingly slow steps, to a small room where he placed it on a good-sized table as carefully as if it might detonate on impact. "Take as much time as you need, ma'am," he said. "I'll be at my desk when you're ready to leave." He shuffled out. Nora locked the door behind him. Alone in the windowless cell, she sighed. Lifting the lid of the box, she looked around guiltily, as if she owed someone an explanation. She wanted to mount a platform and protest her innocence to the world. But if the jewelry in the box was hers, why did she feel like a thief?

This was only the second thing in her life she'd ever done for money. The first was to marry Ned, a decision that had been taken partly to ensure that she would never have to do anything for money again. Whatever personal atrocities were committed against her afterward she chose to regard as expiation for that crime, suffering them sensibly, considering in this manner that she was paying her debt. All this ended for her the moment she took her trinkets and her diamond engagement ring from the box. Her pulse was racing. She felt sick to her stomach. Something was over. Nothing had yet taken its place.

15

Things pulled down; down, then apart. God, how they pulled. This was a physical fact, a concrete thing, not a thought about a fact; not something witnessed by the mind from the sidelines; not a mental construct. To plot an accurate curve or a real history of anyone's freedom, one would have to write down everything, every minute. An exhaustive journal, microminute by microminute. Impossible. Still, the minutes had come to this: Nora thought she might die.

No melodrama. Some wasting illness or other summoned and made welcome by her; a temporary hell. It happens all the time. Those bonds that until now had obliged her to live had all snapped, given way under the freight of the thing she'd dreamed of and prayed for—a great love. Such a love had been granted her, but instead of being reason to live, it was, rather, the very thing that drew her on toward death. The future was known to her—it was the world in which her loss of Lautner would occur. The future hung on the walls of her love like a calendar of death. The past was of no consequence; she hadn't shared it with him. She had only the present moment, the world extant as she drew breath, the present discontinuous moment with all its pain and terror and uncertainty. And she saw how, in the throes of the terrible and wonderful present, she clutched at the coattails of Lautner's greatness as if she would rectify the mistake of her life in him. And, seeing this, she hated herself. She thought her love had obliterated everything fine in her—her loyalty, her unselfishness, her vision of a purposeful life— and thrown her into a drowning pool, a gray pool of ghosts and ghostly emptiness where, although she heard desperate cries for help on every side in the watery darkness, she couldn't stir herself to rescue anyone. How could she, when she felt no kinship for anyone, no pity? And in the absence of kinship and pity everything was degraded, ugly to her. She had expected, having cut herself off from Ned, to make a fresh start. Instead, things seemed dirtier than ever, the failures greater. Lautner's improbability had disrupted the natural process of cause and effect, upsetting all the ordinary balances of her life, estranging her first from the world and then, gradually, from herself. In truth, she was sick to death of her self-righteousness, sick of the excess of her suffering, the excess of her love. She told herself that she had much more than a woman could reasonably expect from life—

hadn't her dreams come true?—and yet she had never been more bitterly despairing. And what was her despair but a morass of self-pity, a vast personal ingratitude to all that was divine?

She saw all this and she condemned herself, and yet, hard as she tried, she could find no way to restart the engine of her will. She was utterly dependent on Lautner for that.

"What would happen if I asked you for proof of your power?" Nora asked him as they strolled, arm in arm, down Fifth Avenue in brilliant sunshine.

"Why? Are you beginning to doubt my identity? Are you turning philosopher on me?"

"I don't understand you at all," she sighed.

"I'm not comprehensible. Why try?" His eyes were narrowed against the sun.

"Why bother to live, you mean?"

"What sort of proof do you have in mind?"

"You know it can't possibly be anything I could imagine."

They paused to look in a jeweler's window. "Do you like that?" he asked, pointing to a filigreed gold bracelet inlaid with rubies and emeralds.

"I don't know. I can't say jewelry interests me much anymore."

"Not even the kind that suggests luscious conversations ending in kisses? You're not greedy anymore?"

"What do I have to be greedy about? I have you for company."

"Be very careful, Nora. Annihilate desire and you annihilate the mind."

"In that case, I'm safe—because as we both know I'm hopelessly greedy for you."

He laughed, thereby acquainting her with the fact that the truth needn't always be a highly somber and fiercely punishing affair. "Are you sure you want proof of my power?" he asked as they resumed their walk. "I know it pleases you to flirt with danger, but I've seen no evidence that you're prepared to surrender to a situation, or to a man, or to an idea, for that matter. You haven't been willing to set foot in my universe. I've had to stay in yours."

If by his universe he meant an imaginative landscape kingdoms richer than her own, one whose climate of temperament was so sensuously transcendent that thought and feeling were inseparable, then surely she wanted to enter it. She was ready. She told him so.

"I'll show you God, then," he said promptly but without undue emphasis, as if it were an everyday offer.

"Oh, no. Thank you very much but no," she said, nearly shouting. "I refuse. I refuse categorically. That's not what I meant. I have no desire to see God."

"Which of the myriad meanings of the word 'see' are you using, Nora?" The abrupt foreshortening from the casual to the dire in his tone of voice frightened her into silence. He paused and faced her. His hands rested on her shoulders like a harness. His contempt and pity mingled with the smoke from his burning cigarette and stung her eyes. "I am offering you a chance to stand in the presence of faultless knowledge. Everything settled, in place, pinned down for all time." His breath was hot and dry with smoke.

"No," she said, timid and courageous by turns. "I don't want to give up my doubts. I have no intention of living a life in which faith is irrelevant. Besides, how would I know that what I felt or saw—whatever—was real, and not just something you'd manufactured for the occasion?"

"Use your head, Nora. It's just that margin of doubt that would leave room for your so-called faith."

"But then it's not proof!"

"You know, my dear, you value me because I don't bore you, and yet when I offer you the ultimate amusement, you turn me down. You use me as a teacher, shamelessly, yet when I offer you the highest form of knowledge, you refuse it out of hand. Why is that?" He loomed over her but his face wasn't unkind.

She sighed again. "I guess I'd rather have less of everything than risk losing it all. A woman's life—my life, I
mean—is geared to prevent the worst from happening.
Who's going to protect me if I don't protect myself?"

"You mean you'd rather be unhappy and ignorant?"

"No. I'm saying I can be smart and happy on less than
what you're offering—and if I can't, well, there are compen-
sations. I mean, one sees everything so much more clearly
when one is unhappy—and things seem worth more, somehow."

They strolled down the channel in Rockefeller Center in
silence. They watched the skaters for a while.

"You're small-time, Nora," he said finally, flinging his cigarette into a potted evergreen. "Your idea of courage is to be
extravagant with your husband's money without his permission."

There was nothing to say. She tried to free her face from
the mask of pain that had settled on it. She tried to make her
humiliation an attribute of dignity, like a skater who falls
executing a difficult maneuver but whose courage, in the
form of perseverance, wins one's deepest respect. She
couldn't let him go. The world was where he was.

"Talk to me," he said, appearing beside her on the bridle
path without warning another day.

"Talk?"

"Yes."

"About what?"

"Anything you choose."

"Now? While we're running?"

"Yes."

"But I can't."

"Why not?"

"Breath, for one thing. Your pace is too fast for me. And
anyway, it's not natural to order someone to talk."

He gave her a withering look which implied that nothing of the commerce between human beings was natural.

"Talk," he ordered, upping the pace. "Say anything. Initiate a conversation. Pretend it's a matter of life and death. See if you can't tell me a story this time."

His tone of voice had become progressively more contemptuous. She was breathless with exertion and dread, her mouth filled with a kind of sawdust of self-absorption. She recognized her state of mind as belonging to that period of her childhood in which most everything but being sweetly and outwardly submissive had been beyond her grasp. Luckily, more had not been demanded of her until one day a hateful, pig-faced teacher tried to frighten her into learning arithmetic.

"The class will remain seated until Nora gives us the correct answer."

She hadn't yet learned to faint. She was too proud to cry. She did what she could. She turned herself to stone—stone being more stubborn than flesh. Eventually the dismissal bell rang. Eventually she grew up.

She groaned, the only story she had. Under his tutelage she'd learned how to respond to serious inquiry, but she didn't know how to initiate it. She might have chattered, but she'd lost the knack. Her eyes were as cold as his, but oddly dry as mouths go dry. His were a labyrinth of cold, jellylike contempt.

"You're hopeless, having your little tantrum of silence. Your self-righteousness is without limits. You say you wish you could believe in God as spirit, yet you treat spirit as if it were matter to be dusted and cleaned, as if God were merely the Supreme Man. You'll mother Him, you'll seduce Him, you'll adore Him, you'll even define Him—which always makes me nervous—but you won't respect Him."

She bit the inside of her mouth. She thought: He must think I'm worthwhile if he's willing to invest this much energy in me. But what if he's right about me? Oh, dear God, what if he's right?

A horse approached from behind just then at a near-gallop. The rider was yelling for assistance and cursing the animal in an almost musical alternation. Nora took her eyes off the track. She stumbled. She tried to maintain her balance and failed. She fell among the cinders; her knees were bleeding, her palms studded with bits of gravel. She tried to get to her feet and failed. Her ankles had somehow become lashed together by a rusted wire hanger. She crawled to the side of the bridle path. The now riderless horse paraded slowly past her. There was immense dignity in the way it raised and lowered its head.

She freed herself of the snare and stood up. A few feet away, the rider was dusting himself off and shaking his fist at the retreating horse. Lautner was gone. She resumed her run. There was no choice, since she'd fallen midway around the track. Seeing her pump her bloody knees, approaching runners smiled benevolently. "Way to go, sweetheart," one of them yelled. "Right on there, babe," someone else said and made a victory sign.

Near the end of her run, Lautner appeared at her elbow and said, "On the other hand, Nora, keep in mind that you have a fineness of spirit, a deep streak of generosity, and real emotional courage. You're a liar but you're also whole-hearted. You're far from hopeless."

Another day he surprised her in the supermarket. She was pushing a wire cart filled with groceries. As long as she lived in Ned's house, she attended to his domestic needs.

"What is it you really want, Nora? What are your ambitions?"

He looked rested, younger, sinewy. Also he'd cut his hair quite short. He resembled Prince Hal in his new and easy intimacy, and his voice was so warmly inflected that she relaxed her guard. "You'll just laugh," she said, in a way that was partly flirtatious.

"What makes you think so?"

"Men always laugh when women are open about their ambitions—if their ambitions are large, I mean." She was debating between two nationalities of bottled water. She chose the Italian in spite of a recent outbreak of typhoid around Naples. "Will you promise not to laugh?"

"Oh, come on, Nora," he said, impatiently, "just spit it out."

"Please don't talk to me like that."

At the sound of her words of warning, his nostrils widened perceptibly, as if he'd suddenly found himself inhaling solid matter. His lips began to twitch, his chin to quiver. He clasped himself around the middle and rocked back and forth. His legs trembled, his feet drummed the floor. The violence of his laughter was frightening. People turned their attention from the bottles and cans.

"And please don't laugh at me," she said, desperately.

This request sent him into another spasm, more convulsive than the first. He was staggering and squeezing his ribs together to ease the ache, pointing a finger at her and howling with the powerful open jaws of a great cat.

"Don't do this. Please." Don't trifle with me, she meant.

He fairly spit his laughter in her face.

Something in her snapped. The line mooring her to caution? She raised her hand and reached back behind her head as if something concrete—courage, maybe—waited there to be grabbed. She started to bring her closed hand around fast and with all her strength, knowing that when her hand made contact with his face there would be a sharp crack like that of a ball well batted, and something in her arched up joyfully at the thought. It remained a thought only. The counterweights of size and sanity saved her from caprice. Her hand wavered.

His hand flicked out and caught her still-uplifted wrist. "I do not take orders from anyone—ever," he said, with an icy gravity.

Her wrist might have been a twig in the jaws of a lion.

"I'm sorry," she said, terrified. "I wasn't going to—"

"I've given you enough latitude. From now on, we'll do things my way," he broke in.

"And if I refuse?" she asked, venturing a bravery she didn't feel.

"You won't ever see me again." He dropped her wrist and with it all pretense of equality. Perhaps love requited is the only true equality.

What had she been thinking? That this was some sort of game to be terminated only at her pleasure? That there would be no consequences? That his psychic stratagems were within her grasp? That he was just another one of us? That, given time and the power of love, she could crack the code?

She must have had brain fleas.

Clearly, he was accountable to no one and nothing, free to come and go as it pleased him. It was she who was condemned, by obsession or love or both, to wait.

"Keep in mind who you are," he raged, knowing his beauty was never more binding on her than when it was infused with terror. "You are not me."

I can live without you, she told herself, discovering even as the thought was taking form the magnificent and shapely truth of impossibility.

I am not you, she wrote on the blackboard of her consciousness.

I am not you.

I am not you.

I am not you.

I am myself. I am my only enterprise. I am my only imperative.

She was haggard with self-consciousness. "I love you," she told him in her most self-pitying voice.

"Do you?" he taunted. "Tell me about it. Do you love me for myself alone?"

"I don't know if I do or not," she said, too frightened now

to lie. "Strip yourself of the world and history. Strip yourself of God. Be like me. Be a supplicant. And we'll find out."

"You're learning," he said, not without pleasure.

"I'm not you," she told him, humbly then, "but without you, I'm nothing."

16

Nora had been two bodiless hours behind the wheel of a rented yellow car before the sun broke through the dense cloud cover like a spotlight burning a hole through paper. Beams of moist pink-and-gold light poured in slanting, celestial lines through the narrow opening and touched the snow-capped peaks of the mauve hills as if in blessing. A fat, sun-fringed cloud gradually assumed the shape of a dragon and breathed fire across the whole vast plain of the sky, which, thus ignited, burst into sudden, brilliant flames. Nora applauded silently.

In dread of being late, she was early. She was always early. Even if she detained her physical self, her nerves raced on ahead. She was already with Lautner. But surely he couldn't have meant to meet her here in this bulldozed and tarred-over developer's tract in the bowels of the mountains. She pulled onto the soft shoulder and checked the map he'd given her. Yes, the intersection was circled in red. She exited at the ramp. The sign that rose over the entrance to the shopping center said PYRAMID MALL. She parked her car on one of the thousand pruned beds of asphalt. The lot was nearly full although it was a Sunday morning.

She took a picnic hamper from the back seat, slammed the door, and started off. The collision was inevitable: she and the child both walking the curve of some rainbow of thought. The child looked up and wailed; a desperate flame-cheeked beauty, a golden fallen apple. She bent to rescue him from the jutting cliffs of her knees and ankles. His will permitting, she would mother away his tears, but his real mother came running. An infant in a swaying canvas sling slept at her breast. The child's mother was fair-skinned and thin-haired, plagued with prominent lips, which crept forward to cover her large teeth.

"Bad boy, Darrell," she said, but her voice was too weary or gentle to carry any conviction.

"It was my fault," Nora said. "I didn't see him. I'm terribly sorry."

The woman appraised her with harshly intelligent eyes. The voice had been a dumb, gentle lie, like so many women's voices.

Below eye level, the compact, wailing little body was once again launching itself into space. The bravery of some children was shaming. His mother's eyes followed him, and then her body was dragged after as if she were attached to him by a leash.

Nora was a few yards from the main entrance to the shopping center when a horn blast tore the quiet Sunday air to shreds. She shied like a doe and bolted from the path. Three silver buses, tailing each other as closely as elephants, drove by. A sign in the window of the lead bus read: THE PRECIOUS GOSPEL SINGERS OF HACKENSACK, NEW JERSEY. The necks of the open-mouthed passengers were arched toward heaven like ebony bows. Through the shaded-glass windows and steel-ribbed bus walls, one could hear the thump and fury of sung prayer.

The buses drew up to the main entrance. The women who emerged were chatty and high-spirited, comfortably overweight, robustly maternal with corseted, oversized breasts. Their choir robes were the color of ruby glass and were slung over their arms in plastic dry-cleaning bags. The men were weary and genial-looking. They walked with effort, like men whose feet hurt, men who ran elevators or waited on tables. The leader of the choir was wearing a hokey, broad-shouldered, spangled white satin suit and a gold ring on every finger. He looked at Nora briefly but with fervent eyes. She felt herself becoming crazily receptive. "Body forth, girl. Send your body forth to God," he seemed to be urging her with his eyes. "You hear me, girl! God is God, girl, and we are who we are." So sure, so sure of who we are. No, no, she argued with her eyes. I'm Miss Nefertiti, sleek-faced as an ancient cat. My eyes can burn flesh from bone.

The leader raised his arms. His rings glittered in the sunlight. "O Lord," he sang.

"O Lord," the choir responded.

All across the parking lot, heads popped out over car roofs. His arm slashed down like a scalpel. There was an abrupt and bloody silence. He winked improbably at Nora, then led his flock through the portals of Pyramid Mall and into, I suppose, the presence of Almighty God.

A number of people were clustered at the foot of a portable stage just inside the main entrance, watching a seedy-complected magician tempt a flock of doves, one at a time, from the crown of his top hat. His act was accompanied by an electric organ. Nora paused and put down the hamper. The birds' eyes were fixed, stupidly staring like the eyes of small-time killers in old movies. Their coats had been dyed the colors of ice cream—peach and pistachio and strawberry and lemon—and their savory tailfeathers fanned out around their plump bottoms like tutus. Once each bird was released, it flapped energetically across the stage to land on the outstretched arms of the magician's assistant, a young woman—more girl than woman—possibly the magician's daughter, with a sturdy, sweetly blank-faced look and an air of hickhood about her that was enhanced by the Alice-blue strapless prom dress she was wearing. When the transfer was complete, the magician rushed to the rear of the stage and returned with a large, covered structure on wheels. He whisked off the cloth drape with an elaborate flourish and the audience, confronted by a cartoonlike replica of Saint Mark's Cathedral in Venice, applauded vigorously.

In response to the opening bars of the "Malagueña," the bird-burdened daughter dropped to her knees and bowed her head. One at a time, the birds left the trembling cross of her body and flew to the golden dome of the cathedral. When they were comfortably settled in, they folded their wings over their heads and cooed. The audience applauded. The magician and his daughter bowed. Nora was about to move on when a meteor shower of canary-yellow particles hit the cathedral dome and sprayed in all directions. The birds soared from the roof, banked like a squadron of fighter planes, and dived straight at the heads of the crowd, bringing on a general stampede. Nora stayed where she was but her hands flew to helmet her skull. She saw the magician running back and forth across the stage, calling to his birds. His daughter covered her eyes and screamed. An appropriately nerve-shattering oratorio, the gift of a vengeful God to some twentieth-century composer, perhaps the organist himself, further agitated the crowd. A group of teen-age boys, carrying empty boxes of popcorn, bolted from the center of the confusion, laughing boisterously and slapping one another's backs.

The clock that had been marking time in her mind since dawn now began to tick as loudly as a bomb. She opened her bag and checked the tiny grandfather clock. Three minutes. She ran the remaining length of the arcade. The cobblestones, though rough to the eye, were by some trick of technology smooth underfoot. Slippery. She glanced quickly at the illuminated floor plan and raced across the main plaza to where he'd instructed her to wait. She took up her post in front of the J. C. Penney department store.

He appeared, after a moment that seemed interminable,

on the opposite side of the small wooden footbridge in the center of the plaza, around which a few park benches had been placed. He approached with a swift, careless yet vehement gait, walking as emphatically as a dancer performing. The soles of his shoes, hitting the cobblestones, made the hard, thudding sound of hoofs. He was dressed in the narrow black clothes of a mime, or a burglar, as she was also, by coincidence—or perhaps by fate. Perhaps it was her fate to be an imitator. His torso was insinuatingly lithe despite his angularity and his height. His eyes were the color of moonlit pools—mercury gray. He was the most brilliant-faced man she'd ever seen. The most solitary. The most powerful.

He stopped to toss a penny into the sunken turquoise pond beneath the bridge, as if by such an act he could claim a strictly human significance, but she perceived his presence as darkness fringed with the possibility of light. She interpreted the lines that traversed his high, steep forehead as hellish trails of sadness and regret which her ministering presence would erase. She would be his Cordelia, with this alteration: love would lend her some of its immortality.

He resumed his walk but broke off again after a few steps, this time to watch a pair of adolescent lovers whose progress across the plaza was hampered by the manner in which they were physically engaged, the girl's head pillowed in the hollow of the boy's neck, she on utmost tiptoe, he with slightly bent knees, their arms encoiled around each other's necks.

He turned his head, shaking it fiercely, ran his fingers through his hair, scratched his cheeks—raked them—with both hands, and, in his preoccupation, jostled against one of the benches. His face darkened with fury—he was hardly tolerant of obstacles—as he skidded backward and nearly fell.

No doubt he sensed her presence, for in the next instant he raised his eyes and found hers, still some distance away. He straightened up and began walking toward her, unhurriedly, with half-opened arms and a kind of smile, a slight parting of the lips which, when paired with the upward curve of his eyelid, may or may not have been a gesture of welcome.

Well, here they were then, nearly met—the guardian of disharmony and his penniless ward—on a morning made blue without end by the extent of her hopes. Silken pennants of many colors flying from the bridge, playthings of an artificial breeze, made smartly nautical sounds, a sort of drumroll of slaps, as if to announce the coming of the tall, darkly attired, shockingly handsome hero who moved toward the waiting woman with all the captured grace of twilight falling. Seeing his beauty, the lady could hardly breathe. She felt her awe as deeply as if it were the only permissible emotion. Her hand flew to her throat.

"Nora," he said. He took her hand from her throat and raised it to his lips, endowing it, poor dead thing, with life.

At his touch, a rush of blood like a false spring heated her pale face, and her cheeks bloomed briefly with the beauty of force-roses, but when the wintry air hidden in the folds of his coat reached her, the blush died away and her cheeks shriveled and she curled inward, away from him. It would not surprise her if one day soon she gave up clinging, gave it up entirely, and dropped, possibly gratefully, to the earth.

She wanted to breathe his name aloud. The occasion called for a name, but only such a name as would awaken nothing by association, a name as entirely without precedent as he himself was. "I wish I knew what to call you," she said, tossing her voice toward the pool as if it were a wish-granting penny.

He smiled crookedly; the cigarette pulled the left side of his mouth into a small inlet off the main body of his lips. It bobbed like a tiny boat on the waves of his speech. "If you like, we can exchange names," he said.

"What for?" she asked, too quickly, and in a voice hinting of alarm.

"For the Pythagoreans, it was a way of sharing the virtues they admired in each other."

They were enveloped in the coarse urgencies, the noisy and unconfinable greed of a growing crowd of Sunday shoppers. Over the din of human wants and human worries, she could hear faintly the reassuring sound of The Precious Gospel Singers as they shoutingly praised the Lord. The heart lifted to certain entreaties whether the mind permitted it or not.

"Did they share each other's vices as well?" she asked.

"Your chronology is a bit self-serving," he said. "Vice is a Judeo-Christian construct. Well, do you accept?"

"What? Call you Nora? I couldn't."

"Not even to learn what I would call you?"

"No, not even then."

"Well, that's an interesting turn," he said, offering her his arm.

She curled outward again at the warmth of his touch. It was the sun of male arms, not a mother's, never a mother's, that she grew toward. They walked for perhaps half a mile up and down the four radiating corridors of that sealed universe, that pyramid, that vault or tomb, which, like its ancient namesake, was stocked with stuff judged to be of worth in the next world because it was touted as having had value in this one.

The shelves held health food and junk food, shoes with leather uppers and man-made soles, no-care clothes, watches and other jewelry, pots and pans, clocks and candles, locks and keys and window bars, and seemingly all of the written expressions of a society save its literature, including one new genre—The Word as printed on a tee-shirt, as in TRY GOD. Or, alternatively, HEAVEN CAN WAIT. Or, for those utterly bored by reminders of the celestial, S.O.M.F. (sit on my face).

Fatso and *The Jerk*, two separate movies, were playing at the local theater.

Nearly everyone was overweight.

"Why did you bring me here?" Nora asked. Their reflections in the window of a smokehouse emporium startled her. Narrow and black, the two of them looked like experienced jewel thieves, cat burglars.

"This is an authentic American invention, like the automobile," he said.

"What does that have to do with me?"

"Oh, let's say I want to reconcile you to your country."

"Women don't have countries. They have families." She remembered she was lately unfamilied. "Reconciliation seems unlikely in a place like this," she said. She had a nervous and utterly humorless horror of popular taste.

"We'll see" was all he said. But, ah, with what sweet male confidence he said it. Did he mean they would see the same thing?

"Here we are," he said, ushering her before him through an archway at the end of one of the arcades and into the high-ceilinged lobby of the Pyramid Mall Motel.

The lobby was paneled in plastic barn-siding; possibly the wall-to-wall carpeting was meant to recall autumn leaves, but leaves whose shrill colors were mercifully unknown in nature. The furniture was large, blunt-brown, and clumsy, Saracen filtered through Chicago. Remembering how history revenged itself on the Saracens, Nora managed a skimpy smile. Off to the right, behind a low wall covered with English ivy that clung with such morose obstinacy that it had to be plastic, was a large indoor swimming pool set under a dome of stately Plexiglas. The rays of the morning sun shone through it, stippling the turquoise water. Guests in swimsuits were lounging at umbrella-shaded tables. The steady breeze—a continuous waft of forced hot air—and the erratic spume kicked up by several noisy children, lent an air of charmless animation to the scene.

"I hate what's happened to this country," Nora said. She longed subversively for Venice (oh, to be with him in Venice), for the cool restfulness of watery palaces, for the light that filtered through sieves of silver and cast Indian-tinsel shadows, and oh, for the greedy suck of the sea at her hem. She was silent as they crossed the lobby, stiff with disapproval.

The desk clerk could hardly rise from her chair. She heaved herself forward at the same time, to conserve motion, pushing the register toward them. Her arms were short and plump, ending in tiny, almost pointed wrists. Nora signed her name. The clerk looked at the sole signature and then, knowingly, at Lautner. She slid the key across the counter.

They climbed a short flight of spongy stairs. They traversed a many-doored, penetratingly dank corridor. Their room was bitterly cold. A sign on the back of the door said, "You have sixty seconds after closing this door to activate the heat. Simply place the plastic card hanging from the lock into the appropriate slot on the opposite door jamb and the heat will come on automatically." High up on the wall over her head, behind a metal grille, a rackety whirring commenced. Nora remembered that she'd left the picnic hamper near the magician's stage. "I'll be right back," she said. As she unlocked the door, the heat went off.

"Not now," Lautner said.

"But it's the food," she told him.

"Not now."

She locked the door and reinserted the card. The heater resumed its clacking. One of the lamps began to flicker like a flame in the wind. She walked over to it and tightened the bulb, grateful to be occupied. Her hands were shaking.

He turned from the window, having drawn the Fiberglas drapes, and motioned her to be seated. She had her choice of two sultan-sized beds separated from each other by a small, wood-grained, brown plastic night table. She lowered herself cautiously to the inside edge of the bed near the window. Her feet trembled in the alley between them.

Where she was, lamps were blazing. The room had no corners. It was an abyss of now hot, now cold, light, a bowl or cave of light, scoured clean of all shadow. She felt as if she were about to embark across an ocean for a newer, harsher place, perhaps to fall off the edge of the known universe into knowingness. Her mouth was dry, her palms were wet. A pulse, tumid with blood, beat insistently in her throat and between her thighs.

He sat down opposite her on the other bed. His head bent toward hers as if for a confession. The dark almonds of his eyes were studded with cloves of light, a killing light. His kiss, when it came, was as swift as the prick of a pin. She closed his eyelids gently with her fingertips. She meant her touch to bring morning to his soul; it was for her to risk the darkness. She stood up and unfastened her skirt. It fell to her ankles in a narrow, dark rush. She stepped out of it.

Seconds fell away.

She knew he was watching her. She heard him suck in his breath, sharply. He sucked up, in one awesome inhalation, time itself, and matter entire, and herself, N O R A—she was sucked up along with the rest, into the great gray maw of timelessness, into the whale's belly of himself.

She didn't like the words he was whispering to her, but a part of the world she had to see resided in the voice that was arching over her body like a whip.

I will do whatever is necessary, only love me, she said silently to him. Teach me. Please. She unbuttoned her blouse and freed the soft craziness, the loose jelly of her breasts, and their reflection in the mirror opposite the bed, and then in the hall of mirrors that his mind was, multiplied so many times beyond her mind's power to grasp what it is she was seeing, forced her to close her eyes, or else submit to a kind of burning lunacy. When she was completely naked, her body revealed and her soul's secrets made transparent, he ran his hands lightly over her. She could feel his will as it was expressed in the dead weight of accumulating desertlike light, light that pressed the air from her lungs and burned her dreamer's thin white skin and the frail parchment of her eyelids. There was no shade anywhere, no refuge from the awful sun of his eyes. Everything was visible in this light, everything was so visible as to be grotesque: the two lopsided breasts, the unrocked empty cradle of the pelvis, the haired triangle, the buttery slit, the browned furrow leading to the rat's hole. She was all parts and no connections. Her skin was raggedy. Her face felt as if it had disappeared, melted in the light or merged with it. The light was making her head ache; her jaw ached too. She would have ground her teeth to dust by the time he'd had his fill of looking. If she remained frozen like this much longer, like a small animal caught in the glare of headlights, the wheels of his eyes would crush her.

She flung herself face down on the bed. She watched him out of the corner of one eye. He stood up and slipped out of his clothes. In this light, the hairs on his body glinted like fish scales or bits of mica in granite. His weight was placed on his right leg, which threw the right side of his upper back into a deeply musical curve, a bass clef—in her mind, anyway. But then her mind's acid would dissolve him altogether into fantasy. Had she ever looked seriously at a man? Had she ever tried to grasp what maleness was? Or were men less what they were than what women thought or felt them to be?

It distressed her to look at him seriously. It was as if her eyes, gliding rapidly (she didn't want him to know of her investigation) over his components, might have activated them, and caused them to do her harm. His back was to her. His buttocks were small and palely neat, creamy and nearly hairless like the skin of an exotic breed of dog. His thigh and narrow hip dovetailed seamlessly. They were joined together with a fitness and harmony that made her wistful and envious both, a sculptor's join, so idealized as to be without threat. (How intent she was on not being threatened.) Long, ribbony strands of cord and muscle were braided to form the structure of his legs, a breathtakingly graceful length of leg, but his ankles put an abrupt and too-thick end to the eye's slide. Their choked clumsiness suggested a peasant ancestry. She would have to make peace with the ankles and with the wrists. She would have to learn to love them.

His feet were squat and muscled like a dancer's or a foot soldier's and had the look of having been broken and rebroken so often that the original shape had been lost in the mending. The toes were crooked and overlapped, the way teeth sometimes did, and to her eyes they were mostly horn and callus. The nails were petrified in brownish postures of age and use.

All this time—only a few seconds, really—he'd been contemplating his reflection in the mirror, or perhaps he'd been watching her contemplate him. She didn't know. But now he turned to face her. She couldn't meet his eyes. She sat up as he approached, feeling dwarfish in her nakedness. She saw the powerful shoulders, the detailed development of the chest, and the virile knowingness in his face, and the sight of this rare collaboration of brilliance and brawn made her wince. She understood she was lost. To have taken up with him was to have contracted for the certainty of a broken heart. Let it break, then.

He was standing in the corridor between the beds, between her legs, so that the complex arrangement of mauve shapes between his thighs was just inches from her face. Her first blurred impression was of a great and pleasing length, of a not-savaging thickness. The blur was partly one of relief at not being disappointed or frightened, although the liveness, the unreasonable, somewhat fantastical nature of a prick, its intensely anomalous reality, always evoked a certain anxiety in her. The relief lasted only seconds and then she began to shiver with cold or nerves. She was brittle with tension, a hateful, comfortless condition of no benefit to anyone. He broke a small vial beneath her nose. She inhaled obediently. She had a queer sense as of furniture being cleared out, whole chambers hurriedly emptied inside her, and of darkness in a rapid, whooshing descent, but darkness that was somehow illumined from within, like a glowing coal or ember; her face was glowingly hot.

Hands rearranged her—or, rather, rearranged *that woman with closed eyes* whose consciousness was but a dimly recognized version of her own—rearranged her from above. Her head, that woman's head, was so placed that it lolled backward off the bed, heavy as a peony on the stem of her neck. Something—a pliant stalk of flesh—broke the crust of air between her lips and sent a strong root down her throat. The man above her uttered the briefest of baritone sounds. The woman smiled inwardly.

Her face was wet. She wasn't weeping consciously; these were tears of physical exertion. Her mouth was swollen, her lips loose and sloppy with moisture, her scalp drenched in sweat. After an interval of some minutes, and with one hand cupping the small of her back, the other laid across her stomach, he gunneled her gently to the center of the enormous bed, and there he drew the bolt of his lower arm between her thighs. The expression in his eyes was royal, coolly far-seeing, like that of a national hero or a prince of the blood.

She was poised on a pinnacle of responsiveness. A corner of the sheet was balled up in her right hand. She hung on to it as resolutely as if it were proof of her sanity, or of her innocence, or, failing these, as if she might somehow need to wave it in surrender. Her knees were bent, her feet flat on the mattress, her buttocks half-lifted off the bed. The muscles in her calves and in her neck throbbed. Her ears buzzed. The soles of her feet burned and tingled. She was quivering with the kind of sexual strain that was indistinguishable from mental exhaustion. When the cold steel of his lips touched her, she gasped, her knees buckled, her pelvis contracted. He ignored her flightiness. His hands gripped the slopes of her thighs like clamps. He burrowed knowingly in the rudimentary darkness, as if in the small squeezing space of a cave, in the not-fully-knowable, in the Atlantis within her, that fabled island, sea-buried, lost to her. His tongue eeled among the dark and slippery flesh cliffs and found her, found it, the hard flesh bud. A mouth, his mouth, warmed it, forced it to bloom showily, a sea anemone with screams for petals. She felt herself being trundled toward the head of the bed, bulkily and somewhat flippantly, as if she were his prey. She dangled, in a state of feverish passivity, between the jaws of his will, her body still warm with struggle, her heart still beating, readying herself to receive him. She had been waiting all her life to receive him.

When he entered, except for a lowish sound, the kind that escaped one's lips in the presence of a brilliant sunset, she was silent. She let go the corner of the sheet. It uncrumpled toward the light.

He was an ambitious lover. With each thrust he strove to empty her of her history. Her story. He arched the upper part of his body away from hers and executed a series of short, steeply angled, almost spading motions. Sensing what he wanted—she wanted it too—she pushed the loosened earth, the narrative of her life to this point, out of their way with little panting thrusts of her own.

He was present to her through all this the way a figure in a dream was, by the sufferance and unconscious will of the dreamer, or as a deity was, by virtue of one's faith or vision; this, even though her arms were locked around his neck, even though he was jacketed in her legs. Abruptly, in one swift and unexpected motion, he dropped his body flat against hers and suddenly they were low and sleek, as if in water, seallike. His strokes now were deep and long and regular with almost no interval between them and she was sculled forward more swiftly than she had thought possible given the weight of her self-control, her watchfulness.

He broke a second vial under her nose and she breathed the fumes greedily this time. Almost at once she felt herself pounded by a wild, foaming, liquidy thing that she recognized as the furthest extreme of appetite. The compartments in the hold of her mind came crashing down; she felt herself breaking up, sinking, and then rising, intent as a murderess.

In this new and watery medium, she was conscious that her hair, floating in tangles on the pillow like seaweed, was being pulled, jerked, sharply enough to cause pain, but whether her destiny was to be rescued or pulled under was unclear. Trying to raise her arms to help herself, she found she had no latitude. She was confined as if to a chute, a slippery vertical tunnel that also ran downward from her consciousness to her stomach, where it opened suddenly, unpleating like a fan, into a fan-shaped space. Lines of sensation radiated from the base of the fan outward along its stays or ribs to her extremities. There was a warm tingling in her scalp and around her closed eyes and in her finger-tips and toes. In the next minute, she felt herself gripped from within by a forward-and-upward-and-outward-pulling force, a force much stronger than she was, almost like a crane or a derrick, that was pulling her toward an awareness of him, of his matchlessness, and of her good fortune, and which was equaled in strength by a downward-and-inward-and-scooping one, a sort of dredge, that pushed her back toward the mound of upturned earth that was herself. There was a look of ferocious, snarling concentration on her face. Catching a trace of her own faintly catlike scent slinking behind the heady, sweetish residue of that other, earlier smell, her nostrils dilated. She sniffed the air near his face with her little cat's nose, but he was without an identifying odor, without any odor at all: her superior even in restraint.

It was borne in on her after a time, registering as if on some gauge in her mind and along her skin, prickling with discovery, that he had sharply accelerated their tempo. She began whimpering inwardly with the cold, mad excitement that came of having put one's life, perhaps wantonly, in someone else's hands. She opened her eyes.

He was in a posture of straight-armed seigniory over her; nearly sitting on his haunches, his palms pressed flat against her breasts, moving them, palms and breasts, in small incantatory circles. His lips were moving, his eyes were closed, his head was turned to one side and lifted goatlike toward the moon of light on the ceiling as he thrust in and out, deeper each time, plunging through her as if through long grass; he was all edge and tusk, trampling her nests under his heavy hoofs, uprooting the shrubs and smaller trees, everything—and speaking words to her of a frankness that made her eyes fly open.

She saw that he was as if pawing the dirt on either side of her legs, digging, moving frenziedly like a dog chasing its own tail. His posture was, oh, heartbreaking. She could sense in him at that moment the hope of homecoming after a life of journeying: an exhilaration, but one overshadowed by suspicion and weariness. She was suffused all of a sudden and in every cell of her body with such a desire to be worthy of him, to help him, that she flung open all the doors to herself and stood naked on the threshold of her life, her narrow, narrow life, and offered him what solace there was in her arms. She promised him with her eyes the allegiance of her heart. She promised to love him forever. She was not lying. She strained toward him in a welcome of such ripeness that the skin of her consciousness, thus touched, burst, and she was drenched in a warm juice. In the narrow strip of sky behind her closed eyelids, an egg of light spasmed and soared and then suddenly, filled the empty cradle of her pelvis with its hatching warmth. She felt a tiny-fingered, fragile-skulled, half-blind second self kicking at the walls of her belly to get out. She was not a young woman. She thought of the years of dependency, the terrors, the pain, but it wasn't in her to deny life to anyone. She uttered a single, tearing scream as something from deep inside her forced its way into the world.

Recovering, she found that her newly born face was clasped between his hands as if it had become his prayer, and that their bodies were more closely joined than obstacles of flesh and bone permitted—so closely that his body had assumed the contours of her mind. Still she continued to hold herself open to him, out to him, in silence and in love, in the diamonded light, not wanting to stoop to words, resisting everything that might decompose her vision or turn it into an obstacle, an ending point, for she knew now that she had always to go further.

They talked for a long time, and when they were finished he went to sleep with his head on her breast and his ear pressed to her heart. She stayed awake until morning to defend him against the dark.

17

This is the last chapter. It's in the nature of endings to sum up the blame and apportion it, but blame is inappropriate here. It will creep in anyway, no doubt.

The light is turning red and gold over the hill to the west as I finish my story. It flames like the sword of an angel, it hovers winglike and low over the land. It suits my mood to think of it as a gleaming harbinger of night.

The table is set for dinner, the fire is laid. I am merely waiting.

I think the most beautiful representations I know of angels are the medieval ones, Duccio's or Cimabue's, not the later beauteous youths of disputable gender or elaborate outerwear, youths of the Renaissance, but those early ones, the lashless and sad-eyed harbinger-warriors, male or female, clearly invested with angelic functions according to gender and winged in fierceness and gowned in simple tunics of dignity.

I myself require no special dress in my existence as an angel. I have no wings. I am a theological creation, not an artistic one. I have known myself to be an angel since I was three. I am afraid I will not be able to be an old woman, but will die almost the instant this weakens in me or vanishes from my life. I do not altogether understand about being an angel; for instance, I have never associated others' fear and envy of me with evil, but I have had moments of private desolation that were unspeakable at the time and are unspeakable still.

I will tell you this: I wake in the mornings in an extraordinary luminescence of will that is part of my ability to live when I'm not unhappy or when I or someone I love is in danger but no unhappiness has broken my spirit. Then I am a spirit. And no demon, no love, not the birthing or nursing of a child can turn my body into only-a-body. How, when I have this shimmer of red and gold on my arms, when my neck holds melodies? No, I wake in the morning with a merciless and unearthly strength and I am directed. I am a hawk of spirit. My body, its presence, does not effect this. Had I been raped in the night, I would have awakened this way. Being despised, being weak, being without volition can break me, but my body cannot break me. I live in a state that is beyond rape or indignity, but which is not martyrdom. I do not show this side of me. I have never revealed myself, except to Lautner. I live in isolation from my kind. I am not part of a choir hymning God. My relation to Him is in my pride and isolation from other women, that I am alone and humble. I do not mean to be a heretic. I simply mean to correct my long silence in these matters.

I was not the messenger sent to remove Adam and Eve from the Garden, for good reason. I would have let them stay. In the deep theological sense, I do lack character. In the lesser theological sense, I can turn my back on some who suffer when I wish it, or when I will it. I am distracted by casual mercies only when I can't avoid them. To look at someone, to see that someone's reality, is, to me, devastating. What I see when I choose to look makes a liar of me: it makes me old and inwardly ill-tempered. I have never loved a mortal qua mortal, only as an immortal soul. Still, under certain circumstances, I would die for love.

I don't think it's that I'm weak. It's that I'm not an archangel, or perhaps I lie and I'm not any kind of angel, not even the serving kind in popular songs, the kind one marries or has for a mother, or the kind that guards the Christmas tree. Perhaps real angels, angels with power, are still exclusively male—they were depicted that way until the fourth century—male like Lautner. Perhaps the androgyny of the later angels is as phony as the femaleness of the Madonna. In my opinion, their androgyny is as bitter and as chastely male as her sweet agreeableness is boylike, boy-sopranolike. I think perhaps it's all male—all, that is, that is not wrested personally by a woman, by each woman separately, from the universe. I include fierceness. That which is not personally wrested is without meaning. It disgusts me. I believe that small illuminations, small strengths are merely forms of politeness, merely etiquette. I believe that only the most overwhelming strength and the most extreme openness to illumination are the minimal requirements for decency, for a decent life, and that such a life is not necessarily ever free of pain.

I know that one cannot hold on to one's decency for very long at a time. I have willingly lived in filth and yet I know it was not willing. You see, the vile moment always comes, the point at which the prospect of more ambition, more flesh, more ecstasy, can cause me to shudder. My patience with humankind—I include myself—exists only as something that emerges from strenuously chanted inner prayer.

The erotic is my weapon, not my fate.

I offer no apologies for this.

Men have made me cry.

Women have given me no comfort.

But I have never really begged, and I wake up in the morning with a shimmer of light inside me, and that light is

as bold or fierce as the light of hell—no, as the light of
heaven—and I know then that I'm not innocent, and that
the God I serve cannot be apprehended theologically or logically. My God is not Aquinas's or Voltaire's. What I know of
God, and my will to know it, is unspeakable. The light is unspeakable.

That's enough.

May I tell you how the dawn comes here? Slowly, in
shawls of light, until the flowering chestnut's dark arms are
clearly visible, spread like a patriarch's in the act of blessing,
and I am one of the flock of morning, being blessed along
with the dew on the grosbeak's nest, the mown-grass smell of
the sky, the ghost of last night's sleep, the song of the yellow
warbler, the unseen worst in the meanest of men. I would
bless them if I could, those crooks and robbers of the heart. I
would save them.

I can feel the presence of my grandfather's ghost here in
this room with me now, saying, No, no, pretty girl. It's the
man's right to receive the blessing of wisdom and to dis-
pense the blessing of salvation; the woman's to wear it second-hand, and then only if she's dear to the man who's being
blessed, or useful to him. My grandfather had his uses for the
devil and for heaven. So do I—or heaven and the devil have
a use for me. I have no gift for life without a heaven, without
a man. My father's fathers saw to that.

These days I wake at dawn, a miracle fetus born from
sleep with my skin loosening from the bone, an old hen too
long in the pot or the bed, my body tough but tiny, very
tiny. I wake huge-headed and squawking with thought, legless, armless, a brain that trembles in the shimmering light.
Mental distensions are the only way I have of accommodat-
ing my few small and toddling truths. And Lautner. He's
with me always. I carry him around in my heart like my
dead grandfather, or like a story demanding to be told.

For a while after I parted from Ned I thought I might be
one of those women doomed to live only once, an espaliered

tree clinging to its crumbling wall. But no, it seems I'm one of the lucky ones. The future's to be filled with love. Perhaps this time I can merge the movement of entering on love with the movement of light on the stony hill outside my house, and my own movement now, as I await the coming of my gray-eyed hero. We'll see. I'm trying to learn not to force the moment but to respect it, to let it unfold itself. Still, there's every reason not to believe me. I'm possessed. I consider it a privilege to be possessed—a kind of miracle I stumbled on. I serve him and yet I'm not his servant. I'm not the woman I was. Not quite. Things have to be as they are and yet things have to change.

Shall I tell you a story while we wait? I'll tell you how the first dawn came—in my grandfather's eyes as he looked into mine and lifted me onto the bar of his bicycle and carried me off to the ocean where we swam in the silvery morning sea while gray gulls dived around us and I was blessed by his smile and his pinches and my own pretty face and by the baker who gave us bread hot from his oven and pressed a warm finger into my dimpled cheek.

A dead giveaway.

Oh, God, what's a woman to do? What is any woman to do? What's intended for a plain woman can't be read in her face; plainness is its own necessity. Well, I won't have it. I won't be pretty anymore. I want the world to be afraid of me. I want to be as ferocious as a nun. I want that ferocity of spirit for my own. How else can a woman grow old without becoming a fool? Or becoming like a man, which is right for some women but not for me.

Leave that. I'll stand by it. My grandfather's fading with the light.

What is it you want, Nora?

I want to love life. I take that back. I want to do my duty. Oh, God, do I dare tell what I really want? Never mind. I'll finish my story instead.

.   .   .

I sold the jewelry. I bought a second-hand car with the money. I packed up my things—Ned, of course, had decreed that nothing but my clothes and a few pots and pans belonged to me personally—and I moved to a tiny rented cottage on the grounds of a horse farm in central Connecticut.

For a while I thought my life wasn't worth much, not worth the trouble. The birds helped there. All that pecking and flitting, useless as it may look to an outsider, does, over the long haul, parent the idea of an inarguable freshness of purpose. At least for me. I'm no one else's advocate in this matter. I had in regular daily attendance a pair of mourning doves, six rosy-breasted nuthatches, four cardinals, a rufous-sided towhee, finches and more finches, a few grackles, too many crows, and the usual assortment of sparrows and chickadees and a couple of downy woodpeckers, and any number of transients I couldn't identify because I'm near-sighted and my binoculars were never immediately at hand, and the birds didn't often wait. The country air helped too. It was so grandly invisible, so sweet-scented with forgetfulness. Living out there, I felt I was out of touch with my century. Everything conspired to protect me from unpleasantness.

And then, one morning shortly after dawn, the morning on which I saw my second Swainson's warbler, I had a call from Lautner. These things are not mere coincidences. He said, "The cards say I can rule the world as long as I have you." Shall I ever be done marveling at my life now that I've learned how?

When I began this story, I was still young. Or at least I felt young. Finishing it, I can see I'm about to be old. An old woman. It's just as well. All my life I've had a horror of becoming an old girl, an old fool. I've promised to change entirely. Lautner and I both know that this is a trick of mine; lying (and then being wholehearted and making promises I can't keep and then insisting I've kept them) is still the principal weapon in my arsenal of evil-doings. I'm sorry to say I was no different with Ned. I really do have to change. But Lautner says, what if my pride and my stubbornness and my worldly vision are what God wants? What if my lying is a form of loyalty? What if this is my way of saving souls?

I know myself a little better these days. I'm a woman of ambition, worldly and moral, but I'm also a woman of limited breeding and limited experience and limited vision, a dependent, a courtesan, really. The difference is that I've chosen to live as Lautner's courtesan rather than anyone else's, on the gamble that it will be like being a courtesan to the truth. And perhaps from there . . .

I wrote this story for Lautner. Tell me a story, he said, and said again. I imagine him listening intently with his head bent forward toward me, the head of a man also about to be old, a man almost past the age of passion, a passionate man nevertheless, a man with strict expectations and a few days' growth of grizzled beard and close-cropped silver hair. A man with a vision and the courage of a kamikaze. I wanted it to be a story worthy of him.

I read a crazy story in the paper the other day, but then these days the crazy is the commonplace. It seems that in my old city a husband, arriving home unexpectedly to find his wife in bed with her lover, was chased from his own house by the bare-chested fellow, who pursued him past a liquor store that, unknown to the pair, had just been robbed. The store's owner, mistaking the husband for the thief, and the lover for a good samaritan, joined in the pursuit. The husband was eventually cornered and subdued; the lover presumably returned to complete what had been so inconveniently interrupted. This being the city, the thief, of course, escaped.

The news is not good anywhere.

Jenny was hit over the head from behind as she was entering her building: and was hospitalized for a week. She wants to leave New York.

No, the news is not good anywhere.

Kasim appeared on network television and was assailing American ethics and the American mind (he described us as a material purgatory), and doing fairly well until he made the unfortunate blunder of ascribing to Jews and homosexuals only a certain museum value (under the heading Fragments of Antiquity in a Modern Political State: he said that) which displeased his American publisher, a Jew with a gay son, and thousands of serious readers. But he has an enormously expanded audience anyway because of the publicity. He won't have to teach next year.

My daughter, Valerie, says he is not an artist.

Connie Blakely is heavily tranquilized. One of Bob's ex-mistresses, angered over the way she was treated, sent Connie a packet of Bob's love letters, and a little black book that she'd taken from his pocket on their last evening together. Connie won't leave someone as rich as Bob but she can't quite accept the situation either—she is not a heartless aristocrat: she is a very, very rich pensioner living now at the edge of a breakdown, too helpless to be charitable, too regretful to be uncharitable.

Matthew died. Marjorie is working in the Division of Nuclear Medicine at New York Hospital. She's been to see me a few times to complain cheerfully about sick people and to laugh at my well-meaningness. I like her enormously.

Kitty and Lloyd Lilienthal's youngest son was expelled from N.Y.U. for drug-dealing while Kitty was in Brazil surgically resisting the ravages of time. In the strain, her left eye dropped to the right and she is skewed but her son has repented and goes to U.C.L.A.

Chester was arrested by an undercover detective in the men's room at Grand Central and charged with soliciting. He was released on his own recognizance. Maudie's secretary moved in with them the next day. Maudie threw a big party to welcome the young man. The three of them are living quite happily—kissily—together. Maudie described it this way to Margaret who hates me for having Lautner. "He likes college girls, you know," she said to me. I told her I looked on her as a mother.

Laurence Ghose flew to his guru's ashram in Northern India for a year of purification. He is not sincere, but then neither is Sylvie Rochas with whom we had dinner last week in Paris on our way to Warsaw. She is impressive—but a liar of complexity, a woman without any simplicity. And, ah, really, she hates me. She hates me because of Lautner. I, of course, hope someday we will be friends.

I lunched with Avery at his club just before I left the city. The portions were unforgivably small. Only by eating slowly did we have time to live out a scene in which he told me I was the love of his life. As sweetly as I could I declined his proposition that he undertake my support. I once did love Avery but now the sight of him is as comically upsetting to me as a tattoo would be.

I'm sorry to say that most of my old friends bear me more ill-will than I can comfortably live with. Lautner says I need everyone to hate me in order to wash myself of my guilt for my past fear of envy. Perhaps. I am frightened all the time now. I feel as cut off from my past sense of decency as if I were living in a savage woods in an Arthurian legend. Yet this fierce place, its light, its shower of leaves, is my home now with Lautner. We are much alone. This saddens me. For all its advantages, for all its claustral beauty, my life is diminished by the general reluctance—no, "refusal" is the word—to let me live in any way different from my past. But maybe I'm being unfair. Maybe Lautner is right and it's that I've become difficult and driven them all away. It's something to think about—when I'm not thinking about money. I think about money a lot. Money is the subtext. But I'm not poor. I'm with Lautner.

About Ned there's only this: he lives on in the absence of the abyss and the miracle, in the absence of truth as it is experienced by the human heart. And he lives this way in order to escape the moral consequences of what he's done, to escape the consequences of who he is, so that he will never have to ask forgiveness of any human being, so that he will never have to make reparation.

A friend of mine, or a former friend, said long before I guessed—she exclaimed, "I know why you left Ned—to save your children." Yes and no. I left Ned in order to have a chance at Lautner and everything has followed logically from that. What I cannot bear to dramatize is that, like me, my children cannot live by principle when they are close to Ned—which means they cannot live but lie and twist in place and torment themselves endlessly. I think they knew this long before I did and hated and blamed themselves. I think children often, in this sense, rightly blame themselves, but of course it's not their fault. My children are remarkable and honorable and after a bad time, without my nagging and without any of Lautner's games, they have let me know as much by imitation as by speech, but by speech as well, that they like my life and they like me and they like Lautner and they want to be like us and not like Ned. Lautner is shy and hesitant toward the young. But these are my children and I am not shy or hesitant. I want them to grow.

Willie has changed. What had been a rich boy's face is now stern with thought and not laughable. He is perhaps the only person who likes Lautner as much as I do. Of course, he is Oedipal and wants Lautner maimed or dead—I really don't understand men.

A week before she left college to work on a farm in the Dordogne, Valerie began to stand up straight—and once she laughed. She sounded like a woman who'd had a father who could be amused. She doesn't have anything to say to Ned. I wonder if he cares.

The extent of human perishability, on the one hand, and the extent of human endurance, on the other—neither is exactly credible. Sometimes things accumulate toward a desire to live. Sometimes not. I don't think there are rules governing this. Lautner says first-rate people choose to live out their fate. (I would agree with Frau Nernst and the mayor and Kasim on this one point: Americans have it easier than the rest of the world.)

Lautner, of course, understands the necessity of rebelling

against God. And, of course, he believes himself godly. Sometimes I want to ask him—how does one save the devil? And if the devil is godly, why does one have to? I don't know what his answer would be but mine is—because it isn't God who saves, or if He does, it's through women. Women save. Even if only temporarily. Even the devil. I guess Lautner really is The Devil. There's a sense, though, in which it hardly matters to me. I'm resigned to the truth that for me all men start being demonic the moment they stop being sons. Those times when I feel closest to Willie—what I would call inseparable—in the dreams that follow, I dress him in women's clothes.

I don't know what Lautner was like before, but since I've known him his displays of generosity and attention have been unmarked by self-serving. His is a genuine outpouring of goodness. Then he steps back and watches as we try to use him for our own purposes, as we become what we accuse him of—rapacious and self-serving and vile. Doomed.

I'm finished now. The day is not quite gone; a burning light streams off the trees, and off the distant mountaintops. Lautner, The Devil, does not quite believe in earthly salvation; he does not believe that he too can be saved. Never mind. The future is happening anyway.

Here is a moment: the woman is thinking how sad he looks, this gray-eyed, stony-faced inhuman human warrior, and she knows him to be unhappy and a fool, and even as she thinks of his eyes and weeps, when she is nearly senseless in his arms, in another universe of story, even then she is saying to herself—Ah, I will save him.

She will.

A NOTE ON THE TYPE

*This book was set, via computer-driven cathode-ray
tube, in a film version of a typeface called Baskerville. The face itself is a facsimile reproduction of
types cast from molds made for John Baskerville
(1706–75) from his designs. Baskerville's original
face was one of the forerunners of the type style
known as "modern face" to printers—a "modern" of
the period A.D. 1800.*

*Composed by American–Stratford Graphic
Services, Inc., Brattleboro, Vermont
Printed and bound by the Haddon Craftsmen,
Scranton, Pennsylvania*

Book design by Judith Henry